Daniel Boone

BOONE

Among Other Books by Cameron Judd

Cameron Judd's The Bridge Burners
Crockett of Tennessee
Jerusalem Camp
Revenge on Shadow Trail
Shadow Warriors
Shootout in Dodge City
The Border Men
The Canebrake Men
The Overmountain Men
Timber Creek
War at Fire Creek

BOONE

A novel of an
American Legend

by

Cameron Judd

High Country Publishers
Ingalls Publishing Group, Inc

Boone, North Carolina
2005

High Country Publishers
Ingalls Publishing Group, Inc.
197 New Market Center, #135
Boone, North Carolina 28607

http://www.highcountrypublishers.com
editor@highcountrypublishers.com

BOONE

An earlier version of this work was published by Bantam Books

Cover painting by Alan Tompkins (c1940)
Interior illustrations from the Miriam and Ira D. Wallach Collection, N.Y. Public Library. Frontispiece: Daniel Boone, from an original painting by Choppell
Cover design by James Geary
Text design by schuyler kaufman

Library of Congress Cataloging-in-Publication Data

Judd, Cameron.
Boone : a novel of an American legend / by Cameron Judd.— 1st ed.
p. cm.
ISBN 1-932158-63-4 (trade pbk. : alk. paper) — ISBN 1-932158-68-5 (hardcover : alk. paper)
1. Boone, Daniel, 1734-1820—Fiction. 2. Pioneers—Fiction. 3. Kentucky—Fiction. I. Title.
PS3610.U33B66 2005
813'.54—dc22
2005006260

First printing: September, 2005

Author's Note:

Daniel Boone's actual experiences provide the frame and foundation of this novel and much of its substance as well. However, this is indeed a novel, and some characters and plot events are fictional, or have been dealt with imaginatively. Where I have fictionalized, I have sought to do so plausibly, to create strands of plot that weave naturally with the true parts of the story, and fictional characters of the sort who, though they were not part of what really happened, easily could have been.

Cameron Judd

Part 1

The Yadkin Valley

"Boone cabin"
undated photo from the Miriam &
Ira D. Wallach Collection, MYPL

CHAPTER 1

Early Summer, 1755

CROUCHED BY THE ROADSIDE, his face twisting in a grimace of pain, a wagoner named Nate Meriwether opened his mouth slowly, gingerly, and allowed a fellow wagoner to peer inside.

"Turn your head a mite, Nate—no, the other way, for the light. That's good. Pull down your lower lip." The sufferer complied, adjusting his posture awkwardly, head tilted back and mouth gaping skyward as the other leaned over him to closely eye a row of yellowed, long-neglected lower teeth. "Nate, that tooth's been let be as long as it can. It'll have to be pulled before it goes to poison."

Nate closed his mouth and looked very sad. "I feared it would come to this," he mumbled. "I dread it."

"Well, a pulled tooth hurts a little while, but a rotten one hurts without end," the other replied. "We'll take care of this here and now. You'd never be able to endure that pain all the way to the Monongahela."

The wagoner about to turn tooth puller was Daniel Boone. He pivoted on moccasin-clad feet and headed for his wagon, which stood in a queue of assorted parked wagons and tumbrels extending far back along the twelve-foot-wide road. Ahead was a moving armory, a conglomeration of horse-drawn cannon, howitzers, and light mortars. Even farther ahead and momentarily out of sight of the wagoners because of the swell of the terrain, were continental soldiers under the immediate command of Lieutenant Colonel George Washington. Beyond them were the soldiers of the British regular army of Major General Edward Braddock, chief commander of this campaign in the Pennsylvania wilderness. And at the very lead and far out of view, chopping away the brush and saplings that had grown on this wilderness route since the Ohio Company had hacked it out three years earlier, were engineers and ax men whose duty it was to broaden the road, to erect crude but stout bridges over the many streams, and to pave marshy areas with logs laid side by side. The entire processional reminded Daniel Boone of a great, long worm chewing a westward course into the hills and mountains. It was a worm that chewed and crawled far too slowly to suit him.

Daniel's pale-blue eyes glanced up the line of wagons, horses, and drivers. *Should have forgone the wagons and used only packhorses and tumbrels*, he thought. He couldn't count the number of times he had run that same thought through his mind since this expedition began. Packhorses and tumbrels alone would have progressed more quickly and easily than those big wagons Braddock had commandeered from Pennsylvania farms, and would have required much less road clearing to accommodate them. Horses bearing packs or pulling light tumbrels wouldn't have tired nearly as fast as the horses they were actually using: big draft horses pulling more than their proper limit in weight. *Should have used only packhorses and tumbrels*. It was simple common sense. Daniel had already discovered that General Braddock's decisions often had little to do with common sense. The man was courageous, dedicated, authoritative, and thoroughly trained, but he was as out of place on the American frontier as a crown prince in a swine pen.

Daniel loosened and pulled back a section of the heavy oiled cloth covering his wagon's cargo and fumbled around until he got a grip on the rawhide handles of a massive, handmade wooden trunk. With a grunt of exertion he pulled the trunk up and out, then put it on the ground beside the wagon, opened the wooden latch, and flipped back the lid.

The trunk contained an assortment of tools: farrier's hammers, chisels, beak irons, a variety of tongs—hoop tongs, hammer tongs, tongs with round bits and square. These tools and others, particularly the wagon jacks, had been called into service time and again since the departure from Fort Cumberland many days ago, because some of the overloaded wagons had literally been jolted to pieces on the rugged, stumpy road. Each time, it was necessary to stop, unload the cargo, fix the damage, then load up again and go on until the next calamity. Occasionally wagons damaged beyond repair would have to be abandoned altogether, their cargo distributed to other wagons. *Should have used packhorses*.

The wagons stood unmoving because the army ahead had halted again. None of the wagoners knew why, and there was little point in asking. If the wagons weren't breaking down and holding back the army from behind, the army was blocking the wagons from the front. It was jolting, monotonous, laborious agony to move Braddock's army across the wilderness, and anyone with a head on his shoulders knew it would only grow more difficult, the deeper they went into the mountains. Often the long processional moved so slowly that the gaggle of camp followers, prostitutes and wives and children, almost outpaced the wagons.

Daniel Boone, like Nate, his neighbor and frequent hunting partner, joined this campaign as a volunteer militiaman from the Yadkin River area of North Carolina. Any who saw Nate and Daniel together inevitably thought that Daniel was several years older than Nate, when in fact he was only two years Nate's senior. Nate's boyish face and the seasoning effects of Daniel Boone's more extensive experience on the frontier accounted for the appearance of greater difference in their ages.

Daniel probed about until he pulled out two tools, one a pair of long, flat-bit blacksmith's tongs, the other a much smaller set of farrier's pincers. Rubbing his chin, he studied both, then rose lightly and carried the tools over to the sorrowful-looking Nate Meriwether. "Nate, I don't know which will give me the better pry on that tooth," he said. "I could wrench harder with the long ones, but these here pincers might bite in some and get me a stouter grip."

" 'Bite in'?" Nate repeated, going pale. "God preserve me," he murmured. "I'm to be tortured like a captive of savages."

Daniel ignored him. Nate tended to whine. Daniel pursed the thin lips of his wide and slightly down-turning mouth and nodded firmly. "Pincers it is," he said. "And if that don't work, we can always try the tongs."

Nate Meriwether looked as if he might jump up and run away. Daniel eyed him sympathetically but sternly, then turned and called to another man still seated on his wagon three vehicles back from Daniel's, his head lolling as he took advantage of the halt for a catnap. "John Findley! Come here; I need thee . . . need you." Daniel blushed, embarrassed by the lapse into one of the old speech habits of his Pennsylvania Quaker youth. It still happened from time to time, even though his Quaker days were long behind him.

John Findley was a thirtyish man whose clever mind, masked by his humble-looking face, was revealed in sharp, intelligent eyes. He lifted his head and tilted back his wide-brimmed beaver hat. He blinked, yawned, and stretched. "Aye, Dan. On my way."

Findley leaped lithely down from his perch, his fluid motions reminding Daniel of the manner common to Indians. Perhaps Findley had unconsciously picked up that manner while living as a Pennsylvania-licensed trader years before, in Indian country few white men had seen. Findley came to Daniel's side, yawned and stretched again, then fixed him with a curious expression, awaiting direction.

"I've got to yank out Nate's bad tooth," Daniel explained. "He's dearly suffering with it."

"What do you want me to do?"

"Hold his head tight. I doubt he has the gravel to hold still himself. He'll probably pee his pants when I yank it."

Nate frowned at Daniel's unflattering words but did not dispute them. Findley grinned, his eyes brightening with mischievous delight; it made him look very much the native-born Irishman that he was. Like Nate, who hailed from Suffolk, England, John Findley was an American colonial by immigration, not birth. His Irish accent had faded substantially in the fifteen or so years he had lived in the colonies, but for Nate's aggravation he deliberately stirred it to life again. "Ah! A chance to enjoy the suffering of a bloody Englishman! What finer pleasure for a man from the Green Isle, eh?"

"May you roast in whatever pit of hell the Almighty has reserved for the Irish," Nate replied. Even though he had been a colonial since age three, he still clung proudly to his English heritage, a fact Findley had ascertained and had much fun with since this expedition had brought them together.

"Get a stout grip on him, John," Daniel directed, opening and closing the pincers to get the right feel of them.

Findley moved around behind the squatting Nate, cracked his knuckles, then bent, looped his right arm under Nate's chin, and fixed his left hand on his brow. "Open wide, Nate," he said. Then, with a wink to Daniel: "You know, these English always do have blasted sorry teeth."

Nate was about to respond, but Findley pulled back on his brow and closed in tight on his jaw, cutting off words and most of his wind, and forcing his mouth open besides. Nate watched Daniel advance with the pincers and squeezed his eyes shut as the cruel-looking tool descended toward his throbbing tooth. As soon as metal touched enamel, he let out a high moan. Tears streamed from beneath his tightly squeezed eyelids. Findley grinned like a cat.

Good thing it's a front-and-bottom tooth, Daniel thought, *otherwise I'd never get these big pincers in there*. He had never noticed before what a small mouth Nate Meriwether had. "Get ready, Nate, you're about to lose her," he said, and closed the pincers tight around the cavitied tooth.

Nate writhed and cried, tongue wriggling about in his up-turned mouth like the head of a snake with its tail in the fire. Findley's strong arms clamped down as if he were trying to crush Nate's head like a walnut. Daniel closed the pincers so tightly they cut into the tooth, and pulled up with a twisting motion. The tooth didn't want to let go; he wrenched harder. Nate's eyes opened wide and rolled back in the sockets so far that only the whites showed as a final twist pulled the tooth free. His mouth flooded with blood. Findley let him go, and Nate groaned and slumped to the ground, eyes still rolled up as if he were trying to see inside his own skull.

"Danged if he ain't fainted," Daniel said. He held up the bloody prize. "And no wonder! The root of this thing must have run nigh to his chin."

Findley knelt beside Nate, turning his head to the side so he wouldn't swallow blood. Then he gently shook him, urging him out of his swoon.

Nate moaned, opened his eyes, and pushed upright, spitting blood onto the ground.

"As courageous an Englishman as ever I met!" Findley said, slapping Nate's shoulder. "Well done, Nate Meriwether."

Nate muttered a curse. Daniel trotted back to the wagon, stuck a hand into his rifle pouch, which lay on the seat, and returned with a couple pieces of patching. "Nate, bite down on these until the bleeding stops. That tooth will be giving you no more pain now."

Nate's color was beginning to return. He bit on the patching a minute or so, then glanced up at Daniel and nodded his thanks. He pointedly failed to do the same to Findley, delighting the Irishman, who had found no greater pleasure along Braddock's Road than getting Nate Meriwether's goat as often and in as many ways as possible. Winking again at Daniel, Findley returned to his wagon, whistling an Irish tune. Moments later an official call came down the line: the advance was resuming.

"Are you fit to drive?" Daniel asked Nate.

"I'm fine," Nate replied through clenched teeth. The bit of patching, very bloodied now, stuck out across his thick lower lip. His sparse beard, usually rich brown, now was rusty red because the bloody drool had soaked into it during his tooth-pulling ordeal. But he grinned weakly, and Daniel knew that though Nate looked a sight, he already felt better.

"A tooth can kill a man if it gets bad enough," Daniel said, wiping the pincers on his trousers. "I seen it happen once, and it's no way to die. It's good we got that chomper out."

The wagons ahead were already creaking into motion. Hurriedly returning to the trunk that bore his blacksmithing tools, Daniel put the tools inside, closed it, put it back into the wagon, and strapped down the cover. He launched himself into the driver's seat and set his wagon in motion just as it was his time to roll out.

TEN MINUTES LATER he was sniffing the air and noting that a marsh lay ahead, its muddy scent distinctive even in the overwhelming reek of the draft horses. Distinctive, at least, to Daniel Boone, who had spent his youth among the scents and sounds of the outdoor world and had become adept at distinguishing and interpreting them. In boyhood days he had roamed the hills and forests of this very colony, keeping watch over his father's cattle, and, until Squire Boone presented him with his first rifle at the age of twelve, hunting rabbits and other small game with a hurling club he had devised from the gnarly-rooted trunk of a sapling. He got very good at this primitive hunting, just as he was very good at doing most anything having to do with life in the wilds. Even in youth he had known that he was unusually skilled at surviving, even thriving, in the wilderness. No arrogance grew out of this knowledge. It was simply a fact Daniel accepted as he accepted any other.

Daniel looked around him as he drove, thinking that by coming to Pennsylvania he had in a fashion come home again. But no, this wasn't home. He wasn't the kind of fellow who looked back once he had left a thing or place behind. Daniel preferred to look forward.

Even so, Daniel's memories of his Pennsylvania Quaker boyhood were vivid and precious to him. He had enjoyed life in this colony, but he was old enough now to understand how different it had been for his parents. They had been affiliated with the Exeter Meeting of Friends, but difficulties had arisen: his sister Sarah married a young man who was not a Quaker, who had gotten her with child before the wedding besides; and a brother, Israel, repeated the offense of marrying a non-Quaker, causing the Friends to come to Daniel's father, Squire, and demand that he discipline his wayward children. Squire declined to do so and soon after was expelled from the meeting, as Sarah and Israel had already been.

Pennsylvania had seemed harsh, alien territory for Squire Boone after that. North Carolina called, and Squire answered, moving south, lingering for a time in the Shenandoah Valley, then continuing on to the Yadkin River. Now the Boones were Carolinians, Pennsylvania Quakers no more. Life in Pennsylvania was part of an increasingly distant past, and Daniel's return there to join Braddock's march against Fort Duquesne was a journey of patriotism and adventure, not of sentiment.

He and Nate Meriwether had signed on with the North Carolina militia together and had headed for Fort Cumberland, Maryland, right on the border of Pennsylvania, with no clear notion of what experiences military duty would bring them. Even without specific expectations, Daniel had been surprised by one thing: General Braddock, for all his arrogance and disdain for colonials, seemed downright inept at his job.

He was condescending to his young lieutenant colonel, George Washington, who commanded the blue-coated colonial troops, a group Braddock clearly regarded as greatly inferior to his red-coated British regulars. Daniel knew that on wilderness soil the opposite was true. Even Nate knew the same, despite his native British pride and the fact that one of Braddock's regulars was his eldest brother, Frederick Meriwether. Frederick was the only Meriwether brother who had not come with the family to the colonies, yet he had been shipped there anyway on military assignment. The middle Meriwether brother, Clive, was a Pennsylvania farmer living west of Carlisle. Nate had talked some about wanting to see him while he was in the area.

Stories of Braddock's arrogance and incomprehension of the realities of wilderness military campaigns had spread through the colonial troops even before they'd set out from Fort Cumberland. Ignoring the advice of Colonel Washington and Philadelphia's noted Benjamin Franklin, who had helped provision Braddock's force, Braddock insisted on a full supply train of wagons, and on marching his regulars at the front of the ranks, placing the colonial men, who were far more familiar than the regulars with the terrain and Indian warfare, farther back. And he would give no heed to any notion that mere savages could prevail over his red-coated army. The Indians that the French had recruited to help them fight might be a threat to "raw American militia," Braddock told Franklin, but against "the king's regulars and disciplined troops" it would be "impossible they should make any impression." As for Fort Duquesne, the French-held outpost Braddock intended to capture, it would fall easily in two or three days at the most.

THE WAGONS ROLLED, and Daniel's anticipation of a marsh ahead proved true. He guided his team carefully onto the makeshift pavement of logs laid across the wet earth, and felt his teeth jar in his skull with every bump of the wagon. What a road! What a campaign! *Should have used packhorses.*

So far Daniel had held his silence about Braddock's ineptitude. Daniel was just a young wagoner, after all. His job was to move the baggage of an army, not to second-guess trained officers. But he couldn't help but worry about one thing: if Braddock was incapable of advancing an army through the wilderness in the most sensible way, would he do battle in the wilderness any better? Would he expect Indians and frontier-savvy Frenchmen to fight by formal English rules of warfare? If so, the lesson he was bound to learn would be painful and bloody.

The wagons trailed the soldiers deeper into the dark and rugged mountains. That night around the fire, John Findley talked about the Kentucky country. Daniel Boone was transfixed. Three times before on this expedition he had listened to Findley's talk of that dark and rich land, where buffalo grazed in herds so vast a man had to look twice to see them all, where broad stands of tall cane gave evidence of the richness of the land, where beaver, otter, mink, and deer roamed in such abundance that a man could make himself rich with their pelts with hardly any effort.

But it was a dangerous land, too, prized and protected by the Indians. A man could gather wealth easily enough, but whether he could make it out with his wealth and his scalp was another matter altogether.

It was only because of such calamities, Findley avowed, that he hadn't come out of Kentucky a rich man.

Daniel asked him if he would ever go back. Findley replied that he surely would, someday, and make another try at riches. Kentucky was a wonderful place, a virtual heaven, except for the Indians. It lay there spread out under the sky waiting for clever men to come pluck its treasures like so many ripe grapes. And if any didn't believe the word of John Findley on how fine a land Kentucky was, they could go seek out Thomas Walker, commissary general of this very expedition, or Christopher Gist, Washington's scout. Both had seen the Kentucky country. And Walker had spied out a big gap through the mountains, the mountain notch the Indians called Ouasioto, through which ran the old Indian trail of Athawominee, what the white men called the Warriors' Path. By this route a man could cross the mountains from North Carolina, or travel down the great valley from Virginia, and enter Kentucky by land rather than river.

Daniel Boone's eyes flashed as he listened to Findley's enticing words. Kentucky accessible by land through a route not very distant from Carolina! Hearing Findley talk about it made the journey seem much more possible. Kentucky was a place he intended to see one day. It was a closed, virtually unknown land now, but not forever. Someday it would be opened, and Daniel Boone would be there when it happened. Or such was his dream . . . the dream of a young man who was at the moment only a wagon driver on a plodding military campaign.

That thought brought him back to his present situation. Before he could turn his attention to chasing dreams, there were challenges to meet: Braddock's Road to travel, Fort Duquesne to capture. No point in getting stirred up by a momentarily unfulfillable wanderlust. Daniel Boone rose and left Findley's fireside with a sense of resignation and regret, resenting the immediate and mundane.

The next morning the march began again, and it was as before, but worse—more wagons breaking down, horses falling exhausted or injured or dying, carrion birds flying above like grim omens, waiting to descend and feed on the fallen beasts. Time and time again the engineers found themselves facing obstacles too big to overcome. The army would divert to a new course, winding along difficult and rocky trails, under massive cliffs, across waterways that threatened to wash away wagons and cannon. Exhausted, frustrated soldiers began to grow sick. Nate heard that his brother was among the ill but was still forced to march, and openly cursed the name of Edward Braddock for having advanced this expedition to begin with.

They crossed the crest of the mountains and struggled on. George

Washington, himself beginning to fall ill, complained to Braddock that their current course was hazardous. By the time they reached Fort Duquesne, the men would be weak and sick, unable to fight. For once Braddock listened and, at Washington's request, divided the force, taking part of it forward at somewhat greater speed and leaving the rest as a rear division, to approach more slowly.

And so it went until the early days of July came, and the army at last neared the Monongahela River. George Washington, carried in the bed of a wagon, was sicker than before. Fort Duquesne was not far away, and barring a French surrender, the battle would soon be joined. From all indications Daniel Boone could see, Braddock still believed the fight would yield a quick and easy victory. What other notion could explain why the general continued to march the more experienced colonial troops to the rear of regulars who knew almost nothing of the frontier? Where were the scouts, the flank guards? Did Braddock not realize the dangers of this approach?

Then came the morning of July 9, and the shining Monongahela. And across the water, disaster that awaited like a crouched catamount ready to spring and kill.

CHAPTER 2

ALL HIS DOUBTS about Braddock's way of making war were not enough to overcome rising excitement in Daniel Boone as he drove his wagon across the Monongahela River. The crossing was quite a spectacle, done in typical British military fashion. Certainly there was no secrecy about it. The "Grenadiers' March" rang out across the river, shrilly piped on fifes, and the soldiers resplendent in their bright uniforms, sunlight glinting off their weaponry. The British military knew how to put on a proper show, Daniel would say that much for them.

Fort Duquesne was within easy marching distance now. Knowing the French were surely aware of the force coming against them, Daniel wondered if they were afraid, and if they would fight hard or give in easily, as Braddock was predicting. So far no opposition at all had arisen.

When the entire force was across the water, a brief rest was called, and the officers conferred. Where were the French and Indians? Might they have fled already, or might they be waiting to surrender at the fort? Hope and concern made an uncertain mix.

They decided to advance with great caution. Braddock sent out a small lead unit, followed by a larger force under Lieutenant Colonel Thomas Gage, with the ax men coming behind. The rest of the army followed, wagons and cannon proceeding after, and more soldiers backing them. The arrow point of the force moved into a narrow wooded slash in the mountains, the Turtle Creek Ravine. It moved through without difficulty, followed by Gage's men. The rest of the force was about to enter when trouble began.

Nate's wagon was directly behind Daniel's. "They ain't going to fight us, I don't believe," he was saying. "I'm hearing rumors that the Indians have run off and maybe killed the Frenchies their selves!"

"I don't put much reliance on rumors," Daniel replied.

A popping noise rose far ahead, followed by others. He pulled his wagon to a halt and stood on the seat to see what was happening. Commotion, smoke rising through the trees. More pops—gunshots—and shouts in English and in French. And the unmistakable war cries of Indians.

"What's happening, Dan?" Nate asked from behind.

"Ambush!" Daniel shouted.

The shots and yells grew closer. There were screams now, death yells, cries of pain. Daniel saw red coated men running, falling, crying, bleeding. There! He saw Braddock himself, mounted, moving among his men with sword uplifted, urging them back into formation, to fight an enemy who was invisible. Braddock tried to force his troops into tight ranks in their brilliant scarlet coats. And now, among the colonials, Daniel saw Washington. Fevered or not, he had left his wagon bed, mounted a horse, and was moving with reckless abandon among his troops, who were taking to the cover of trees to fight on terms this enemy understood.

One of the wagoners was trying to wheel his big vehicle about; an officer swept past on a horse, ordering him to remain where he was . . . there would be no surrendering, no retreat. As soon as the officer was gone, the wagoner continued his effort, then gave up, leaped from his seat, and began running back toward the river on foot.

"Frederick . . ." Nate said. "My brother's up there, Daniel!" He grabbed his rifle and jumped down, obviously intent on running into the thick of the fight to find his brother.

Daniel vaulted out of the wagon seat and alighted directly in front of Nate, cutting him off. "No, Nate. You can't do any good up there. You won't help him by dying."

"I can't let him . . . I have to . . . Get out of my way!"

Daniel put out a hand, grabbed Nate by the shoulder. Nate shrugged it off. The sound of rifle fire and death screams grew closer, and the wind carried the stench of spent gunpowder.

"I'm going up there, Dan!"

Daniel Boone drew back his fist and hit Nate squarely in the jaw, knocking him down. Nate lay stunned, gazing at the bright sky. Daniel followed up with a kick to the head that knocked him senseless.

Drawing his knife, Daniel raced to his draft horse and slashed the lines binding it to the wagon. The great beast's eyes were big with fear. Daniel led it around and stopped to scoop up Nate and throw him across the horse's back. The horse lunged forward, and Daniel raced to catch up. He managed to grab one of the lines and guided the horse to a stop. Clumsily, he gathered up his rifle, then Nate's, from the wagons, while still holding the horse and leaning against Nate's legs to keep him from falling off the beast. Daniel feared he would never be able to ride and keep Nate in place at the same time. Could he tie Nate in place somehow? Was there time? He could abandon the rifles, but he didn't want to be left weaponless, not with a horde of French soldiers and Indians close behind.

John Findley rode up; he too had cut free a horse and was fleeing. He saw Daniel's predicament. "Give me the rifles!" he directed. "You just get Nate out of here. Was he shot?"

"No," Daniel replied. "Struck in the face." There was no time or need to explain further. He shoved the rifles up to Findley, who immediately galloped away toward the river. Danie leaped astride the horse. The fighting was much closer now; his heart was hammering and his mouth was dry.

Holding Nate's limp form with his right hand and guiding the horse with his left, he let the animal run hard toward the river. He splashed across, as Findley had already done, then up the far bank and away, going as fast and hard and far as the horse would take him, leaving the smoky, bloody Turtle Creek Ravine behind.

DARK STORIES SPREAD among the soldiers fortunate enough to survive the two-hour carnage in the gorge. Everyone knew that Braddock himself had been shot and was expected to die. Officially it was said that the foe had brought him down, but the story among the men was that Braddock had lifted his sword against a Virginia soldier who had angered him, and the soldier's brother had put a ball into the major general's back.

Daniel Boone didn't know the truth and didn't think it mattered much; a rifle ball was a rifle ball, and dying was dying, so it was all the same for Braddock no matter who shot him. Daniel wouldn't grieve much over the man, who he believed had endangered his own troops by insisting on formal battle tactics against a very informal foe. Only the continental troops under Washington had fought sensibly, taking to cover in the trees and behind rocks, but Braddock's battle style had put even them in more danger than necessary, and far too many had died. About all the credit Daniel was willing to give Braddock was that the man had displayed tremendous grit. Witnesses were saying that five horses had been shot from beneath him before he finally received his wound, and not once had he balked before the enemy, even though it was an enemy he couldn't comprehend.

Daniel was glad that George Washington had come through unscathed. It was surely an outright miracle that he had. After the fight he had found four bullet holes in his coat, and combed fragments of lead from his hair. It had appeared to some witnesses that several Indians had specifically targeted the brave Virginian, yet none had brought him down, even though he rode defiantly in the most exposed areas. Two horses had been shot out from under Washington, but still he had fought on, reckless in the face of slaughter. Divine protection, several solemnly declared. Daniel would never forget the stalwart soldier's courage.

Daniel was afoot now, as were most all the former wagoners. The horses that had come out of the fight had been given over to carrying the wounded and dying. Groans and cries of pain punctuated the unending rustle of trudging feet and plodding hooves. Some men whistled softly, trying to put a bright touch on a dismal retreat, but most didn't even try. Shoulders slumped, eyes vacant, faces gaunt, they moved like hollow men along Braddock's Road, grateful only that they were still alive and that the French and Indians had not pursued them. Beyond gratitude there was little to feel but a general soul-sickness and the pain of whatever injuries they had received in battle or flight. The sorrowful, defeated mood was heightened by the gloom of the thick forest, so shaded that even at noon little sunlight pierced the foliage arching overhead.

Daniel grimaced and rubbed his jaw. It was very sore, thanks to Nate Meriwether, who at the moment marched several paces ahead, keeping away from Daniel. Nate was very angry, when he had regained consciousness after Daniel kidnaped him away from the ambush. He had exploded in anger at having been restrained from "helping" his brother and struck Daniel with his fist. Daniel did not retaliate. He understood how Nate felt. Still, he knew he had been right to stop his friend from plunging into the fight. If Nate had done that, crazily hoping to find a single individual out of all the milling British regulars in that hellish ravine, he would surely have died, just as most of the redcoats and half the provincials had died. Out of three Virginia companies in the fight, only thirty men remained alive. The officers had fared about as badly. Of eighty-six English officers, sixty-three had fallen wounded or dead.

The dead had been left behind with the supply wagons and artillery. Daniel could easily imagine what desecrations the Indians had performed upon the corpses, and what had happened to the dozen or so English troops who had been unfortunate enough to be taken prisoner by the Indians. If they had expected decent treatment and later release, they surely had already been relieved of that vain hope at the fire stakes of their captors. He hated to think of it, especially as Nate's brother Frederick had not shown up among the surviving British regulars. The odds were he had died or had been captured. If the latter, he was probably doomed for execution at Indian hands.

Daniel approached Nate cautiously that first night. Despite his assurance that he had done the right thing, he was bothered by Nate's anger. At first Nate rebuffed him, refusing even to talk to him, but then emotion suddenly broke through and he cried like a child. He was not the only man to cry without shame on the shadowed road back to Fort Cumberland.

"You couldn't have helped him, Nate," Daniel said. "You'd have died out in that ravine. That's why I stopped you."

"I know," Nate replied through his tears. "I know."

Braddock died the third night after the Fort Duquesne battle, declaring in his final breaths that the next time he met such a foe, he would know better how to deal with him. Daniel thought that comment not only pitiful but also terribly ironic. There had been plenty of advisers around Braddock who *had* known better how to deal with the foe. Braddock had simply refused to listen.

By torchlight Washington read Anglican funeral rites over Braddock's grave, dug in the middle of the road that had come to bear his name. The army tramped and rode over the grave so it would not be found by the enemy, who would certainly exhume and desecrate the general's corpse if they had the chance.

The retreat continued until the remnants of the army reached Fort Cumberland, only to find it abandoned. They marched on to Philadelphia. Washington departed with his troops, and Daniel Boone and Nate Meriwether headed back to the Yadkin.

But not directly back. Nate had not yet visited his brother Clive, the Pennsylvania farmer. Now there was more reason than ever for Nate to see him. He had news to give—tragic news about their brother Frederick.

"I have people of my own here I'd like to see before I go home," Daniel said to Nate. "I'll be glad to go with you to see your kin if it won't belabor you to come with me to see mine."

"It will not," Nate replied. "Now, let's be off. I'm eager to leave this cursed army, though I dread to tell my people what has happened."

"All trials are easier when their weight is shared, or so my mother has always said," Daniel replied. "There is another thing she says too, and that's that heaven will seldom let a man be smitten without soon giving him a good thing to make up for it. If that's true, then there will be good things coming to you soon. Or at least you'll be spared more tragedy."

"Your mother is a fine woman, Daniel," Nate said. "But I hold no faith in proverbs. And there's nary a thing good enough to make up for losing Frederick. Nary a thing."

THEY RODE TOGETHER to the little farming community where Clive Meriwether lived. Nate had never been to Clive's home and had to inquire about its whereabouts. It seemed a simple question, but from the first time it was asked, the responses it evoked were inexplicably, disturbingly odd.

One woman went pale and withdrew silently into her house after Daniel identified himself and Nate and asked about Clive Meriwether's whereabouts. A man farther down the road stammered and declared he knew nothing of Clive, when obviously he did. By then Daniel was full of dread, fearing that, contrary to the sentiments of his mother's proverb, the heavens were about to hand Nate another tragedy, after all.

Obviously something was wrong with Clive, and nobody wanted to say what it was.

Finally, at a cabin about a mile from the creek upon which Clive was believed to live, Daniel's worst fears were confirmed.

"Aye, aye, Clive Meriwether's gone," a toothless old man there told them. "A sorrowful tale, his is. The redskins, cursed murdering savages, slaughtered his family and carried Clive hisself off with them, slapping him with the very scalps of his loved ones. Burned his place to the ground behind them. The dead wife and children were left behind amongst the ruins. A boy who seen it all from hiding said the red devils took Clive off with them to kill somewhere else for sport, no doubt. Poor Clive was a friend of you men, was he?"

"He was my brother," Nate said in a whisper.

"What was that?" the old man cocked his ear toward Nate, cupping it with his hand.

"Clive was his brother," Daniel said. "Nate here didn't know nothing of this until now."

"Brother, you say? Oh, aye, aye. I had heard Clive speak of a brother or two. Mighty sorry to be the one to tell you such sad news. Clive was a good one."

"You don't know for a fact that he's dead, do you?" Nate asked in a noticeably tightening voice.

"Well, he must be. It was redskins who took him. Ottawas. They show no mercy I've ever heard of. He had fought hard and angered them. They surely killed him."

"Where did Clive's house stand?"

The old man pointed west and gave directions. "But there's naught there to see no more," he added. "I told you they burnt it to the ground."

"I'm inclined to see it, anyhow," Nate said. "Thank you, sir, for your help."

Daniel could see little point in going to Clive's place, but this was Nate's business, not his, so he followed along in silence. Though he ached to comfort his friend, he could find no counsel to give. Life had handed Nate Meriwether two hard trials in succession, and there was nothing for him to do now but suffer through them. It was as simple as that.

They found the cabin, now merely a burned-out shell. The sad remnants of the meager furniture of the humble place still sat within the blackened walls. Nate dismounted and walked to where the front door had been and stared sadly, then lifted his eyes and looked around.

Nearby were three graves, marked with wooden crosses, all made of charred wood left after the fire.

"That's where his wife and children are buried, I reckon," Daniel said. "He had but two young ones?"

"That's all, last I knew of it. Merciful heaven, what's happening to my family, Daniel? Smote down right and left by battle, fever, redskins . . ."

"I don't know what to say to you, Nate."

"God himself is against me, Dan. It ain't fair. It ain't right. Here I am, coming out here to do my righteous duty and fight the French, and what happens but my brothers are killed! There's nothing fair nor right in it."

"It don't seem so, no; though I won't presume to judge the Almighty."

Nate shook his head and swore, first beneath his breath, then louder and louder again, until he was shouting curses to the sky. Words yielded to tears, and he sobbed pitifully nearly half an hour until he had no strength left. He was seated cross-legged beside the grave of a sister-in-law he had never met, rocking back and forth from the waist, like a distraught child, sniffing quietly, wiping the last of his tears on his sleeve. Daniel saw he was wept out, scoured to the soul by his grief, and knew that was good. The only thing a man could do in a situation like that was to get past the tragedy and get on with living.

Daniel went to Nate's side and knelt, putting his hand on his shoulder. "Nate, you ready to move on toward the Yadkin?"

Nate sniffed and nodded. His face looked very puffy and blotched.

"I am, too. But I'm right hungry. Yonder is a promising-looking grove that I've seen three fat squirrels poke their heads out of in the time we've been here. If you'll build us a fire, I'll wager you half a horn of powder I can bring back all three before another half an hour has passed."

Nate grinned weakly. "You're a cocksure old crow-bird, Dan Boone. I'll wager you won't bring back more than two."

Daniel won the bet, and better, bringing in four squirrels before Nate had even got the fire coals worked down to a good cooking level. They skinned and spit-roasted the squirrels and ate some hard, dried biscuit Nate had carried all the way from Carolina. Afterward, they kicked dirt onto the fire and left. Daniel was pleased that Nate didn't pause to look back on the destroyed cabin or the graves. Not looking back was the best way. The only way a man could get by, oft times.

DANIEL PICKED UP a stone, squinted upward at a knot on a branch above him, took aim, and threw. The stone shot upward, falling short of the targeted knot, and arced over and down, splashing into the water of the Schuylkill River. Daniel shifted about to a more comfortable sitting position on the riverbank, dug another stone from the mud, and tried again. He missed the knot by an even greater margin than the first eleven times he had thrown at it. Sighing, he lay back on the bank and put his hands behind his head, staring up into the sky.

All was amazingly peaceful there along the familiar old Schuylkill. Alone, far from home, free now from military duty, Daniel could close his eyes and almost convince himself that all the intervening years since his boyhood on this very river were but a lazy afternoon's daydream, and in the evening he would rise and find his family awaiting him at the supper table in the old Squire Boone house in the Yadkin Valley, young manhood, and the sorrows of Braddock's Road still far in the future and unseen. Along this beautiful stretch of river there seemed to be no such thing as time, and Daniel found its lack nothing to grieve over.

Farther down the stream he heard a faint splash. Opening his eyes, he saw that Nate had reappeared with a bottle in hand. Daniel didn't know where he had gotten it, but it didn't surprise him. Nate always found liquor when he wanted it. Probably he had obtained this bottle somewhere in nearby Exeter. The splashing sound had resulted when Nate kicked something into the river, probably a stone, judging from the painful grimace on his face and the way he was limping. He slumped down to the riverbank and rubbed the injured toe with one hand while unstoppering the bottle with his teeth. Daniel decided to keep quiet and not draw Nate's attention just yet. If Nate was intending to get drunk, Daniel figured solitude to be a preferable companion.

Enjoying the sun's warmth, Daniel closed his eyes and forgot about Nate. His mind drifted back across the years to this very riverbank, to a spring day, when the shad were running and the sky was clear and warm.

His mother had been with him then, cleaning shad he had caught after a particularly good morning of fishing. The Schuylkill on such spring days was always lined with Pennsylvanians out to take advantage of the abundance of fish, and several neighbors had been nearby as well, harvesting catches of their own.

The warm sun had lured Daniel onto a flat rock ledge jutting out into the water. The rock wasn't occupied by a fisherman at the moment, which seemed a great stroke of luck to Daniel, who knew this rock had perfect contours for a young fellow to fit the lines of his body into, a process which, if done just right, would make the hard stone as comfortable as a feather bed. Within minutes Daniel had found that perfect niche and was drifting off into sleep, the voices of chatting neighbors blending with the rippling of the river into a soothing backdrop of sound. It was wonderful, heavenly existence as it was meant to be enjoyed.

All came to an abrupt end with a cold and shocking splatter. Roaring in surprise, Daniel jolted upright, breathless, swiping at the unidentified and gruesome something that had been thrown onto him from somewhere.

He realized the foul substance consisted of water, blood, and fish entrails when he heard the insulting sound of feminine laughter. Fury rising in him, and with fish guts hanging from his hair and smearing his face, he looked up and saw two neighbor girls enjoying his predicament. One of them held an oaken bucket from which the mess had been thrown.

Daniel roared. He wanted to swear, but he was too angry for that and at least subliminally aware that his mother was within earshot, so he merely roared, like a provoked beast. Lunging forward, he pounded one of the girls in the face with his fist, drew back, and gave the same to the other. It was done before he even realized what he was doing.

For a good Quaker boy to strike anyone—even worse, a girl—was unheard-of. After the deed was done, Daniel stood panting and heaving, the girls gaping up at him from the ground, the first signs of bruising showing where his fist had struck them. Bursting into tears, they leaped up and ran to their mother and told what the terrible Boone boy had done to them and for no reason except that they had played a simple prank on him.

Lying on the bank now, with that spring day years behind him, Daniel still had to smile as he recalled how his mother had risen to defend him for the indefensible. Challenged by the girls' mother to account for her son's act, Sarah Boone had stood up straight and declared, "If thee has not raised thy daughters to behave better than they have toward my boy, then it is time they be taught manners. My Daniel has given them no more than they deserved."

Down the bank Nate dropped his bottle and it broke. Opening his eyes, Daniel sat up. Nate was cursing, stomping clumsily about with a jagged piece of the bottle in each hand and his clothing wet with spilled and wasted liquor. With a final oath Nate threw the pieces of the bottle into the river, walked back up the path, and sat down against a tree, arms crossed over his chest, back turned toward the river. A petulant child, he seemed to Daniel Boone. An unappealing characteristic, but Daniel supposed if anyone had cause to be childish at the moment, it was Nate.

Daniel stood, yawned, and stretched. Giving one final look to the peaceful river, he turned reluctantly and headed toward the pouting, semi-drunken Nate. It was time to begin the long journey home to North Carolina. Already he had visited with his kin and a few old friends in and about Exeter, including the family of the girls who had slopped him with fish guts years ago. The incident was long ago forgiven on both sides, and now the subject of much nostalgic laughter.

In any case, there was no longer any reason to linger in Pennsylvania and lie about on warm riverbanks, pleasant as that might be. There were loved ones to return to on the Yadkin, kin who were probably even now worrying over him. They deserved to know he was safe, especially since word of the disaster near Fort Duquesne might reach home before he did and make them worry even more. And besides, Nate needed to get away from Pennsylvania, back to a place associated with home and happiness, not tragedy and death.

CHAPTER 3

DANIEL AND NATE didn't hurry home. They were dog-weary from the campaign on Braddock's Road, and of the temperament to enjoy relaxed travel.

All along the way, blue mountains loomed to the west. Daniel's eyes were constantly drawn to them. There was something about mountains, something that both pleased and challenged a man of his type. He had never seen one he didn't want to cross, and in his time he had crossed many of them, big and small. It was that urge that had sometimes led him to wander too far from home when he was a Pennsylvania boy assigned to watching his father's free-ranging cattle. How many times had he chased a deer or even just a rabbit into an unfamiliar hollow and looked up to see some unexplored ridge gazing haughtily down at him, all but taunting him to come see what lay beyond? And what lay beyond, of course, was almost always another such ridge, issuing the same call and luring him yet another three or four miles. Sometimes it seemed that the mountains must go on forever.

He knew they didn't. Eventually the mountains gave way to more open country. His mind went back to John Findley's fireside talks of broad rivers and wide cane lands; of vast grassy meadows cleared by fire and teeming with buffalo, deer and other game; of streams rich with beaver and otter and mink, and filled with fish a man could catch bare-handed—fish so big that two would more than fill a skillet. It sounded like paradise to Daniel Boone.

They rode through Virginia and at last into North Carolina, making their way along the eastern slope of the Blue Ridge, until finally they reached the Yadkin and home.

Once there, Daniel let his mind wash free of the strains and trials of Braddock's failed campaign. He possessed the fortunate ability to lay aside mental burdens once the reasons for bearing them were gone. Serving under Braddock had been a wasted and tragic time, but it was behind him. He had survived, and there was no reason to look back.

He wished Nate Meriwether would learn that lesson. Nate's homecoming did nothing Daniel could detect to ease his grief. He wasn't the same carefree young man as before. Whenever Daniel encountered him, Nate was either brooding and distant, or irritable. Occasionally he turned up drunk and quarrelsome. Daniel felt sorry for Nate, but also perturbed. Nate was acting as if he held a monopoly on suffering and tragedy, which was nonsense. The Boones themselves had recently suffered the loss of Daniel's older brother, Israel, who had died in June of consumption, an illness that had killed his wife earlier. Now Israel's four children, Jesse, Elizabeth, Sarah, and Jonathan, were left orphaned, to be cared for by their relatives. They and all the Boones were saddened by Israel's untimely death, but Daniel saw no value in bearing the grief forever, like an eternal shroud.

Daniel knew nothing to do but leave Nate to be healed by the balm of time, if he would allow it. In the meanwhile, he had much happier thoughts on which to dwell.

Specifically, thoughts of a young woman named Rebecca Bryan, a daughter of Joseph Bryan, friend of Daniel's father, Squire, and head of a family that already had close ties to the Boones as neighbors and through marriage. Daniel's younger sister Mary had wed herself into the Bryan clan, and at her wedding Daniel had first cast his eyes upon the dark-eyed, fifteen-year-old Rebecca. She was a striking figure—pretty, brunette, very tall for a girl. He had been stunned. Smitten.

At that first meeting he was already a far-roaming fellow with about two decades of life experience behind him, and Rebecca was merely a shy, gangly girl-child. Even so he had found it hard to get up the courage to speak to her, and oddly difficult to look her in the eye once he did. He hadn't met another girl who had that effect on him, and frequently, throughout the long drudgery of Braddock's advance upon Fort Duquesne, he had diverted himself by thinking about her. Not all that seriously, perhaps, and certainly not with the thought of marriage. He had mostly just pictured her, looked her over in his mind's eye, and imagined scenes in which he performed acts of courage and manliness while she looked on in admiration.

On the retreat from Duquesne, however, his thoughts had become more focused and far less frivolous. Brushing against death had in one thrust injected much more sober maturity into his view of life. He began to realize that a man couldn't just assume he would live long, with boundless opportunities rising before him to be claimed at convenience. When a door worth going through opened for him, he should step through at once, else the door might close and not reopen again. With such a fine female as Rebecca Bryan close at hand, and he himself still single in a day when many men married well before age twenty, perhaps he should think about marriage. The death of his brother Israel had driven the same conviction even further home.

IT WAS THE TIME OF YEAR when the cherry trees hung laden with their red fruit, ready for picking. The job was drudgery in itself, but like many dull tasks the people of the frontier created ways to put some fun into it. A field needing reaping, a cabin needing building, a pile of corn needing shucking—such things were ready excuses to get together a group of neighbors, along with a fiddler or maybe just a good singer or whistler, and use the work as an excuse for a frolic.

Daniel was in a bright mood, all full of himself and feeling vigorous and handsome. At the moment he was kneeling by a spring, washing his hair and face. He had shaved earlier, with a freshly sharpened razor lubricated with a little grease, taking care not to nick himself. This was no day to look anything less than his best. He was bound for a cherry-picking frolic over near the Bryan place, and Rebecca was to be there. He'd made sure of that earlier in a secret visit to see her, and had secured her promise that she would keep company with him today. In fact, she said, she would pack some victuals for them to share on a blanket in a particularly pretty spot at the edge of the cherry grove. Daniel had no plans to do any cherry harvesting. This day was reserved to spend time with Rebecca.

Finished with his splashing, Daniel watched the water settle. His reflection shimmered and shook and grew still, and he studied it. The face looking back at him from the surface of the spring was fair and ruddy in complexion, with a mouth tending to wideness, lips quite thin, nose hooked ever so slightly, eyes blue and hooded by thick, somewhat arched brows. His hair was sandy but dark, curling around his ears and sweeping back from his high forehead, trained into that style by the wide-brimmed flop hat he usually wore. All in all, he looked rather fine, as best he could judge. The question he couldn't answer was how he looked to Rebecca.

Rising, he straightened his clothing. Nothing fancy or new, just his usual woolen trousers, deer hide moccasins, sashed hunting shirt, wide-brimmed hat. He'd washed the clothes the day before, hiding out in the woods in an Indian-style loincloth until they dried. They didn't look all that different for being clean, but they did smell much fresher.

He spied a large blue jay feather on the ground, picked it up, and stuck it into the band of his hat. There. Now he was outfitted properly for courting. Whistling, he picked up his long walking stick and began treading toward the cherry orchard, where she would be awaiting him.

SHE LOOKED PRETTIER than ever, and it gratified him that she had made up for him. Her hair was pulled back and tucked into a freshly washed limp-brimmed sunbonnet, and her linsey dress obviously had been scrubbed, dried, and pressed out to remove wrinkles. Daniel glanced down and was amused to see that Rebecca had even trimmed her toenails and wore no shoes. It was common for females to go barefoot as long as the weather was warm, but Daniel had never seen a girl who seemed to relish feeling the earth against her feet more than Rebecca. It was slightly on the cool side today, but she had forgone footwear all the same.

But more flattering to Daniel even than washed clothing and trimmed nails was the fact that Rebecca had brought out her most prized garment, a beautiful cambric apron as white as mountain snow, that she wore only on special occasions. She had worn this apron at the wedding where Daniel had first seen her; its crisp linen whiteness was one of the things that had initially drawn his eye her way. Now, as they sat together beneath the cherry trees, Rebecca was taking great care not to let any scrap of their food fall to mar the linen cambric. Before they had seated themselves, she had carefully checked the ground and cleared away all the overripe cherries that had fallen there and would have stained the ties of the apron. Daniel found her carefulness endearing, as most everything she did was endearing to him. He liked the way she curled her lip, the way her hands moved, the way she walked and laughed.

She was laughing now, telling him how a habitually bashful friend of her father's had gotten himself into a scrape with a wounded bear that ended with him up a tree, minus his buckskin trousers, which the bear chewed to pieces before dying beneath him. This had forced the man to make rough breeches out of the untanned bearskin so as to maintain modesty as he went home. Daniel knew the man but hadn't heard this tale, and thought it was hilarious. He was in the midst of laughing when he glanced up and saw Nate approaching. Humor died away; he didn't want Nate around. Not now! Not with his hangdog, sorrowful manner, his way of bringing clouds over the clearest skies. He had been ever like that since the loss of his brothers, and though Daniel pitied him, he didn't want Nate's grief interfering with his courting.

"Howdy, Dan. Hello there, Rebecca."

Daniel grunted but said nothing.

Rebecca smiled prettily and said, "How you faring, Nate?"

Blast it, Daniel thought, you didn't have to ask him that. He'll go on with his sorrows till sunset.

"Well, Rebecca, I ain't doing too well, to tell you the truth. I'm still grieving over my loss."

"Yes," Rebecca said. "That was a mighty hard thing that's happened to you."

"It is," he said. "Two brothers, killed by savages. Killed dead!"

What other way but dead can you be once you're killed? Daniel thought grumpily.

"There's always hope, ain't there, that the one the Indians got might have just been took prisoner?" Rebecca asked.

"I reckon it's possible, but I know in my heart he's dead. When you lose family, it's something you can feel right down in your bowels."

Good Lord, Daniel thought disgustedly. His peevishness was mounting quickly, but a glance at Rebecca showed her face touched with true sympathy for Nate. To fuss at Nate would make Daniel look heartless in her eyes. Biting his lip in frustration, he reached down, drew out his hunting knife, and began jabbing it into the moss on the ground between him and Rebecca, just to pass the time.

Nate continued talking, sharing his grief and receiving abundant sympathy from Rebecca. Daniel jabbed the knife harder, then harder again, driving the blade deep into the mossy turf. It appeared to him that for all Nate's whining about loss and grief, he was beginning to have quite a good time conversing with Rebecca. Down went the knife, then up. Wiping the dirt from it across his knee, he probed the sod again.

Then disaster struck so quickly, Daniel didn't realize it had happened until it was too late. Raising his knife for another thrust, Daniel unconsciously shifted a little closer to Rebecca, just as she herself moved a little closer to him. A corner of the white cambric apron slipped to the side, and the blade plunged right through it.

Daniel, Rebecca, and Nate saw it all at the same time. Conversation stopped dead, and Rebecca blanched, staring in disbelief at the knife that pegged her apron to the ground. Her eyes lifted and looked in bewilderment at Daniel, as if asking the question that Nate was brash enough to put into words: "Dan, did you do that on purpose?"

Daniel felt flustered. Hurriedly he pulled the knife out of the apron and put it away. "Rebecca, I'm sorry. I didn't mean to."

"You've ruined it, Dan!" Nate said in an oddly bright tone of voice. "Plumb ruined it!"

Daniel came to his feet, face red, anger surging. He wanted to shout some particularly fierce words in Nate's face, but the presence of Rebecca and an overwhelming sense of consternation allowed him to do no more than stammer a few half words, grow even redder, then turn and walk away. A dozen strides out, Rebecca rose and came after him.

"Daniel, wait!"

He turned, looking at her but wishing he could sink into the earth and be gone. She surprised him with a smile.

"Dan, don't go off. You didn't mean to. It don't matter none."

"That's your prize apron, and I've ruint it."

"It's just an apron. Come back and sit with me some more."

Daniel looked across her shoulder at Nate and sent a message with his eyes that Nate picked up on right away. *Be off with you*. Smiling with only the corners of his lips, Nate lifted a finger and gave Daniel a little salute, then turned and walked off the way he had come, softly whispering a morbid-sounding old hymn, shoulders slumping.

Daniel took Rebecca's arm, led her back to the mossy patch beneath the cherry tree, and sat down beside her again. Conversation came easily and with pleasure. He knew now that she did treasure his company. He was important to her, more important even than an apron of real cambric, made of fine linen.

GENERALLY SPEAKING, Daniel Boone never felt more in his element than when he was hunting. It was so natural to him, so easy and gratifying, that he had come to believe he was born to the purpose.

Not, however, to the kind of hunting he was taking part in that night. Though hunting was far more necessity than sport on the Carolina frontier, Daniel generally believed that wild game deserved a sporting chance unless, of course, a man was desperately short of meat, as happened to be the case at the Squire Boone cabin just then. At such time a man had to obtain his game the easiest way it could be had, whether by salting the ground to draw deer, killing bears hibernating in their winter dens, or fire-hunting with torches in the forest, shooting the game that came to investigate the unusual light.

Tonight's hunt was a variation on the latter system. Standing carefully in the back of a long dugout canoe, Daniel poled the craft a little closer to the riverbank. The night was clouded and very dark; the only light visible was a faint glowing smudge in the clouds, which showed where the moon was hiding, and the yellow flicker from the pine torch that burned upright in the prow of the canoe. Daniel could not see the actual fire of the torch itself, which was shielded from him by an upright screen of bark strips woven around a wooden frame. In the middle of the canoe sat his older brother, Jonathan, helping to balance the craft.

Directly before Jonathan, with rifle barrel poked through a view hole in the screen, was little brother Squire, namesake of their father. Even though he was a decade younger than Daniel, Squire was one of Daniel's favorite siblings. A good-looking boy with ruddy features and bright eyes, Squire admired Daniel and tried to learn all he could from him. He was a fast learner and showed promise of being a fine partner, once he had a few more years on him, for the long-range hunts Daniel had planned for his future. Daniel's affection for his little brother had led him to put Squire into the privileged position on tonight's hunt: he would be the one to actually make the kill.

All three in the canoe were very silent at the moment, having heard sounds of movement in the trees on the riverbank. It sounded like deer to Daniel, who poled the canoe around just a little farther so that the flaring torch cast light onto the bank. Daniel found it frustrating not to be able to see beyond the bark screen and hoped that Squire was keeping a sharp eye. A few moments later he saw the boy slowly lift the rifle butt to his shoulder, carefully click back the flint-bearing lock, and sight through the hole in the screen. Daniel rooted the pole in the river bottom to steady the canoe. His mind gave silent instruction. Easy, Squire. Just aim it easy. You'll only get one chance.

A couple moments of total silence followed as Squire steadied his aim. Then slowly the boy's finger squeezed down. The rifle blasted fire and sound and smoke, its recoil strong enough to make Squire rock back and the canoe itself push against the restraining pole in Daniel's hands.

Jonathan peered around the side of the bark screen. When the gun smoke cleared, he declared, "You hit it, Squire! A clean dead shot!"

"The eyes was a-glittering in the torchlight when I fired," Squire said, trying not to sound as proud as he obviously was. "I aimed right between them."

Daniel poled the canoe to shore and the three got out, Jonathan taking the torch from its stand. Jonathan and Squire examined the dead game, a young buck, by the light of the torch as Daniel dragged the canoe onto the shore. They had come intending to bring in one doe or buck, and now that they had, they would hunt no more that night, even though the same ploy would certainly work just as well again, farther down the river.

"Look there, Squire," Jonathan said. "Right between the eyeballs, just like you said."

Daniel came over. "That's a good kill, Squire. Your aim is getting better by the day."

"You couldn't have shot him better yourself, Dan," Squire said proudly.

Daniel grinned. "Reckon not."

Jonathan helped Squire field dress the buck, and they loaded it onto the canoe. They took down the blind shield, and Daniel could see where he was going much more easily. He laid the pole in the canoe and took up a paddle in its place, Jonathan doing the same. The canoe moved along the quiet, dark river, the dip of the paddles in the water a soothing, pleasant sound.

Jonathan was in a good mood, proud of his younger brother. Abruptly, he began singing:

I went up to London town
To court a fair young lady,
I inquired about her name
And they called her Devilish Mary . . .

Daniel grinned. Jonathan had a decent voice, knew many songs, most of them from England, and sang them quite well in an untrained baritone. Not a few of his favorite numbers told of taverns and bad women, songs he had somehow managed to pick up despite a strict Quaker upbringing.

We sat down to courting,
She got up in a hurry,
Said she had it in her mind
To marry me come Thursday . . .

Marry. The word seemed to ring in Daniel's ears. Ever since the cherry-picking frolic a few weeks back, he had not been able to shake out the notion of marrying Rebecca. He'd realized the very moment when she overlooked his destruction of her beloved cambric apron that she was a prize indeed. Even better, she thought of him as the same; otherwise, she would have sent him packing because of the apron.

Well, she filled my heart with sadness
And sewed my sides with stitches
And jumped and kicked and popped her heels
And swore she'd wear my britches . . .

Not Rebecca, he thought. *She wouldn't be that way.* Since the cherry picking Daniel had seen Rebecca five or six times. Just walks together, or conversations beside the creek. Daniel had told her of his restlessness, his feeling that the future for him lay west across the mountains. He said these things to her not only for the sake of conversation, but to see how she would react. Might she be able to envision herself as part of Daniel Boone's future? Would the idea of a life farther west put her off as intolerable? He had studied her reactions and found nothing in them to discourage his hope that she would consider entwining her life with his.

If ever I marry in this wide world,
It'll be for love, not riches.
Marry me a gal about four feet high
So she can't wear my britches!

"I like that song, Jon," Squire said. "Sing us another one."

Daniel stroked the water, then sculled to move the canoe farther toward the center of the river. Unexpectedly, he felt a literal aching in his heart. God in heaven, he longed to marry! He was as ready as he would ever be, and all but certain that Rebecca would accept his proposal. As best he could see it, there was only one barrier he would have to hurdle.

"Let's see, Squire," Jonathan said. "How about this one?" He cleared his throat.

Oh, hard is the fortune of all womankind,
They're always controlled and always confined.
Slaves to their fathers until they are wives,
Then slaves to their husbands the rest of their lives . . .

Again Jonathan's choice of songs had struck close to the very thing on Daniel's mind. Slaves to their fathers. Rebecca was still under her father's hand and part of his household until he relinquished her. So far Daniel and Rebecca's courtship had been entirely between the two of them. He had not asked her to marry him, nor her father for her hand. Would he be accepted? He knew he could easily fulfill the tradition by which young frontier men showed themselves ready to provide for a wife: killing a deer and dressing it out before the eyes of her parents. But even then, would the Bryans think him worthy of their daughter?

Your parents don't like me because I am poor,
They say I'm not worthy to enter your door.
I work for my living, my money's my own,
And if they don't like me, they can leave me alone.

That's right, Daniel thought. *I'll not be denied Rebecca Bryan, whatever they think about it. I'm as fine a young man as they'd find for their daughter, and if I'm poor now, someday I won't be.*

If they wouldn't give her hand to him, who would they reserve it for? Some coarse soul like Nate Meriwether, who had given Rebecca an interested glance or two in his time? Surely not . . . but then, what if somebody finer than Nate came along? Daniel might see Rebecca snatched away from him.

He made up his mind right then, and from that moment on, his resolve never wavered. Back home again, he hurriedly helped his brothers put the deer in the cold springhouse to await further dressing and butchering the next morning, then headed off to bed, where he lay long into the night, listening to the hammering of his heart and trying to think of how best to say what he had to say when the morning came.

Before dawn, Daniel was at the Bryans', awaiting the sunrise. As soon as he heard the family stirring to life inside, he went to the door and knocked. Joseph Bryan answered, obviously surprised to see him.

"I've come to speak with Rebecca," Daniel said.

"She ain't dressed," Joseph answered.

"Just have her throw a frock across herself and send her out. What I've come to say won't take long."

Joseph Bryan studied young Daniel Boone with a suspicion that slowly gave way to understanding. His eyes sparkled and he grinned. Calling over his shoulder, he said, "Rebecca! Come out soon as you're fit! You've got a caller this morning."

Rebecca looked pleased, but surprised to see Daniel so early in the day. He took her hand and led her away from the cabin as her family gathered around the door, watching them. Daniel turned his back on them; having to look at them while he said what he'd come to say would just be too difficult.

"Rebecca Bryan, I reckon you know I think highly of you. You're as fine a woman as I've ever met, and there ain't a minute goes by I don't have you on my mind. I reckon what I'm trying to tell you is, I don't think I can make it through the rest of my life without you, and I want you to become my wife." He spoke it all in a rush. When he was through, he drew in a breath. "There. I've got it all said. Now it's your time to answer."

When they returned to the porch, hand in hand, Daniel was filled with a greater joy than he had ever known. He looked Joseph Bryan in the eye. "Sir, I'll be back later, this evening if I can, with a deer to dress out for you and your family. I've asked your daughter to marry me, and she's said she would. I'd like to have your blessing on it, if you'll give it."

Joseph Bryan put out his hand. Daniel extended his, and they shook. "Daniel, I've wondered how long it was going to take you. Welcome to the Bryan family, young man. You want my blessing, then you have it."

Daniel grinned. "I thank you, sir. I thank you."

"You had breakfast?"

"No."

"Then come in with us. There's always room for you at our table. There always will be."

Daniel nodded his thanks. He hoped nobody would ask him to say anything for the next few minutes. If they did, he wasn't at all sure he could manage to speak without sobbing right out loud, and that was something he had never done in front of anyone, for any reason, since he was grown.

CHAPTER 4

August, 1756

THROUGHOUT THE MONTHS of Daniel and Rebecca's engagement, folks in the Bryan and Boone clans laughed about the jest Daniel made the day he'd performed the customary deer dressing for the Bryans. He had killed and skinned out many a deer in his life, and the Bryans knew it, so the act was really no more than a symbolic bow to tradition anyway; but Daniel approached it with dead seriousness, working so hard that he thoroughly smeared his hunting shirt with blood and grease from the dead deer.

This had prompted plenty of teasing from Rebecca's mother and sisters, who had turned Daniel's face red with embarrassment. He took it well, but at the supper table that night, he managed to turn the joke around when a bowl was set before him. Picking it up, he had looked at it closely and said, "This bowl is like my hunting shirt—both 'pear to have missed many a good washing."

The Bryan women had turned as red as Daniel had earlier, and Joseph Bryan thought it the finest joke he'd heard in a long while. He spread the story all around the neighborhood, to the chagrin of his wife. The Bryans were well-off folk in comparison to many of their neighbors, and Mistress Bryan had always taken pride in the cleanliness of their home.

There was no church close at hand, so the ceremony took place outdoors near the Bryan cabin. Nate attended, but he was a poor guest, being back in his melancholy state, and suffering the effects of having gotten drunk the night before. He was dirty and his clothing was ragged and, all in all, he looked like the no-account people were beginning to take him for.

Daniel paid no heed to such matters. His mind was fixed on Rebecca. He was standing in the yard, guests all around, and his own father, a justice of the peace, ready to perform the simple ceremony. All eyes turned toward the road when Joseph Bryan came riding around the bend with Rebecca behind him on a pillion. Daniel smiled; she saw him there, wearing a new pair of trousers and a fringed linsey-woolsey hunting shirt he had scrubbed to nearly the whiteness of her old cambric apron, and gave him a gentle, loving smile.

Joseph Bryan dismounted and helped his daughter down from the pillion. Perhaps he felt some sorrow or dismay at the idea of losing his daughter to another man, but Daniel saw no evidence of it in his manner. He was grateful that he could enter wedlock without any obvious burden of disharmony with soon-to-be in-laws.

If anyone felt emotional, it was Squire Boone. Daniel was surprised by the unusual quiver in his father's voice and the way his eyes reddened as he went through the ceremony. Then, in the nervous tension of the moment, it began to seem funny, and Daniel strained not to laugh out loud at Squire's discomfort. Thus father and son struggled against opposing emotions, and only with effort did Squire and Daniel manage to get the ceremony behind without tears or guffaws, respectively.

When they were declared man and wife, Joseph Bryan shook the hand of his new son-in-law, and together they went back to the horse. Joseph removed the pillion upon which Rebecca had ridden and handed it to Daniel, who put it on his own horse. He climbed into his saddle, rode over to Rebecca, and put down his hand to help her swing up. Ceremony and symbolism were done, and they were together, husband and wife at last. As badly as Daniel had been aching for this moment, now that it was here he realized it was going to take a lot of getting used to, being a married man.

Daniel and Rebecca led the wedding party back to Squire's house, where a tiny cabin Daniel and his father and brothers had built in the yard would be their first home. Once they were there, the spirit of ceremony was overtaken by one of celebration. A feast awaited, with deer meat, beef, corn, vegetables, loaves of bread, pies, molasses, cakes, and corn whiskey. Good humor bloomed like spring flowers, and before long the wedding guests were laughing and joking and having a fine time all around. Nate Meriwether delved heavily into the whiskey and quickly shook off his moodiness. Before long he was off behind the Squire Boone cabin engaged in a knife-throwing contest with Daniel's brother Edward, who went by the nickname of Neddy.

Daniel wasn't fully happy about being the center of attention, but he appreciated the company and the happiness all seemed to feel about his marriage. As evening came on and the western sky darkened, he grew eager for everyone to leave and for him and his bride to be alone. They had already talked about children; both were of the frame of mind to let them come along as quickly as nature could provide them, and in whatever abundance. Being the middle child in a family of eleven children, the idea of a small family was totally out of his experience. Daniel wouldn't mind it at all if they conceived their first little Boone that very night.

When the fires of celebration began to cool, the young women gathered around Rebecca and escorted her to bed in the loft of the new cabin, and Daniel was immediately hustled up afterward by his own brothers and friends. They tucked the couple in side by side, pulling the covers over them and handing out coarse advice that neither was at all comfortable hearing. They left them alone, and headed back outside for a little more liquor and much more laughter. Daniel and Rebecca lay for a long time, listening to the guests out in the yard, whispering to each other, and letting themselves grow accustomed to being close together in such an intimate way. Someone came up with another couple plates of food and some knowing winks and talk of "keeping up your strength," then retreated.

Daniel and Rebecca nibbled at the food, having had plenty before, and their laughter came more frequently and their conversation with greater ease. Bit by bit, the guests outside drifted back to their own homes, and by the time Daniel's parents finished removing the platters and trenchers from the makeshift tables set up outside, and the dogs that had been penned were set free to forage for scraps, both the twenty-one-year-old bridegroom and the seventeen-year-old bride were lost in each other and lost to all the world except the blissful, intimate one that existed in the tiny loft of their little cabin.

Afterward Rebecca gently stroked Daniel's face. "Promise me there will never be no other but me," she said. "Promise me that. No matter what happens, no other but me."

"I promise," Daniel said. "Before God Almighty, I promise. And you promise me the same."

"No others," Rebecca said. "No others but my own dear Dan, from now until the day I die."

A WEEK AFTER THE WEDDING Rebecca received an unexpected call from a small-framed, thin-faced woman named Rennie Lowell, wife of John Morgan Lowell, a distant neighbor even by frontier Carolina's standards. Rebecca had known Rennie slightly before she married. Rennie was quiet, plain, and unimposing—"mousy," Rebecca's father had once unkindly put it—a woman hard to read and harder to know. Rebecca never thought of Rennie as a full-fledged friend and was surprised to see her striding across the yard toward her, a baby boy on one hip, an older girl walking along behind, and a third child, still unborn, swelling her belly to an absurd-size on her tiny frame.

In her free hand Rennie held a tied-up bundle of dried wildflowers, which she thrust toward Rebecca as she approached.

"Rebecca, I've brung you a gift from John and me," Rennie said in her distinctive, breathish whine. "I'm sorry I couldn't be at your marrying. I wanted to come, but John, he needed me at the cabin, he said."

"Rennie, I'm grateful," Rebecca said. "Have you walked so far just to give me a gift? You needn't have done it."

"I wanted to. You've always been a good friend to me."

Rebecca was stunned. Rennie had considered her a good friend? She had been blind to it, nearly blind to Rennie herself. Rebecca felt shamed. She shouldn't have been so unnoticing.

"The flowers are so pretty, Rennie. Thank you." Rebecca lifted them to her nostrils. "You can still smell the scent of them, even dried."

"I love flares. I'd let wild ones grow right up to the door if John would let me. But he likes his cabin yard clean to the dirt. He don't like flares."

"Is he with you today?"

"No. I come alone, just me and the younguns."

"All them miles? Why, Rennie, you get in the cabin and rest yourself. I'll fetch us up some cold water to drink."

Rennie sat very straight and unmoving, eyes darting about while she sipped on her water. Her children sat beside her on the floor, as still and uncomfortable-looking as their mother. It made Rebecca feel uncomfortable herself. She wondered if Rennie had come there against her husband's wishes or without his knowledge.

"Where's your man?" Rebecca asked.

"Out a-hunting. Where's your'n?"

"Hunting. He hunts a lot."

"A man, he seems to want to be away from home as much as in it," Rennie said. She took another tight little sip of water.

"It does seem that way," Rebecca replied.

"Your Daniel, does he spend most his nights at home?"

"Yes," Rebecca said.

"I'm glad to hear it. My John, he spends most his nights out in the hills, a-hunting. Men stay home more at the first. Then time goes on by and they take to roaming about, days and nights on end, hunting and doing all the other that men do."

"All the other? What do you mean?"

"Oh, nothing. Don't know. Just roaming about. Tomcatting. Being men. They all do it."

Rebecca was cooling toward the conversation. "Well, Daniel hunts when he has to, and other than that, he's home."

"He'll be that way for a time yet. You treasure these days, Rebecca. Time will come you'll think back on them and pine."

The rest of the conversation was more mundane—a welcome change—but Rebecca remembered little of it when Rennie and her brood finally left. What lingered were Rennie's dire, fatalistic ideas about the nature of men. Unsettling notions . . . the first such that had entered Rebecca's marriage, and she hated Rennie for having been their vehicle. She felt no more pity, no more shame over having never realized that Rennie thought her a friend. Rennie Lowell was a cold and unhappy woman who spoke cold and unhappy words.

When Daniel came home that night, Rebecca greeted him with a hard, hot kiss and a strong embrace that she wouldn't let go. "Has something happened today, Becca?" he asked.

"No," Rebecca replied. "I'm just happy you're home."

"Where'd you get them dried flowers yonder on the mantel?"

"Somebody brung them in. A wedding gift."

"Who was it?"

"Just a woman I knew before we married."

"They're pretty."

"I don't care for them."

"I thought you liked dried flowers. What have we for supper tonight?"

That night before she retired, Rebecca burned the dried flowers in the fireplace and crawled into bed with her young husband. With deliberate forwardness far bolder than any she had yet shown, she made herself his while the smoke of Rennie Lowell's flowers curled up the chimney.

THE COUPLE DIDN'T LINGER long in the little cabin in Squire Boone's yard. Now that Daniel was married, he was determined to gather some sort of wealth for himself and Rebecca, and a man couldn't do that living in the shadow of his father's house. He needed a place of his own, land to work, a place to run livestock, a cabin that could be expanded as the family grew.

And so they moved to land Daniel had cleared along a Dutchman's Creek tributary called Sugartree Creek. This was the region occupied by Rebecca's kin, who retained ownership of the lot. Daniel and Rebecca's lack of ownership of the property made little practical difference; it was theirs to use as they desired. Family bonds were strong in the little Carolina community, and now that the Bryans and Boones had intertwined their broods twice through marriage, the two families had become something of a single unit.

Rebecca would have enjoyed the privilege of occupying her new home with only the company of her husband until their own little ones came along, but such was not to be. Daniel's nephews, eight-year-old Jesse and five-year-old Jonathan, sons of the late Israel Boone, came to live with them. They had always loved Daniel above all their other uncles, and in his typical easy-mannered way, Daniel agreed to take them into his home as if they were his own sons. Rebecca would have preferred it otherwise, but she never spoke a word. She was accustomed to life among lots of relatives, and after all, they were fine, well-behaved young boys and would be helpful around the house as they grew older.

Daniel and his wife entered into marriage in a better situation than did many of their time and neighborhood. The Bryans had been lavish with gifts, providing them furniture, pots and pans, dishes, linens—a dowry that the newlyweds were justly proud to own. Such fine possessions needed a goodly house to hold them and inspired Daniel to make their new home as fine a place as he could. Working with the Bryan men and sometimes helped by Nate, he hewed the logs as squarely as he could. The one-story house had but one door, south facing, and a large hearth with a soapstone-and-stick chimney. Daniel dug a well in the yard and built an exterior kitchen house. After they moved in, he made plans for future additions to the house—a puncheon floor, clapboard siding, and so on. Rebecca clearly relished hearing such plans, so he talked them up frequently.

Rebecca planted flowers outside and cleared the yard of weeds, then set about to ready herself for the arrival of their first child. Just as Daniel had hoped, Rebecca had become pregnant not far into the marriage, maybe even on their first night together. He thought she looked prettier than ever all big with child, even though her almost perpetually bare feet did tend to swell around the ankles and her face looked somewhat puffy. He teased her about it, but she took it well and teased him back. Their marriage was a playful one in those youthful, forward-looking days, and therefore a happy one as well. The cloud that Rennie Lowell had brought into Rebecca's mind faded and moved off to the horizons of her consciousness; not gone, but nearly forgotten.

The baby came along in due course; Daniel was thrilled that it was a son. They named him James, and his presence added a whole new flavor to the household. More than ever Daniel felt as if the cabin on Sugartree Creek housed a real family. He was fond of Jesse and Jonathan, but they were nephews, after all. James was a true son, the first life that owed its existence to Daniel and Rebecca. Daniel couldn't look at the infant without grinning, and his plans for the boy were big and unrealistically grand.

Daniel made his living like most around him: farming, trading livestock, hunting, trapping, driving a wagon from the outer settlements to the big towns; also doing blacksmith work for his neighbors. It was an acceptable working life, but the only part he actually relished was the hunting and trapping. The other jobs he more or less lived with, taking whatever pleasure he could in them but more often than not merely enduring them, with his eye casting longing glances toward the forested hills.

Whenever he could, Daniel ventured out with Nate Meriwether, his younger brothers Squire and Neddy, and occasionally others, hunting for two or three days at a time. He noticed Rebecca didn't seem to like his leaving, but a man had to bring in meat. He gave little heed to her barely masked unhappiness, a state Daniel silently dismissed as "womanishness."

Nate was somewhat better off that year than the one before. He didn't talk as much about his lost brothers and had a new, though intermittent, spark of life about him. Nate confided at length that he had begun seeing a woman. Oddly, he refused to say who she was.

Daniel and his fellows made occasional trips to Salisbury for militia musters that were motivated as much by the desire for fun as by the need for military readiness. The musters amounted to little more than drilling on the green, firing off a few practice rounds, and generally imposing a minimum of military form and order on independent backwoodsmen.

After the drills the men would get together at a local tavern for drink and talk, cards and dice. Outside in a clearing they would conduct target shoots, dogfights, cockfights. Like most, Daniel placed the occasional bet, but generally he had little to put up. Still, he greatly enjoyed the male fellowship and found the musters to be the best source of news from across a wide area.

Sometimes the news was disturbing: Cherokee Indians, Daniel learned one evening, had been killed in Virginia so their murderers could turn in their scalps, claiming they came from French-supporting Indians, and reaping the English bounty paid for them. The Cherokees, who maintained an often shaky alliance with the British, were enraged by such atrocities.

Indian problems were nothing new. In 1754 Governor Dobbs had arranged for a company of 150 men to protect the frontier settlements; commissioners in Salisbury had met with members of the Catawba tribe to gain their support in protecting the settlers against French-allied tribes.

Seventeen fifty-five had brought Indian dangers to the Moravian settlements of North Carolina, and finally the North Carolina Assembly approved the construction of a fort on the South Yadkin, named Fort Dobbs in honor of the governor. It was an impressive building, three floors high, fifty-three feet long, forty wide, and almost twenty-five feet tall. Shortly thereafter other forts went up on the upper Catawba River: Fort Prince George across from the South Carolina Cherokee town of Keowee, Fort Moore on the Savannah, and way over on the westernmost fringe and in the Overkill Cherokee country, Fort Loudoun.

Daniel had uneasy feelings through the first year of his marriage. Indian affairs were becoming all the more delicate as time went by. They made the future seem uneasy, and now that he was the head of a household, he had more to worry about than he had before. He had never worried much for himself. But Rebecca, little James, Jesse, and Jonathan—they made some things different. No, not some things. Everything.

Worries notwithstanding, life went on. Daniel did his best for his family and enjoyed the blessings that had been given him. But he wasn't fully settled. He couldn't conceive of life continuing as it was, and no more. He often cast his eyes west, across the mountains, and wondered when, and how, and how far.

DANIEL LIFTED THE HAMMER and slammed it down on the glowing horseshoe, making sparks fly. His sweat-drenched forehead was wrinkled, his broad mouth set in a thin line. He looked angry, acted angry, and in fact was angry, and the source of it all sat across from him in the little smithy shed, hardly noticing the effect he was having on his friend, being caught up in anger of his own.

It was Nate, though he looked so different from usual that it had taken a few extra moments for Daniel to recognize him when he'd come riding in about an hour before. Nate's face was swollen and bruised, his eyes blackened, his cheek marred with a deep scratch, and a thumb-sized section of his scalp raw where hair had been yanked out.

"A fight?" Daniel had asked as Nate dismounted.

"The cruel beating of an innocent man. Namely, me," Nate had answered. "He took after me with an ax handle, and I had done nary a thing to deserve it except pay call on his daughter."

Right then Daniel knew who had done this to Nate. A few days before, Nate had finally confessed that the woman he had been seeing for the past several months was Nora House, daughter of Pyler House, a farmer and hunter, and man of violent temper, who lived about ten miles from Sugartree Creek and seemed to relish possessing the worst of reputations. Nora's reputation was hardly better, for that matter. Daniel had never liked Pyler House and had been displeased when he first learned it was Nora who had caught Nate's fancy. He claimed he had been "courting" Nora. Daniel didn't believe it. No one "courted" Nora House. Her father was possessive and had put out word that only men of his choosing would have the opportunity to pay call on his girl. Nate was one of several who had defied him, seeing her on the sly. Daniel had warned Nate it would be only a matter of time before Pyler learned what was going on and made Nate pay for it. The battered man seated on the other side of the shed was proof that Daniel's prophecy had been accurate.

For almost an hour now Nate had been seated there, grumbling, cursing, vowing his vengeance on Pyler House and his intention to marry

Nora no matter what the man said about it. He had moaned and complained and drunk from Daniel's water bucket, meanwhile offering no help to Daniel as he forged horseshoes, and Daniel was getting bone-weary of it. But Nate's growlings were only growing more intense and threatening.

"I'll kill old Pyler next time I see him, Daniel. I ain't lying. I'll do it. I really will."

"That right?" Daniel laid a couple more blows onto the shoe. "You figure that murdering a man is going to solve your problems?"

"I figure it'll sure make me feel better," Nate replied, gently examining a tender place on his left jaw with his fingers and making a face of pain. "He came on me from behind, you know it? Yanked me right up off of Nora and commenced pounding me with that ax handle right before her eyes, and her crying and begging him to stop. 'Oh, please, Pap, please, don't hurt him!'—that was how she was a-shouting the whole time."

"You were on the ground atop Nora, were you, your back to the sky?"

"Yes . . ."

"Well, it don't take much to figure why Pyler was so mad! I don't blame him. What father wouldn't be?"

"Be that as it may, I'll kill the sorry old devil." Nate was working himself up as he talked. He lifted his hands, fists clenched side by side. "I'll choke the life out of him with these very hands. I mean it, Dan."

"If you do, then I'll have to testify that I heard you making that threat when they try you for Pyler's murder. If you even get to trial, that is. Pyler's a tough old knot. He might kill you instead of you killing him."

"Don't try to talk me out of it, Daniel."

Daniel laid down his hammer and closely examined Nate's damaged face. "Nate, are you drunk this early in the morning?"

"I ain't drunk. I ain't touched a drop of nothing for days."

"So you mean to tell me you're sitting there, cold sober, and swearing you'll murder a man who did no more than react like any man would who found a scoundrel dallying around with his daughter?"

"Scoundrel? Is that what you think of me, Dan?"

"Right close, Nate, right close. I'm just trying to understand how serious you are about this threat you're making. You ain't just flashing your pan, talking about murdering Pyler House?"

"I'm dead serious, Daniel. Some things a man can't stand for. I'm telling you gospel truth when I say I intend to see Pyler dead." He lifted his hands again. "These hands, his neck, and that will be all for Pyler House. I'll choke the life out of his body and send his black soul right to the ee-ternal fire."

Daniel didn't laugh now. He could tell that Nate really meant his words, and it sent an icy chill down him. He picked up the finished horseshoe with his tongs and dunked it into the water bucket. Then he hefted up the hammer in his right hand and slipped it behind his back. "Well, do you aim to wait for Pyler to come to you, or are you going to him?"

"I hadn't given it that much thought. I reckon I'll go find him."

Daniel glanced around as if to make sure no one was within hearing distance. "Well, if you're set on it, come here then," he said more softly. "I'll show you a way to do it a lot cleaner and easier than strangling him, and it will kill him quicker than lightning."

Nate drew near, looking curious. Daniel stepped back and laid his left hand out on the anvil, palm down. "Now, let me show you how you can do. Say my hand here is old Pyler, laid out in bed at night. Now, lay your right hand there atop mine."

Nate looked puzzled. "What are you trying to show, Dan?"

"Just lay it out. I can't explain it. You'll have to see it to understand."

Nate shrugged and put the back of his hand atop Daniel's.

"No, the other way. Palm down."

Nate complied. "I don' see what you're—"

In one fast motion Daniel jerked his left hand from beneath Nate's and grasped Nate's wrist. At the same time he brought up the hidden hammer and slammed it down toward Nate's fingers. Nate screeched in terror just as Daniel averted the blow to the side, making the hammer ring against the anvil, barely missing Nate's fingers. Had he struck them, they would have been shattered.

Nate jerked free and drew back his hand as if it actually had been hurt. "You deuced bloody fool! Are you trying to smash my hand?"

Daniel stalked around the anvil and stood before Nate, shaking the hammer in his face. "I should have. When I swung down that hammer, I wasn't half-sure I wouldn't. That way I'd be sure you wouldn't use that hand to hurt Pyler House or nobody else. As it is, I hope it was enough of a jolt to make you think about all the fool things you've been saying."

"Fool! You're calling me a fool, Dan?"

"I'm calling you nothing but what you're making yourself to be. Your feelings pull you along like runaway horses pulling a wagon, Nate. It's been that way since Braddock's Road. You ain't been fully your old self since all that happened. But never till today have I heard you talk like a murderer—and you not even drunk, so you can't blame whiskey for it! You've been my friend for a long time, Nate, and you're still my friend, and I'm hanged if I'll stand and listen to you talking murder—even if next time I really have to bust your hand to stop you!"

Nate's stare was cold and distant. He had never been one to like being preached at, and showed it. Daniel didn't care. He'd endured plenty of cold stares in his day and hadn't suffered the first case of chilblains yet.

"Get up, Nate, and out of here," Daniel said wearily. "Go set down somewheres and think real hard over whether Nora House is worth murdering for. Think about the way Nora has acted the common harlot with you and ask yourself if that's really the kind of woman you want to spend your life with, or be hanged for because you killed a man over her. You think about that, Nate. Now, get on with you, and don't come back till you've got some sense in your head."

Nate turned without a word and walked across the yard. With one icy glance back at Daniel, he mounted his horse and rode out of sight.

Carrying James on her hip, Rebecca came out of the cabin. Jonathan and Jesse raced up behind her. She had noted Nate's demeanor. "What's wrong with him?"

"He was just worked up, that's all. And I helped work him back down again. Nothing to give two more thoughts to." Daniel leaned over and kissed her lips, then tousled James's downy hair. "Well, I've got plenty to do yet. Jesse, you stay here and give me a hand; there's a good fellow."

CHAPTER 5

NATE SHOWED UP again at Daniel's two weeks later. Daniel was the first to see him coming. He rode in with the sunset behind him while Daniel was chopping firewood. Daniel took off his hat, combed back his hair with his fingers, and resettled the hat while he watched Nate draw near. When Nate rode around and the sunset light fell on his face, Daniel was confounded to see his face bore a strange, distracted, oddly placid expression, like a mystic who has seen a vision of angels.

"Howdy, Dan," Nate said.

"Howdy, Nate. How you been?"

"Well enough, well enough."

"You ain't killed Pyler House or nothing, have you?"

"Lord, no! Did you think I really meant that?"

"You surely seemed to mean it."

"You know me, Dan. More bark than bite. But forget that; it don't matter now. I've learned something that makes everything different. Everything." He smiled, and that beatific, awed look became even more pronounced.

"What is it?"

"Daniel—Clive is still living."

"What?"

"Clive, my brother Clive, he's still living! The Ottawas captured him, like that man told us, but they didn't kill him."

"How do you know?"

"From this," Nate pulled a folded piece of paper from beneath his belt and handed it down to Daniel. "It come to me just yesterday. It's from a second cousin of mine in Pennsylvania, and he's seen Clive, had him right there with him in his very house!"

"That's grand, Nate. Mighty grand, nigh a miracle! How did he get free?"

"I don't know—the letter don't say. All it says is that Clive is alive and that he's coming to North Carolina to find me."

Daniel looked over the letter, written by one Amos Harding and addressed to "Nate Meriwether, Salisbury, N. Carolina."

"Salisbury?" Daniel said. "Why did he post it to Salisbury?"

"You remember, I lived in Salisbury a few months before I came to

Dutchman's Creek? That was the most recent place Amos knew me to be. It was sent on out here by way of a Salisbury merchant who knew me in the town."

The letter itself was raggedly written by an obviously inexperienced correspondent, and contained little information. The relevant portion stated only that "Clive lives and come by my house. He was took by the Indyins and now is free and shall journey to N. Carolina with a companion and find you Nate. Be ready, Clive is much changed by his trials."

" 'Changed by his trials,' " Daniel quoted. "What does that mean? And who is this 'companion'?"

"I don't know. Soon I will, though. He's coming here to see me. Coming right here! Glory be! Hallelujah!"

Daniel quietly marveled at the unusual sight of an exultant Nate, then thought deeply for a few moments. "When you consider it, Nate, he's more likely to go to Salisbury. If your cousin don't know you are no longer there, will Clive know any different?"

Nate obviously had not thought of that. "No, no, I reckon he wouldn't. Lordy! He might go to the wrong place!"

There was no date on the letter, so it was impossible to know how long it took to travel from Pennsylvania all the way to North Carolina.

"Do you think he can manage to find his way to you in Rowan County if he does show up in Salisbury?" Daniel asked.

"Well, I don't know. I suppose he will, somehow or another. I hadn't much thought about it. All I've thought about is how much a miracle it is that I've thought him dead, but he's alive. I can scarcely believe it."

Daniel handed back the letter. "I'm glad, not only for his sake but for yours, Nate. All that grieving you did over Clive, it 'pears it was wasted."

"Yes." Nate grinned. "I don't think I'm going to grieve anymore, Daniel. Not even over Frederick. I've grieved enough. You're going to see a changed man in a lot of ways. No more getting drunk, no more running with sorry women like Nora, no more fighting and moping around and threatening folks. Pyler House can have his daughter. I don't want her." He held up the letter. "This here is a miracle from heaven, Dan, a miracle that's going to change the way I live my life. You wait and see."

Daniel grinned at the welcome words. "I'll look forward to meeting Clive whenever he shows himself," he said. "And I wonder who this companion of his might be. Climb down from that horse, Nate. Becca's putting supper on the table right now, and there's aplenty for you. Venison stew, with lots of taters."

"Sounds good, Dan. Sounds mighty good." He smiled broadly. "Life is grand, Daniel. My brother's alive, and he's coming to find me. Life is grand."

"Yes it is," Daniel said. "Grand indeed."

Nate returned to Daniel's house the next day, far more somber this time. He had been thinking about what Daniel had said about Clive trying to find him in Salisbury and had grown seriously worried that Clive would not be able to track him to his current area of residence.

"What if he gives up trying to find me?" he asked. "I might not see him at all. I might lose touch with him for good."

"The thing to do is to go to Salisbury, then," Daniel said.

"That's the same thought as mine. I hear something about a load of freight you're hauling—"

"Ah! Now I see why you've come."

"Yes. I could go alone, but the truth is I was hoping you'd linger with me there a day or two and search for Clive. I have the strongest feeling he's already there looking, and I'm afraid I'll miss him. That letter might have taken as long to get here as Clive himself, maybe even longer. And the part about his being changed by his trials it was like a warning. I'm fearful for his welfare; I must find him, quick as I can."

Daniel put a hand on Nate's shoulder. "Come with me on my wagon run. I reckon I can spare two or three days to give a hand to a friend."

"Aye, and a true friend you are, Daniel Boone. Even in wanting to bust my hand, you were a true friend. God bless you, Daniel. God bless you."

"Don't gush on me, Nate. I don't much like that kind of thing."

THEY SET OUT that very afternoon. Both rode in the wagon, with Nate's horse tied behind. All along the way Nate talked about his memories of life with Clive in their younger days, their parents, the voyage from England. Nate jabbered at top speed, looking rapidly about with almost birdlike jerks of the head, as if he expected to see Clive appear from the roadside coppices. Nate was so intense, he was almost too much for the easy-mannered Daniel to endure. When they paused to eat by the road, Nate bolted his food and paced about impatiently while Daniel finished his. Then it was back in the wagon, Nate declaring that he wished he could drive the team at a decent speed, instead of poking along as Daniel was doing. Daniel replied he was going as fast as he could without driving the horses to exhaustion.

Salisbury was a market town, one feeding end of a lifeline extending to the Yadkin-country settlers. It provided a place where furs, crops, and the like could be sold, and stores where goods could be bought. For men of the frontier, if not for the women, it was a place of occasional refuge and entertainment. Daniel was not prone to wild revelries, but never had he entered the village without being swept with a desire for fun and diversion. Normally, this was even more true for Nate, but today he talked not of taverns and cards and dice, but only of finding Clive. When the wagon rolled onto the street, Nate was actually standing on the seat beside Daniel, cupping his hand over his brows and looking around furtively at every face, drawing quite a bit of attention in the process.

"Nate, you're making us 'pear like fools that ain't never been in a town before," Daniel whispered.

"I'm all a-boil inside, Dan. He's here—I can feel he's here."

"Even so, you'll not likely find him like that. The thing to do is get this wagon unloaded and begin visiting the inns and public houses. We'll look into every one of them, leave your name in case he hasn't come yet, and if he's to be found, we'll find him."

Eagerness notwithstanding, Nate's common sense made him concede it was the best way. Daniel steered the wagon to a log-and-clapboard warehouse on a side street and made quick work of disposing of his load and receiving his pay. He arranged to park the wagon and stable the horses for a couple of days, then went with Nate to a nearby inn, where they paid in advance for lodging. "Is there a chance for a room where we won't be crushed upon by strangers?" Daniel asked the innkeeper.

"A chance," the little man replied. "But only the slimmest of them."

Nate asked the landlord whether he had recently had a guest by the name of Clive Meriwether. The man checked his book and shook his head. "No, sir. Nary a Meriwether until you. Are you kin?"

"He's my brother, coming from Pennsylvania to find me. He believes me to live in Salisbury. There will probably be another man with him, whose name I don't know."

"Where do you live?"

"Rowan County, in the Yadkin Valley, on Dutchman's Creek. If he comes to you after I've left this town, tell him he can find me there, if you would be so kind."

"If Clive Meriwether appears, I'll tell him. Dutchman's Creek, you say."

"Indeed. And if you guide him to me, I'll see you rewarded for it."

Daniel wondered what Nate had to give for a reward but kept silence.

"You remember now, landlord—I'm Nate Meriwether of Dutchman's Creek. The man who I'm looking for is my brother, Clive. You bring us together, you'll benefit for it."

They began going from inn to inn, tavern to tavern, looking for Clive but not finding him, leaving similar messages behind. By the evening Nate was growing discouraged.

"Don't be worried, Nate," Daniel said. "Hearing nothing of him may be the best thing we could have found. The most likely event is that he's not reached here yet. If he had, we'd have surely picked up some mention of him somewhere. But now you've got your name and where you live spread all over town, so whenever he does come in, he'll be bound to hear of it and come on to Rowan County."

"I'd hoped we'd just happen across him."

"Who can say we won't? We'll be here a day or two more. Now, what would you think of us finding some good victuals and a tankard or two to wash them down, eh?"

"Sounds fine, Dan."

They selected an inn based mostly on the delicious smells wafting from its doorway, even though they came primarily from the bakery next door. They ordered plates of beef and potatoes, two loaves, and big cups of ale. This time they were so weary even Nate ate slowly. Once finished, they felt revived and set out to explore the taverns again, pleasure rather than business in mind this time.

Daniel was not prone to excessive drinking. Throughout youth and into young manhood he had always been basically a sober, prudent fellow. Only once so far had he acted differently. A time years back he and a friend named Henry Miller had hunted and trapped for about a year all the way to the headwaters of the Yadkin, then hauled their peltries to Philadelphia to sell them. After that they had remained for three weeks, living the unfamiliar but thoroughly enjoyable life of the idle, frolicking rich, and came home with nothing much to show for their year's labor but a few gifts for their relatives. Daniel's mother had quoted him scripture about the prodigal son, but, all in all, little rebuke was given beyond that. After all, it had been Daniel's own money.

That one round of wild living had been enough to satisfy Daniel Boone. Tonight he planned to drink no more than he could handle and to mind no one's business but his own. Nate selected the next tavern, a place that Daniel would have passed over, a low-ceilinged, smoky, dirty place, full of the stench of humanity in its crudest, most drunken form. Nate and Daniel waded through the crowd and ordered more ale. Daniel took a sip, noted the poor quality, and set it aside. Nate seemed to like his, however, and drank it down, followed by Daniel's as well.

"Any more of that, and you'll be violating your pledge to turn away from drunkenness," Daniel said.

"I ain't hurting nothing or nobody. It's been a long day, and the liquor relaxes me."

"Well, if you think that there's a—" Daniel cut off as a human form slammed against him and knocked him from his stool onto the floor. The man who had fallen against him was heavy and ended up crushing Daniel's chest in just the right way to drive the breath from him. Struggling for air, Daniel's nostrils rebelled at the stench of the drunk atop him, who was now clumsily struggling to get off. Something wet and hot trickled onto Daniel's cheek. Shoving the man off him, he rolled to the side and rose, wiping at the moisture. It came off red on his hand. Blood. The drunk hadn't fallen against him accidentally. He had been driven against Daniel by a blow delivered by another man. The impact had shattered his nose and set the blood to flowing. The drunk groaned on the floor, then got up, his antagonist standing over him with fists moving in circles and ready to stab out again.

"Dan! You cut?" Nate asked, having vaulted off his seat as soon as Daniel went down.

"No," Daniel replied, still fighting for breath. "He bled on me . . ."

The man who had knocked down the drunk moved in and hit his victim again, making him pivot, flinging blood out like a spray. Some of it hit Nate in the face. He stepped hack, grunting in disgust, swabbing at his fouled cheek with his hand. A third man entered the fight, intervening to help the victim. This brought a fourth into the fray, and a fifth, and suddenly a full scale brawl was going on all around Daniel and Nate, blocking them from getting away, jostling them, bloodying them. A stray fist hit Daniel in the jaw and his temper surged.

He struck back; a man grunted and fell across a table, tilting it and sending himself and everything on the table to the floor. Cups and liquor flew, splattering the filthy floor. Curses rose; more joined the fight. Nate was grabbed by someone and hit across the nose, and suddenly he too was bleeding. Daniel moved in to help him but was cut off by another man sailing past him in virtual flight. Groping, the thrown man got a handful of Daniel's hair, dragging him down and evoking a bawl of pain.

For the next minute all was utter confusion. Daniel flailed about, hitting this jaw and that gut, lifting his arm to deflect blows, sending out jabs in all directions. Meanwhile he searched the room for Nate. He caught a glimpse of him, fighting while also making for the door. Good, Daniel thought. The best thing now was to get out of that place. A path opened around the surging scrum line of fighting men, and Daniel lunged toward the door. He reached it just as Nate did, and they butted against each other. In the confusion Nate apparently didn't realize he'd collided with Daniel and raised his fist to strike. The blow would have hit home had not a third man with thoughts of escape launched between them, pushing them aside. Once outside, the man turned and gaped openly at Nate, looking confused, then backed off into the darkness.

Nate recognized Daniel, lowered his fist, and together they pushed through the door into the street. Turning left, they darted down a few yards and ducked into a dirty alleyway to catch their breath and dab away the blood.

"Nate, never again will I let you pick the taverns we go to," Daniel said. "We hadn't been in there but—how long? A few minutes?—until that ruckus began. You've got a touch for finding trouble, you know it?"

"Clive?" The voice came from the end of the alley. Daniel and Nate wheeled as one to face the man who had left the tavern just before them. He was staring at Nate, who was slightly illuminated by light from a window behind him.

"Clive? Is that you? No, no—now I see that it ain't." The man acted nervous and sheepish suddenly, touched his hat, and began to stride away.

"No," Nate said, stepping forward so quickly the man started. "Wait—don't go. I'm Nate Meriwether, Clive's brother." The fellow turned, eyeing Nate more closely. "His brother! Aye, he told me of his brother Nate in Carolina! It was you he came to find. You have the look of Clive about you, my friend, judging from what I can see of you. When I caught first sight of you, I said to myself, 'Jim Cable, that there fellow could be Clive himself, come back again.' That's how much like him you are."

"You say Clive is already here? I've come looking for him."

"He was here," the man said. "But no more."

"Where did he go?"

"I don't know. You never know with Clive, not the way he is now. But don't you hold fault to him for his ways, Mr. Meriwether. No, sir. Had you witnessed what his eyes and mine have, you would be a right bad case yourself. To see Christian men painted black by savages, to see them lashed to poles and put to a death only a demon could want to inflict on a man—oh, you'd have turned to the liquor, too, just like Clive did. You mustn't judge him too harsh. Better men even than him have lost themselves in the bottoms of their cups."

"What are you talking about? Clive is drinking?"

"Aye, yes. He drinks to forget what it is to have seen his own brother burned to death by savages outside the walls of Fort Duquesne, curse the place! May the fires of hell rise to burn it and every Frenchman, and every savage, that ever set their foul feet in the place!"

Suddenly the man began to cry. He was very drunk, obviously. Maybe more than drunk. Daniel wondered if this man's mind was right. Something about him was odd, distorted.

Nate's voice took on a tremble. "Wait. You're saying that Clive's brother—my brother—was burned by savages outside Fort Duquesne?"

The man slapped his hand over his mouth, red eyes bugging. "Oh, forgive me, sir, forgive me! I had forgot for the moment that the poor wretch was your brother too! I would have told you a gentler way, had my wits been with me!"

Nate leaned back against the wall and stared at the dark sky, silent.

The man turned and began to hurry away

"Stop right there, friend," Daniel said. "We've more talking to do."

The man paused, on the verge of either stopping or making a hard bolt for freedom. Daniel reached him in three quick strides, snagged him by the shirt, and pulled him back toward the alley.

"Don't hurt me!" the man said. "I'll not run!"

"Not now, you won't. Come with us."

"Where?"

"Back to the inn where we're staying. And there you are going to tell us from beginning to end everything you know about Clive and Frederick Meriwether, and what has become of them. What did you say your name was?"

"Cable. Jim Cable."

"Let's take a walk, Mr. Cable. Our inn lies yonder."

Cable seemed worried at first, but Daniel gave him repeated reassurances that they had no intention to harm him. By the time they were inside the inn and made the pleasant discovery that the room they had been given had not been infiltrated by other boarders during their absence, Cable seemed more at ease.

"Tell me what happened to my brothers," Nate demanded.

"It's a tale you'll not like hearing."

"Tell it. I must know."

"Very well, then, though you must be patient with me if I don't tell it well—I've been in my cups tonight, as you can see."

In fact, he told his story very capably, though his voice was slurred. Cable described himself as a Pennsylvania gunsmith by trade, and a friend of Clive Meriwether and his family long before ill fortune came upon them. "I was with Clive at his home when the Ottawas came," Cable said. "Came without warning, they did. Clive's always been good to me, even though I turned too much to liquor after my wife died, and most everyone else thought me of no account. My cabin had burned—my own fault, trying to build a fire when I was too drunk to see the sky—and I had lost my gift as a mechanic of guns because of the drinking." He held up his hands, which trembled badly. "See that? How can a man with such a shake hope to whittle out a decent gunstock, or put a good rifling into a barrel? I lost it all—but Clive, he and his were evermore good to me.

"When the attack came, Clive fought hard for his family, but the Ottawas were too much for him. I tried to help, too, but there was naught I could do. They murdered Clive's wife and children, but they didn't kill Clive, nor me, and God knows if I understand just why. I think it was the way Clive fought that made them spare him . . . but me, well, it's yet a mystery. Such mercies happen sometimes."

He paused, considering his own words, and gave a cold laugh of irony. "Mercies, I say. Bah! The truth is, they didn't intend to give us mercy for long. They were planning to take us off and kill us slow, for sport, except that Clive was clever. He made them believe he and me both had knowledge of what the Brit army would be doing soon against Fort Duquesne and the French, and so they spared us. Hauled us off to Duquesne and turned us over to the French there."

"So Clive was a prisoner inside the fort when the battle happened!" Nate exclaimed.

"Yes, indeed he was, and me right beside him, standing on the rifle platform and looking out across the walls." Cable closed his eyes and shuddered. For a few seconds he did not speak. "We couldn't see the battle itself, but what happened after the battle we did see, and it was that what changed Clive from the strong man he had been to the drunkard and sad soul he became. The Indians, you see, had took some prisoners, British soldiers, Mr. Meriwether, and one of them was Clive's brother—your brother—Frederick. They blacked their faces, stripped them down, and burned them to death at stakes set up beside the river. They treated them fierce, with hot irons and sharp pieces of burning pine shoved into them. Clive watched it all, watched his own brother die that way. God. God help us. And the damned Frenchies, sitting there in the fort and hearing it all, and never even raising a brow while good white men were being treated so, right outside the walls! The screams of them poor men, they still ring inside my head, and all the liquor I can down won't wash them out. I hear them in my sleep. God!" After a moment or two of silence he opened his eyes again. They were red and moist.

"Poor Frederick," Nate whispered. "Poor, poor Frederick."

"How did you get away from the French?" Daniel asked.

"They set us free when they discovered we knew nothing. Some of their soldiers beat us good and threatened to turn us over to the Indians for the same treatment Frederick and the others took, but in the end they just let us go. And Clive, he was much changed. Seeing his wife and children killed, and then his brother after that, he become like me. I reckon it's partly my fault. I was already lost to liquor, and I helped him lose himself the same way."

Nate's head was lowered, his shoulders quaking slightly as he cried and tried to hide it.

Daniel said, "Nate got a letter from a cousin in Pennsylvania, saying that Clive had come on a visit and would come to Carolina to find Nate."

"Yes. We did go by one of Clive's kin for a time, a man named Amos Harding, I recall. He was bad disturbed by the news of what had happened, and even more by the state Clive was in. He began to tell Clive he ought to go to North Carolina and look up Nate. I believe Harding was mostly trying to get Clive out of his house because of how he disturbed him. Clive decided he would come find Nate, and I came with him. Nothing better for me to do. I didn't know nothing about Harding sending a letter to Nate, though. I reckon he must have felt the need to warn him."

Nate looked up. He had brought his emotions under control. "I reckon that's right. And Amos Harding, curse his soul, didn't even have the decency to tell me in the letter that Frederick was dead. I expect he wanted to leave that dirty kind of work to Clive."

"When did you reach Salisbury, Mr. Cable?" Daniel asked.

"Two weeks back, maybe. We looked about for Nate, asked for him, found no sign of him. It got Clive terrible worked up not to find him. After a week or so, he went away. He was just gone, like blowed-away smoke. Don't know where or why. I've been looking for him ever since."

"The reason you didn't find Nate was that Nate wasn't here. He hasn't lived in Salisbury for quite a long time, though Harding didn't know that," Daniel said. "He had no notion at all that Clive was looking for him until that letter came too late to do any good."

"So it would seem, sir," Cable said. He fingered the hat he had swept off his head when he entered the room. "Might I go my way now, sir?"

"Go on . . . unless you have more to say to him, Nate."

Nate had turned his face to the wall. He shook his head.

Cable rose. "I'm terrible sorry about having to bear such bad tidings, Mr. Meriwether," he said. "If I should see Clive again, I'll tell him you came looking for him."

"Tell him more than that," Daniel said. "Tell him Nate lives now in Rowan County, along the Yadkin at Dutchman's Creek. If he'll come asking there, he'll find his brother."

"I'll tell him, sir, if I see him. But it's been days and he ain't showed himself. I think he's run off for good and left his old friend Jim Cable behind. The fact is, sir, I fear harm might have come to Clive, maybe by his own hand."

Upon hearing those words Nate gave a sharp little spasm and grew even more pallid.

Daniel put his hand out and gently pushed Cable toward the door. "No need to add a bunch of idle surmising to a matter that's bad enough as it is."

Cable gave a wince of embarrassment. "No. No, sir, there's not. Speaking too freely and supposing too much, I was. Clive is probably well and fine wherever he may be. Yes, I'm sure he is . . ."

"Good evening, Mr. Cable," Daniel said.

"Yes, indeed, good evening to you both. Good evening and fare you well, with God's blessings . . ." And then he was out the door and stumping quickly away, stammering as he went.

"Remember, Mr. Cable!" Daniel called after him. "Rowan County, Dutchman's Creek! That's where to tell Clive he can find his brother."

"Yes," Cable said, his voice receding. "If I see him, I'll tell him that very thing."

Nate stood. "I'm going to get drunk."

"What good do you think that will do, Nate?"

"Not a bit. But it'll sure make me feel better. God knows there's nothing else that'll do that right now." He pushed past Daniel and out the door.

Chapter 6

In his years in the forests Daniel Boone had observed and adapted to his own person the same skills that kept alive the creatures of nature who lived there—the quick, evaluative, observing power of the rabbit, the athletic celerity of the gray squirrel, the keen scenting skill of the wolf, the silent stalking ability of the mountain panther, the statuesque stillness of the hiding buck. At the moment, he employed the latter skill, standing with rifle half-lifted in the midst of a copse of maples, his form so still that it blended into the background of the forest. Even another awl-eyed hunter might have passed him by with no suspicion of his presence.

He had frozen in place when he heard the voice. It had come from somewhere across the wooded ridge that rose before him and sent a chill of horror through him. A human voice, it had seemed to be but not quite. The closest thing he had heard to match it was the keening wail of a grieving squaw back in Pennsylvania, whose daughter had suffered a terrible seizure that had first sent blood coursing from her nose, then stiffened her in sudden death. Daniel had witnessed the event as a young boy, and the impact of it had been tremendous. The wail he heard from across the ridge spurred all the boyish horror he had felt when he'd seen the Indian girl die.

He heard it again. Indeed, it was a human cry. A man's voice distorted in pain or grief, but vaguely familiar.

Daniel broke into motion. Lowering his rifle, he left the copse and ran up the slope. It had rained earlier in the morning, and the mast was soft beneath his moccasins, allowing him to move with hardly a sound. Near the top of the rise he slowed and cocked the rifle, just to be ready.

The wailing changed to a low moaning and weeping by the time he crossed the ridge. Daniel quickly determined from where it came, a little rocky enclave at the base of a shallow bluff, a natural depression in the mossy bluff wall, in which he himself had nestled during past deer hunts on wintry days, sheltered from the wind and cold while waiting for prey to come by. Moving to his right for a better view, he peered down at the nook and saw a man kneeling there, leaning against the bluff as if it were an altar, crying and shaking his head. Stepping closer, Daniel saw that the man was John Morgan Lowell, whose cabin was less than a mile away. There was blood on Lowell's forearms.

"John!" Daniel called out—after first looking carefully to see that Lowell didn't have his rifle close at hand. He didn't want to risk startling the distraught fellow into grabbing his weapon and shooting him. "John, it's Dan Boone! Are you hurt?"

Lowell came to his feet. His face was ruddy and wet from crying, his chest was heaving, and now Daniel saw that it was not only the man's forearms that were bloodied: his hunting shirt was encrusted with blood across the front—drying blood, not fresh, indicating either that Lowell had stanched his bleeding—or that the blood was not his own. "Boone? That you, Boone?" Lowell's voice quaked terribly.

"Aye, it's me. I'm coming in—don't go shooting me for an Indian or something."

"I can't shoot. My rifle is back at the cabin. Oh, God! Back there, in that place, where I dropped it when I seen—oh, God!" He burst into tears again, and Daniel filled with dread. What could be so terrible as to bring a grown man to such tears?

Daniel came near, but held back from Lowell a few yards. He didn't put down his rifle. The thought crossed his mind that perhaps Lowell had gone mad. Daniel had never encountered a madman and didn't know what deviltry such a man might perform. "What's wrong, John? Are you hurt?"

"Rennie, my Rennie . . . the children—oh, the children!"

"They're injured?"

"Dead, Boone. They're dead, all of them, dead in their blood right in my own cabin!"

Daniel's first thought was of Indians. Some isolated, wandering band of disgruntled Cherokees, perhaps. They must have come upon the Lowell cabin while John was away. Like Daniel, John Morgan Lowell loved the woods and the life of the hunter and trapper, and he was often away from his family, ranging for miles to the west.

"Was it Indians?"

Lowell sobbed loudly, which Daniel at first took for confirmation. But Lowell shook his head, then lowered it.

"It warn't Injuns. It was her. It was Rennie."

"Rennie . . . you mean . . ."

"Go look, Dan. Go see the evil she done to herself and the children. I found them in their blood. Cradled their dear heads against me, but it was too late. Too late. Go see it . . . I can't bear to go back there myself."

There was no sleeping for Daniel Boone that night. He sat up in bed, back against the cabin wall, and stared into the darkness. Rebecca lay at his side, her head nestled against his arm, her hand caressing his shoulder, as she vainly sought to comfort him.

"How could she have done it, Becca?" he asked in a whisper. "How could any mother ever take the life of her own babes? One by one she shot them, and herself last. Why?"

"Maybe because she was so much alone," Rebecca replied.

Daniel looked at her. In the darkness, her form was an imprecise outline. "There's many a woman alone much of the time, but they don't do such evils."

"I know. I can't excuse her. It's just—I know it was hard for Rennie to be alone. Her man left her so much. It made her sad and hard of soul."

"How do you know so much about her?"

"Do you remember the dried flowers that were given me a little while after we were married? You asked where they had come from."

"I remember."

"It was Rennie who brung them."

"Rennie! She came a far distance just to bring a handful of flowers."

"She said I had been a friend to her, and it was important to her to give me a gift."

"I recall you said you didn't like them flowers. You even burned them that evening, didn't you?"

"Yes I did."

"Why?"

"Because of things Rennie said. Things I didn't like hearing."

"Tell me."

Rebecca hesitated before speaking. "She said that her John was always leaving her alone. That men were like that, staying home at the beginning of a marriage, drifting off later, staying away from home, leaving their wives alone to get by."

"All men ain't like that. John has done his share of roaming and hunting, but such has to be when you live in border country."

"She said you would do the same in time."

"Me? Why, I reckon I'm home often enough."

Rebecca was silent a time. "Not as much as you were at the start. You roam more, hunt more. Many a night you don't come home at all."

"Becca, you can't hold me to fault for doing what I must to keep meat on our table." He sat up straighter. "Lord have mercy, Becca, here I am, sick to soul and stomach for what I saw today, and you sound as if you're chiding me!"

"I'm not chiding you. It's just that I . . . I understand just a little of what must have tormented Rennie."

"You'd make excuses for a murderer?"

"I told you already I don't excuse her. Understanding ain't excusing."

"I'm glad to hear you say that. Because there ain't no excusing what I saw inside that cabin today. And there ain't no understanding, neither. I'll not forget it. If you had seen it, you'd not feel any softness toward Rennie Lowell. You'd not even say you understand it."

Rebecca lay silent for a few moments, then said, "I wish you hadn't have seen it."

"So do I."

"And I wish Rennie had never come here that day with them flowers." He felt the tension in her. Reaching over, he stroked her hair. "Put it behind, Becca. What Rennie did was terrible. There's no forgiving it. And there's no changing it. So just put it behind."

"Yes." They held each other for a time. Daniel stared into the darkness, still vividly imagining the hellish scene that he had found inside the Lowell cabin. But with Rebecca's warm touch soothing him, bit by bit the images faded and sleep approached. He was about to drift off when Rebecca's soft voice partially roused him.

"Dan?"

"Hmmm?"

"Always try to remember how hard it can be on a wife and family when a man stays gone too long. Always remember. Will you?"

"I will," he replied. But even as he said it, he was falling asleep, and the words held no meaning for him. He slept without waking but dreamed of scenes too terrible to remember in the morning, scenes of blood and corpses and death.

Early Spring, 1758

REBECCA BOONE, hands on hips, stood in the yard and looked down the road, brows knit, as she watched the lone rider approach. In a moment she turned to Daniel, who stood nearby. "It's Nate, just as I thought. Coming to drag you off to war!"

"He'll not drag me anywhere, Becca, and I've told you already I'm not going to fight, but to drive a wagon. Just like the first time."

"But this time it's different. You'll be leaving me alone with one child still a baby and another on the way. How can I know you'll even be here to see our secondborn? How can I know you'll come home at all?"

"No one knows such things, Becca. A man can go into the woods to hunt squirrels and be whumped on the head by a falling branch and whoosh! There he goes, off to Glory Land. I could get killed or hurt just staying home." Seeing she was unswayed, he went on. "It's unfinished business for me, Becca. We run off from the first try at taking Fort Duquesne. Now I want to go back and do better on the second."

Rebecca sighed. "I believe it's Nate Meriwether's wanting to pay back for his brothers that has you riled up, Dan. For the life of me I can't see what need some Scottish general has for Daniel Boone running all the way to Pennsylvania from North Carolina just to roll wagons across the wilderness." She stopped speaking now that Nate was closer. Turning on her heel and making no greeting, she walked into the cabin.

Nate watched her go. He had become aware long ago that Rebecca Boone didn't think too highly of him. "Hello, Dan."

"Nate. How are you today?"

"Ready to throw my weight behind General Forbes. What about you?"

"I've talked to Becca about it. She ain't happy. But be that as it may, I'm going and she knows it."

"Good. Good."

Daniel was talking with the kind of devil-may-care, manly aggressiveness Nate would respect, but inwardly he thought that maybe Rebecca had a good point. Was there really any need for him to head off to join the second thrust against Fort Duquesne, a thrust that had taken three years to come about since the disaster under Braddock? Would he even be considering taking part if not for Nate's continual prodding?

Probably not. He too suspected that Nate was using this new campaign to be led by Scottish-born Brigadier General John Forbes, under the orders of William Pitt, as his way of striking back for the family loss he had suffered.

Sadly for Daniel, Nate hadn't even tried to live up to all the promises of reform he had made when he'd first learned that Clive was still alive. The disappointment of not finding him had broken his will. He still drank too much, still had been seen from time to time with Nora House, even though her father openly despised and threatened him, and still brooded over his lost brothers. He seemed to assume that Clive was dead, probably the result of suicide or some disaster brought on by his reported heavy drinking. Daniel couldn't fathom what sense Nate saw in bringing himself to ruination along with his brothers. The best he could figure was that it had little to do with sense. Nate was driven too much by feeling, too little by reason.

Yet on the matter of joining Forbes's military expedition, Daniel was of the same mind as Nate, for a cause almost as personal. Ever since he had fled in stark fear across the Monongahela on the horse he had cut free from its traces, he had felt that nagging sense of unfinished business, of an offense left unanswered. Forbes's campaign would provide that finish, that answer. The prospect of being present when Fort Duquesne at last fell into British and colonial hands was very enticing, and Daniel had easily convinced himself that the Forbes campaign couldn't fail, and that it was his duty to be part of it.

Nate dismounted. "I've learned of a few others who'll be going as well, Dan. We'll leave the morning after next. Can you do that?"

Daniel heard Rebecca's voice inside the cabin, scolding little James for having knocked over something or another. Daniel didn't look forward to having her turn that same scold on him. The thing was, it wasn't typical of Rebecca to be that way; generally, she was the most amiable of women. He could only conclude that her feelings on the issue were unusually strong.

"Rebecca fixing supper?" Nate asked.

"Yes, I believe so."

"Reckon there's enough for me to join you?"

Daniel grinned at Nate's typical directness. "Come join us—but be warned. Becca ain't happy about the notion of my going off to fight."

They entered the cabin. Rebecca was stooped over a pot, stirring the squirrel stew that was to be supper. Straightening, she brushed a strand of hair back from her sweat-dewed forehead and cast her dark eyes on the two men. James rolled on the floor, making loud noises in his throat.

"Hello, Nate," she said.

"Howdy, Rebecca."

"Nate's not had his supper. Reckon we could—"

"Why, of course. There's plenty, and we're happy to share."

Daniel flickered his brows, a subtle gesture of relief. He had been afraid Rebecca might be harsh to Nate, even though she usually wasn't the kind to treat folks ill.

Rebecca dished bowls full of stew and tore hunks of bread from a big round loaf for each of them. There was nothing to drink but water. They ate with little conversation, typical of the Boones, while James lay on a pallet of flax in a high-sided wooden crib. Jesse and Jonathan jabbered to each other about an elaborate game of white-man-and-Indian they had played the day before, oblivious to the adult conversation. They bolted their food and raced out the door, Rebecca watching them. Nate concentrated on his food until his bowl was emptied three times, then leaned back to talk about the coming campaign.

"This shouldn't take so long if it's done right. I say go back to Duquesne by Braddock's Road, take six, seven thousand men if need be, and smite them hard and hold out long. And buy the Indians into it with gifts and such. You can always buy the loyalty of Indians, don't you think, Dan?"

"Don't know I'd say that as a rule, Nate."

"Well, no matter about that. If Forbes can learn from what was done wrong by Braddock, damn his soul, Duquesne can fall, and my brother Frederick can lie in peace at last."

Daniel glanced at Rebecca. Her face was beginning to show signs of strain. Nate kept on talking, following the same lines, growing ever more explicit in his descriptions of the cruelties of the French and Indians and his own retaliatory intentions, unrealistically combative ones for a man signing on as a wagoner. The more Nate talked, the more pronounced Rebecca's strain grew. Finally, Daniel pushed away his bowl and stood, interrupting Nate in midsentence. "Nate, let's step outside and talk awhile."

Nate looked puzzled, but shrugged and nodded. Outside, he dug tobacco from his pocket and bit off a chew of it. "What's the matter, Dan? Did I say something wrong?"

"Becca's getting fretful, I can tell from her looks. The more you talked, the worse it was. A man has to be careful around womenfolk."

Nate shot Daniel a sly grin. "That so? Well, I reckon I'll be learning that lesson myself, once we're back from this campaign."

"What are you talking about?"

"I'm getting married."

"Married! Who to?"

"Nora."

Daniel took a step back. "Nora! Are you that great a fool, Nate? Why, her father'll murder you!"

"I don't believe so. He's gone."

"Gone? Dead gone?"

"No, just gone, though he may be dead, for all I know. To tell the truth, I hope he is."

"Nate, you tell me something straight out: you haven't gone and killed that man, have you?"

"Lord, no! When you about busted my hand, you managed to drive that notion plumb out of my head. What it comes to is, nobody knows what's become of old Pyler. He got into a fight of some kind and had the sheriff looking for him over it. Nobody's seen him since, and that's more than a month ago. Some say he's gone to Virginia, where he has kin. For all the protecting way he's acted about his daughter, he surely up and left her behind without so much as a batted eye."

"How has Nora been getting by?"

"On her own, and with me providing for her. I've hunted game for her, brung her food I've raised. I told her that since I was providing for her like a husband, I might as well just be one. She accepted right off, with only one condition."

"Well, I should congratulate you, though I worry that Pyler might come back and put you in your grave if he finds you hitched up with his little girl."

"You're getting to that one condition I mentioned. Nora has come to believe her father is probably dead, but she wants to be more certain. Go off on your fight, she says, and if he ain't returned by the time you get back, I'll marry you. So that's how it stands."

"Nate, I don't know what to say. I wish the best for you." Daniel didn't feel free to speak his doubts fully about the proposed marriage. Nora House was known to be no more than a harlot, respected by no one and just as untrustworthy as her father. She was the kind who looked out for herself first, and it wouldn't surprise Daniel at all if Nate returned from Forbes's campaign only to find Nora had taken up with some other man in his absence.

"Are you talking open about this marriage?"

"Not yet. No point in it until we're ready to take the vows."

"Should I tell Becca?"

"Suit yourself. It don't matter." Nate spat and scratched his neck. "Well, Dan, I'm heading home." He peered through the door into the cabin. "Rebecca? Thank you much for the supper. It was prime fare!"

Daniel watched Nate ride away. Quite a marvel, that man was. Up one minute, down the next, riding through his life on the rise and fall of however he felt at a given moment, and those feelings constantly changing. Most of it wasn't Nate's fault, he allowed. Until the tragedies that had come upon him, Nate had been nothing but a typical young frontiersman with no more flaws or problems than the average man. Now his future seemed as unpredictable as the wind.

DANIEL SPENT THE EVENING cleaning his rifle, mending a tear in his rifle pouch and wrapping a supply of jerked meat for eating on the way to Pennsylvania. Rebecca watched him without comment, knowing that his actions marked the final confirmation of his plans. He really was going to join the Forbes campaign. Further discussion of the matter was to no avail, and she would not pursue it.

It was sad to think of Daniel heading off so far, for heaven only knew how long. She was accustomed to having him gone on fairly extensive hunts from time to time, but this was different. This was war. Even if he was no more than a wagoner, he might be killed.

She rocked James to sleep that night, thinking about her future. Daniel had talked to her of his dreams of someday moving over the mountains. He spoke of hunts that he would take, confessing that he might be gone for a year at a time, maybe more. She had wondered how serious he was about such things. Could he really leave his family alone for such a long period? She had doubted it before. Now, with Daniel getting ready to go off to Pennsylvania again, she wasn't so sure.

She was beginning to learn an unwelcome lesson: Daniel Boone was a good and sincere husband, but he was still very much his own man, living life his own way and not necessarily hers. And Rennie Lowell, despite the evil thing she had done, had been basically right about one thing: men did roam, men did leave their wives and families alone. Even good and loving men like Daniel Boone.

CHAPTER 7

DANIEL ENTERED THE CAMPAIGN with hopes that Brigadier General Forbes would prove a more savvy leader than had Braddock. It was difficult to judge either way at the outset. Forbes's approach to Fort Duquesne was going to be different both physically and tactically. In Daniel's mind it counted to Forbes's favor that he was a man with ideas of his own and the will to enforce them. If he would make mistakes, they would be his own, not mere repeats of those made by Braddock.

Forbes would have to face one problem that Braddock had not: personal illness. Forbes was a very sick man, maybe a dying one. When Daniel first saw him, he was surprised that a man not yet fifty years old looked about fifteen years older than that. On Forbes's face were the kind of lines only pain can etch, and often he was in such poor condition he could not bear to sit his horse. An abdominal ailment of some kind, the story had it. Supposedly no one, Forbes included, knew just what it was, and this even though Forbes had originally been a physician in his native Scotland before entering military life. He had distinguished himself as a military man, serving as lieutenant colonel of the Scots Greys in 1745 and acting as quartermaster general under the Duke of Cumberland. In 1757 he had come to America as a brigadier general, and the success or failure of the campaign to seize Fort Duquesne would inevitably be the test by which his record would be judged forever after.

Forbes had made clear his determination to plan every detail of the campaign. This was time-consuming, leaving the soldiers themselves stalled, with impatience mounting. Daniel perceived soldiers to be a contradictory folk. Whenever they were stalled, they were eager to get on with whatever campaign lay before them, but as soon as they did, they always grumbled and declared they wished themselves still at rest in camp.

Fort Cumberland was crawling with military men from the moment Daniel Boone and the other Yadkin volunteers arrived. Swiss-born Lieutenant Colonel Henry Bouquet had brought in more than a thousand Highlanders from Carolina, along with three hundred Royal American troops and even a band of English-supporting Cherokees. George Washington, the battle-tested Braddock campaign veteran, had led in about two thousand Virginia colonials. All in all, there were about nine thousand men at Forbes's disposal, and this at a time when it was known that Fort Duquesne was poorly garrisoned. Prospects were bright for a successful effort.

But there were disputes at high levels. George Washington favored basing the campaign in Virginia and moving in on Braddock's Road, which, though covered with brush and scrub trees that had grown up since the earlier campaign, still seemed the quickest route. This had some obvious secondary, nonmilitary advantages to Washington's native Virginia, where he served in the House of Burgesses. Reopening Braddock's Road would create a commercial route to the west leading right out of Virginia.

Forbes had a different idea. He favored advancing along a more direct route across Pennsylvania, cutting a new road as they went while building fortified supply depots along the way, where provision would he held temporarily until the main army was within reach of Fort Duquesne. At that point the supplies in the depots could be quickly moved forward to reach the army, and the siege could begin. In this way Forbes hoped to avoid the problem that had plagued Braddock: moving a full wagon train of supplies the full distance right along with a massive army.

But there was more to Forbes's proposal than that, the insightful believed. He had been influenced by Pennsylvania land speculators looking for some of the same political advantages Washington had desired for Virginia. Whatever his reasons, Forbes settled on the more direct route, leaving Washington frustrated.

They set out late in July. Initially it all felt very familiar to Daniel Boone, like a repeat of his experiences under Braddock. Looking ahead, he anticipated long summer days dragging by as they tramped and rolled their way into the Alleghenies, fording creeks and building bridges across the rivers, creeping along the rutted, stump-filled route. All along they would build their depot stockades and fill them with supplies. Leaving behind a force to guard each depot, they would go on. It would be grueling and slow, but no one could complain that Forbes was having it easier than his men. In fact, he would have it much harder. His physical condition had already deteriorated to the point that he had to travel on a litter slung between two horses. He was in pain at all times.

Soon all the grumbling Daniel had anticipated from the troops occurred in abundance. Word had it that Forbes was deliberately planning to move slowly, believing that the French-supporting Indians had little natural patience and would probably desert if forced to wait a long time for battle to be joined. They might even be lured to the English side by diplomacy, and this he attempted through selected emissaries.

Daniel despised the diplomatic stops. For the wagoners they provided long, dull hours when nothing much happened. Not usually, at least.

DANIEL BOONE PAUSED at the end of the high, rugged bridge and eyed the lone man standing in the center of it. The fellow was an unusually large Indian with a big, peculiar grin on his face that was very disconcerting, especially when a glance about revealed to Daniel that there was no one else around toward whom that grin could be aimed. From the way the man wavered, Daniel guessed he had been drinking.

Hanging fire there at the end of the bridge, the only way across the watery mountain gorge that cut the landscape like a great wound, Daniel grew increasingly worried. The Indian wasn't retreating or advancing, leaving Daniel with the option of remaining where he was and inviting the Indian to perceive him as afraid, which in fact he was, or go on and try to get past the man. Every instinct he had told him that would not be easy. The Indian had a look about him that was a silent dare for Daniel to try, just try, to get past him.

Daniel cursed his luck. He had crossed this high bridge earlier in the day, carrying two large sacks of flour needed by one of the expedition's cooks. He had lingered about the cook fires for conversation and food and was now returning to his own camp across the gorge. His timing couldn't have been worse. If ever he had seen a man looking for trouble, it was this grinning Indian.

The Indian took one step closer and moved more to the center of the bridge. Standing tall, he folded his arms across his chest and motioned with his head for Daniel to come on. For a moment Daniel considered turning and walking back to the camp, but the fact was that he needed to get to the other side. And with no one else around, the Indian might come after him if he turned his back. Daniel was fleet, but so were most of the Indians he had known.

Steeling himself, he assumed a blank expression and advanced along the bridge, veering to the right. The Indian stepped in that direction, cutting him off. Daniel veered the other way. The Indian stepped in that direction too. Daniel drew to a stop.

"Hello," he said.

"Hello," the Indian replied. "You are a Long Knife," he added, using the typical Indian expression for white colonials.

"My name's Boone." He was glad that the Indian spoke English. Maybe he could talk his way out of this.

But the Indian drew a knife. "The headmen are at the council fires with your English Long Knives, talking of going to war at their side." The grin vanished. "I hate Long Knives and will never fight beside them. I kill many of them. Today I will kill another."

Instantly, Daniel understood the broader implications of the situation. He knew that Forbes was making overtures to Indians in the area, seeking to gain their support against the French. This Indian apparently hoped to end the diplomacy by killing a white man.

Daniel's dilemma was terrible. He wasn't about to let himself be murdered, and the only way to stop that might be to kill the Indian. But this would be difficult. Daniel doubted he was a physical match for this giant of a man, and for once he didn't even have his knife or belt ax with him. Even if he did manage to kill the man somehow, the act would certainly infuriate the Indians and destroy the council talks. It could lead to retaliation and other killings. If only he could get past him.

The Indian swung the knife in a big circle, laughed, and lunged forward. Daniel had no more time to think, only to react. Lowering his head, he charged toward the Indian, dodging as the knife swung. Shoving his shoulder forward, Daniel butted the Indian in the gut. The Indian doubled over and fell back, letting out a loud woof!

By now Daniel was past. He turned on his heel as he realized what was happening and gaped at the sight. The Indian teetered on his heels at the very edge of the bridge. Sensing that he was on the brink of falling backward, the Indian straightened and swung his arms in big arcs, his face wild with fear.

He still gripped the knife with which he had intended to dispatch Daniel Boone. He still gripped it when he lost his struggle for balance and pitched back into empty space.

Daniel rushed to the side of the bridge in time to see the Indian crash against the rocks forty feet below. For a moment the Indian lay spread-eagled on the rock that caught him. Then he slid off into the dark, rushing water and washed downstream. A red liquid stain on the rock slowly disintegrated in the rushing water.

The body itself washed under an overhanging rock and did not come up again within Daniel's sight. Perhaps it had hung up on something beneath or was caught in an underwater current.

Daniel sank to his knees, panting. His head swam so badly he feared standing, feared he might stagger and fall off the bridge himself. He had killed a man! And he wasn't even sure he had done it on purpose.

Finally he stood and made his way across to the other side, feeling queasy. Pausing, he looked all around. No one. As best he could tell, there had been no witnesses to the incident. He turned his back to the scene and went on to his camp.

"DEAD? You're certain of it?"

"Not so loud, Nate!" Daniel said in a sharp whisper. He was seated beneath a big pine, his supper spread on a trencher balanced on his lap as he sat Indian style. Hardly a bite of it had been touched. He had just finished telling Nate in a whisper what had happened on the bridge. "And yes, I'm certain. You know how high that bridge is. He fell flat out on a rock and slid under the water."

"You ain't told nobody?"

"I've been thinking maybe I should report to one of the officers."

"No," Nate interrupted. "Don't you do it. They're talking with the Indians hereabouts, trying to gain their help. If word gets out that one of their own was thrown off a bridge, that'll be the end of any talk."

"I know that. It just seems to be something I should tell. What if the body washes up somewhere and gets found?"

"Nobody saw what happened?"

"Not a soul I could lay eyes on."

"If there had been anybody there to see, you'd have seen them. That's just the way you are, Dan Boone. So that means that if the body's found, as best anybody knows, that Indian just got drunk and stumbled off the bridge." Nate grinned. "Lordy, I right envy you, Dan. I'd like to have the death of a redskin to my credit, after what they done to poor Frederick. Someday I'll get my chance to send a few redskin souls to hell myself, and when I do, you'll not find me getting quiver-hearted over it!"

Daniel shot Nate a withering look that went unnoticed. "All I wanted was to get past him. I never killed a man before."

"It's not really a man, just one more dead redskin. That's all the tally that counts in Nate Meriwether's ledger. You just keep your mouth shut about what happened, Dan. That's one Indian who'll never threaten another 'Long Knife' again. Be glad it all fell out like it did." He paused, then laughed at the unintended irony of his words.

Word spread among the men that a particular Indian was missing and being sought by his companions. Did anyone have any knowledge about what might have happened to him?

Daniel said nothing, keeping to himself and minding his business. Though he felt as if he would burst from holding in the truth, prudence kept him quiet. To speak might cost peace and lives, and surely there was no sin in silence, even if that silence was uncomfortable.

IT SOON APPEARED that some of Forbes's anticipations about the Indians deserting the French were true. Intelligence indicated that France's Indian allies were open to influence at the moment, and Forbes took advantage.

English emissaries met with leaders and members of the various tribes, giving out gifts and liquor and telling them that if they would switch allegiances and help drive out the French, they would be given the support and friendship of the king, and a promise that no white settlers would move across the Alleghenies. The Indians listened and responded positively. The French now had less chance than ever of holding out.

But the army crawled on so slowly that Daniel wondered if any advantage gained by the shifting allegiance of the Indians would be erased by the sheer sluggishness of the advance. By September the army still had not crossed the Allegheny range. Bouquet, second in command to Forbes, was sent across the mountains with an army of two thousand to Loyal Hannon, there to build a fort in advance of the main force.

From Loyal Hannon, Bouquet sent out Major James Grant with a force of Highlanders and Virginians to take a look at Fort Duquesne. Grant took his orders a step further. Dividing his group, he sought to draw the French out and ambush them. He did find the French, but from there his plan went awry. They had recently been reinforced by four hundred new troops. They engaged the English, who gave way, leaving the real fight to the colonials. Despite their efforts, the French came away victorious, then went on to attack Bouquet himself at Loyal Hannon. After a four-hour battle they withdrew, but the spirits of the English were much sobered. Word was sent back to Forbes.

In response, Washington was sent forward to Loyal Hannon with a thousand provincial troops. The main army dragged behind, arriving in November. A bleak winter loomed, and spirits were lower than ever. Forbes himself seemed ready to give up and put the fight off until the next year.

George Washington was livid. If his original plan had been followed, Fort Duquesne would have been under British control long before. To abandon the effort now seemed absurd to him.

News obtained from three prisoners gave impetus to Washington's view. The fort was extremely weak, its manpower down to about four hundred. The Indians at the fort were leaving; none seemed to have the spirit to fight. Washington seized upon the information and urged Forbes to let him advance with a band of provincials.

His request granted, he advanced with a force of about five hundred toward Fort Duquesne. On November 24, as they neared their destination, they heard a boom like thunder in the distance, though the skies showed no evidence of bad weather.

The next day showed the true origin of the booming noise. Fort Duquesne had been destroyed, blown up, by the French themselves, and what remained had been set ablaze. Later information would reveal that Indian scouts had seen the advancing army, had exaggerated its numbers to the French inside, and persuaded the fort's commanders to abandon their post. Now the shattered remnants of Fort Duquesne stood empty, and the French and Indians were long gone, having fled down the Ohio River by boat.

The British flag was raised above the remains of the fort. Forbes arrived to find that after all his months of struggle and labor, there was no battle to be fought, a situation both relieving and anticlimactic.

He ordered that a new fort be built in place of the old one. Its name would be Fort Pitt, after the British statesman William Pitt. If a town happened to grow up around it, as it probably would—what good were promises to the Indians about no settlers moving west of the Alleghenies, now that the Ohio basin was in the hands of the English? It could be called Pittsburgh.

The day after the English flag went up, Daniel went looking for Nate and couldn't find him. He searched and at last saw him pacing along the riverbank, his movements odd and fast. Daniel was about to approach him and make sure he was well when he realized why Nate had come there. It was along this very riverbank, in sight of Fort Duquesne, that his brother Frederick had been killed by Indians.

Daniel turned and slipped away before Nate could see him, and stayed clear of him that night. It seemed unfair that a campaign as big and important as this one could be settled without a battle, while Nate seemed to have to fight endlessly in the worst kind of battle, the kind that rages inside a man's mind and soul.

Forbes stationed a couple regiments of Virginia troops to man Fort Pitt, and soon the rest of the army marched off, back toward the east along Forbes's Road. Daniel felt certain this road would enjoy a much brighter fate than the shorter Braddock's Road, which was twenty or thirty miles farther south, roughly paralleling a portion of Forbes's route. Forbes had carved out a major thoroughfare through the Alleghenies to land previously dominated by the French. The inevitable result would be westward movement of land-hungry settlers. The promise made to the Indians to entice their allegiance would amount to little, as was usually the case. Forbes's Road would become a highway to the west, and lands that the Indians thought their own would be infiltrated by white men.

The new passage would cause mistrust and violence. Others would die in this region as Frederick Meriwether had died in the shadow of Fort Duquesne. Already there were growing strains with Indians elsewhere, including North Carolina. Frightening stories had made their way to Daniel during this campaign: raids on the Carolina frontier, people taking to forts. He was eager to get home and see that his kin were safe and well.

CHAPTER 8

RETURNING TO THE YADKIN, Nate found that Nora House had not taken up with another man in his absence. And Pyler House had still not shown himself since his apparent flight from the region. By now, most had concluded he had deserted his daughter. Daniel found it amazing that a man who had been so jealous regarding his offspring in the past wouldharden his heart sufficiently to abandon her. But Pyler was undeniably gone, and no one knew to where.

Nora was as eager as ever to marry Nate. They wed in the summer of 1759 with little ceremony and virtually none of the kind of celebration that had marked the marriage of Daniel and Rebecca. Nora moved into Nate's little cabin on Dutchman's Creek and seemed to become a better woman for having a husband. Nate was happier too, worked harder, and actually gave up drinking. He seldom spoke about his lost brothers. Daniel decided his doubts about the marriage had been misplaced. Nora and Nate were good for each other, a combination that went together as nicely as their names.

Daniel's own household grew with the birth of his second son, named after his late brother. Israel also had been a secondborn child and one of Daniel's first teachers in woodcraft. Young James, now an active little boy who constantly challenged Rebecca to keep pace with him, dearly loved his new little brother despite an initial round of jealousy. Jesse and Jonathan continued to live in Daniel's house, now having nearly the status of sons themselves. Daniel enjoyed being with his family but felt an increasing sense of pressure and responsibility.

A settled life was something of a strain for him to maintain, for reasons beyond his own natural disinclination toward farming and living in close quarters with others. The Indian troubles that Daniel heard rumor of while away with Forbes had not been exaggerated. Raids small and large had occurred fairly frequently all across the Carolina frontier since the year before. No one slept well at night, and farmers kept their rifles close when they worked in the fields. It was a trying time, particularly for Rebecca. She worried about her little ones constantly, and when she soon found herself pregnant again, she had even more to worry about.

Daniel felt frustrated because so many of the Cherokee hostilities were due to unalterable circumstances. The Cherokee system of vengeance was somewhat formalized, yet not overly discriminating: a family of settlers who had done nothing themselves to harm the Cherokees could find themselves attacked in revenge for some atrocity committed by another group of whites far away. Many people began fleeing the frontier, moving into the towns. In some cases families would be divided, the husband and older sons remaining behind to work the farms. As 1759 went on, many men died in fields along the Upper Yadkin, more than a score of them in the planting season alone.

From time to time Daniel Boone's young family was forced to undergo the frightening trial of midnight flight, moving in silence, snatching up what they could, praying the children would remain quiet, sometimes fleeing on foot because there was no time to take horses. Fort Dobbs was the closest refuge. They fled there so frequently that it began to feel like a second home. The strain on Rebecca was tremendous.

Daniel and the other local men did not remain confined to the fort at such times. Parties of armed men were sent out as rangers to patrol the area and scout for Indians, and if this was desperately dangerous work, it suited Daniel better than being penned up in a fort. The woods was his element, his accurate rifle a protection he preferred over stockade palisades or blockhouse walls.

The Cherokees seemed fearless to the point of being brazen. A huge mounted band of them attacked one big body of travelers and left about fifty dead and many others wounded and scalped alive. Individual families died in raids by smaller bands, and the bodies of unfortunate travelers or hunters were found all too frequently on the roadsides or in forest clearings, lives and scalps gone.

Rebecca began to talk to Daniel about moving away from the Yadkin, maybe into Virginia, at least until the troubles were over. He didn't relish the idea. Moving deeper into civilization meant being farther from the wilderness, where he felt at home, and which he still couldn't resist ranging into for hunts, Indian trouble or not. Certainly times were dangerous, but to withdraw seemed an extreme answer. Daniel resisted Rebecca's pleadings as long as he could, and when 1759 ended, the Boones were among those still on the Yadkin, holding on, holding out.

IN FEBRUARY OF 1760 Cherokee aggression reached a new peak when Fort Dobbs, commanded by Captain Hugh Waddell, was attacked. Waddell had noted a small party of Indians lingering for days around the fort and had sent out numerous small bands of rangers to reconnoiter and, if possible, to drive them away. They had little luck; the Indians would show themselves, then vanish like smoke in the wind. Waddell grew suspicious that the Cherokees had a major assault planned and were trying to lure large numbers of the fort's defenders into exposing themselves simultaneously.

On the night of February 27, dogs around the fort set up an uncommonly loud ruckus and ran toward a spring that flowed nearby. Waddell immediately suspected an Indian presence, but something about it didn't seem quite right. "They're trying to draw us out for ambush," he told his confederates. "I'll not have big numbers of us leave these walls; to do that would be the very thing they want."

He pulled together a band of ten men, including himself, and they left the fort bearing rifles loaded with one bullet and seven buckshot each. About three hundred yards out they were attacked by a group of sixty or more Cherokees, who came out from cover firing and yelling and bearing down toward the isolated little band. Waddell had anticipated just such a thing and tersely repeated an order he had given even before they left the fort: "Don't fire until I give the word."

It was terribly straining for each man, standing there with rifle in hand while dozens of Indians came in upon them from the darkness, rifles firing, lead balls raining around them, smacking the ground at their feet. But each held his position, rifle aimed and ready, waiting for Waddell to give the order to fire.

Waddell had counted on the Indians firing their rifles before they were in good range and while they were on the run, throwing off their aim, which was poor anyway because of the darkness. They acted just as he had anticipated. As nervous sweat poured off his brow despite the cold night weather, Waddell kept a rough tally of shots until he felt sure that most of the Indians had emptied their rifles. The closest Indians were only a dozen strides away, knives and tomahawks upraised. They were close enough now for the men to see as well as the darkness would ever allow. At the last possible second Waddell ended the aching tension of the tiny band of men.

"Fire!"

Rifles blasted with ear-jolting concussion, hurling bullets and buckshot and doing a good deal more damage than the Cherokees had anticipated from so small a band. They fell back in surprise and confusion. Waddell shouted for his men to retreat to the fort.

But in the meantime, a second body of Cherokees had attacked the fort itself. Those outside were at risk of being cut off. Waddell had not anticipated this scenario.

The battle was hot for a time, but almost miraculously, Waddell and most of his men fought through and safely made it inside. The battle now turned fully in their favor. From behind the thick walls they fired heavily upon the Indians, killing about a dozen. Before long the Cherokees picked up all the dead they could find in the darkness and carried them away on the backs of stolen horses. The fight had been hellish but short.

Fort Dobbs had been successfully defended, at least for one night. Waddell's tally showed two men wounded, only one of them badly, and one boy killed. Tragedies, but everyone in the fort knew it could have been much worse.

Waddell carefully recorded the battle the second day after it was past. At the end he wrote words touched with a certain lilt of pride: "I expect they would have paid me another visit last night, as they attack all Fortifications by Night, but find they have not liked their Reception."

Early Spring, 1760

DANIEL WALKED SLOWLY behind the wagon, his rifle cradled across his arm and incompatible feelings warring in his mind. Rebecca sat in the driver's seat, leads in her hands, a smoking pipe stuck between her teeth, and her belly large with child. James sat beside her, the baby in a box at his feet. He had been given the job of "helping" his mother watch after Israel, and took the job very seriously, looking all around while imitating the serious, lowered-brow expression he had seen on the face of his father when Indians were thought to be about. The wagon rolled heavily, laden as it was with boxes and bundles and casks. The milk cow and a few head of beef cattle that had not been sold lumbered along behind, herded by Daniel with the aid of a couple of hounds. The wind moved softly through the trees and was cool against the skin. Jays and titmice and wrens poked through the brown forest mast as squirrels and chipmunks scampered among the treetops. It was an incongruously peaceful scene, difficult to reconcile with the violence that was motivating their move.

They were leaving at last. Daniel had given in to Rebecca's pleas. In one sense it was a relief to go. Almost everyone else had, it seemed, including Nate and Nora Meriwether, who had gone to Salisbury. Daniel's father, Squire, had left the Yadkin the year before and gone to Virginia. Samuel Boone, another of Daniel's brothers, had left about the same time and gone into South Carolina. Daniel had held out so long, it now would have seemed unreasonable not to go ahead, give in, and move his family to a safer place. His brother Neddy and younger sister Elizabeth and her husband were already on the road somewhere ahead, waiting for Daniel's family to catch up with them sometime in the afternoon.

Daniel sighed, steered a wayward cow back onto the road, and shifted his rifle to his other hand. Dissatisfaction showed on his face. It might be reasonable to leave, but it wasn't pleasant. Despite all the Indian troubles, he had been thinking of making a hunt come autumn, penetrating farther into the mountains than ever before, maybe even crossing them to the rich hunting lands beyond. He was sure a lone man with the proper skills, or a small band of such men, could hunt those lands and avoid the Cherokees at the same time. Yet here he was, heading the opposite direction, bound for Virginia and whatever work he could round up there.

They met the others sooner than anticipated and went on a few more miles before pausing to build a fire and spit-cook some squirrels Neddy had shot. Daniel had little to say, but Neddy was talkative, chatting happily with Rebecca, who had always been fonder of him than any of Daniel's other siblings. Daniel might have found grounds for jealousy except that Rebecca had told him she liked Neddy because he looked so much like her Daniel. He couldn't help but be flattered by that.

They went on. Along the way they met other travelers fleeing the Yadkin and joined their parties for the sake of safety. No trouble arose. They posted guards for the night camps, but no sign of Indians presented itself. The farther they traveled, the less the danger, and by the time they reached Virginia, even Daniel had to confess it was a relief not to have to be so constantly on guard against an enemy who could appear like a phantom and vanish likewise, leaving death behind him.

THE BOONES SETTLED in the tobacco country of Culpepper County, where they had friends, and Daniel began to earn a living as a wagoner, hauling freight into the Rappahannock River market town of Fredericksburg. The work put him in contact with the rather high-browed planters of the Old Dominion. They seemed to take a low view of him as a simple laborer and treated him with little more respect than they gave their slaves.

He was ready to haul a load of casks for one of the most aristocratic planters early one morning when a man came striding over the hill, carrying an oddly shaped, lumpy burden. He was limned against the sun, and Daniel had to put his hand to his brow to make out who the man was. It was Tom, a slave of his current employer. But Daniel still couldn't tell what it was he was carrying.

The broad-chested black man stopped. "Mr. Daniel, sir?"

"Howdy, Tom. How are you this morning?"

Tom came on. "Fine, sir, fine. I brung some food."

Tom held out the item he had been carrying. Daniel took it and gave it a wry look. "What's this? Bull neck?"

"That's right, sir. Mr. Tate, he sent it for you and me to eat today."

"You and me? You're coming along?"

"Yes, sir, that's what Mr. Tate wants. He says for me to help you with the load and bring back some mahogany timber he's bought from a Mr. Winston in Fredericksburg."

"Timber, eh? You reckon he aims to pay me extra for the return load?"

"I don't know. That ain't the kind of thing he'd tell me, Mr. Daniel."

"Well, throw this thing up in the seat there and let's be off."

Tom was a quiet man and as friendly and outgoing as his life's station would allow. Daniel would later describe him to Rebecca as "having a way of saying things without saying them." Daniel picked up all kinds of subtle commentary on the difficulties of a slave's lot from things Tom said, things that in themselves were entirely innocent on their face. A clever fellow, Tom was. Daniel liked that.

When they paused to eat, Daniel decided to send a message himself for Tom to take back to his master. Daniel took down the bull meat and carried it to a rock on the roadside. "Tom," he said, "fetch up that stick lying yonder . . . yes, that one. Bring it over here."

Tom, looking puzzled, picked up the stick and walked back with it.

"Now, whop that neck meat good and hard."

"What's that, Mr. Daniel?"

"Whop that neck meat. Hard as you can."

Tom raised the stick and gave the bull neck a hard blow. Afterward he glanced around uncertainly as if afraid someone would come along and see the strange activity.

"Hit it again. Lay into it and just wallop the devil out of it."

"Well, sir, if that's what you want."

He gave it seven or eight good blows. Daniel nodded. "Good work, Tom. Now let's see if it helped." He picked up the meat and worked it in his hands. "Nope. Just like I feared—still plaguey tough!" He fired a meaningful, mischievous glance at Tom, and the spark in Tom's eye and the subtle grin on his lips told him he had got the message and would certainly pass it on to the man it was intended for.

They made the best meal they could of the nearly unchewable meat and went on their way into Fredericksburg, where they loaded off their tobacco and headed elsewhere, with Tom driving now because he knew the way and Daniel did not, to pick up the mahogany.

The curving road led around a large copse of maples and alongside a creek for about a mile, then narrowed and veered left while a secondary avenue cut off to the right. Tom took the latter way. The wagon road climbed a low hill, and at the top Daniel looked down the other side and raised his brows at the sight of a large plantation house bathed in sun light. A wide green yard spread around it, enclosed in an excellent fence that separated it from broad fields spreading back to the forest and river. Barns and outbuildings stood in an orderly cluster to the rear of the house.

"Right there's a place that speaks of wealth," Daniel said.

"Yes, sir, Mr. Winston is a rich man. My brother Joe, he's a slave here. Mr. Winston treats him fine, just fine. I wish I could be here too." Then he clamped his mouth shut and looked worried. It didn't pay for a slave to express too much dissatisfaction over his situation, and he had just come close to that. Daniel could have told him he needn't worry. Nothing would pass his lips to bring trouble to Tom. He wasn't the kind to cause trouble for anyone if he could help it. And being treated something like a slave himself by Virginia's uppity planters, he had much sympathy for Tom's situation. A white man could work his way out of bad situations, or at least give it his best try. But a black man had all the world against him. Even when a slave was set free, few opportunities opened for him.

The wagon rolled up toward the house, around it, and toward one of the barns. A big grin broke across Tom's face when he saw another black man just closing the gate of a calf pen, telling Daniel that they had just encountered the aforementioned brother, Joe. Tom pulled the wagon to a stop and leaped down. Brother met brother in happy reunion. Daniel climbed down more slowly, looking around at the big house, admiring it while thinking he would never really feel at home in such a place.

They were not long at the house. The mahogany had already been paid for, and all that had to be done was to load it onto the wagon and drive off. Daniel took the reins this time. Along the way Tom talked more about his kin, several of whom were the human property of various plantations around the region. Tom said he was thankful that most of his brothers and sisters were not far from him, even though he almost never was able to see them.

"Are your parents living?" Daniel asked.

"My mother is dead, sir," he answered. "My father, his name is Burrell, and he's yet living as far as I know. He's a cowboy who's been all the way across the mountains."

"The mountains?"

"Yes, sir. All the way over the ridges in the Indian country."

Daniel was impressed. Herdsmen, or "cowboys," such as Tom's father, were a hardy and self-sufficient breed. They often lived for months at a time in the wilderness areas, grazing the stock of their employers or masters in distant meadows, protecting them as much as possible from predators, branding and earmarking new calves, and eventually rounding them up and driving them east again to the market towns, where they would usually be fattened on rich meadow grass for one more season before being slaughtered. The cowboy's life was substantially the one Daniel had lived as a boy in Pennsylvania, watching Squire Boone's cattle, far from his bed and supper table, learning to support himself off what he could find and kill.

"When did you last see your father, Tom?"

"Years ago, sir, years ago. I know where he is, but there's no chance for a man like me to go see him. I don't know for certain if he's even still living." Tom swallowed and looked misty-eyed a couple of moments.

They rumbled on back to where they had started and unloaded the wood. "Don't forget to tell Tate about our meal today."

Tom grinned. "I won't. And I believe he'll understand what you're trying to say, sir. Of course, I don't understand it myself, being just a poor Negro." He gave the subtlest of winks.

A couple of days later Daniel was back again to haul a load into Fredericksburg. When Tom joined him this time, he was carrying a pail and wearing a sly smile. He held up the pail. "Good ham meat, bread, and some apples," he said. "I think Mr. Tate will be victualing us out a lot better from here on out."

They rode toward Fredericksburg. It was a cloudy day with thunder rumbling from beyond the horizon. Daniel was about to comment about the likelihood of their getting wet before the day was out when he heard something that caught his attention. Tom heard it too, and frowned. He and Daniel glanced at each other and cocked their ears toward the forest. Daniel stopped the wagon.

"That sounds like a man crying out in the woods yonder," Tom said.

"So it does."

The cry sounded again. No doubt now: it was a man, and from the tone and edge of his cry, he was in great pain. Then another cry, and a moan, and another cry. Another sound, too—a swish and slap, the sound of a long switch being applied at full force, against bare flesh.

Daniel declared, "My God, I believe some poor feller is taking a right fierce beating back in them woods. I'm going to take a look." He took up his rifle.

"You can come too if you—Tom? What's wrong?"

Tom had a terrible look on his face, eyes wide, brow furrowed. "I know that voice," he said. "That's my brother Joe, Mr. Daniel. My own brother Joe."

Chapter 9

THEY CAME UPON a shocking scene of cruelty. Tom's brother Joe, in a forced kneeling position, was tied by the wrists to a sapling. He was shirtless, and his back was bloodied in stripes laid on with a long, supple willow switch wielded by one of two ragged-looking white men. Both were bearded, dressed in filthy, worn-out clothing. From what could be seen of their faces under whiskers and dirt, they looked to be brothers.

"Joe, Joe, what've they done to you?" Tom exclaimed. He started to rush forward to his brother, but Daniel reached out and gripped his shoulder. "Wait." A quick glance showed the rifles of Joe's abusers leaning against a tree to the left, fortunately out of quick reach of the men. But Daniel knew that if the advantage was to be gained, it would still have to be done carefully, not impulsively.

"What's this?" Daniel asked loudly. "Why are you whipping that man?"

"Who the bloody devil are you?" the switch wielder asked. Already Daniel could tell he was the man to deal with. The other fellow had a scared look, this one's face showed nothing but belligerence.

"I might ask you the same," Daniel replied.

"I can tell you who they are," Tom said. His voice was strained with fury. "Them's the Kincheloe brothers. They been up to bedevilment around here for a year now since they come in from Carolina."

Kincheloe . . . the name was vaguely familiar to Daniel. Now he remembered: his brother George had run across the pair once on a trapping expedition and had almost lost his pelts to them. They were a couple of hunters and trappers who ranged along the far border in North Carolina, who, like Pyler House, were known to be troublemakers and were generally avoided by most. They must have fled to Virginia because of the Cherokee war.

"You Kincheloes got any business whipping on the slave of—What's his name, Tom? Mr. Winston?"

"Mr. Cedric Winston," Tom said. "No, sir, they ain't got no business doing that. They don't work for Mr. Winston, and I know he don't stand for nobody hurting his Negroes. They ain't nothing but devils causing trouble like they always do."

"Let them answer for theirselves, Tom," Daniel said. "Speak up, now! Why are you hurting that fellow?"

"Ain't no affair of yourn," the belligerent one said.

"That one's Lucas Kincheloe," Tom side-spoke to Daniel.

"You'd best lash down that free tongue of yours, boy," Lucas Kincheloe said to Tom in a loud and venomous voice. "You don't call a white man by his name 'less he tells you to, and I'll let no damn slave call me scoundrel!"

"It's you who'd best mind your tongue," Daniel said, leveling his rifle. The scared-looking Kincheloe had begun edging toward the rifles leaning against the tree, but he stopped and moved back closer to his brother.

"You," Daniel said to him. "Get out your knife and cut that man free."

"Don't do it, Willie," Lucas said.

"Do it!" Daniel countered, brandishing the rifle.

Willie Kincheloe obeyed. Joe collapsed, whimpering, at the base of the tree.

"Back up, both of you, hands above your heads," Daniel ordered. Willie obeyed at once, but Daniel had to repeat the command before the snarling Lucas complied.

"Go to your brother, Tom. Help him up and bring him back here, then go get them rifles."

"You touch them rifles, you're as good as dead," Lucas Kincheloe spat.

But Tom ignored him. He went and eased Joe to his feet. Blood streamed down Joe's back and dripped onto the leafy forest floor. He leaned against Tom and staggered over to where Daniel stood, then sank to his haunches, moaning softly, his pitiful back turned toward the men who had hurt him. Tom went and fetched the rifles.

"Take out the flints and keep them, then toss the rifles into them bushes," Daniel directed. Tom quickly followed orders.

"Them's our flints!" Lucas said. "That's theft you're doing right there, and we'll see you whipped at the post if you go on with it."

"I'm not stealing your flints. You'll find them out on the road when we're gone," Daniel replied. "If I was you, I'd sure be slow to show myself. I just might lie in watch, and if you look to be a threat, I'll do what I have to. Now, I'm asking you one last time: why did you whip that feller?"

Lucas ground his teeth, his anger making his ugly face uglier. "He—he was . . . we seen him . . . We seen him peeping at a white woman swilling herself off in a creek," he said.

"It ain't true, sir, I swear it ain't!" Joe said.

"I know it ain't," Daniel replied. "He stammered around too much trying to think it up."

"I was out looking for some calves that had got out of the pen," Joe said. "That's all. I had a pass paper to let me be off the plantation, but they just tore it up, tied me up, and commenced to whipping me . . . Lord save me, I'm hurting mighty bad, sir. Lord save me."

"I aim to give the Lord a hand at that, Joe," Daniel said. "We're getting you out of here right now. And you two—" he raised the rifle a little higher, aiming it right at Lucas Kincheloe's head—"stay right where you are. I wouldn't show myself on the road for at least an hour after I'm gone, if I were you and prized my life."

The Kincheloes didn't move while Tom helped his brother back toward the road. Daniel backed out of the woods, keeping his eyes on the pair, just in case one had a hidden weapon. Lucas Kincheloe gazed at him with the most undisguised look of hatred Daniel had ever seen.

Back on the road Daniel, Tom, and Joe climbed hurriedly into the wagon. Daniel took up the lines. With a snap and yell he set the horses in motion and drove off so fast the tobacco in the bed bounced about, shaking off dust that made Tom sneeze.

"Where we going, Mr. Daniel?" Tom asked. His hand rested on Joe's trembling arm. Joe was leaning forward, his battered back oozing and raw. He was struggling hard not to faint.

"We're going to Mr. Winston's plantation," Daniel replied. "I have a notion he's going to be mighty interested in knowing what the Kincheloe brothers have done to his slave."

A little way down the road he tossed away the flints Tom had removed from the Kincheloes' rifles. He made sure they landed in the weeds by the road, where the brothers would have to search to find them. No point in making it too easy for them to be armed again. If they had sense, they wouldn't come after him, but you could never count on men like the Kincheloes to have sense.

CEDRIC WINSTON was a tall man, about fifty years old, with an amiable face and congenial manner not eclipsed by the aura of wealth and power he exuded with his long embroidered waistcoat, white stockings, and cravat. But at the moment, fury animated his sweeping movements. Daniel had come there with a positive predisposition toward Winston because of what Tom said about his kind ways, and nothing the man had done so far gave the lie to his expectations. Winston's anger itself spoke well of the man in Daniel's mind, because it was not the impersonal anger of someone who had been stolen from, or who had lost money in a business gamble. Winston's anger was the personal kind. He deplored the Kincheloes, not because they had damaged some of his legal property, but because they had brought suffering upon another human being. Winston was tender of heart, and Daniel Boone admired that quality.

Joe was bandaged now and soothed by several swallows of corn whiskey. Tom was with him out in the little clapboard house where he lived, near the barn. Winston was pacing, waving his hand like a House of Burgesses orator as he expounded upon the situation to Daniel, who stood by a big carved mantelpiece, puffing on one of Winston's long churchwarden pipes. He had been invited to sit but had declined because he knew he would not feel at all comfortable in one of Winston's big velvety chairs.

"The Kincheloes have been a bane in these parts since the cursed Cherokee wars drove them off the border," Winston said. "They're like a stench blown on a bad wind. They've caused trouble for many, and I'm certain they were involved in the theft of some livestock from a plantation south of here. They seem to hold a particular hatred of Negroes, but never have I seen such brazenness as what they demonstrated today on poor Joe. I would not have sent him after those calves alone if I'd had any notion such louts were roaming about. I'm confounded by it all, Mr. Boone. How could they expect to treat a man so and not be punished for it?"

Daniel took the pipe stern from between his teeth. "The truth is, sir, I expect they intended for him not to be able to tell nobody who done that to him."

Winston frowned, probing out Daniel's implication. "You mean they intended to beat him to death?"

"I wouldn't put it past them."

"Zounds and damnation! I'll have them in the noose, those scoundrels!"

"They'll likely be hard to catch now they've been found out," Daniel said. "If they've got any wit about them, they're bound for far parts."

"Yes, aye, that's probably true. I don't know whether to be glad of it or disappointed. On any road, however, I do owe you a great debt of thanks, Mr. Boone. Your courageous intervention almost certainly saved the life of my Negro. I'm fond of Joe. I wouldn't see harm come to him."

"Nor would I, Mr. Winston."

"I wish to reward you, Mr. Boone."

"No reward needed. I had no such notions."

"Oh, quite, quite! But be that as it may . . ." He reached beneath his waistcoat and produced a purse. From it he drew five pounds and handed the money to Daniel.

"Sir, that's a big amount of money to be handing a man who ain't done nothing to earn it."

"Oh, you have earned it, sir. And believe me, five pounds is a small reward in my estimation. Yes, sir, Mr. Boone. I'll be remembering your name, and if ever there is anything more I can do for you, it will be done. Keep that in mind, sir."

Daniel nodded his thanks. Winston had surprised him indeed with his generosity. Joe was fortunate to have such a master, if any slave could be considered fortunate. Even though some of the Boone family had owned slaves, Daniel still held a trace of the Quaker disdain for slavery. He wouldn't himself be a slave to any man and felt pity for those who were, but for those trapped in slavery, certainly it was better to have a humane master than a tyrannical one.

A thought came to mind. "Sir, may I ask one thing more of you now?"

"You need but speak it."

"If you would, sir, I'd appreciate your letting Tom stay here with his brother tonight. We were to be in Fredericksburg until the morning, but I believe he'd like to be able to tend to Joe this evening. He has his pass to be away from his plantation, if you wish to see it."

"No need. He is welcome to stay; in fact, his help tending to his brother would be welcome."

"Thank you, Mr. Winston." He held up his reward. "I don't think I should keep this money."

"I insist, good man. It's a pittance compared to my gratitude."

Daniel shrugged, then nodded. "Well, sir, then keep it I will. I'm grateful."

DANIEL WENT ON into Fredericksburg alone. He had no plan to inform Tom's master, Tate, that Tom had remained behind with Joe for the night. They were to have spent the night in Fredericksburg in order to pick up a load of rails early the next morning, but Daniel could handle that job alone.

He had another motive besides the one he had given Winston for leaving Tom behind. He was sure that the Kincheloes had watched him from the woods and probably knew where he had gone. They might have watched him when he left Winston's plantation, might be following him even now. He wasn't as sure as he had purported to be earlier that they would actually flee. They might be lingering, plotting to even the score with him. If so, he preferred to face that problem without Tom about, without encumbering himself with worries over the welfare of another.

Daniel rolled into the town near sunset without encountering trouble. He drove the horses carefully, mindful of the town children, who were none too cautious about where they darted in their play. Looking about, he watched the wheels of commerce turning in the little hamlet. On one side of the street, in a dirt yard full of sawdust and chips, a carpenter labored on a pine coffin, one of the most demanded products of his craft. Down from him a short distance, past a couple of little houses, a cooper was carefully using a wood-and-rope windlass to draw together the curved staves of a large barrel while shouting at some dogs that wouldn't stay away. A woman came out of a bakery, carrying a fragrant basket of bread on her head, and in a stock pen beside a stable two men were arguing over the price of a draft horse. Daniel smiled to himself, enjoying the bustle, yet feeling choked by it. Even a small town seemed cramped and airless to him, and he couldn't abide it long.

But he thought again of the Kincheloes and decided that staying in town wasn't a bad prospect that night. There was more safety in a crowd, so if the Kincheloes did come looking for him, they would be less likely to try to harm him where there would be witnesses. He wasn't afraid of the pair unless they chose to take a shot at him from hiding.

When the wagon was unloaded and parked in a lot beside a low-roofed log warehouse, and the horses turned over to the local livery, Daniel went looking for a meal. Taking his rifle with him, he headed for a two-storied clapboard building with a low door standing ajar, its thick coat of greenish-black paint shining in the sunset light washing over the building. He walked through the door, stooping to avoid bumping his head. A young woman with dark eyes and curled hair, which was sweat-dampened at the end of a long day, was just beginning to light lamps in the darker corners of the room. She wore a dress and corset that fit her narrow waist and full bosom very flatteringly. She smiled at Daniel as he entered.

Sitting around a table, a cluster of tradesmen rolled dice, their voices exclaiming in pleasure or disgust at the results. A counter made of heavy varnished planks extended along the back wall, and Daniel went to it, scooting out a stool and sitting down. He leaned his rifle against the wall nearby and hung his horn and shot pouch on the end of the ramrod.

A greasy-looking man in stained wool trousers, over-loose stockings, heavy shoes, and a loose-sleeved baggy shirt that was half tucked in, half hanging out, came to Daniel, wiping out a cup with a cloth and asking for his order with his expression instead of words. Daniel ordered beer. When it came, he quickly downed about half of it, then turned on his stool and leaned back on the counter with his elbows, sipping slowly on what remained. Trying not to be obvious about it, he surveyed those in the tavern, just to be sure. He couldn't get the Kincheloes out of his mind.

They weren't there. Relieved, he turned back again and ordered bread and whatever meat could be had. It turned out to be salted pork, which suited him, and he enjoyed the meal. Invigorated, he had a second beer, then took his rifle and headed out, ignoring the sly and possibly inviting smile the pretty barmaid gave him. He thought with mild amusement how Rebecca would bristle if she could see such flirtation with the man who had vowed his eternal fidelity to her alone.

The sun had edged down while Daniel was in the tavern. Now it was almost dark outside. Commerce had substantially ended, the cooper having put aside his barrel and the carpenter having finished his coffin, which now sat upright beneath the overhanging shingled porch of his shop, an unintended but effective reminder to all passers of their mortality. The men arguing over the horse were gone, and the horse was too. Daniel thought about seeking out an inn to sleep in, then decided against it, even though he felt very well-off with Winston's reward money in his pocket. He would content himself to turn in on his blanket beneath the wagon over by the warehouse. There he wouldn't have to worry about bedbugs or lice or any of the other loathsome things that were part and parcel of inn residency.

He turned to his left, intent on a leg-stretching walk around town, when to his dismay he caught a glimpse of Lucas Kincheloe, looking at him from around a corner of a log shop that sold glassware, fabrics, and women's goods. Kincheloe stepped back when Daniel's gaze swept across him, and Daniel knew at once that they had been following him in secret, and intended to strike at him unexpectedly.

Daniel slid into the closest alley and stood leaning on his rifle, pondering how best to deal with the situation. Blast the luck! What kind of men were these? Obviously not the kind to let a perceived offense against them go unanswered. Like Indians, they would not abide an insult.

The best response would be a direct and aggressive one, he decided. Checking his rifle, he stepped out of the alley and toward the place he had seen Kincheloe. When he got there, no one was about. He looked around for places the Kincheloes might be hiding and found no sign of them. Dropping to a crouch, he tried to examine the ground for tracks that would tell him which way they had gone, but it was too dark to make anything out. Rising, he circled around to the street and stopped in front of the tavern he had left earlier.

Something moved across the street, behind a stack of lumber. He ran lightly in that direction, rifle at ready, feeling odd to be playing out such a furtive cat-and-mouse game right there in town. He rounded the lumber pile and came face-to-face with Lucas Kincheloe, who raised his rifle. The flint was back in place, and Daniel regretted having kept his pledge to leave the flints where they could find them.

"We have you now, damn you!" Lucas Kincheloe chortled. He pulled back the hammer of his rifle.

Daniel lunged out with his own rifle and knocked the muzzle of

Lucas's weapon aside. Lucas swore and began to swing it back, but Daniel kicked him in the groin, making him grunt and double over. Daniel raised the butt of his rifle and struck him on the back of the head, knocking him to the ground, where he writhed and made blubbering sounds.

Arms closed around Daniel's middle, pinning Daniel's own arm. Someone had grabbed him from the rear—Willie Kincheloe, who had sneaked up behind him. Fearing he might be knifed at any second, Daniel jerked forward and down, lifting his antagonist, then pushed off the ground with his legs, falling backward. Daniel's weight landed hard atop Willie, driving the air from him and breaking his grip. Daniel rolled off and up, never having lost hold of his rifle. He rammed the butt of the rifle down on Willie's forehead, and the curved metal butt plate laid open the skin. Willie howled as blood streamed into his eyes.

Lucas was trying to rise. Daniel turned and kicked him down again, then took away his rifle. Willie's rifle was on the ground nearby, where he had laid it while sneaking up on Daniel. Daniel swept up that weapon as well and walked casually around the lumber pile, bearing both Kincheloe weapons and his own. He doubted they would bother him again, but he wasn't about to make the mistake of leaving them armed.

The ruckus had drawn men from the tavern. Some stopped when they saw Daniel; others ran around him and examined the defeated pair behind the lumber pile. Daniel heard scraps of exclamations: the name "Kincheloe," the word "scoundrel," and a comment to the effect that whoever that lean fellow with the rifles is, he should be rewarded for having treated two thieves and ruffians to what they deserved.

"Is there a constable or such about?" Daniel asked the crowd in general. "I'd like to make a complaint against them two men."

"I'm a constable," said a stoutly built man in a tricorne, vest, woolen pants, and heavy square-toed shoes. He stepped up to Daniel.

"Them two need to be took in custody," Daniel said. "They attacked me, and earlier on they switch-whipped a slave belonging to Cedric Winston. If you send to Mr. Winston, he'll want to prosecute them, I believe."

The constable fired Daniel a surly glare. "I'll take them into custody—and you too. I'll not stand for brawling in the streets without knowing full well what caused it. Two street brawls in as many days! I'm growing bloody tired of it. This was a more peaceable town before the Indian wars drove in so many border ruffians. Hand me them rifles, and be quick about it!"

Blinking in surprise, Daniel handed over the weapons. A moment later he was all but dragged away, feeling like a criminal instead of a man who had brought two criminals down, at no small degree of risk.

CHAPTER 10

THE NEXT FEW HOURS involved such bother and harassment that Daniel began to believe the Kincheloes had actually succeeded, however indirectly, in avenging themselves upon him. For a time he was locked up in a small, filthy room with log walls; then he was abruptly dragged out and put through a harshly toned interrogation by the constable. Then it was back into the locked room again. This time he could hear the voices of the Kincheloes filtering back to him, Lucas cussing and Willie whining as they gave the constable their own—no doubt distorted—version of the fact.

Another voice, stentorian and authoritative. Daniel sat up. He had been asleep. The light sponging its way through the walls via cracks in the chinking told him it was morning. He had spent the night locked up. Standing, he moved to the door and listened more closely to the new voice, then grinned. Cedric Winston! He must have been called in by the constable to verify what Daniel had told about the beating of the slave Joe.

A few minutes later the door opened, and the constable, now presenting a downright amiable face, told Daniel he was free to go. He was very sorry he had been locked up, but such had been necessary until the facts were clear. There had been a similar brawl earlier in the week, you see, Mr. Boone, in which a man had suffered some stab wounds, and so it was only natural, sir, that he as constable should react very, well, firmly, and sternly, to any new instance of violence within the town . . .

Daniel waved off the explanation. He hadn't really minded spending the night locked up. At least there had been a roof over his head and he had been safe from any further violence by the Kincheloes. But now he had work to do—a load of rails to be picked up.

Winston had brought Tom with him and now turned him over to Daniel, which was a good thing, since Daniel was late to pick up his load and could use Tom's help after all. Further, it would save him from having to pick up Tom at Winston's plantation on the way back to Tate's.

"It seems you've had your opportunity to do me a return favor far earlier than either of us would have figured on," Daniel said to Winston, who laughed pleasantly while digging a silver snuffbox from his vest. After taking a deep sniff of the fragrant powdered tobacco, he tucked away the snuffbox and patted Daniel on the shoulder.

"You are a good man, sir, and I'm very regretful you were ill treated by our constable. I can see to it that he is called to task for his manner, if that would suit you."

"He was trying to keep the peace. I don't fault him. Just leave him be. Now, sir, if Tom could come with me, we'll be off."

"Very well. And keep it clear in mind, Mr. Boone, that I am available at your service anytime you might need me."

"Thank you, sir. Tell me: how is Joe faring this morning?"

"He is in pain, but beginning to heal. A good crust of scabs on his wounds. He's a healthy fellow who will be mended straightaway."

As Daniel urged the horses anxiously toward their destination, Tom said, "I reckon them Kincheloes will get their due now, won't they, Mr. Boone?"

"I expect they will, Tom. I'm glad to have them out of the way."

"Yes, sir. So am I."

They fulfilled their purpose and headed back the way they had come, traveling more slowly because of their load. Daniel was in a good mood, whistling an old fiddle reel and tapping his toe in time. Tom had little to say, though, and seemed weary. He'd sat up with his brother most the night, and what sleep he'd gotten had been light, just dozing in his chair.

They were nearly out of town when Daniel jerked the lines and brought the wagon to a halt so suddenly that one of the horses nickered, the rails in the bed slid and knocked about, and Tom was almost jolted off his seat onto the ground.

"*Oof!*" Tom righted himself, with a frown. "Mr. Boone? Something wrong, sir?"

Daniel was looking past Tom, into a shaded grove beside a small smokehouse. "Wait here," he instructed, and leaped off the wagon.

"YOU THERE!" Daniel called out. "You there! Stop!"

A man had been peering out of the shadows, a face so much like Nate Meriwether's that for a moment Daniel believed that was who it was. At that point he jerked the wagon to a halt. A second glance, very fleeting, revealed that the man wasn't Nate. But when he had noticed Daniel looking at him, he turned to run.

This was Nate's missing brother, surely—what was his name? Daniel couldn't remember at the moment; it was extremely frustrating.

Tom waited in puzzlement on the wagon. Daniel chased the fleeing man, who kept glancing back over his shoulder fearfully. And he was gripping his side as if it hurt—was that a bandage of some sort making his shirt bulge?

"Wait!" Daniel called. "Wait . . . Clive Meriwether!" Thank heaven he had remembered the name. "Clive Meriwether, is that you?"

The man stopped, turned. He still looked scared but also cautiously intrigued. He was very pale as if sick. When he spoke, his words were the unpolished vernacular of the common colonial, but there were still traces of a British accent at their edges. "How you be knowing my name?"

"Your brother Nate," Daniel replied. He had stopped now, well away from the man so as not to spook him. "My name is Boone, Daniel Boone. I'm a friend and neighbor of Nate's. I knew when I saw your face that you had to be Clive Meriwether. Nate has been—whoa, there! What's wrong?"

Clive, who had been going whiter by the moment, had just keeled over to the side in a dead faint. He was gripping his side, and blood showed between his fingers.

Daniel roused him again, though he looked very weak. "Well, Clive, I suppose it must have been you who were knifed in that brawl the constable spoke of."

"Aye . . . How do you know of that?"

"I had a brawl of my own and heard there was another," he replied. "You've broke open your wound a-running, but the blood is beginning to staunch up already. I feel partly to blame, frightening you as I did."

"Never mind it. I don't care none . . . God, I need a drink."

"Mighty early in the day for drinking."

"When you've suffered the hell I have, friend, there's no time of day too early, nor any hour too late."

Daniel gave him an evaluative look. "Well, Nate and me heard you turned to drink. 'Pears it was true."

"Where'd you hear of that?" Clive Meriwether's expression showed his astonishment at having encountered a stranger who seemed to know everything about him.

"Heard it from a feller name of—" Daniel screwed up his brows—"Cable. Jim Cable. Met him in Salisbury. Said he was a friend of yours."

"Old Jim! Aye, Jim's an old friend and neighbor of mine. He was with me when the bloody Ottawas come and killed my dear . . ." Clive trailed off, his eyes going vacant and sad. He held brief silence, smothered by sorrowful memories, then gave a little shudder that seemed to push him past the moment. "He came with me to find Nate. But I up and left old Jim alone there in Salisbury. Shouldn't have done it, I reckon."

"Had you remained in town, you'd have found Nate. We came looking for you after Nate got a letter from one of your kin in Pennsylvania."

"Nate was there?" Clive smiled. Though he still gripped his bloodied side, he suddenly took on a little more color and sat up straighter. "When

I reached there and didn't find him, I thought maybe he had died, too, like all the ones I ever cared for. Do you know of my tragedies, Mr. Boone, did you say?"

"That's right. Daniel Boone. Yes, sir, I know of them. I'm sorry you've had to face such sorrows."

"When I left Jim Cable behind in Salisbury, I had it in mind not to face them no longer. I planned to end my days by my own hand. But I couldn't. I lacked the courage even to put an end to my own suffering."

"I'm happy you didn't do it," Daniel said. "There's better ways to end suffering than a rifle ball through the noggin." Daniel smiled, shaking his head in amazement. "Lordy, but you do look like Nate! When first I seen you, I thought you was him just like Jim Cable thought that Nate was you. It's like me and my brother Neddy. We've been mistook for each other more than once."

"Nate . . . how is he? And where?"

"Married. He's been a neighbor of mine on the Yadkin and was still there at the time you come to find him. Since the Cherokee wars he's gone to Salisbury. As far as I know, he's still there."

"I'd surely like to see him."

"You will."

"No. No. I've thought more about that since the first time I set out from Pennsylvania looking for him. It was my cousin there who spurred me on to do that. But it's a good thing I never found Nate. What I am now—it is nothing to show to my own brother. I can't let him see me as I am now."

"Then let him see you as you used to be. Throw away your bottle. Come with me and I'll help you through it, sober you up. Then we'll go and find Nate together."

Clive looked astounded. "You'd do that for me?"

"Aye, I would. Or perhaps it's more for Nate that I'd do it. He's been a good friend, and I know how much store he's laid by finding you."

Clive looked past Daniel, red-rimmed eyes wide and thoughtful. Slowly a sad look drained down across his features. "No, it can't be. I'm too far gone. I'm bound to the bottle now. I'll never break free."

"You will. Others have done it. I'll stay by your side until the hard time is past, and you can make yourself fit to see Nate. Don't you worry—Nate knows you've come upon hard times. He knows all about the liquor and such. He is not looking for you to be a saint. He just wants to have his brother back."

Clive opened his mouth to speak, but nothing emerged. He dropped his gaze and stared at the ground, troubled.

"Come with me, Clive. I'll open my own home to you. It's naught but a rented cabin, a place to live until the Cherokee wars are done, but you're welcome to share it."

Clive looked up at Daniel, appearing on the verge of yielding. But suddenly his lower jaw thrust out and he shook his head. "I don't know you, Boone. You're a stranger to me, come talking big words about my brother, talking about rescuing me from liquor. You think I'll put myself into the house of a stranger, a man I never laid eyes on until a few minutes before? Go away. Leave me be." He turned and began striding off.

"Clive, wait," Daniel said. "Don't go off—what would I tell Nate?"

"Tell him . . . tell him I'm dead, just like his other brother who the damned savages put through hell at the stake, too cruel even to let him die with mercy. Tell him I got into a fight on the streets of Fredericksburg and got myself killed. Tell him to forget about Clive Meriwether, and love that wife of his as long as he's got her, for a man never knows when he'll lose all that matters in this world."

He strode away. Daniel had to restrain himself from going after him and forcing him back. Clive passed across the back-side of a log building and entered an alley, heading for the street beyond. Daniel went back to the wagon.

"Who was that?" Tom asked.

"Nobody. Just a man that reminded me of somebody I knew," Daniel said. He snapped the lines and the wagon jerked into motion. As they drove along, he glanced back across his shoulder. Standing at the front end of the alley he had entered was Clive, watching him. When Daniel's eye caught his, he backed into the alley and did not emerge again until Daniel was out of sight.

REBECCA BOONE squinted, straining to see in the dimming light that spilled in through the west-facing window. Her fingers worked a thick embroidery needle nimbly, probing it in and out of previously punched holes in the leather flap of the hunting pouch in her lap—a lap, she noticed with private amusement, that was increasingly less and less of a lap now that her pregnancy was advancing. This was Daniel's hunting pouch she was stitching, a nicely fringed and embroidered one that she knew he was proud of despite his pretense of denigrating anything that seemed frivolous or "prettified." A lingering vestige of his youthful Quaker days, she figured. She knew the ways of Quakers, their insistence on plain, almost shapeless clothing, their disdain for "worldly" display. That was fine for them, but Rebecca was determined that when her Daniel went hunting, he would do so with at least a modicum of ornamentation. There was a prudent side to her desire as well. A wilderness hunter never knew when he might encounter Indians; and having a nicely ornamented item like this embroidered hunting bag at hand could provide him something to trade for safety.

She glanced up at the sun, which rested now at the tree-lined crest of the hills. There would not be enough time, after all; the sun would be down before she could finish threading the holes, and she had no intention of working at it by lamplight. Detailed work by lamplight always made her eyes itch and the back of her neck ache.

With a sigh she laid down the hunting pouch and stood. The children were quiet at the moment, occupied with play, and the cabin was pleasantly still. Slipping outside, Rebecca arched her back and looked about, cupping her hand above her eyes when she gazed into the sunset. She saw Daniel coming, bearing a string of squirrels. Good. For the last two days she had been developing a craving for a good squirrel stew but had been without enough meat. Daniel had been busy with his wagonering lately, and she had planned to go out the next day and hunt some squirrels herself. It appeared that would be unnecessary.

"Dan, I didn't know you'd gone hunting today," she said when he was close. "I thought you was out on the wagon again."

"Was, up till a mite after noon. Then I took out to the woods. Should have told you where I was, I reckon, but you was busy down by the creek, and I didn't come down to you."

"No matter. I'm glad to have the squirrels. Bring them over here and we'll get them skinned."

They worked at the task together. Rebecca soon detected that Daniel wasn't his usual self. He seemed despondent, distracted. Tossing aside a peeled-off squirrel pelt, she said, "You're thinking on Nate's brother still, ain't you?"

"I am. I dread telling Nate how low he's sunk."

"We won't see Nate for a good while, likely. Maybe by then matters will have changed."

"Maybe."

When they went to bed that night, Daniel lay close to her, arm around her, hand on her large, pregnant belly. As the children drew the steady, slow breaths of sleep, Daniel gently kissed Rebecca's cheek. She turned her face to him and their lips met. "I love you my dear, my Becca," he said, and she yielded to his silent advances, eager for the special intimacy of their frequent conjugal unions. Before long her pregnancy would be too advanced to allow them to love each other physically, so now such times of intimacy seemed all the more precious.

Later she held him while he slept. She was a woman at peace, contented with her life. Her children slept around her, her husband snored softly in her embrace, and all was well. Daniel murmured and spoke in his sleep, saying a single name: Clive. A tinge of sadness invaded Rebecca's happy world. Even in his sleep Daniel was plagued by the tragedy that had befallen Nate's brother. She regretted that the sad state of a virtual stranger could trouble him so—but on the other hand, was not Daniel's sensitivity to the sorrows of others one of the things that made him a good man and a husband a woman could be proud to claim? She was glad he was tender of heart. So many men weren't.

Clive Meriwether. She had never laid eyes on him, so she pictured him looking much like Nate, an accurate perception based on what Daniel had said. What a sorrowful thing it would be to lose one's loved ones in the way Clive Meriwether had lost his. She couldn't imagine it—no, she could, and that was the terror of it. She had known what it was to hear the alarm of Indians in the night, to fear even to breathe too loudly or to speak a single word because any noise might become a fatal betrayal. Rebecca knew the grim things that befell those who were victim to raiding Indians . . . how even children died in terrible, merciless ways. It was this more than any other aspect of wilderness life that was impossible for her to take in and understand. Such cruelty simply couldn't find a place in her view of the world. She was glad right now to be living far away from the Yadkin, where the warring Cherokees could strike at any time.

She hugged Daniel closer. Was there ever a man who loved the wilderness more than her husband did? She didn't mind it; or, when she did, it was when she thought about the dangers of such a life. So many men plunged into the mountains and across into the Indian country, never to return. Even now, she knew, Daniel was restless, tired of this tied-down, domestic existence and the drudgery of wagonering from settlement to settlement. It would be only a matter of time before he broke away and headed into the far blue country that attracted him, and this whether the Indian dangers had subsided or not.

She prayed in her mind: Lord God, keep my man when he is far away from me. Keep him well and safe in the wilderness, and may he never, never fall at the hand of Indians. And my children as well, Lord. May the savages never harm any of them.

She slept after that and awakened in a bright mood the next morning. As so often happened, the terrors and worries that darkness could impose on a weary mind seemed unreal and trivial. Daniel was already up, chopping wood in the yard, and the children were scurrying about outside, alternately arguing and playing. She heard Daniel tell Jesse to leave James be and go milk the cow as he was supposed to. Then the sound of more chopping, Daniel grunting with each swing.

Gathering up her skirt, she went to the springhouse and brought out some cooked pork, boiled potatoes, and a crockery pitcher half-full of buttermilk from the previous night's supper. Daniel smiled at her. "You look hungry," she said. "A man shouldn't work so hard before breakfast."

" 'Taint hard, chopping wood," he replied. "I like doing it."

"I'll have you a plate filled in a few minutes, as soon as I can put some heat back into the taters."

When the food was ready, she poured Daniel's favorite cup full of buttermilk and called him in to eat. They sat together enjoying a meal without the loud presence of the boys, who would come in and eat later. Their intimacy the night before had left Rebecca in the mood to be close to Daniel. She was glad he had no wagon work to do that day and would stay near the cabin.

"I've got half a mind to put a new roof on that smokehouse out there," Daniel said. "It leaks fierce. And it would be good work for the boys."

"I've noticed the leaking myself."

"Them boys spend too much time snuck off into the woods to hunt and such, anyway."

"They are Boones."

He chuckled, knowing she had his measure. "So they are."

And then he sat up straighter, eyes turning to the door. "Somebody's coming," he said.

Rebecca had heard nothing, but then, Daniel always was the first to detect anyone approaching the cabin. He swiped buttermilk off his lips onto the back of his hand, rose, and went to the door.

Rebecca followed him. As Daniel swung the door open, she saw a man walking around the nearest bend in the road. He was ragged and thin and looked very much like Nate Meriwether.

"Hello, Clive Meriwether," Daniel called. "Is it me you're looking for?"

"Aye, Boone, it is. I've come to do what you said, if you'll still be willing for it to be."

"I'm willing. I welcome you, friend." Daniel turned to Rebecca. "That's Clive Meriwether out there, Becca. He's come to join our household and put aside his liquor. That's a good thing, eh?"

She smiled as brightly as she could while trying to absorb what Daniel had just said. Come to join our household . . . what exactly did that mean? She wasn't at all sure she liked the sound of it.

"Yes," she said haltingly. "That is a good thing."

CHAPTER 11

DRENCHED IN SWEAT, sodden hair hanging loose in his eyes, Daniel strained to keep his arm-pinning grip around Clive Meriwether, who struggled and screamed and declared that spiders were upon him—hundreds, thousands of them, big and hairy and trying to bite. "Get them away, get them away . . . God in heaven, get them off me . . ." His screams and pleas were pitiful and loud in the cabin.

Rebecca and the children were gone. Daniel had sent them to a neighbor's house until Clive's drying-out period was over. He had known it would he difficult to be nurse and guardian to a drunkard abruptly deprived of his liquor. But he hadn't known it would be this difficult, this absolutely hellish. Clive must be a determined man to let himself go through this. He'd told Daniel that after fleeing from him in Fredericksburg, he'd been unable to force Daniel's offer of help from his mind. The idea of being free of the liquor that was his demon grew so enticing that he'd asked around as to how to find the Boone cabin. With effort, he'd finally succeeded. He had come to the Boone house and declared himself ready to endure whatever it took to liberate himself from liquor.

Neither he nor Daniel had fully understood what a wrenching, painful liberation that would be. They understood now, grappling and struggling alone in the cabin.

Clive quit screaming abruptly and fell to silent weeping. No more struggle; his body went limp. Daniel relaxed, but cautiously, because several times over the past twelve hours Clive relaxed like this, only to jolt into furious violence again. Daniel took several deep breaths and said, hoping against hope, "Clive, let's get you to bed, maybe you can sleep."

He wished he would sleep. Clive hadn't enjoyed even a solid two hours of rest from the time he arrived at the Boone house, and as a result Daniel had not either. As Clive went longer and longer without alcohol, tension turned to discomfort, discomfort to irritability, irritability to terror and suffering. At this point, Daniel sent his family away, and settled down to see Clive through the terrible delirium that liquor-addicted men had to endure when they gave up their habit.

"God help me, please help me," Clive whispered after Daniel got him back into bed. His chest was heaving, wet with sweat. His skin was pale and sheened.

Daniel sat back and closed his eyes, wondering if he would have taken on this task had he known how hard it would be. All this for Nate? Well, he would have wanted the same kind of compassion for one of his own brothers. If only he could make it through . . .

Clive began to snore and Daniel smiled in relief. Exhaustion had overcome all the mental and physical travails striving to keep Clive awake. Maybe now there would be a time of respite. Daniel was sorely in need some rest himself. How long could Clive's delirium go on? Daniel had never dealt with such a thing before and couldn't know. Maybe, God willing, it was almost finished.

Daniel yawned. He folded his arms across the table and laid his head on them. Clive groaned and stirred; Daniel bolted upright. But Clive didn't awaken. Daniel laid his head back on his arms. Within a few minutes he too was sleeping.

Three Weeks Later

REBECCA BOONE FELT SADDER than she had expected as she watched Daniel mount his horse. Clive Meriwether, looking haggard but clear-eyed, now that he was through his liquor withdrawal, was already in the saddle of the horse, borrowed from Daniel, and seemed eager to go.

As Daniel swung into the saddle, she realized why she felt so sad. This parting reminded her of the time Daniel and Nate had departed to make their second military journey to Fort Duquesne. Clive's remarkable resemblance to his brother only made the similarity stronger. She felt better, knowing her sadness came from the memory of wartime fears past, not from any immediate threat. Daniel and Clive were traveling no farther than Salisbury, where Nate was. Surely no harm would come to them on such a relatively short journey. Surely the travel would be quickly done and Daniel back home before the baby came.

She and Daniel had said their good-byes the night before, and now there was little to be said between them. The children looked sorrowful. Jesse and Jonathan appeared envious, too, to see Daniel about to go. Daniel settled himself in the saddle and gave them a smile as he touched his hat. "We're off now." He lifted the hunting pouch, its embroidery now complete, and winked his thanks to Rebecca. Despite his professed indifference to ornamentation, he was truly pleased to have such a finely decorated item to display on his person.

"Good-bye, Dan!" Jesse called. "Don't let the Indians peel your roof thatch!"

Rebecca gave the boy a gentle, remonstrative swat. She didn't believe in speaking specifically of potential dangers before a journey, fearing the words would somehow bring about the fact. But Daniel simply grinned anew, lifted his hand, and said, "I'll be careful. Don't expect we'll encounter Indians. Farewell for now, folks! I'll be back soon." Then they were off, and Rebecca led her charges back into the cabin, feeling the unborn one kicking inside her.

THE FARTHER he and Clive rode, the more Daniel sensed his companion's mounting excitement. It gave him a good feeling and made the time he'd spent helping Clive dry out seem worth the torment. He could imagine Nate's face when his lost brother suddenly appeared before him. That would be a joyous reunion indeed, assuming they found that Nate was still in Salisbury. He and Nora might have moved on for some reason or another. If so, that would generate a problem for Daniel. Rebecca was due to give birth sometime in November, and he planned to be home when that happened. He wouldn't have time to roam all over creation with Clive, trying to track down a straying Nate. Clive would have to go on alone, but that would leave him without a companion to keep an eye on him and steer him away from the inevitable temptations presented by taverns and backwoods stills. After nursing Clive out of hell, he didn't want to see him fall back in again.

Clive made for a fine companion now that he was sober. He was much like Nate in voice and manner, but seemed to be a deeper-thinking, more serious man. Daniel could see how such a fellow could be the devoted family man he apparently had been up until the Ottawa raid wiped out his loved ones. Daniel didn't like to think about what effect such a tragedy would have on Nate if, God forbid, it ever occurred. He might become just as pitiful and self-destructive a specimen as Clive had been at his lowest.

Clive talked volubly as they traveled, words bubbling out as if they had been held back too long. Daniel took it for a good sign. The man's mind, no longer clouded, was sorting through its contents, putting things back in place again.

Daniel learned that Clive was like him in loving the land. But his love was different from Daniel's. Daniel favored the open wilderness and the dark forest, land as it was in its natural state, teeming with game, fish, fruits, and vegetables no man's hand ever had to plant. Clive loved the land as a farmer loved it. The soil was there to be broken and planted, to be turned from its natural condition into a productive entity a man could control. Clive, in short, loved the land best when it was fenced and conquered, while Daniel loved it when no fences had yet been built and the conquering was yet to be done.

Clive talked of his past, from his English childhood on to his marriage and settlement as a Pennsylvania farmer. He talked of his family in detail and wept when he recounted their slaying by the Ottawas. Daniel, pitying him, tried to divert the subject by asking questions about Nate, but that only turned Clive to talking of his brothers in general, leading to a harrowing account of how he had watched his brother die outside Fort Duquesne, and more tears. Daniel began to worry about Clive. Though he had sweated out his addiction to liquor once, the demons that had led him to it in the first place still remained. Daniel began to hope even harder that they would encounter no difficulty in finding Nate. The truth was that he was eager to turn Clive over, so that he would no longer have to feel responsible for him.

They were about a day's ride from Salisbury and making camp for the night when three travelers caught up with them on the trail. They were horse traders, heading to Salisbury with money in pocket after having made a transaction in Virginia. They were friendly, jovial fellows, in good humor because of their successful venture, and Daniel was pleased to have their company for the night until one of them, a yellow-haired, bearded man who had given the name David Caine, brought out a jug of whiskey. "Any of ye care to take ye a swallow?" he asked politely, offering the jug all around.

One of Caine's companions quickly accepted and passed the jug on to the next man. Daniel glanced at Clive, who caught his eye and then broke off. Clive's fingers were trembling, and he looked as if a fever had gripped him.

"Mr. Boone, have you a drink, sir," one of the others said, handing the jug to Daniel. Daniel was about to turn the offer down when he thought better of it. Clive would not long have Daniel at his side to keep him from falling back into drinking again. Nor would Clive be able to expect the rest of the world to change its ways to make things easier for him. If he was to survive without his addiction, he would have to learn to do it with liquor close at hand and available. If he could not do that, there would be no hope for him.

So Daniel took the jug and drained off a swallow. Clive, beside him, looked very fevered now. None of the others seemed to notice, being caught up in conversation.

"Clive?" Daniel said, handing the jug toward him.

"For God's sake, man, what are you doing to me?" Clive whispered at him sharply. "You stay with me while I suffer my way out of the bottle, and you want me to jump back in it again?"

"No, I don't. What I want you to do is make the choice yourself."

Clive licked his lips, eyes fastening on the jug. "And if I choose to take a drink?"

"Then my hands are clean of you, and you can go on and find Nate on your own."

Clive hung fire for several moments, licking his lips over and over and blinking too rapidly. Then he closed his eyes, sucked in his breath, and said, "No. Put it away."

Daniel smiled. "Good man, Clive. Good man." He handed the whiskey jug back to its owners.

Clive still looked ill and was shaking almost as badly as he had at the worst of his withdrawal. "I'm going to lie down now," he said. "I need some sleep."

CLIVE WAS GONE the next morning. He had left his rifle, bedroll, and pack behind, but the whiskey jug was nowhere to be found in the camp. Daniel, sick to his soul, told the others of Clive's situation and paid them for the whiskey, which deterred them from their initial impulse to go after the sorry liquor thief. They went on toward Salisbury, and Daniel set out to track down Clive. He took Clive's rifle as well as his own so that there would be no risk of their being stolen. It was an easy job. Clive had made no effort to cover his tracks. He'd gone less than a quarter mile. Daniel figured that as soon as the jug was in his hands, Clive had thought of nothing else, not safety, not common sense, not precaution. His tracks were obvious and led straight toward a patch of ivy-tangled blackberry briars that grew thickly along the side of a path, where the sunlight had a clear way in.

Daniel heard Clive's voice well before he entered the thicket. Clive was crying and talking at the same time, his words a slur that angered Daniel, made his heart pound with fury. What he had gone through with this man, this near-stranger, only to have him throw it aside at the very first jug of liquor that came to him! It even made Daniel angry at Nate, who knew nothing of any of this, because it was for Nate's sake he had bothered to try to help Clive at all.

"Clive, it's Dan Boone. I'm coming in there," Daniel said.

"No, no, Daniel, don't do it. I'm drunk in here. That's right. I took the jug and now I'm drunk, and there's no more good to be done for me. I've sealed my fate and more than likely damned my own soul this very day."

Daniel wasn't about to take orders from a drunkard. He poked the barrel of his rifle into the thicket and pushed the briars aside. They tugged at his clothing and pulled the hat from his head as he pushed into the thicket.

"You figured you could hide from me in no more than a briar thicket?" Daniel asked sternly. He stopped and eyed Clive, who was leaning back against a dogwood tree around which the thicket had grown, his legs straight out before him and spread, the jug, lying on its side, on the ground between them. His hat sat askew on his head and his eyes were bleary from drinking.

"I ain't fit to live, Daniel. I've turned around and undid everything that was done." Then he laughed, though there were tears on his face.

"You've undid it indeed," Daniel said. He was filled with disgust at Clive, yet he pitied him too. Here was a man who had lost everything of worth outside himself, and now it appeared he had lost himself, too.

Clive turned his face upward and sobbed aloud. "Oh, why did I do it? I knew it would destroy me, but yet I did it. I lay there in my bedroll, and all I could think of was that jug sitting there. Everyone was sleeping, just a-snoring, and so I just got up and took it. Sneaked off with it and drank. God, it was good. You don't know how good it was, Daniel."

With those last words Clive's expression changed. Regret abruptly vanished and he no longer cried; he spoke as a man glad to have done what he did. Then just as quickly he sobbed again and said, "God help me, Daniel. I'll never be free of it, never."

Daniel said nothing. He just stood looking at Clive, not knowing what to do.

Clive said, "I ought to pick up this jug and smash it and never take another drink again."

That was true, but Daniel saw no reason to comment.

"I'll do it," Clive said.

"Then do it."

Clive picked up the jug in shaking hands, lifted it. Then he lowered it again. "I can't."

Daniel sighed. "Come on, Clive. Stand up, if you can. Let's get back to camp and sober you up, then we'll go on and find Nate."

"No, no. Not now. I can't let him see me."

"We'll sober you up, I said."

"For how long? Until we reach Salisbury and there's an open tavern door to lure me?"

"That's up to you. Only you can decide whether you're going to give in to it or not."

"I'm a weak man. So weak . . ." He shoved the jug away; a little of its meager remaining contents splashed out. "I hate the bloody stuff, yet I love it too."

"Get up, Clive. Let's go."

"You should have never let them bring out that jug with me in the camp," Clive said suddenly in a very bitter tone. "It's your doing!"

"Don't blame me for this. It wasn't me who lifted that jug to your lips. Now, get up and get on, or I'll leave you here and head back to my family. Maybe I should have stayed with them to begin with."

"Go on. Get the bloody hell away from me. I don't need you, don't need Nate. No use for nobody. My family, my brother, dead by the hand of savages . . . what does it matter what happens to me? Hell with me . . . Nate is best off never seeing me again."

"Maybe so," Daniel said. He turned to leave the thicket, fully intending to abandon Clive where he was. If the man had no desire to save himself, Daniel Boone couldn't do it for him and wouldn't waste his time trying.

He was surprised when Clive came wobbling to his feet and lurched forward. "Wait for me . . . I'm coming . . ." He fell into the briars, tearing the skin on his face and arms. He whimpered and tried to rise. Daniel sighed again, walked over, and helped him up and then out of the thicket.

The jug still lay on the ground in the thicket. Clive stopped, glanced back through the briars at the jug.

"Leave it," Daniel said. "Leave it or I'll leave you."

Clive lowered his head. "Aye. I'll leave it."

They went back to the camp. "We'll stay here today and let you sober up," Daniel said. "Tonight you'll sleep, and tomorrow you'll be like yourself again. We'll go find Nate, and after that the rest is up to you. I've done all I can for you." Clive was terrible company well into the afternoon, when he at last fell asleep. Daniel sat and whittled, despising his situation and wishing he had never laid eyes on Clive Meriwether.

WHEN DANIEL AWAKENED the next morning, he felt vaguely ill. His vision was blurry, his stomach ached, and his head was hurting in dull throbs, dulling his hearing. Lord above, what a time to grow sick! Daniel wasn't accustomed to even minor illnesses, seldom catching anything worse than a bad case of sniffles.

A slightly muffled blast rang out without warning and made him start. He came to his feet, his stomach turning over in the process, making him feel nauseated. "Clive?" he called. "Where are you?"

Clive's bedroll was empty. Again! The man had managed to slip away yet again! Daniel wondered why he hadn't heard him—for he had gone to sleep intending to keep both ears and one eye open for any unusual movement on Clive's part—and then realized that his illness probably accounted for it.

"Clive!" he called out. "Where are you?"

Then he realized where he must have gone—back to the thicket, where that jug remained. Fury surged. This time Daniel Boone would show no softness, nor would he put up with any excuses or new, empty promises of reform. What he just might do was put his fist firmly against Clive Meriwether's jaw.

Rubbing his aching stomach, he picked up his rifle and headed off toward the briar thicket. Now his muscles and joints were aching, too. No question about it, he was sick. Wincing, he rubbed his belly as he walked. Clive's rifle—he had forgotten it. Turning, he went back to the camp and found that the rifle was gone. Clive must have taken it with him and—

He stiffened, eyes growing wide with horror. That muffled rifle blast he'd heard . . .

Forgetting his aches and nausea, he ran hard all the way to the thicket, then stopped. He didn't even have to look to confirm his worst fears. The smell of powder smoke drifting out through the briars and the ivy told the story.

It took Daniel a minute or so to steel his nerve to enter the thicket. When he did, he saw Clive lying there, the muzzle of his flintlock in his mouth and the top of his head gone. He had triggered the shot with his toe. Daniel felt tears rise, then his stomach heaved and he was sick.

When he was through retching, he noticed that the whiskey jug lay to the side of the corpse, unbroken. Before he had put the muzzle in his mouth and brought it all to an end, Clive had drained away every drop.

CHAPTER 12

DANIEL BOONE RODE into the streets of Salisbury in the gray light of a very bland sunset. He was slumped, weary, defeated, regretful of having ever intervened in the life of Clive Meriwether. Daniel even wondered if the tragic end that Clive had brought to his own life was somehow his fault. If he hadn't enticed Clive with the prospect of a life free of liquor, Clive might never have taken such a drastic step when that prospect slipped out of his reach.

Daniel had buried Clive's body near the little briar thicket and marked it with a pile of stones. He stood beside it for a full hour, debating whether to go back to Rebecca in Virginia and let Nate live on in relatively blissful ignorance about this tragedy, or to search him out and tell him the truth. He finally decided on the latter, though he had little spirit for it and much real dread. Nate had lost one brother tragically already, and now he would have to learn for the second time that the other sibling had also come to a bad end.

Salisbury had changed little since Daniel had been there last. He looked around listlessly, thinking that it should be pleasant to be back in a place associated with the Yadkin life he much preferred to wagonering in Virginia. Tonight, pleasure was a feeling unknown. He was numb and empty, and the vague sickness that he had detected that morning was still there, adding physical distress to his mental and spiritual sorrow.

He stabled the horses and went to a tavern for his supper, which he ate without once looking up from his plate. Meanwhile, clouds gathered outside and thunder rolled in from off the horizon somewhere. Rain was on its way. Daniel didn't mind it. A good storm would suit his mood.

He would not attempt to find Nate until the morning. He wanted only to sleep. He stopped at two inns, hoping to find a room where he could sleep alone, but both had nothing but shared rooms available. A third try was successful, and he was sent to a little second-floor room that was cramped and smelled of burned peppers. The landlord apologized for the smell, saying his wife, a hater of gambling, had recently detected that some of the guests were playing cards in that particular room and had driven them out with the acrid smoke of a pan of burning peppers held just beneath the floorboards. The stench hadn't gone away yet, he was sorry to say.

Daniel didn't much care. His sickness stuffed up his head, and the pepper smell actually seemed to clear him up a little. After telling the landlord he was feeling poorly and would probably sleep through breakfast, he undressed, rolled into bed, and fell asleep at once. He didn't fully wake all night, though once he was conscious enough to be aware that the storm had hit, wild and vigorous, with lightning. Water was dripping from the ceiling somewhere in the room, but it wasn't falling on his bed, so he didn't worry about it.

He awakened about eight o'clock the next morning, very late sleeping for him, and sat up to evaluate his condition. Physically he felt better, having sweated profusely in the night. But the dread of telling Nate of Clive's tragedy was heavier than ever. Sighing, he dressed and went downstairs, paid his bill, took a couple of dried chunks of cornbread for his breakfast, and asked if the landlord knew Nate Meriwether. The man had heard the name but didn't know where Nate lived. Daniel headed into the day to begin his search.

Asking here and there, he finally found a man who sent him to the Boar and Stallion tavern, whose landlord was a friend of Nate Meriwether. If Daniel inquired there, he should have some luck.

It was after noon by now. Daniel sought out the tavern, a big, fine-looking, clapboarded building with large chimneys on each end, and bought himself a dram, loaf, and bit of ham. When he was done, he asked the landlord about Nate Meriwether. To his pleasure, the bewhiskered man nodded resolutely.

"Aye, indeed I do know him, sir, though it's been upwards of a week since I've seen him here. Nate lives east of town, you see, an hour's brisk walk. His cabin lies north of the road—a rented place, I believe, shared with that devil of a wife of his." The landlord caught himself short and looked at Daniel warily, making Daniel suspect he had just realized that this stranger asking about Nate Meriwether might be friend or kin of Nate's wife. Daniel grinned to put him at ease.

"A devil of a wife, you say? Is it Nate or the rest of the world that she's the devil to?"

"I've not laid eyes on the woman in my life, and all I know is what Nate has told me. She has made him suffer, he declares. I don't know all of what their difficulties are, but Nate tells me she has become a plague and pox that he wishes he had never brought upon himself. You, eh, are a friend of his . . . not hers?"

"That's right. Nate and I were neighbors near the Yadkin, and Lord willing will be again. I'm sorry to hear he has troubles with his Nora. I thank you for your help, sir."

"Indeed, sir. If you see him, send him greetings from Big Charles at the Boar and Stallion."

"I will. Obliged to you, sir."

He obtained clear directions to the road that would take him to Nate's, then went to the stable, where he retrieved his horses and saddled them. He was immensely conscious of the emptiness of the saddle on the horse Clive had ridden. Eager to find Nate, yet dreading the moment, he rode north out of Salisbury on a muddy, puddle-filled road.

NATE LOOKED THE SAME, except not so youthful. There were lines on his face now, around the eyes and the corners of his mouth. Trial-lines, Daniel's mother had always called such. The tracks left on the human face by trials of the human spirit.

"What brings you, Dan? I'd never have looked for you, not for nothing!"

"Well, I've come . . . just to see you, Nate. Just to talk to you a bit." Daniel paused, wondering if he should pretend ignorance about Nate's troubles with Nora, then deciding not to. "There was a man in town at the Boar and Stallion, Big Charles was the name he gave. He's the one who told me how to find you and Nora here."

Nate nodded, the lines on his features suddenly looking darker and deeper. "Nora's gone." He chuckled coldly. "I should have danced a fling for happiness the day she went away, but Lord help me, I've missed her. You get used to living with a woman, you miss her when she's gone, no matter how she's bedeviled you."

"You two were striking it up right fair last I seen you."

"It was good for a time, but once we come here, a different side of that woman showed itself. God! A spirit out of hell she was! Spiteful and harpish, shrill as a tin whistle! That woman taught me how it is for them trapped critters who chew off their own legs just to get free. But you know, Daniel, I would have stayed with her if not for what she told me . . . but never mind that. I need not speak about that."

"So you left her?"

"She left me, I throwed her out—I ain't sure. We separated. It's all the same in the end." He grinned sadly. "I will tell you that on the way out she threw the stove wood ax at me and nigh split my head. Then she grabbed up some clothes and such, wrapped them in a bed blanket, and out the door she went. Never even looked back, and I ain't seen her since."

"I'm sorry. I'd hoped you'd be happy."

"We were, for a time. It just wouldn't last for us—couldn't, after what she told me. I should have listened to you, Daniel. I recollect you had doubts about me and Nora from the start."

"I just didn't trust old Pyler House. That was the main thing."

At mention of Nora's long-missing father, Nate's eyes widened for a second, and he actually blanched a little. But it was so quickly past that Daniel couldn't swear it wasn't just a trick of the constantly changing sunlight that dappled Nate's features as it filtered through the windblown oak in front of his little cabin.

"Aye, yes." Nate straightened his shoulders and slapped on a grin. "Well, gone is gone and past is past, and there's naught more to say about it than that. Come inside and let me see if I can round us up something worthy to drink. I believe I've got a jug with a few good swallows yet remaining."

Mention of the liquor jug brought Daniel's mission rushing back to mind. It must have shown on his face, because Nate looked wary and worried all at once.

"Daniel, what is it?"

"Nate, I have news for you of your brother."

"Brother Clive, you mean?" Nate's face was suddenly the boyish one Daniel had known before. "You've found Clive?"

"I did. But, Nate, it's not well with him. It's not good news I'm bringing to you."

Nate went solemn. He swallowed visibly. "He's dead?"

"He is."

"Oh, God. Oh, no." There was silence a few moments. Nate looked past Daniel, into the green, upreaching boughs of the great oak. "How?"

Now was the truly hard part, the most dreadful thing. He now had to tell a friend that the brother he had longed to find, his only remaining kin, had put a rifle muzzle into his mouth and blown off the back of his skull. Daniel's lips suddenly felt gummed shut, his mouth dry.

"Nate, he was . . . what happened to Clive was . . . he died of a rifle ball."

"Someone killed him?"

Daniel found it hard to speak. "Yes. Aye."

Nate was very pallid now. "Murder?"

Daniel's throat felt even drier. "It was . . ." He struggled, then yielded. "Aye. It was murder. Or nigh like it."

Though he kept his face straight, he gave himself an immediate fierce chiding in his mind. *Now take a look at what you've done, Boone! You've gone and lied to him, and now there'll be no going back*.

"What do you mean, 'nigh like it'?"

"He was killed helping out a poor man along the road on the way here to find you," Daniel said, desperately making up his lie as he went along. If he was going to lie about what had happened to Clive, he might as well do so in such a way as to make Clive look as fine and good as possible. To give himself time to contrive a story, he went back to the beginning and told as much of the truth as he could. "I ran across Clive in Fredericksburg, up in Virginia. Pure chance it was—I was on my wagon, heading home, when I saw him there in the town. I went to him, we spoke; I found he was ready to put aside his drinking and such and get his life back on the straight and narrow again. I took him home with me, and he put aside the liquor, just like he said he would. It was hard for him, but he did it. You would have been proud of the way he fought it out, all the dreams and visions and such that come to drunkards when they do without. He was strong and set, and he come through it.

"After that he was ready to find you. And so we set out here together, but along the road we found a poor fellow who had been robbed and struck in the head. He was nigh dead, and Clive and me set about to patch up his skull. Then we headed into the woods, looking for tracks, hoping to trail the highwaymen. After a time Clive grew concerned again about the hurt fellow back on the road, for it had commenced to raining, and he went back to cover him. And he had the bad fortune of finding the highwaymen, two of them, back on the road again, too. They came back and killed the man they'd robbed, I suppose thinking he might be able to name them to a constable or judge. Clive must have took out after them, for one of them turned and shot him through the breast. He died where he fell. I heard the shot, run back, and found him. His last word was for me to come ahead and find you, and tell you what became of him, and that at the end he'd set things right in his life."

Daniel stopped, his throat burning and face red. He was generally an honest man, and it went against his nature to tell such a falsehood even out of such a high motive as protecting Nate from hurt. He stood there in silence, feeling as if his lie were revealed on his very face.

But Nate's own stare was blank and unprobing. He absorbed Daniel's talk in silence a few moments, then swallowed and went moist in the eyes. "So he died noble. Died well."

"Yes. You would have been proud of him."

"I am. I am. Clive, he was always the best of us. If any of us was to die well, it would be Clive. I doubt it will be me."

"I laid him to rest in the woods," Daniel said. "I can take you to his grave on our way to Virginia."

"*Our* way? What? I'm going with you?"

"I want you to. Come back and stay with me and Becca until we can move back to the Yadkin. I'd covet your company, and you can work with me at wagonering."

Nate thought it over, then looked around. "There's nothing to hold me here now, God knows. Very well, Dan. I'll go back with you. And then, come fall of the year, you and me will head across them distant mountains and hunt, like we've talked about so many times."

Daniel was surprised by that notion. "Hunt? With the Indian trouble still going on?"

"Why not? That's a vast forest. Two men could lose themselves in it easy enough."

Nate's words stirred the restlessness that was always beneath the surface calm of Daniel Boone's thoughts. He had yearned for a long hunt for years, a truly long hunt, and the relatively short jaunts and trapping ventures he had undertaken off the Yadkin had never satisfied the craving. Could Nate's idea be worth carrying out? Could a man really undertake a long hunt in the midst of Indian troubles?

Had Rebecca and the young ones been standing there at his side, Daniel might have put down the notion at once. But they weren't there, and Daniel allowed himself the pleasure of mulling over what might look absurd if considered in the context of his temporary Virginia home.

Fall of the year—October? No. The baby wouldn't have come by then. But in late fall or early winter the birthing would be done. There would be nothing to hold him back. He and Nate could spend winter in the distant wilderness beyond the mountains and bring back enough pelts and deer hides to put the Boone family in the best situation they had known all their days.

"Maybe we will take us a hunt this winter, Nate," Daniel said. "It'd be a right fair one, wouldn't it?"

"Aye, indeed. But for now, Dan, I want you to take me to where Clive is buried. I want to see it and pay my respects to him."

"In the morning," Daniel said. "We'll leave before the first light. For now, I could use some food in my belly and a bed for the night."

NATE KNELT by the fresh grave and said nothing. Daniel stood to the side, feeling awkward and in the way, even though Nate hardly seemed to be aware of him. He felt exposed, too, as if being near the place Clive had ended his life would somehow expose his lie. This spot gave him feelings bordering on the superstitious.

Nate stood at last, after reaching out to pat the mounded soil gently. "My good brother," he said. "Clive, I wish to God I could have seen you before the end." He turned to Daniel. "Where's the other grave?"

"Other grave?"

"Yes. The man the highwaymen killed."

Daniel felt a hot flush creep over his face. "I—I didn't bury him here."

"You buried him somewhere else?"

"No—I hauled his corpse on into Salisbury and turned it over to the constable. Figuring, you know, that someone might be able to name him. He was likely to have family, you see."

"Oh. Aye. Did they know him?"

"No. Well . . . the constable didn't, on any road." Nate poked about in the woods a bit, looking for a stone to place at the head of Clive's grave. He drew closer and closer to the blackberry thicket where Clive had ended his life, and where a great rusty stain of his blood still marked the ground and a portion of a tree trunk. Daniel actually feared Nate might find it and notice it, but he never entered the thicket. Soon he found a big, head-sized chunk of mica-flecked quartz, which he brought back to the grave and set up.

"That's all I can do for him, Daniel," Nate said, his voice breaking. "Just mark the place he lies. All I can do."

"It's a fine thing. No one wants their bones to be forgotten."

Nate wept silently, head turned away, and then he straightened his shoulders, drew in a deep breath, and wiped his sleeve across his eyes. He turned back to Daniel. "I'm ready to leave here."

"Then let's leave."

They rode out, heading north. Daniel felt an overwhelming sense of relief to be putting this terrible spot behind, and that his lie had gone undetected. He knew Nate well enough to realize that he wouldn't appreciate being lied to, especially on so sensitive and personal a matter as the mode of his brother's death. The fact that Daniel's motive had been kind wouldn't go far with such a man as Nate Meriwether.

As the miles fell behind, Daniel felt much better. The brief portion of his life spent with Clive Meriwether had brought nothing but trial and sorrow, but now it was over. Daniel regretted that it all had ended as it had . . . but at least it was ended. It was past. Daniel Boone was content to leave it there.

Part 2

The Long Hunters

undated photos from the
Miriam & Ira D. Wallach
Collection, NYPL

Beech tree where
D Boon "called a bar" 1760

Reconstruction of
Shawnee village

CHAPTER 13

THE BABY CAME the second day of November and, as Rebecca hoped, it was a girl. Together father and mother settled on the name Susannah, and Daniel almost immediately turned his attention to the hunt he and Nate had been talking about ever since they'd shown up together after Daniel had set off with Clive to find Nate.

Rebecca found it all rather consternating—especially the intrusion of Nate into their home. Intrusion, she thought of it, even though she knew Daniel had invited him. She felt sorry for Nate, especially since his wife had left him and he had lost another brother so tragically—though according to the story Daniel had told her (in an oddly sheepish, averted-eye way) there was at least the consolation that Clive had died in a noble effort to help another person. But she still didn't want Nate to be a part of her home. It was as simple as that. He was the kind of person whose presence seemed to permeate the place so that she never felt at ease or even fully at home within her own walls. It had always been that way with her where Nate was concerned. Her displeasure at his presence had gotten so bad that she actually had looked forward to his and Daniel's departure for the West—just so she wouldn't have to have Nate about.

Of course, then Daniel wouldn't be about either, and she dreaded his absence. Men were thoughtless and selfish by nature, she had decided. Poor Rennie Lowell had been right about that. Here she was, having freshly given birth, and Daniel was occupied with Nate and plans for a coming hunt that seemed to have no anticipated ending. Whenever she asked him how long he would be gone, his answers grew more and more indefinite. A season, maybe two or three. It all depended on how the hunting and trapping was, and whether they could avoid losing anything they gained to the Indians.

Indians. There was another worry for her. Trouble with the Cherokees had grown hotter and deeper throughout the year. There had been a massacre of some Cherokees at Fort Prince George down in South Carolina, which had led to a retaliatory starvation siege and massacre at Fort Loudoun, a British military outpost deep in the country across the mountains. It had fallen in August, and it had stood uncomfortably close to the regions Daniel and Nate could be penetrating on their long hunt.

Daniel knew his wife's displeasure at his coming long absence and sought to give comfort by assuring her that his brother Neddy would be coming by frequently to see that all was well. "Don't be fretful," he said to her more than once. "What I'm doing is for the good of our family. There'll be rich game, hides, and peltries that will pay off our debts. Being apart for a time is a small price to pay for freeing ourselves of debt."

She wasn't convinced, though she knew that their debt situation was indeed in need of attention. So far Daniel had made little money in his life, and often he would take out small loans just to purchase lead, powder, and hunting supplies. Little debts for the most part, but they had added up. There had been whispers about lawsuits back on the Yadkin.

He would be going, and she knew it. There was no point in trying to stop him. Daniel was a headstrong fellow, not prone to swerve once he had fixed his mind on something. The only comfort Rebecca could find was that maybe he really would bring home a rich enough harvest of furs to better their situation.

And in the meantime there was Neddy Boone to keep an eye on her and the children, and relative safety among family and friends in Virginia. She would have to be content with that.

Daniel made a visit to Tom before leaving. It was a crisp autumn day, the wind brisk and the scent from the forest clean and sharp. "I've had it in mind to see if I might find your father and see if he would guide me on a hunt, Tom," Daniel said. "He must know the Overmountain right well."

"He would, Mr. Boone, he would. I know the general parts he lives in, though I don't know I can for certain put you onto right where he is, considering. He roams far, 'way out into the wild country. But I'll tell you the best I can."

When Daniel left Tom, mentally going over the directions given him, the slave was wiping away tears. Daniel knew why: Tom was missing his father, longing to see him, but couldn't go to him because he was bound. It was a sad thing and made Daniel rejoice in his own freedom even while he pitied Tom for his lack of it.

All was ready now. Daniel and Nate were outfitted with one good saddle horse each, and two packhorses that would carry supplies into the woods; and, if all went as hoped, bales of peltries back out again. Rebecca had sewn him two new hunting shirts out of plain linsey, and he wore heavy wool trousers that he tucked into leggings that covered him from ankle to thigh. His moccasins were of deer hide, as were Nate's, but both hoped to replace them with more durable elk hide moccasins after they entered the wilderness, where elk could be found grazing on the great mountain balds. They would make the footwear themselves, peeling off the elk leather with their skinning knives, curing it Indian fashion right in the field, and shaping and sewing it into moccasins with awls and some of the rawhide strips, or whangs, that they had packed along with them.

Both men carried two rifles, along with extra screw plates, vises, files, bellows, and other gear they would use for maintenance and repair. They'd molded a large supply of rifle balls in the evenings leading up to their departure, and they carried several bars of soft lead and a couple of melting pans as well. They anticipated using much ammunition before returning, and would have to mold new bullets in the forests.

In bundles on the packhorses and inside their bedrolls they stashed other assorted tools and goods, from extra knives and axes to mittens, tow, flint and steel, punk, tea, jerked meat, skillets, kettles, cups, flour, and an abundance of parched corn, a staple of the wilderness traveler. Nate had even rounded up some excellent coffee that would brighten many a mealtime in the vast wilderness.

They set out on a chilly morning, Rebecca standing in the doorway and tossing an ax toward Daniel as he left, a traditional act, believed to bring luck. Daniel rode until the little cabin was almost out of sight before turning and waving one final time at his little family. For a moment there was a burst of regret at leaving them, but then he turned and smelled the sharp, moldy scent of the trees and was filled with a joy of nearly religious proportions. At long last the hunting time had come again, and this season he would plunge deeper and come back better off than any other such time in the past.

They rode south into North Carolina and on to the familiar Yadkin country, where they paused to make an inspection of their old homes. There was no guarantee they would find them standing, but standing they were, unmolested by the Cherokees. They were badly overgrown with weeds and brush, the undergrowth encroaching and making them look sad and lifeless. There would be plenty of work to do when the Yadkin was at last fully reoccupied.

Visiting old neighbors who had opted to stay in their homes despite the Indian threat, Daniel and Nate learned that retaliation against the Cherokees was planned for the next year, and Hugh Waddell was talking of raising a force on the Yadkin and joining the excursion. Daniel regretted hearing it, not because he didn't think such a move was needed or because he feared the idea of war, but because he had been mulling the possibility of continuing his long hunt well into the summer. If Waddell raised a Yadkin force, continuation would be impossible, because Daniel would feel obligated to volunteer for Waddell. His only hope was that somehow the Cherokee war would come to an end before the next year.

He and Nate left the Yadkin eagerly, anticipating the plunge into the wilderness. The autumn was already beginning to give way to the winter, and they wanted to make as thorough an exploration as possible before settling in for the winter.

They knew they had time only for a cursory effort toward finding Burrell, Tom's father; and frankly, they didn't expect that they would succeed. But inquiries at a couple of outlying farmsteads that had almost miraculously survived the troubled year gave them new direction. Following it, they found the old slave in a small hut at the base of the mountains. He was a stooped, gray-haired, pleasant-looking man with a strong resemblance to his sons. Initially suspicious, he became open and friendly as soon as he understood that Daniel and Nate knew Tom and Joe. He wept with joy at the news that they were well, and Daniel was discreet enough not to mention the trouble Joe had suffered at the hands of the Kincheloes. He saw no point in laying unnecessary burdens on the old fellow.

Conversation turned to the hunt, and Burrell agreed without hesitation to take them to a rich hunting ground seldom touched by white men, high on the crest of the mountains. Burrell was assigned to graze and guard the herd of his master, who lived many miles distant. Though he was a slave, he had the trust of his master, lived a generally isolated life that seemed to suit him, and enjoyed great physical freedom.

He led them up an old buffalo trail that wound through brown hills and beneath great crags. In the end it came out in what Burrell called the "high meadow," a wide expanse of grassy land at the top of the mountains. Here stood a rough shelter of logs, cut green and left unhewn, but snugly chinked and roofed with puncheons and peeled bark. Daniel stood before the low little door, looking about at the beautiful land stretching all around, and thinking that this might be the finest place he had stood in all his years.

"This here's a shelter me and other herders have used through the years, grazing cattle here on the balds and high meadows," Burrell said. "From here a man can reach some of the best hunting land he'll ever find. It's headwater country, rich as can be, and filled with every type of critter the good Lord ever made, I reckon."

They made the shelter their station camp and set off on hunts, though for the first days they did more simple exploring than hunting. They found the country as rich as Burrell had declared. In this region the Yadkin, Watauga, and New rivers had their sources. They were gorgeous rivers, filled with fish and pure, clean water, sullied only by the droppings of the game that grazed and watered along the bottoms.

At length Burrell ceased accompanying Daniel and Nate on their excursions and settled into the job of cook and hide dresser, tasks he seemed to relish. Daniel and Nate explored the rivers and their tributaries, establishing temporary camps for two or three days, where they scaffolded their harvests of deer hides to keep them out of reach of animals. When they had a sufficient bundle, they would haul the hides back to the cabin in the high meadow and Burrell would dress them out fully, fold and bale them, and store them in the rear of the shelter.

And they would eat. Burrell was a cook like neither man had ever met; the fare he made them became the focus of anticipation when they wound their way back to the high meadow, and the subject of nostalgic conversation for a day or so after they left again. Buffalo hump, stews with a mix of venison, buffalo, wild turkey, and bear, and once a delicious breakfast of marrow bones cooked on hickory embers. Burrell caught fish in the streams, using a combination of a trout line strung with Daniel's fish hooks and white-oak fish traps like baskets made Cherokee-style, and roasted his catches seasoned with sage. He used a Dutch oven stored at the cabin to bake plump loaves of bread made from flour and corn he had ground to meal in a log mortar. They drank tea, coffee, rum, and some of the most delicious, pure water any of the men had ever tasted. Daniel considered that if paradise ever descended to earth, it could surely have little more to offer than this. The only part of it he didn't relish was the beaver tail that Burrell enjoyed cooking. Daniel had always despised the taste of beaver tail, though most hunters thought it a delicacy.

Frost-mellowed persimmons fell in abundance to the earth—fruity, pulpy manna that the hunters happily added to their diet with beechnuts, hickory nuts, and the chestnuts that Nate particularly relished. As the weather cooled, they added more fat to their diet, cooking tallow down to a thick liquid with which they dressed their meat and bread.

Eventually Burrell made his way back down the buffalo trail to the world they had left behind, a world that now seemed very distant and almost unreal to Daniel Boone. The hunters remained alone, grieving philosophically over Burrell's departure for reasons both affectionate and gastronomical, and began ranging farther across the great divide of the mountains. They had less to draw them back to the high-meadow station camp, with Burrell and his cookery gone, and if they ate less well, they covered much more country and found more new hunting grounds, which was why they had come, after all.

They explored the country along the Watauga River, camping in different places, while the weather grew ever cooler. Around Christmas, Daniel roused a bear from its winter sleep near the Long Island of the

Holston River, killed it, and skinned it out for a coat, wearing it with fur turned inside and leaving the skin of the forelegs unsplit to serve as naturally lined sleeves. Nate considered it so fine an animal that as Daniel skinned it out, Nate recorded the event with his knife on the bark of a nearby beech tree:

D. Boon
Called A. Bar on
tree
in the
YEAR
1760

TWO DAYS LATER Nate killed a bear of his own and made himself a similar coat. Daniel didn't return Nate the compliment of recording his bear kill in wood, being off following another tributary of the Holston, just to see where it led.

As winter grew colder, deer and other game became lean and less palatable, but otter and beaver came into their prime. Daniel and Nate strung trap lines along the rivers and built themselves a half-faced camp in a secluded spot that they approached along a rocky path to avoid leaving tracks.

So far they had seen no sign of Indians. Now that winter had come, Daniel was optimistic that they would have no encounters at all. Except for isolated hunting parties, the Cherokees should be far from there, in their towns along rivers a hundred miles or more to the south. There should be nothing for Daniel and Nate to worry about except making sure they had sufficient horse power to get their furs and peltries safely back to the eastern market towns for sale.

STRAINING NOT TO MOVE and hardly to breathe, Daniel crouched beside a big gnarled maple, peering intently at the three Indians passing through the ravine below him. That he had managed to avoid being heard or seen by them so far was astonishing, and for once he knew he couldn't credit his own woodsman's skills for it. He had been absorbed in following the track of a fox, so much so that he had failed to keep a careful enough eye out. Only an odd-sounding rustle in a copse of trees had warned him that all was not well. He had slipped over and crouched by this maple, watching in astonishment as three Indians emerged from the trees.

Daniel was surprised to see a hunting party this far from the Overhill towns in the heart of winter. Or perhaps these were Shawnees ranging south out of the Kentucky country. Whatever their tribe, they were a surprise and a potential danger.

He examined their weapons. They were trade muskets, cheap and short and poorly made, the kind the licensed Carolina traders sold the Cherokees in the towns. So these were indeed Cherokees—so much the worse for him, considering the current warfare between the Cherokees and whites.

Daniel all but held his breath and felt the most overwhelming need to shift his position. He didn't. He held still and wondered just where Nate was, and if he had any notion there were Indians about. They had parted ways that morning, planning to rejoin at sunset in a temporary camp along a creek about two miles from where Daniel was now. He had left his horses there today. Knowing he would be in hilly country, he had preferred to rely on his own feet.

The Cherokees seemed oblivious to his presence, and he thanked heaven that the wind was not blowing from him to them. If he could remain as he was, and no scent or sound or footprint betrayed him, maybe they would go on past and he could escape. In his inside-out bearskin cloak he blended very naturally into the background of winter brown.

It was a blue jay, of all things, that shattered all hope of remaining unseen. Blue and black and crested, it flew in from somewhere behind him, settled on a branch fifteen feet above him, and gave out a raucous cry as soon as it saw him. Daniel was not a man prone to hatred, but right then he hated that blue jay, hated the entire bird race of jays—intrusive, spiteful birds, squawkers that would not abide even so much as a squirrel within twenty feet of them.

One of the Indians glanced up the rise at the jay, and then his eyes dropped and locked on Daniel. For a few seconds the two men stared into each other's faces, the Indian's expression changing swiftly from one of blank incomprehension to surprise to alarm.

The Indian sent up a yell, and the others swung about and saw Daniel, too. Daniel might have stood and tried to bluff friendliness, a technique once recommended to him by John Findley, but one of the Cherokees had already raised his musket. Daniel turned on his heel and ran across the ridge just as the musket fired and the ball made a flat, dead slap into the maple he had been hiding beneath. He felt his scalp tighten as he imagined what it would have been like if that musket ball had found its way into his skull instead of the tree.

They yelled and came after him. Holding his rifle close to his cloaked body to avoid losing it, Daniel ran hard, his moccasins making a faint slapping sound on the ground. He dodged right to miss slamming into an oak, then left again to avoid the grasping branches of a dogwood. Another of the muskets fired, the ball ripping through the branches above Daniel's head, sending up a flurry of chickadees and titmice. Two shots fired, both misses. That much was good. Daniel ran on, the rough ground tearing at his moccasins, chestnut burs stabbing his heels. Unheeding of the pain, he ran on. His hat blew from his head and he didn't even notice.

At one point he was about to wheel and fire at the closest of his pursuers but chose not to. There was the risk of missing; and even if he didn't miss, he would be left with an empty rifle and two determined enemies, one of whom still had a loaded musket. The other two had not taken time to reload after firing their own failed shots.

The best hope was that the third man would also fire and miss, which would leave Daniel with the advantage of having a loaded weapon while they had none. Even so, he would be in a precarious situation, for the moment he fired out his charge, he would still face, at best, a two-against-one fight.

All he could do, it appeared, was run until he escaped them . . . if that was possible.

Another ridge loomed up before him, a shallow rise that quickly became much steeper. Marshaling his strength, he willed every pulse of it he could spare into his legs, pushing his way up the slope. A glance back showed the Cherokees closing in, the third one raising his musket. Ducking, Daniel anticipated the shot, but it did not come. He made it over the ridge too fast for the man to fire it off.

It was a downhill run now, for quite a distance. Daniel used both muscle and gravity to full advantage, leaning forward so that he raced down the slope almost like a flying arrow. A narrow rivulet ran at the base and he leaped it in one stride, then pounded up the gentler rise on the far side. His breath came in great gulps now, ragged and burning in his chest. There was pain in his legs, calves and thighs tight and cramping. He ignored it. He could afford to do nothing else.

Beyond lay a wide shallow filled with ivy, vines, and scrub brush. There was no time to go around it, so Daniel pushed off and leaped as far into it as he could. He reached down with his feet to find the ground hidden below the undergrowth. It wasn't there. Unseeable from above the tangle, the ground had given way to a pit. Daniel was swallowed by the vegetation, disappearing from sight.

He wound up on his side, lying atop his rifle. The fall had knocked the breath from him and disoriented him slightly as well. He rolled onto his belly and was about to push up when he realized that the Indians might not know where he was. To continue his run might be precisely the wrong thing. Twisting his head, he looked through the tangle and saw the Cherokees at the edge of the shallow. They were peering into the ivy and vines with the intent expressions of spear fishers looking for fish in a pool. The two who had emptied their muskets were taking advantage of the time to reload.

That made Daniel's decision for him. Obviously they knew he was somewhere in the tangle, and it would only be a matter of time before they found him. And giving the other two time to reload was the last thing he wanted. He sprang up and bulled his way out of the vines, almost having his rifle torn from his grip. There was a shot—the last musket had been fired. He didn't know where the ball struck, but it hadn't struck him, and that was all that counted. The two who were reloading had no time to finish, and now the third musket was empty.

Knowing that the Indians now lacked fire power gave him a new burst of strength and will. If they wanted him, they would have to catch him, not simply shoot him from a distance. And he would run himself into the dirt before he would let them catch him.

For the next while Daniel lost all sense of time and distance. All he knew was running, as hard as he could go and as far. His lungs burned and ached, his legs were pillars of pain, his feet torn and bleeding, the bottoms of his worn moccasins having long since given way. He longed to stop, but he could not. They were still after him. His bearskin coat became hot and heavy, but he had no time to shrug it off.

Over the gasps of his own breath and the noise of his running he heard the sound of running water. A creek ahead . . . and now he knew what creek it was. This was a stream he and Nate had camped alongside three nights before. He looked behind and saw the Indians had lost ground. There was hope.

He entered the stream and splashed through, heading up the far bank and into the woods a short distance. Wildly, he looked for a way to get back to the stream that would not leave a path, and found it in the form of a fallen poplar. Long, straight, limbless along most of its length, it lay at an angle down the bank, reaching almost to the water. Daniel leaped atop it, then ran down it and into the water.

Just ahead was a small waterfall that he had noticed when he'd been hunting there before. It was about three feet high, rapid, and with a heavy flow. Daniel reached the edge of it, leaped down to the stream bed below, and rolled back under the wall of water. There was just enough room for him to lie there without having to bury his face in the water.

He curled his knees up to his chest, wrapping his arms around them, while clinging to his rifle. There he panted, as softly as he could, grateful for the masking sound of the water. He hurt terribly, but he was hidden, and there was enough room for him to breathe and rest, and if all went as he hoped, the Cherokees would not find him.

He stayed there, drenched by the waterfall, tired and knowing that he might be found at any time. Long moments passed and he heard them moving about, talking, looking. They did not find him. He lay still for about an hour, then closed his eyes. Amazingly, he slept. When he awakened, the light was different; at least a couple of hours had passed, as best he could judge. He felt alone but would take no chances. He shifted his position a little but did not emerge.

Only when darkness fell did he come out. As quickly as he could, he made his way to the camp, where he found a tense Nate waiting without a fire.

"There's Indians about," Nate said. "When you didn't come, I was fearful they'd kilt you."

"They nigh did. But I believe they're gone now." He pawed at his head. "I lost my hat in the run. Doubt I can find it again."

"I've got an extra one rolled up back at the station camp. You can have it."

"Thank you. Lord, I'm tired, dog-tired. And hungry. Any food on you?"

"Jerky, and some dried biscuit."

"Good enough."

He ate wordlessly, rolled out his blankets, and fell asleep, having never even removed his ragged moccasins or the waterlogged bearskin coat. Nate watched him, frowning, and stared around at the darkening forest as if it had suddenly become an alien, threatening place.

CHAPTER 14

THE HAT NATE GAVE Daniel to replace the one he'd lost was on the small side and had a slightly narrower brim than Daniel preferred, but it was far better than nothing, and he accepted it with thanks. He managed to improve the fit by stretching the hat down over a small stump for two or three nights; as for the brim, he just put up with it.

The encounter with the Cherokees had cast something of a pall over the long hunt, particularly for Nate. Now that their presence in this wilderness was known, they would have to proceed with greater care. For several days they forsook their usual separate ventures and hunted only together, built nothing but hidden, virtually smokeless hardwood fires, and kept a close watch for any sign of danger. Several times Daniel thought he detected an Indian presence, but it never proved out, and he began to think that perhaps the danger he had so narrowly escaped was gnawing at his nerves more than he wanted to admit.

Or perhaps Nate's tension was beginning to rub off on him. Nate had grown abnormally quiet, furtive and birdlike in his movements, starting at every sound and suspicious of every bird call. Daniel could only imagine how much worse Nate might be if the Cherokees had stumbled upon him rather than Daniel. Nate's softened nerve was a serious concern. In the wilderness a man had to keep a balance in his mind, not waste fear on things that did not merit it, nor withhold it from things that did.

In late January the temperature made a sudden plunge, and the wind shifted and came from the north, blustery and slicing cold. The forest floor teemed with birds frenetically scavenging for seed to fill their stomachs. Clouds gathered and hung low, heavy and thick as mud. Snow was coming. Daniel and Nate checked their trap lines, and moved back to the herdsmen's shelter. There, they chopped firewood, and daubed the old chinking with fresh mud. Nate chopped saplings in the nearby woods and built a half-faced shelter big enough to stable the horses through the worst of it.

The snow began by night, falling rapidly, in big, moist flakes. The cabin creaked and groaned as the snow piled onto the roof, weighting it down and making it sag. Daniel worried that it might collapse, and built up the fire high and hot so that the thin roofing would warm and the snow atop it would melt and slide off. He and Nate ate buffalo hump and drank the last of the coffee, and Nate grew less nervous, knowing the weather would keep the Indians huddled by their fires in their camps, wherever those might be. The snow drifted against the wall and weighted the door shut so that they had to fight it open the next morning. It lay knee-deep, bending tree branches to the earth, sparkling in the sun as if diamonds had been sprinkled through it from the sky. The clouds had thinned and cleared away almost entirely as the sun rose, and the light reflected off the white blanket was so stark and bright there in the high mountain country that it was nearly unbearable to look into, but the scene was so wildly beautiful, they looked anyway.

Two days before the snow Daniel had killed a big elk on a mountain bald and skinned it out. Snowbound in the shelter, he used his time to soften the best portion of the hide on a straking board until it was supple, and with awl, knife, and rawhide whangs, made two pairs of moccasins, one for Nate, one for himself. They had their elk hide footwear at last and welcomed it, for the flimsiness of the deer hide moccasins had been a bane to them since the hunt had begun.

They hunted only a little in the snow, game being hard to find and even harder to surprise against such a brilliant background. It didn't matter much; they had sufficient supplies laid away in the shelter to see them through several weeks of bad weather. They continued their trapping, adding beaver, otter, and mink to their rising store of peltries.

In the evenings there was time for talk, and Nate began to speak of Nora. Daniel had made a point of asking no questions about her, not considering it his business, but when Nate raised the subject on his own, he listened.

"I loved that woman, Dan," he said. "There ain't no question of that. Sometimes, hard as she could be, she would have a way about her, a sweetness you don't often see. If the sweet side had been all there was to her, she'd still be at my side today. It was the other part of her that drove us apart."

"A man can't know all he needs to know, sometimes," Daniel said. "Not soon enough, leastways."

"If I'd have knowed what I learnt later, I wouldn't have married her. No question about that. She was a hard woman at her heart, Dan. Not a bit less than a demon in the shape of a woman. The Nora what walked off and left me wasn't the Nora I thought I knowed. She surely wasn't the Nora I loved first. A demon, she was, with the spirit of hell in her."

Daniel was puzzled by the harshness of Nate's words. Nate had spoken similarly about Nora when Daniel first came to Nate's farmstead outside Salisbury, but not then nor now did he seem inclined to elaborate.

"Them's fine moccasins," Nate said. "You make as fine a moccasin as I've ever seen, Dan Boone." The comment marked the end of all discussion of Nora House, and Daniel wondered if he would ever know what Nora had done that had so turned Nate against her.

By the first of February the weather warmed for a bit and the snow went away, melting its beauty into dripping, muddy ugliness. They roamed out farther again, and once more Nate became nervous about Indians, though not as much as before. They lived a quiet, repetitious life throughout the month, which brought them another snowstorm, smaller than the first one, to end the month and bring in March. After this one melted, Nate announced that he was ready to head home.

"It's early for leaving, Nate," Daniel said. "There's still the spring to come; we can go as far as we want in that weather. I even thought about trying to reach the gap of the Cumberlands, if you shared the notion."

"No," Nate said. "I'm set on going back."

"To Carolina?"

"Just long enough to sell my share. After that I'll go into Virginia. Help your brother Ned see to your family's care."

Daniel felt a vague sting at those words. Rebecca and the children were his responsibility, not Nate's, yet it was Nate and not he who was talking about their welfare. It made Daniel feel guilty, and angry at Nate for making him feel that way, until he realized the truth. Nate was leaving because he knew the spring weather would increase Indian hunting activity. He was leaving because he was afraid. The presence of Indians in the region had touched the part of Nate Meriwether that still ached from the pain of a brother killed at the stake outside Fort Duquesne, and another whose family had been massacred. Daniel could understand his fear, but he could not abide it. He could not afford to.

"Go on, then, if it suits you," Daniel said brusquely. "Tell Rebecca I'll be home later in the spring with money in hand for her. Then I reckon I'll head back to the Yadkin to join up with Hugh Waddell 'gainst the Cherokees, if that's still the plan."

"I'll tell her," Nate replied, very noticeably omitting any similar intention to become an Indian fighter. Daniel felt slightly contemptuous. It was he who had nearly been killed by the Cherokee hunters, but Nate who had been spooked out of any courage he might have had.

Daniel didn't ride any of the initial homeward distance with Nate, as he had with Burrell. He said his farewells there in the high meadow and stood watching until Nate was out of sight, his laden packhorses trailing after him. For only a few seconds did Daniel feel any loneliness. He seldom minded being by himself, and the deepest, most shadowed groves of the forest roused no fear in him. It was a trait few people shared, one that he had noted in himself in his boyhood, one that helped him know he was set apart from most other folks.

Before Nate was long out of sight, Daniel was already gathering his possessions for another excursion westward. There were miles of the westward-flowing Holston he had not yet followed, and he was curious about how far the river continued until it reached whatever end it did. He might explore its entire length, if he could, or at least a long stretch of it.

He was just setting out when the thin sound of a distant gunshot reached his ear. A second shot followed, echoing across the mountains, then a third. Their sound was so faint he could scarcely detect them, and a listener with less of a woodsman's ear might not have heard them at all.

The shots came from the east, and judging from the volume, they had been fired from about the vicinity Nate would have reached by now.

Daniel moved quickly. Throwing aside everything but his most basic gear, his rifle and ammunition, he leaped upon his saddle mount and rode east as hard as the horse could go.

DANIEL SLID SILENTLY off his horse and led it into the trees beside the buffalo road. Keeping his eyes in constant motion, scanning the forest all around, he took a hobble from his saddle pouch and hobbled the horse. A quick check of his rifle showed his loading and priming in good shape. He took off his hat, hung it on the saddle, and slipped into the trees.

The sign he had found indicated Nate had followed the buffalo road about that far and then abruptly left it. In the woods his tracks were harder to trace, but Daniel managed to follow them. A few paces on he sniffed the air. Wood smoke, a faint, lingering scent. Someone had camped near there very recently, probably the night before and into the morning.

Proceeding with greater caution, Daniel made his way from tree to tree, vigilant, listening. The wood smoke scent was stronger there, though still faint. Kneeling, he looked through the undergrowth in all directions until his eye fixed on something a few yards to the north. He held his position for a full minute, moving only his head and eyes, trying to ascertain if the half-hidden something he saw was what it appeared to be.

Rising, he advanced with a mounting sense of dread. There was no responding motion or sound from anywhere around, and his instinct told him no one else was nearby—no one living, at any rate. Even so, he would take no chances. Instinct was a good thing, but his older brothers had long ago beaten into Daniel's mind the maxim that a man who trusted instinct alone followed an unreliable and sometimes deadly guide. A woodsman's best guide was his senses, and his best counselor was caution.

This time Daniel's instinct was validated. By the time he reached the edge of the little Cherokee camp, he knew that he was alone. There was no one there except himself and the obviously dead Indian lying on his face beside a barely smoldering fire.

Daniel moved to the Indian's side, his elk hide moccasins making no more than a whisper on the leafy ground. Kneeling, he examined the corpse, then touched it. Still warm. Oddly, one of the dead man's legs was splinted with two stout oak rods held in place by strips of deerskin. This man had already been treated for a broken leg before the attack that killed him. Rolling the body over, Daniel winced when he saw the man's chest. The Indian was wearing an open-fronted deer hide shirt, sleeveless. There was a large, ugly bullet hole near the area of his heart, and the volume of blood blackening and clotting on his skin and the pain-racked expression frozen on his features showed that this man had not died instantly. He had suffered out his last moments there on the ground, weakening and dying from loss of blood. He had not been scalped.

Daniel stood, then looked about the camp. A deer, stripped of its skin and its choicest meat, hung from a branch at the perimeter of the camp circle above a darkened area where its blood and juices had drained and dried. An English trade musket stood against a tree nearby, powder horn and bullet pouch hanging over the end of its sheathed ramrods. A second musket, of better quality than the trade musket, lay on its side near the standing musket, its horn and shot pouch lying beside it. Nearby, a third powder horn also lay on the ground, unstoppered, some of the powder spilled out around it. A few stray rifle balls lay scattered beyond. Here and there were great dollops of dark blood on the leaves and dirt, drying but much fresher than the blood of the skinned deer. Daniel examined all the evidence and interpreted the story it told.

He knelt and studied the ground closely, both where he was and all around the circle of the campfire, particularly around the muskets. All he saw, from footmarks to the position of the muskets, confirmed the same thing. Whoever killed the Cherokee had surprised two Indians in their camp. The man with the broken leg had been shot first and had not moved from the spot he fell before he died. The second Cherokee had been wounded and managed to grab one musket and fire off a shot before fleeing. It was to this musket that the fallen, unstoppered powder horn belonged. The fleeing Indian had been pursued by the man who had attacked the camp. A lone man, the footmarks showed.

Nate. It had to be Nate.

Daniel picked up each musket and removed the flints, tucking them under his belt sash. Then he left the camp and headed northeast, moving slowly, following footmarks and bloodstains, until he came upon an animal path that led toward a looming rocky hill nearby, so steep it was nearly a bluff on the side facing Daniel. He examined the face of the escarpment, then turned his eyes to the ground again and advanced, pausing frequently to look about and listen.

The path led to a cave that smelled heavily of musk and droppings—a frequent den, obviously, for bears, or a lair for bobcats. The fresh footmarks on the damp ground indicated that the most recent occupant had been human. There were blood drippings, too, bigger than those at the camp. Either the wounded Indian's bleeding had increased, or—

Daniel felt a chill of dread. He had an impulse to turn and flee from the cave, but he didn't. He stepped inside, allowed his eyes time to adjust to the darkness, and advanced.

It was not a deep cave, and in fact hardly a cave at all, he found. Instead, it was a natural tunnel, about thirty feet long and bearing to the left, that passed through an outcrop of the hill. There was water through part of the passage, flowing out of the hill itself and passing out of the cave on the side opposite the one Daniel had entered.

Daniel reached the other opening and paused there, looking around carefully before leaving. As soon as he did leave, he realized he was not alone. A shuffling sound to his right made him wheel, leveling his rifle.

"Dan," Nate said weakly. He was leaning on his two rifles as if they were a single crutch. His left hand gripped a bloody spot on his right side. "I'm cut, Dan." He collapsed, falling atop his rifles and closing his eyes with a groan.

NATE OPENED HIS EYES and stared straight up. Slowly they rolled in their sockets, first left, then right, and locked on Daniel's face.

"I'm still alive."

"Yes. You just fainted out on me for a while. I've swabbed off that cut and tied it up, so don't roll around and get it to bleeding again."

"Was it deep?"

"Not bad." Daniel raised a forefinger and with his other forefinger touched it just below the knuckle. "He just hit you in the right place to draw a lot of blood."

"God, I thought he'd cut me to the gizzard, the way it felt."

"Why'd you kill that old Cherokee, Nate?"

"Why do you think? He was an Indian."

"The way you've put on lately, I would have figured you would stay far away from any Indian camp."

"Well, I'll tell you what happened." Nate moved and winced, and Daniel again admonished him to remain still. Nate went on. "I smelled the smoke of their fire and stopped. Hid my horses and took both my rifles and sneaked down closer to see if they were red or white men. When I saw they was Indians I nigh made water right then and there, and I won't lie and say otherwise. I thunk about turning and sneaking back, but I was afraid they'd hear me, and then I got to thinking about poor Frederick, and Clive's family, and the rage got up in me. It come to me that here was a chance to set right the balance for what the savages have done to me and mine. I had two rifles, and there was two Indians, and one of them hurt, at that. Had his leg all swaddled up with sticks and whangs, like he'd busted it somehow."

"I saw that."

"He's the first one I shot. Just marched right in there and shot him as he twisted to see me. Shot him right through the chest." Nate grinned. Daniel gazed at him but did not grin back. "I confess, Dan, I've been afraid of meeting up with Indians since you got chased under that waterfall. I know you've noticed it, even though you ain't spoke about it."

"I've noticed it," Daniel said.

"Well, when I stepped into that camp, there wasn't a bit of fear in me. I'm proud as I can be to say it. Not a bit of fear."

"So you walked in and killed a man laid up with a busted leg."

"I did," Nate said proudly,oblivious of the coldness in Daniel's tone.

"What about the other one? He didn't hear you or see you?"

"There's a queer thing for certain, Dan. I don't know why he didn't notice me. He was young, sitting there with his eyes closed like maybe he was sleeping, but I never heard of an Indian you could sneak up on easy even in his sleep. I had figured he would jump a lot faster than he did, so I had both my rifles raised, one in each hand, so I could shoot at the same time if need be. But he didn't even know I was there until I'd already shot the old one. Anyhow, when he did light up, I shot him too. Pop, pop. That's how it went. One Indian shot, then the other."

"But I heard three shots back at the high meadow."

"That's right. My shot didn't bring down the young one. He grabbed a musket and fired it at me, but he missed. Looked scared as a rabbit and took off like one, too, even though he was bleeding."

"Just how young was this one, Nate?"

Nate frowned. Something in the way Daniel had asked the question clearly hit a nerve. Nate's answer was in a very defensive tone. "He was a boy, or hardly more, and I don't feel no shame at admitting it. Let me say it this way: he was old enough to kill a white man or misuse some poor white woman or take the scalp of a white child. He was a savage, just like them that have shed Meriwether blood in Pennsylvania. He was old enough to jump me from hiding and put a knife hole in my side on yonder side of that cave-tunnel yonder! And you know the saying, Dan: nits make lice. Kill them while they're young, and they won't grow up to kill you while you're old."

"So you killed him too?"

"Reckon so. I wounded him good when I shot him. Hit him right in the side."

"But you didn't hurt him again beyond that?"

"No. I reloaded my rifles and took out after him. Found his tracks at the mouth of that cave, and that's where he jumped me and cut me. He scampered off into the cave and on through, and I followed him, but this side of the cave I never laid eyes on him." Nate's face suddenly whitened. "God, Daniel! He might be watching us now, and he had his musket with him when he ran! He might be beading down on us right now!"

"He had his musket, but he dropped his powder and shot back at the camp. So he can't shoot us, and I took the flints out of all the muskets left behind, just in case somebody sneaked back there."

"You're a fine woodsman, Daniel. You know how to think."

"I wish I could say the same for you, Nate." Daniel's eyes sparked as he finally gave vent to an anger that had been building from the time Nate had begun his story. "What you've done is bloody wrong, bloody foolish too. That old Cherokee didn't burn your brother nor murder Clive's family. Likely he was just an old man out on a winter hunt who busted his leg and was laid up with a boy to tend him. I want to sing your praises, Nate Meriwether: you've killed an old man and put a bullet in a boy who, if he don't die too, might just make it back to his town to spread the word about what you did. It's fools like you who start Indian wars in the first place, fools like you who keep them going."

Nate raised up, face twisting first in anger, then in pain as his stab wound hurt him. Daniel put out his foot and shoved him to the ground.

"Lie still. You get that cut to bleeding, and I'll not waste my time trying to stanch it again."

DANIEL HAD NO MORE WILL to continue the long hunt alone. Nate's actions had greatly increased the danger of their situation and cast a dark shadow over the entire venture. In a state of great disgust, Daniel recovered his horses and Nate's, took the entire processional back to the high-meadow cabin, and began preparations to depart.

He boiled lynn-tree bark into a paste and used it as an ointment on Nate's stab wound, which was showing signs of festering. Covering the anointed wound with elm bark and a linen bandage, he told Nate to lie still and keep quiet a couple of days: he had no desire even to converse with him. In this sullen, unpleasant atmosphere Daniel finished all the baling of hides and peltries, loaded the packhorses, and within a few days, when Nate was beginning to heal, set out for the east.

In the Yadkin they sold their harvest for less than Daniel had anticipated. There, confirmation reached them that Hugh Waddell was in fact going to raise a force for the summer campaign against the Cherokees. Daniel and Nate indicated they would both be taking part, then mounted and headed north to Virginia in a relationship that at the moment seemed to hold as much enmity as affection.

For Daniel Boone it had been a fine long hunt, but it had turned bad. He resented Nate for ruining the expedition, and despised even the physical process of moving east instead of west. If not for the fact that his family lay at the end of this journey, he would find nothing happy in his circumstances at all.

CHAPTER 15

REBECCA HELD HIM CLOSE, her arms wrapped around his lean form and her face pressed to his chest, but still he could feel the tension and restraint in her. Almost from the moment he'd returned, it had been like this, and he wasn't yet sure why. It was troubling.

Daniel Boone forced a smile onto his face and put his hands on her shoulders, pushing her back and examining her up and down. She was wearing a pretty cambric apron, just like the one he had ruined during their courtship. He'd bought it for her out of the money his peltries had brought. That and a couple of baubles for the children was all the extravagance he had felt free to indulge in. Most of the money would be needed for the family to live on while he was away, fighting the Cherokees under Hugh Waddell.

Daniel looked her over. "You look might pretty, Becca. Just prime. That apron makes a girl out of you again." As he spoke it, he knew it wasn't the truth. Rebecca didn't look nearly as girlish as she had even a couple of years ago. Though she was only twenty-two years old, her most recent birthday having passed unheralded while Daniel had been still on the hunt, she looked as if she could be ten years older. Now that he thought about it, she looked much older than when he'd left her last year. Her eyes were hollow and weary, with lines around them almost as deep as those developing along the sides of her mouth. This was a woman who had gone through a difficult winter indeed. Rebecca had already told him as much, but only now did it truly sink in.

Now she smiled at him, wearily, and thanked him for his compliment. "It's the finest apron I've ever owned, Dan," she went on. "I'll put it away in the chest and take good care of it."

She pulled away from him and removed the apron, which she folded carefully and put away in a cedar trunk he had made her shortly after their wedding. It contained the treasures of her life. Daniel looked inside as she put away the apron and noticed with a pang how few those treasures were. A couple of combs, one nice but very simple blue dress, a kerchief, a brooch, and a couple of pretty quartz stones she had found in the garden and called her "jewels." God help me, Daniel thought. About all I've given that woman is debt and labor.

"Becca."

She closed the chest and turned to him. The lines he had seen looked deeper in the light. Her shoulders were stooped, her breasts heavy with the milk that was the sustenance of little Susannah, who just now was stirring out of sleep in the rugged little crib in the corner. "What's wrong? You ain't yourself today."

"Nothing's wrong," she said.

"You act as if there is."

"What wrong could there be? You're home again, and you've brought money. And you'll be here a few days before you take out again, so there'll be time for you to patch the roof hole and clear the saplings out to make the garden bigger. That's all in the world me and the children need from you. What could be wrong?"

He stiffened, his expression turning cold, even as his insides felt hot. "Becca, you ain't being fair to me. You know that if I had my choice, I'd be here with my family."

"If you had your choice, Dan, you'd be out with your traps and rifles in the mountains, hundreds of miles away from here, and you know it."

He did, and couldn't deny it. "I must hunt for this family to live, wife."

"There's other ways to make a living. You could farm, drive a wagon, trade horses and such."

"Aye, and we'd starve out right fast. There's hardly a farmer who don't have to take to the forest to make enough extra money to keep a roof above his head."

"That's true enough, but at the least those farmers spend what time they can beneath their roofs. You're happier far from home. It's a hard time for the rest of us when you're away, husband. Do you know what it is to be here with one baby squalling in the crib for its suckle while another one's turning over the churn and another one's nigh setting the cabin afire with piling too much wood on the hearth, and me trying to take care of it all alone? And all the while not even knowing if you're still alive or if maybe some savage is showing off your hair to his squaw? And now you're home again at last, and what have you told me but that you're set to head off again to fight the redskins!"

"Becca, now listen to me . . ."

She would not stop. Her feelings had been restrained through a long and lonely winter, and she could not stanch the flow of them now that it had started. "No, you should listen to me, Daniel Boone. I know you never wanted to come to Virginia. We both know it was me who led you here. You know why I did it, husband?"

"Because you were worried about the family being safe with the Cherokees a-warring."

"Yes, but mostly because I was worried about you, Daniel. Because

I knew that as long as we were on the Yadkin, you'd feel obliged to be off rangering and fighting after every Indian raid anywhere within a hundred mile, and sooner or later you'd wind up dead, and me left a widow. You remember the time you buried poor old Fish after the Cherokees murdered him?"

"Aye." William Fish, a settler in Yadkin Valley living at the mouth of Fish River, had been killed by Cherokees before the move to Virginia. Daniel himself laid the man's corpse away after Fish had been slain.

"That night I dreamed of William Fish coming to our door and knocking and taking you off with him. It was a portent of you a-fixing to die just like Fish had, sure as the world. That was when I knew we had to go. It was for your sake more than anybody else's I pleaded with you to come away from the borderland. And it's been all for naught. You've left us here a full winter's season while you hunted in the heart of the savage country, and now you're ready to leave us again and go marching off to fight the very Indians I wanted to get you away from!"

Daniel stood aghast. Rebecca had never spoken so forthrightly and angrily to him before. He was touched to realize it was for his welfare, primarily, that she cajoled him off the Yadkin. He was chagrined and shamed to think she'd suffered such worry over him while he was away. But what she seemed to want of him was something he could not give.

"Becca, I can't stand idle and let neighbors of ours smite the Indians. I could never show my face back home again if I did such a coward's act!"

His objections meant nothing to her. "Daniel, don't go. Don't come back to me only to run off again."

Daniel could find no words. Rebecca's eyes were fixed on him, and her expression was uninterpretable: maybe pleading, maybe angry. He had never seen her look at him like that before.

When it became evident Daniel was not going to speak, Rebecca sighed. Her shoulders slumped even more and she seemed very weary. "If it wasn't for your brother, Dan, I'd feel there wasn't a Boone man alive who truly cared for me," she said. "Neddy has been good to me, coming by and making sure we were getting along."

"Well, I'm glad he's been good to you. Neddy's a man to be relied on." Daniel winced at his own words, realizing they invited a comparison between himself and Neddy that he didn't want made.

At that moment James came running in through the front door, playfully yelling in feigned terror that he was being chased by an Indian. Israel bounded in right behind him, laughing in his high toddler's voice as he chased his older brother with a twig that represented a tomahawk. Tiny Susannah was frightened by her brothers' noise and began to cry loudly.

Rebecca turned away from Daniel and went to the crib.

"Look at Israel, Pa!" James yelled, circling his father. "He's an Indian, going to ax me in the head!"

Daniel smiled tightly, his wide mouth curving up for an instant. At the moment even so feeble a cordiality required great effort. He watched Rebecca as she put Susannah to her breast. Rebecca's eyes lifted and fixed on Daniel's face. He turned away and headed for the door, pausing only long enough to take up his rifle, horn, and pouch, and to slip his hat off its peg and onto his head. He left the cabin and headed into the nearby woods, his stride even wider and more rapid than usual.

DANIEL REMAINED AT HOME only a few days more, then headed back to North Carolina, ostensibly to begin repairing the Sugartree Creek cabin and preparing for the family's return, even though no return would be possible until after the upcoming campaign against the Cherokees was through. He'd left in anger, and both he and Rebecca knew it.

Naturally, his parting from Rebecca was unhappy, but the prospect of remaining with her while she held her current attitude seemed much more unpalatable than being alone. She had hardened in her way of thinking, and he had done the same. She had stung him, and he resented it. At the moment she was as much a foe as a wife.

The Sugartree Creek cabin was a sad, lonely place for Daniel, and his labors around it didn't suffice to throw off the gloom. There he was reminded continually of his family. He finally gave up doing much work and spent his days hunting, heading west again, ranging along the creeks and ridges, searching for the contentment he had enjoyed all too briefly at the outset of the hunt the prior fall.

This time contentment was elusive. Rebecca remained constantly in the back of his mind. Knowing that she was unhappy with him was an eternal ache that ruined every moment. He dwelled on her rebukes and began to resent them. What did she expect of him? Did she not understand that he had debts that needed paying, and the best and fastest way to deal with them was to sell the wilderness bounty that nature had so well equipped him to harvest? Did she care so little for her husband's happiness that she would be content to see him a farmer and wagoner for the rest of his days, living out his time on earth in drudgery while the mountains called? And how could she resent his plan to join Hugh Waddell's expedition against the Cherokees? Did she not understand that to fail to do so would be to bring the name of coward onto himself? No man could abide such a stigma among his own people.

He gained some satisfaction from mentally railing against Rebecca's perceived injustices toward him and her stubborn refusal to see good sense. Yet this satisfaction didn't make him happy. What good was being right if it cost a man the best things in his life? Daniel felt hollow inside, empty. He missed his wife and his family and the happy relationship they had enjoyed before.

At last, he deliberately began to try to think of things from Rebecca's point of view, and discovered she might not really fit the stubborn, unreasonable mold he had cast her in. Truly, it must be hard to be alone and with a houseful of children, not knowing whether her husband was even among the living. Maybe he hadn't been completely right, after all.

He knew matters must be set straight. Gathering his gear, he readied himself to return to Virginia. He paused long enough to find Waddell and sign his muster roll as a volunteer, then headed to Salisbury, where he sold the relatively few skins and pelts he'd taken in, then rode to Virginia.

Halfway home he met Nate, who looked at him as if he were a dead man come back from the grave. Daniel returned Nate's stare coolly, still ambivalent about his old companion. He wouldn't soon forget how Nate had endangered them earlier in the year and forced the hunt to be cut short. Come to think of it, had Daniel not been compelled to return to Rebecca when he had, all the subsequent heartaches he and she had suffered might not have taken place at all.

"Dan, I came looking for you," Nate said. "You're needed back home."

The weather lines on Daniel's face grew taut. "Is there sickness?"

"No. But if you don't get back and set things right with your wife, you may not have a wife much longer. She's been in a state since you left again. Mad at first, nigh ready to cast you off, but I believe that she's mellered out since. If you go back to her now, matters could be set right."

"You took it on yourself to butt into my business, did you, Nate? You think I need you to watch out for me?"

Nate lifted his hand. "You recall when you near busted this hand with your forge hammer? Seems you were butting into my business then. But it was for my own good. And what I'm telling you now is for yours."

"It happens I was on my way home to set things square with Becca, even before you showed up," Daniel said. "I've thunk it through, and it seems to me that Becca's about the finest treasure I'm likely to own. I'll be hanged before I'll lose her."

Nate grinned, revealing the dark gap from which Daniel had pulled his tooth years before on Braddock's Road. "Glad to hear you say that. Having been married to a hell-demon myself, I'd hate to see you lose an angel. It's good you ain't dawdled around too long, too. Much longer, and I believe there'd be a new Mr. Boone living in your place."

Daniel frowned. "What'd you say?"

Nate's eyes went wide, and it was evident he had said more than he'd intended just then. "Nothing, Dan. Just saying it's a good thing you're heading home again."

"What was that about a new Mr. Boone?"

"Nothing. I didn't say that. Your ears need a swilling out, Dan. Come on, now. I'll ride back with you, if you want."

REBECCA HELD DANIEL close to her, listening to his soft breathing, feeling his chest rise and fall as he slept. The touch of his skin against hers was soothing and pleasurable. They had reunited the day before, both saying words that had needed saying for a long time now, and wounds had been healed. Last night and tonight as well they had given themselves to each other in the darkness while their children slept. Rebecca had felt truly happy for the first time in many months. She clung to his sleeping form, warm outwardly from the touch of his body and inwardly from the deep love she felt for him.

It was difficult for her to believe they had quarreled so seriously over matters that now seemed, if not trivial, at least not nearly as momentous as they had before. Of course Daniel had to leave his family to hunt; otherwise, he would be the most miserable of men, and there would be little hope of ever getting free from debt on the meager profits of farming and wagon driving. And of course he had to help fight the Cherokees, as she knew he was still planning to do. Anything less would leave him open to suspicions of cowardice. No man could live on the frontier under such a stigma. She had accepted the situation as it was. She would not complain to him again.

But, oh, how she wished he didn't have to leave so soon! Why was it that a woman had so little control over her world? Why was life so uncertain not only for herself, but also for her children and her husband? She wondered if there would ever be a time when she could rest securely in the knowledge that all her little ones were at hand and safe, and her husband at her side and not to leave again.

As she drifted to sleep, a song was going through her mind, a tune she had heard Nate Meriwether loudly singing when he'd ridden past just a few days ago, one that rang so true to her situation that she wished she knew how to write just so she could record and keep them:

Oh, hard is the fortune of all womankind,
They're always controlled and always confined.
Slaves to their fathers until they are wives,
Then slaves to their husbands the rest of their lives. . . .

DANIEL AND NATE were back on the Yadkin by the time hot weather set in. They put themselves under Waddell's service. For the pair, the feeling was much like that of their two Fort Duquesne military expeditions, except for one notable difference: this time they were going as soldiers, not wagoners. Waddell had raised five companies, and the men within them were but a few of the total number being sent against the Cherokees.

The summer and fall of 1761 were seasons of suffering for the Cherokees. In June, Lieutenant Colonel James Grant, an aide to the commander of a force ambushed by the Cherokees during an attempted relief of the besieged Fort Loudoun the prior summer, led a force of nearly three thousand men, including not only soldiers but also Chickasaw and Catawba warriors, and marched out from Fort Prince George. They passed through Rabun Gap and headed down the river that would someday be called the Little Tennessee, moving into the heart of the Cherokee country.

Attakullakulla, called the Little Carpenter by the whites, was a Cherokee leader of great influence and with a general disposition to live peaceably with the English and settlers. He had been one of the Cherokees who had come to General Forbes's assistance in the Fort Duquesne campaign, though Forbes had reportedly found the small-statured Indian with the big ego very irritating and untrustworthy. Now, with the English as enemy rather than ally, Attakullakulla dispatched a request for peace to Grant. The overture was coldly rebuffed. It had already been decided that the Cherokees would suffer in retaliation for the suffering of the victims of the Fort Loudoun massacre.

Grant's force, which included the North Carolina militiamen, met the Cherokees near the place they had come against the Fort Loudoun relief force the year before. The battle lasted several hours and was intense and bloody. The Cherokees inflicted heavy damage on Grant's force, but in the end a shortage of ammunition did them in. Having nothing except empty muskets and rifles with which to fight—they had left their bows, arrows, and spears back in their towns—they fled into the mountains.

Grant let them go. To pursue them in that mountainous country would be futile. Dividing his force into detachments, he sent them out to strike the kind of blow that would bring the Cherokees to the treaty table more quickly than any direct battle. He sent them to burn the Cherokee towns.

Over the course of a month town after town fell to the torch. Refugees in their own country, the Cherokees fled before the advancing force. No mercy was shown them. The mist that rose amid the laurel thickets, lush fern beds, and towering woodlands of the Cherokee high country now mixed with the acrid smoke of burning towns and cornfields. Dark native eyes watched from hiding as the white men, the unakas, wiped away their homes. Over the remaining days of summer and the colorful days of autumn, a full fifteen towns were devoured by flames, along with cornfields totaling fifteen hundred acres, and countless granaries that held the foodstuffs that would have seen the Cherokees through the winter. Some five thousand Cherokees, including many women and children, were left homeless, living on roots and berries, growing weaker by the day, facing the approach of the cold seasons with no shelter, no crops, no food laid by, and no ammunition with which to fight back.

There was no way to answer such a powerful blow, but the Cherokees initially resisted surrender because of a harsh term laid out by Grant: four Cherokee warriors should be sent to the white army's camp to be executed in front of the soldiers, or in the alternative, four fresh or "green" scalps should be sent. Only when negotiations eliminated this demand did the Cherokees finally agree to terms.

Daniel and Nate were on hand at the famous treaty ground on the Long Island of the Holston when the Cherokees signed their surrender on November 19. Daniel was a changed man, now, from what he had been when he'd set out under Waddell in the summer. Only a few months before he had been furious at Nate for having so cruelly shot to death an injured old Indian. Now, after all the suffering that Daniel had seen and even helped inflict, that seemed a relatively minor brutality. If Nate was cruel, he was no more cruel than Grant and his army.

Daniel was very glad that the campaign was behind, and as for the peace being promised at the Long Island council fire, he hoped it would last a long time. He had no desire to play soldier again anytime soon. He had seen atrocities he did not like to remember. He had watched soldiers laugh while they fed the bodies of dead Indians to their dogs, had seen scalps taken from the corpses of women and even children.

But there was a brighter side to this dark campaign. As heartless and harsh as the warfare had been, it had brought about certain results that Daniel couldn't help but be pleased with. The boundaries of the frontier had been extended many miles, and the Cherokees had pledged themselves to peace. Country that had been Indian country was now open for all, and there Daniel stood right in the heart of it with the winter hunting season just ahead. It was all tremendously convenient. Here at the Long Island, Daniel was standing in the very country he and Nate had secretly hunted just a year before. Only a few miles away was the tree upon which Nate had carved the record of Daniel's bear kill, and the creek with the waterfall under which he had hidden from the Indians.

With the treaty signed, what had been done in secret could be pursued much more openly. The natives were beaten back, their will shattered, their hopes now dependent upon the good graces of those who had defeated them. The time was right for another hunt, bigger and better and more profitable than before. It was a prospect Daniel had no desire to resist.

Of course, he had been away from home all the summer and fall. Rebecca was surely very ready for him to be back again. But this opportunity was just too promising to pass up. Even Nate, who had worried about the state of the Boone household a few months before, was encouraging Daniel to make another winter's hunt in this newly opened country. But what about Rebecca? Daniel had asked. She would understand, Nate had quickly replied with a shrug and a dismissive curl of the lip.

Rebecca would understand. Daniel supposed that was right. She might not like it to begin with, but she would understand. In the end, Rebecca always understood.

There were others going back to Virginia, and Daniel made arrangements for a message to be taken to Rebecca. All was well with him, and the Cherokees were defeated. He and Nate and certain others were remaining to hunt, and he would be home sometime the next year. In the meanwhile she should do the best she could, and if she lacked anything, she should ask Neddy. Neddy was reliable and would give her whatever she needed. "And oh," he added, turning away from his messenger in self-consciousness. "Tell Rebecca I love her. Make sure you tell her that."

The army disbanded. Most of the soldiers, weary and tired of violence and blood, turned east and eagerly headed back to farmsteads and families. For them, the wilderness was a place from which to escape with gladness. Homes and domestic life, plows and cattle, fields and towns called to them from the east.

But Daniel Boone, along with Nate Meriwether and a handful of others, answered a different call, turning to the west and vanishing into the wilderness.

CHAPTER 16

January, 1762

HARD FLAKES OF SNOW pelted against Rebecca Boone's face, stinging her eyes. The wind was icy cold and made her face feel frozen stiff. She wasn't sure she could relax her long-held snow squint if she tried. Her hands were cold, too, despite the thick, fingerless fur mittens that enwrapped them and softened the feel of the stock of the long rifle she held.

Before her stood a buck, shaking, thin, weak, and maybe sick, its outline blurred by the driving snowfall. So far, accumulation had reached halfway to the buck's belly. It was a pitiful creature and obviously on its last legs, a victim of the winter. Puny as it was, though, it was meat, a commodity in short supply in the fatherless Boone household.

Fatherless. Rebecca had come to think of her brood in that fashion. As so many times before, she didn't know whether Daniel was dead or alive, whether he was approaching over the next ridge or hundreds of miles away across the mountains. Wherever he was, he wasn't home, and no man could be a real father apart from his children. The messenger who had brought Daniel's message from the Holston country had said only that Daniel would return sometime during the year. Instinctively Rebecca felt it would be more late than early in the year, and against her will a good part of the old bitterness returned. She told herself that Daniel was doing the right thing and for the right reasons, and probably that was true. But it was also true that she was alone, and alone was a difficult condition to endure—a condition Daniel left her in altogether too frequently, altogether too long.

The buck took a difficult step forward, the snow hampering its motion. Too weak to lope or bound, it made a sad sight. Rebecca leveled the rifle, took more careful aim. Ammunition was in as scant supply as meat in her house, and she didn't want to waste the shot. She squeezed the trigger slowly, struggling not to tremble from the cold and the weight of the long, heavy rifle. The flint snapped down, sparking the powder in the pan, which almost instantaneously touched off the charge she'd carefully loaded into the muzzle. The rifle cracked and slammed against her shoulder. Smoke and flame filled the air. The buck jerked, staggered to the side, and fell.

Rebecca lowered the rifle and drew in a deep breath, and exhaled a white cloud of steam. It had been a good shot, a clean kill. What little meat this buck would provide would be a welcome addition to the stews that had become the biggest part of the Boone diet. Stews were easy to make, took almost anything as an ingredient, and stretched further than most meals. Rebecca was constantly amazed at how much food her family could consume, particularly the boys.

"Rebecca!" The voice called from somewhere behind her, back near the cabin. "You out there?"

"I'm here, Neddy!" she called back. A burst of excitement filled her. Neddy is here! He visited frequently whenever Daniel was away, making sure everyone was well and that there was enough food on the table. Seldom did he come without some sort of gift, usually food, other times powder or lead. And the last time he had come, he had brought Rebecca a shawl—and not some threadbare old homemade shawl, either. It was a new one, made of lfine lamb's wool and bought in a real store. Neddy had wrapped it in a crisp piece of real paper and even decorated the package with holly leaves. He acted shy about giving the gift to her, as if he were doing something he shouldn't. Rebecca felt shy about taking it, too, but also thrilled. It was the first kind gesture she had received from any man in the longest time, and the fact that this particular man was Daniel's brother—and the very spitting image of Daniel himself when he'd been five or six years younger—made it all the more exciting to receive the gift. When she unwrapped it, she gasped out, "Oh, thank you . . . Neddy!" She had been on the verge of calling him Dan.

"Was that you who fired that shot?" Neddy called. His voice sounded closer now. He was advancing through the snow.

"It was, Neddy. I killed a buck."

"Did you? Well, I'll wager he's a thin one, this time of year."

"Thin as a stick."

He emerged through the white veil, which was thicker now than before. In the brief time since Rebecca shot the buck, nearly another inch of snow had piled up. She worried for a moment about the cabin roof, but then Neddy was beside her, grinning that open, handsome grin of his, and she didn't worry about anything. As self-reliant a woman as she was, it was always a comfort to have a man about, particularly one who so reminded her of her missing husband.

"You should have sent Jesse out to hunt," Neddy said. "No reason you should have to bear the cold when there's an able fellow like him to do it."

"I don't mind the cold," she said. "Sometimes I like the peace of being alone."

Neddy looked around. "No peace out here, not in this weather."

She smiled. "Yes, there is."

He shook his head and chuckled, handed her his rifle, then went over, backed up to the fallen buck, crouched, and picked it up by the legs. When he stood, the buck was on his shoulders. He carried it as if it were nothing. Neddy was strong, like the brother he so uncannily resembled.

They walked back to the cabin, following the landmarks of familiar trees to get them there, the snow falling so thick and rapidly now that they could scarcely see the way. Within minutes they reached the cabin. Neddy, the deer still on his shoulders, nodded toward the nearby smokehouse. "Have one of the boys bring some light to me and I'll dress it out in there."

Rebecca went inside and sent Daniel's two nephews out with pine-knot torches, a sharp hand ax, and a couple of good butcher knives. Then she built up the fire and settled down before it, letting the blaze warm her until her face was reddened. The children went to their beds one by one, retiring early, lacking anything else to do. Eventually Neddy and the two other boys came in, bearing lean, dripping portions of raw meat.

"Well, there's more there than I thought there'd be," she said. "Thank you, Neddy, for saving me the butcher work."

"Glad to do it. Where do you want me to put it?"

"Yonder. I believe I'll go ahead and cook up a stew with it tonight, while it's fresh, and we'll have breakfast awaiting when we rise in the morning." Neddy cut up the meat while Rebecca sliced up the few vegetables she had taken earlier from the straw-filled potato bin buried in the backyard, now covered with a foot of snow. The two Boone nephews went to their beds, Jesse soon snoring loudly, as he always did. Jonathan muttered and complained about the noise, but soon fell asleep himself.

Rebecca put the stew on to cook slowly. It took only a few minutes for the aroma of simmering meat to fill the cabin. Neddy's stomach rumbled loudly, and Rebecca grinned at him. "Why, you probably ain't ate a thing tonight, Neddy. I'll put the kettle more on the blaze, and you can have a trencher of good stew."

"Well . . . I ought to be going on, with the snow still falling." He sniffed. "But I reckon that stew would be worth the wait."

They sat silently, the only ones awake in the crowded cabin. Neddy whistled beneath his breath and examined a cedar soldier Jesse had been whittling out for the last week or so. Rebecca did nothing but stare into the fire and glance from time to time at her brother-in-law. She had slipped on the shawl he had given her, and it seemed to please him.

"I believe the stew is done," she eventually said, and hustled up to get him a serving of it. She got a trencher for herself, too, and sat across the table from him, eating slowly.

When they were finished eating, Neddy grinned at her and thanked her. She detected something different in his look—a touch of discomfort, perhaps? He rose and went to the window, opening the shutter enough to peer out.

"I'll have a time, traveling home in this snow."

She came to his side and touched his shoulder. "Don't go, Neddy."

He looked at her, his expression serious. "What?"

"Don't go."

"Well, I don't think I should . . . are you saying . . ."

"Don't leave me," she said again, and put her arms around him, reaching up to stroke his cheek.

With that gesture a memory flashed into her mind. She remembered herself, lying beside her newlywed husband in the loft of the little cabin outside Squire Boone's house back in the Yadkin country, her hand stroking Daniel's face and a promise passing her own lips: *No others but my own dear Dan, from now until the day I die.*

She pulled away from Neddy, suddenly troubled. God help her, what was she doing?

Neddy came to her, put his hands on her shoulders, and made her look at him. It was like looking into the face of Daniel himself as he had been at the time of their marriage. She felt weak, confused, trapped . . . yet she wanted to be in the trap and knew it. She was so lonely there, so much in need of comfort and affection, and for all she knew, Daniel would never return. For all she knew, he was dead.

Neddy pulled her close. She told herself it was out of her control now, no longer her responsibility. This was Neddy's doing, not hers. How could she resist him? And he was so like Daniel . . .

HE WAS UP AND GONE before daylight. The children awakened about dawn and opened the door, looking across the snowy land. Jesse said, "Look—them's Neddy's tracks!"

"Ain't much snow in them," James said. Already he was learning to think like a tracker. "Neddy must not have left till this morning."

Jesse glanced at Rebecca, who was unusually silent. She was busying herself with Susannah, seeming to ignore the boys at the door.

"When did Neddy leave, Aunt Becca?" Jesse asked.

"Last night, after you were asleep."

"But his tracks is fresh."

"I said he left last night, after you were asleep."

"But how did—"

"Hush, boy. I've no time to waste trading words with a young fool."

Chastened, he held silent for a long time thereafter. It proved to be a long, dreary day, with everyone pretty much trapped in and about the cabin because of the snow. Bitter cold passed through the log walls as if they hardly existed, and the fire did little to knock the chill out of the cabin. Jesse noticed that despite the cold, Rebecca didn't wear her shawl that day. It remained folded on the mantelpiece. He thought about that a lot, and the tracks, but was wise enough to keep his thoughts to himself.

DANIEL KNELT BESIDE the icy water of a rocky creek and carefully extracted the stopper out of a little bottle from his pouch. Instantly, a foul, pungent scent rose to his nostrils, making him wrinkle his nose. He dabbed a little of the bottle's smelly contents onto a leaf and from the leaf onto a twig. Stoppering the bottle, he put it away, then made a final check. The trap was in place and set, and the twig bait was well scented by the beaver castor he had just dabbed on.

"That one's ready as she'll get," he said to a man standing just behind him. It was Nathaniel Gist, a fellow in whom Daniel had found the same kind of companionship he'd found in John Findley back on Braddock's Road and for the same reason. Nathaniel Gist was full of tales of the Kentucky country.

Nathaniel hadn't been to Kentucky himself, as Findley had, but his father had explored that land and brought back vivid descriptions of its riches. Nathaniel shared those same stories with Daniel, who gave them a gratifying reception. Some of his tales sounded almost too good to be true, but because that was a commonality in almost all Kentucky tales, Daniel still gave great credence even to the parts that Gist might be exaggerating for entertainment's sake. Daniel always had an innate sense that somewhere, somehow, there existed a perfect land where a man could live exactly as he had been created to live. A piece of Eden must surely remain somewhere on the earth. Maybe in Kentucky.

Buffalo herds that made the earth rumble, canebrakes filled with game and waterfowl, salt licks that attracted deer, elk, and bison in such numbers that a hunter simply had to make his selection and take aim. It was no marvel that so many Indians viewed the Kentucky country as the best hunting ground in the land.

The men moved downstream until Daniel found another good trap site. "When you reach Kentucky, Daniel, you'll not have to use bait to catch beaver," Gist said, leaning on his rifle as he watched Daniel setting and baiting the trap. "They're just like otter there . . . they'll slide right down the bank into your trap just to oblige you."

Daniel stoppered and put away his bait bottle, casting a wry look up the bank at Gist. "That so? Well, maybe you ought to head to Kentuck right now and make yourself a rich man, instead of standing around watching an old fool like me try to make a shilling."

"Maybe I'll do just that," Gist replied. He yawned broadly and arched his back. "Lord A'mighty, I'm weary of sleeping on the ground. I get tired of it sometimes, don't you?"

"Never do." It was the truth.

"I ain't never met nobody as much at home in the woods as you, Boone. You're a downright fool for wild country."

"I don't deny it."

A sound in the woods caught the attention of both men. They looked warily, then relaxed as Nate Meriwether emerged. Nate had left off shaving during the Cherokee campaign, and now his beard was rich and full. He was proud of it, combing it every night despite the taunting this brought him from the other woodsmen.

"Look here," he said, grinning and lifting a fat beaver.

"Pretty," Daniel said. "Worth at least two doe skins, maybe more."

"Oh, more, for certain," Nate replied. "Hey, you men hungry?"

"I'm always hungry," Gist said.

"Come back to camp. That turkey's ready to come out of the ground."

They set one more trap and followed Nate to their camp, a half-faced shelter built near a bluff. Nate had plucked, eviscerated, leaf-wrapped, mud-coated, and buried a wild turkey in a bed of coals the night before, and the bird would be cooked through by now. Nate dug up the turkey and broke away the leaf-and-mud shell. The scent of hot fowl filled the air. They sliced off great hunks of it with their knives, and ate like kings.

They'd hunted over a wide stretch of country, ranging from portions of North Carolina, into the Overmountain region that some were beginning to call the Tanasi or Tennessee country, because of the great river by that name that drained it, even into Virginia. Daniel felt content with his fine companions, all of them capable woodsmen. He'd heard so much talk of Kentucky from Gist that he had talked up the notion of heading on to the big gap of Ouasioto, which Dr. Thomas Walker had named Cumberland Gap in his Kentucky explorations a little more than a decade back. No one else seemed that eager to go on. And Nate annoyed Daniel by reminding him several times that come spring, the best thing to do would be to return to the Sugartree Creek settlement, put in a crop and finish repairing the cabins, and bring the kinfolk back in the fall. It annoyed Daniel because he knew it was right and sensible, and being right and sensible wasn't always as gratifying as following your nose to a new country.

They ate and talked and chewed tobacco after the meal. Gist, as usual, led the conversation. Daniel felt concerned when Gist wound around to the subject of women and put a question straight to Nate: "Nate, you ever been married?" Daniel cleared his throat and tried to think of something to say to shift the talk in a new direction. Nate generally disliked having to talk, even to close friends, about his failed marital life. So Daniel was surprised when without hesitation or flinching Nate said, "I was married, but we parted. I reckon she's still my wife on the law papers, though I don't know I'll ever see her again."

"I'm sorry things went bad on you," Gist said.

"Couldn't be helped. She turned out to be something other than what I thought she was." In response to a questioning look from Gist, he went on. "She had done an evil thing I knew nothing about until long after we was wed. When she finally told me, I knew there was nothing that could save us."

"What did she do?"

Daniel watched Nate out of the corner of his eye while busying himself with picking the last meat off a turkey bone. Gist was far more forthright in his questions than Daniel had ever dared to be, but Nate didn't seem to mind it. At long last the mystery of what Nora House Meriwether had done to estrange herself from Nate might be answered.

But Nate just coughed uncomfortably and said, "Nothing I need to speak of. Just an evil thing, that's all."

That evening Daniel thought back on the afternoon's conversation, which led to thoughts about Rebecca. It had been a long time since he had seen her, and if he put in a crop on the Yadkin as Nate was suggesting, it would be a long time to come before they were together again. He missed her, though not with an unendurable ache. For the first time he found that aspect of himself a little disturbing. Many men seemed to pine for their women when they were away from them. They rushed back to them at the first opportunity. But he wasn't like that. He could spend months away from Rebecca without feeling matters between them were askew. Was something wrong with him? Did he not love his own wife?

He knew the answer to that at once. Of course he loved her. He loved her more than anyone else on earth. If need be, he would die for her without a moment's hesitation. She was his wife, the woman he'd pledged himself to, and his love for her was no less than it had been in the first days of their life together. And he was sure she loved him, too. If not, why had she grown so perturbed at him last year for being away so long?

If there was no lack of love, then all he could conclude was that the lack was in him. *Lack* . . . he didn't like that word, so he revised it.

Difference. The *difference* was in him. He just wasn't like most men. God had made him that way. He loved his wife as much as any man ever loved a woman. The difference was that he didn't naturally show his love by his physical presence and required solitude—what he often called "contemplation"—to an unusual degree. Far more than most people, he was able to love from a distance. When he was roaming the far mountains with his wife and children far away, he did not perceive himself as having abandoned them. No, he was away for only a time, searching for a better life not only for his sake but for theirs. Why was that so hard to understand? Why did folks seem to think that a man loving his family had to mean he craved sleeping crowded up with them in a stifling little cabin?

These thoughts gave him a sense of vindication until a new facet of the same issue arose. If he was different from most people, then was it right for him always to let that difference determine his actions? Shouldn't he more frequently take into account the perceptions of others as well, and particularly the feelings of his own wife?

He lay down on his blankets and huddled beneath his bearskin cloak. Nate was snoring on the other side of the camp. Nate had no wife at all now, not in any but the strictest legal sense, and yet his life and Daniel's weren't all that different. Nate lived without a family because his family had dissolved; Daniel lived without a family because he had chosen to. Maybe he shouldn't have stayed away so long. Maybe he should leave immediately and head back to Virginia until spring came and he could put in a crop on Sugartree Creek. As he fell asleep, he had it clearly in mind to do just that.

But the next day the traps were found full of good beaver and otter, and Nate killed a deer that actually had a decent hide, despite the season. Daniel decided that it made little sense to head back to Virginia when he could do better things for his family by staying right there and gathering more wealth. He would not leave, at least not right away.

He remained with his fellow hunters the rest of the winter, and when spring came, returned to North Carolina, where he sold his furs. He bought seed and tools, and worked hard preparing the house for re-occupancy, plowing the land, planting crops. There was more to do than he had anticipated, and before he knew it, harvest time had come. He took in his crop and stored it for winter, and then at long last headed back to the cabin in Virginia to fetch his family home again to Carolina.

REBECCA HEARD from a neighbor that Daniel was on his way home; he had been seen on the road. Rebecca said thanks, then withdrew for a few moments to ready herself for an encounter that she had come to dread.

She managed to shoo all the older children away and to occupy the young ones behind the cabin. This was a meeting that needed to take place without their presence.

Her heart raced when she saw him ride into view, leading a couple of packhorses that were saddled but unladen. Swallowing hard, she stood straight and held the bundle in her arms despite a crazy impulse to try to hide it. Daniel rode up before the cabin and looked at her a few moments, then down at the burden she carried. He dismounted and walked slowly to her. The first thing he did was lean forward and kiss her lips; then he straightened, looked down, and pulled away a corner of the blanket bundled in her grasp.

A small red face looked back at him. A baby, very new, and looking much like her mother. Rebecca studied Daniel's face as the truth settled in and thought his eyes might have reddened for a moment. If so, it was the faintest, most indiscernible of reactions, and the only one he showed.

"When was it born, Becca?"

"October."

"Boy or girl?"

"Girl. I've named her Jemima."

Daniel smiled, just a little, but Rebecca could now see he was shaken.

"Jemima. That's a fine name. Pretty." He paused and looked into his wife's eyes. "Whose is she, Becca?"

"Neddy's. She's Neddy's baby."

"Neddy . . ." He looked away a few moments.

Rebecca longed to read his thoughts but could not. She couldn't tell if he was about to curse, to rage, to hug her, to kiss her, or do nothing. Tension mounted as she waited.

"Daniel, I know I've wronged you. I have no excuse. I'm asking that you forgive me and accept this girl as our own."

Daniel opened his mouth, faltered, reddened, turned away. Striding across the yard, he walked into the woods nearby and sank down on his haunches, trying to absorb this unexpected event, and to figure out just how he did feel about it, about Rebecca . . . and Neddy.

Back at the cabin Rebecca stood staunchly, her face set like stone. She had not called out after him. But she was waiting to see if in fact he would forgive her, as she had asked.

He sat thinking for long moments. *Forgive me*, she'd said. *Forgive*. To forgive, one must first assign blame. But the longer he thought about it, Daniel found he couldn't fully blame Rebecca. After all, he'd made it easy for her to slip into infidelity because of his continued absence. She wasn't the first lonely wife of a missing hunter to do such a thing. Nor could he hold even Neddy at great fault. Neddy was little more than a score of years of age, still boyish and easily overcome by his own passions. He'd done wrong, but temptations were strong for a young man. Daniel himself had made a bad choice or two in his own youth.

He recalled with chagrin the cryptic warning Nate had once given him, talk about a "new Mr. Boone" who would be taking over in his household if Daniel didn't spend more time there. Obviously, Nate had noted something unusual in Neddy's and Rebecca's behavior and foreseen what would happen. Neddy surely was the "new Mr. Boone" he had been speaking of. Daniel had been warned, but the message just hadn't gotten through.

But what did it matter now? Nothing could be changed. Daniel had once heard a preacher say that not even God could change the past. If that was true, what could he gain by grieving over it?

He rose and returned to Rebecca. She remained where she had been, though she had seated herself. She stood as he came to her.

Daniel cleared his throat. "I've been gone a long time, Becca. Too long. If there's any fault here, it's mine for leaving you lonely. The way I see it, you've got more to forgive than I do."

Rebecca took in his words, then let go her anguish in a flood of tears. She had dreaded this moment for a long time, but Daniel had just taken the sting out of it. With little Jemima cradled on one arm, she put her other around Daniel's neck and buried her face against his shoulder. He smiled at her. "Besides, if the last name's the same, I reckon everything else is all the same, too."

"I missed you, Daniel," she said. "Missed you so and . . . I was afraid you were killed. That's why it happened. Neddy came by, and I was so lonely . . . I didn't plan for it to happen. It just did."

"It's all the same now, Becca. It's all the same. She's a fine and beautiful child, and I'm proud to claim her." He kissed Rebecca squarely on the lips. "Fine and beautiful, just like her mother."

CHAPTER 17

THE WAGGING TONGUES of a few nosy neighbors notwithstanding, the birth and rearing of Jemima Boone brought about good for the household of Daniel and Rebecca. Daniel loved Jemima in a special way, and though he never said as much aloud, it was evident to all who observed that she was becoming his favorite child. That she had been fathered by Neddy was known by all the older children and soon by the younger ones too—along with a few outside observers who figured things out on their own, but the matter was never discussed within the Boone family, and hardly ever mentioned between Daniel and Rebecca themselves. Daniel had declared it was "all the same," and he was true to his word.

Rebecca was a happier woman during the months following Daniel's return than she had been since the first days of their marriage. Simple circumstances accounted for much of this. The Cherokee had been put down, meaning the Yadkin country could safely be occupied again, and now Rebecca was eager to return. As badly as she had begged to leave in the dark days when they were so frequently besieged and fleeing for safety to Fort Dobbs, Rebecca loved the Yadkin country and the fine, sturdy log house on Sugartree Creek. That house was home to her, even though it technically remained the property of her family, and they were mere squatters on Bryan land. She felt very attached to the place, much more so than Daniel, who never seemed deeply rooted to any given spot. He was a landowner, thanks to the acreage he had received from his father, but it was on Bryan property that he still made his home.

The return to the Yadkin meant hard work for all the Boones. Rebecca relished it and even appreciated that it seemed to keep Daniel closer to home. Something was keeping him around, at least. He continued to hunt, but mostly throughout the Yadkin region, never traveling as far as he had on his recent long hunts. The diminishing of the human population in the Yadkin Valley during the Cherokee hostilities had led to a return of game to the region. No one expected this to last, but for the time being the hunting was fine and the living gratifying and good, if not easy. Rebecca was satisfied.

But there were threatening pressures, particularly on Daniel, though sometimes Rebecca was too distracted by her own busy daily life to see them. He was still constantly in debt, a common condition for hunters and trappers, whose livelihoods were so dependent upon uncertainties. Furthermore, he simply wasn't a good manager, tending to spend what income he received rather than paying off debts. From time to time creditors' suits were filed against him in the court of Rowan County, and the judgments against him generally forced him deeper into debt.

Social problems abounded. Now that the Yadkin was open again, newcomers came in along with the returnees, and some were of a much fouler breed than the prior populace. Highwaymen and bandits began terrorizing the outlying farmsteads and travelers on the shaded, lonely roads. As time passed, the scoundrels became ever more bold, eventually actually began luring or driving people out of their homes, then ransacking the places. Victims were stripped of what few possessions they owned, and, a time or two, cabins were burned down for no reason but sheer meanness. The law-abiding folk of the Yadkin were infuriated.

Frontiersmen were not the sort to take criminality lightly or to endure wrongs against them for long. Daniel found his woodsman's skills called into an unusual use after one bandit gang kidnaped the daughter of a neighbor. Joining the posse formed by the girl's father, Daniel was pressed into service to guide the group, because no one knew better than he the ways through the hills.

They were pleased to find the girl in no need of rescue; in fact, she had managed to escape her captors on her own while they quarreled drunkenly over who would take the first turn at raping her. Daniel stood aside and the girl took over as posse guide. She steered the group to the bandit hideout and enjoyed the spectacle of the capture, by a far superior force, of men who had intended the most foul use of her. The ruffians were jailed in Salisbury, and Daniel felt a certain satisfaction when he heard the news that they were convicted and hanged.

At the same time, he was disturbed that such terrible events could transpire at all. The Yadkin wasn't what it had been when the Boone clan had first settled there. More people meant more troubles, more crimes, and less game. Within a year after his return, Daniel noticed that he had to range much farther to find the same level of game. It was growing harder to make a living.

Making it even more difficult was a secret inner pledge he'd made after finding that Rebecca had been unfaithful. All the earlier justifications he'd made to himself about his free-roaming ways, and the long time he spent away from home, had been swept away at the first sight of the baby's pink, pinched face. He'd pledged inwardly that he would think less of himself and more of Rebecca, and avoid such long stretches of time and distance away from her.

While the game nearby had been in good quantity and quality, that pledge hadn't been particularly difficult to keep. Now that the game was being driven out again by a fast-rising population, things were changing. How could he do enough hunting to make a good living and yet maintaining his pledge to stay closer to home?

He could think of only one answer, one he wasn't quite ready to propose to Rebecca, and that was to leave the Yadkin country and go farther west. The high meadow where he and Nate had lived and hunted out of Burrell's cabin called to him, and often he lost himself in a fantasy of building a home right there in that meadow, putting him far from neighbors and within easy range of the best hunting grounds. He toyed with actually presenting the idea to Rebecca but kept putting it off.

He was sure her answer would be no. Rebecca liked the settled life and enjoyed the protection and company of kin close at hand. She would not be pleased with the idea of moving far away from them.

And from 1763 on, another barrier stood between Daniel and his high-meadow dream. A royal proclamation was issued, barring white settlement beyond the mountains. Any encroachers would be living there illegally—a notion that didn't particularly bother Daniel, but which would probably cause concern for Rebecca.

She was pregnant again by the end of '63, but tragedy came when a fall made her miscarry. Daniel plunged into the forest shortly after that, carrying his grief and a copy of the Bible with him. After that he seldom went into the forest for any lengthy period without carrying his Bible and, almost as frequently, his copy of *Gulliver's Travels* by Jonathan Swift, a satire that had become his favorite book. In its pages he could hide from the steadily encroaching, over-populated world around him—only to have it intrude upon him again with the crack of some distant hunter's rifle, echoed by another somewhere else. Too many people, too many cleared fields, too many lines of smoke rising to the sky from too many cabins. And too little game. It wasn't the kind of world in which Daniel Boone could be happy.

In the fall and winter of 1764 Daniel began taking his son James with him on a few of his hunts. The boy was past his seventh birthday now, old enough to begin seriously learning the skills of a woodsman. Daniel's times in the forest with James were happy ones, and he passed many a contented hour in the dead of winter, seated before a fire, his cloak draped over him, and James huddled beneath it, leaning back against his chest. Nate would accompany them sometimes. James took a great liking to Nate, beginning to call him "Uncle," much to Rebecca's aggravation and Daniel's amusement.

Daniel didn't mind James thinking of Nate as an uncle. Nate had his faults, and Daniel couldn't yet forgive him for the foolish and merciless thing he had done to the crippled Cherokee and the boy with him, but all in all, Nate was improving with the years. He had a settled quality about him now and seemed to have put the pain of his various tragedies behind him. He was a good friend and an excellent hunting companion, and if James looked up to him, Daniel could see no harm in it.

Salisbury, 1764

THE MILITIA DRILL had ended several hours before, and late-November dark was falling across the town. Daniel strode beside Nate, grinning at a joke Nate told, and anticipating a good round or two in a lighted tavern just ahead. It was cool but not cold, the kind of weather that stripped away the years and made men feel like boys again. Daniel was in the mood for fun, had a few coins in his pocket, and a good companion at his side.

The tavern was the Boar and Stallion, where the landlord who called himself Big Charles had steered Daniel to Nate, the time Daniel came bearing news of Clive's death. When he passed through the door, the memory of all that surged through Daniel's mind, momentarily chilling his good humor. He was reminded that even today Nate still believed the lie he had told about the circumstances of Clive's death. Surely it had been easier on Nate not to know the truth, but Daniel was an honest man by nature, and it didn't rest easy on him, knowing he had lied. He couldn't shake off the worry that somehow Nate would find out the truth. When that familiar concern stabbed him as he made his way to a table in the corner of the tavern, he reminded himself that Nate couldn't possibly learn the truth, not unless Daniel told it himself. There had been no one else there to know that the death of Clive Meriwether had been by Clive's own hand.

"Nate Meriwether, b'gum and golly!" a boisterous voice boomed as Nate dropped into his chair. "How have you been, my old friend?"

It was Big Charles doing the talking. Swabbing his hands on a greasy apron that covered knee-length pantaloons, a bulky shirt, and sleeveless waistcoat, he approached, grinning broadly. Nate bobbed up again, thrusting out his hand. "Charlie, old man! Fine to see you, you old sod, you! You know my friend Dan Boone, here?"

The landlord looked closely at Daniel. "Seem to have seen you in here before, sometime or another."

"Yes," Daniel said. "I've been in a time or two." He didn't want to get more specific and risk bringing the subject around to Clive.

"Are you men in need of a tankard?" Charles asked.

"Aye, indeed we are, or maybe two or three," Nate replied. "But first you tell me something, Charlie: have you left off dallying with the trollops behind your wife's back yet?"

The landlord blustered and reddened, then laughed. "Why, Nate Meriwether, you bugger you, you've asked me a question that a man can't answer without damning himself either way he goes! Ha! You always were the one for the clever jest, Nate!"

The two laughed. Daniel merely smiled, not as easily amused. Nate put an arm across the landlord's shoulder and accompanied him back to the kegs stacked behind the heavy varnished bar, and the pair laughed and talked above the volume of all others in the place all the way there and back again, carrying big sloshing tankards on the return trip.

"Bottoms up, my dandies!" Charles bellowed, hoisting his tankard up to salute his companions, then back for a swallow. From the bleariness of his eyes and the pattern of tiny red blood vessels emblazoned on the tip of his bulbous nose, Daniel surmised that Charles made quite a common habit of tippling with his patrons.

Daniel drank more slowly than his companions and found himself growing less amused by them, and more embarrassed, as time went on and liquor did its work. Nate was in high form, bolstered by alcohol, and in turn bolstering a similar condition in Charles. Eventually, Daniel pushed his tankard aside, and with his own head buzzing from the effects of the strong drink, rose and excused himself, saying he would be back when he had cleared his head and lungs a bit.

He headed out the door into the night, which was growing chilly. Salisbury looked quiet and settled, carts and wagons rattling by, shops closing for the night, people out for an evening's stroll speaking to one another, tipping tricornes and clumping heavy-heeled shoes on the cobblestones. It was much quieter there, away from the revelry of Nate and the landlord. Daniel dug beneath his hunting shirt for a twist of tobacco.

"Mr. Boone? Is that you, Mr. Boone?"

Daniel turned, surprised by the soft, feminine voice. The speaker was between him and the open door, her face turned toward him so that it was silhouetted. Even so, he thought he knew who it was.

"It *is* you. I thought it was. It's a long time since I've seen you last."

"Indeed it has," Daniel replied. "Indeed it is."

NATE GAZED AT HIM almost stupidly, eyes red and face flushed. "What did you say, Dan?"

"You heard me, Nate," Daniel replied. He was leaning over, talking almost directly into Nate's ear and keeping his voice low, meanwhile resenting the way the landlord stared at him and obviously strained to hear what was being said. Daniel shot him a hard glance, and Charles cleared his throat, rose, and literally staggered back to his bar, so drunk it was hard to see how he could hope to tend decently to his own business. Daniel repeated to Nate what he had said before. "It's Nora out there, Nate. She's in a bad way and asking to see you."

"Nora!" Nate said, all his joviality suddenly gone. "I've got no wish . . . to see that banshee . . . no more!" He was so drunk he could hardly speak.

"You have to see her," Daniel said. "She's with child, Nate. And due to travail before long at all, judging from the look of her."

"Tell her . . . to go away. Leave me be."

Daniel reached out and grabbed Nate by the scruff of the neck. "Up, Nate. You'll not turn her away. She's your wife, man! You must see her."

"You think this . . . is your affair, Dan?" Nate shrugged Daniel's hand off him. "You don't know what I know about that she-demon."

"Up, Nate. Up or I'll carry you out myself—and as drunk as you are, there ain't a thing you could do to stop me."

Nate, with lowered brows and quivering lip, looked like an angry dog. He glared up at Daniel a moment, then stood, wobbling and almost falling until Daniel caught his arm.

"Steady, Nate. I told her you were drunk, in case that matters to you, her seeing you this way."

"It . . . don't . . . matter."

They were halfway to the door when a late-coming comprehension seemed to dawn on Nate. He turned and exclaimed: "With child? You say . . . she's got a babe in her?"

"She does."

"Curse the woman! A harlot and strumpet she is, to the very foul heart of her!"

"You've been no saint yourself. She looks ill to me, Nate. She needs help."

"She'll find naught . . . from me."

Nora Meriwether was standing directly in front of the door when they exited. Daniel felt Nate tense at the sight of her and had to all but push him out. He closed the tavern door behind him.

"Nate, oh, my dear Nate!" Nora said, coming forward and stroking his face. He turned his head as if her touch were dirty and pushed her hand away with a murmured curse.

"Oh, Nate, I don't blame you for despising me. I'm an evil woman, and you've every reason to hate me for what I am. I'm so sorry, husband."

"Not your husband. Not no more. I won't . . . lay claim to you."

"If you won't be my husband, Nate, at least be my friend. Give me mercy. You see what terrible thing I've done and what a bad state has come upon me." She stepped back, spreading back her ragged clothes with her hands, making the swell of her belly visible against the coarse fabric.

"It wasn't my doing, Nate. I was . . . used. Several men, scoundrels and drunkards they were, they forced themselves upon me and shamed me. Now I carry the seed of one of them, and I have no place to go."

"You can . . . go to rot, and take your . . . bastard brood with you!"

Daniel was overwhelmed with rage. He gave Nate so hard a shake that he groaned and cursed. "You'll not speak that way to a woman, and most of all not to the very woman you wed!" he said.

"I need no nurse or guide, Dan!"

Nora, very weak-looking and pallid, sank to her knees with a murmur, as if sick or in pain. "Oh, Nate, will you not have mercy on me? Will you not take me back?"

"I'll not."

"But you must, husband, or I'll be left to nothing but sorrow! When I found our old home empty, you gone away, I thought there was nothing left for me, no hope . . . I came to town, not knowing what I would do, and there, like a miracle, I saw Mr. Boone a-standing, and when he told me you were inside, I knew that I'd surely been forgave my sins, and God was giving me mercy and help at last. . . . Oh, you can't turn all that away from me now, Nate! Don't forsake me, please don't, I plead of you!"

Nate made a deep, guttural sound, pulled away from Daniel, and heaved up the contents of his stomach right there on the street. Ugly and foul as he was right then, Nora rose and came toward him, hands outstretched and tears on her face. Nate wheeled, staggered, bumped her and knocked her back. Daniel caught her before she fell, and after she righted herself, she moved toward Nate again. He was standing with arms dangling, shoulders stooped, drool still clinging to his lower lip.

She reached him, and he struck her across the face with the back of his hand. Crying out, she fell back onto the ground, moaned, tried to rise, then fainted.

Daniel walked up and hit Nate in the jaw as hard as he could. There was a popping noise, and Nate screamed. He stumbled backward, bumping into the tavern door, where he leaned until someone inside opened it. He fell back, landing face up on the spittle-covered floor, his jaw pushed to one side, dislocated by Daniel's blow.

"Nora, are you hurt?" Daniel asked, going to her. She was coming out of her faint now and crying hard. He reached down to her, but she pushed him away.

"Nora, wait!" She came to her feet and ran away down the street and around a corner. Daniel headed after her, but a strong hand grasped his shoulder.

"What's this, now?" a gruff voice said. "Are you harming that man and woman?"

"She's injured," Daniel said, turning to face the big constable who had stopped him. "She's carrying a baby—don't let her be lost to us!"

As if from nowhere, a fist swung up and hit Daniel in the left temple, very hard. In a blur he saw the ground rush up from the right and strike him hard. Stunned, he rolled over and saw it was Nate who had hit him. While the constable was talking, Nate had risen and come back out of the tavern door. His blow had come without warning.

Daniel grasped the side of his head as the constable struggled with Nate. Others surged in and restrained him. Angry and swearing, the constable demanded to know who Nate was, who Daniel was, and who the woman had been. Nate tried to answer and couldn't for a moment, but then there was another popping sound, a spasm and yell from Nate, as his jaw moved itself back into proper position. Nate spoke again, though it was hard for Daniel to understand him because of his own ringing ears and the distortion that Nate's painful jaw imposed upon his voice, but it sounded for all the world as if Nate said that the woman was a "damned murderess."

"Murderess?" the constable repeated skeptically. "And who might she have murdered?"

"Pyler House," Nate replied, his words nearly incomprehensible. "She's Nora House, the demon of a wife I was cursed to have, and she's the murderess of her own father."

CHAPTER 18

DANIEL WALKED toward Nate's cabin with real caution. He hadn't seen Nate since their fight in Salisbury two nights before, but word reached him that Nate was furious at Daniel's intrusion in his marital affairs, humiliated that Daniel had struck him down in public, and bitter over the harassment he had received from the constable. Only the most fervent pleas and the intervention of Charles the landlord, to whom the constable apparently owed a favor, kept Nate and Daniel from being jailed as brawlers.

As usual Daniel was carrying his rifle—Ticklicker, he had begun calling it, because it was so accurate he liked to claim he could shoot the tick off a dog at a good distance. As he neared Nate's place, he thought better of it and set the rifle against a tree in a hidden spot, hanging his horn and pouch there with it. When he approached Nate, he wanted to look as harmless and peaceable as he could. Making peace was his intention; though he still faulted Nate for his callous dismissal of his pregnant wife, he didn't like living at odds with him. They had been friends a long time.

"Nate!" he called as he came into view of the cabin, a small, pretty hewn-log dwelling in a grassy clearing that at the moment was filled with morning mist. "You there?"

He saw a shutter move, then close. A moment later the front door cracked open. "What are you doing here, Dan?" Nate called back, his words still slightly muffled because of the swelling of his injured jaw. "No call for you here!"

"I want to talk to you. We need to set things right."

"Just be off with you!"

"Hang it, Nate, I'm coming down there."

He walked down rapidly, wondering if there was any chance Nate would actually take a shot at him. The door opened as he advanced, and Nate stepped out onto his porch, rifle in hand. It wasn't cocked and he did not raise it.

"Well, say what you have to say and be off."

"There's no cause for us to talk so to each other, Nate. I'm sorry I've angered you, and sorrier that I struck you."

Nate's expression was belligerent, but Daniel knew him well enough to see that he held the look only with effort. Passing time had cooled both their tempers substantially.

"Sorry I struck you, too," Nate said. "Not that you hadn't earned it."

"Maybe I had," Daniel said, and risked a small grin.

The ice was broken now. Nate waved for Daniel to come inside.

"Let me run back and fetch my rifle first," Daniel said. "I was afraid to come in carrying it for fear you'd think I'd come to fight."

When he had his rifle in hand again, Daniel entered the cabin. It was a cramped, smelly place, lacking the touch of a woman or even of a man who cared half a penny for any sort of cleanliness. Three dogs shared the quarters with Nate, eating their meals on the dirt floor and leaving their droppings in the corners. Nate's odd habit of seldom opening his shutters left the place stale, dank, and moldy. Daniel demanded no frills and niceties of life, but even he had trouble abiding Nate's foul place. He'd enjoyed better accommodations living in caves while hunting.

"Ain't got no food to offer but some squirrel and rabbit meat, and squirrel being on the old side," Nate said.

"I ain't hungry."

Nate changed the subject abruptly. "You had no call to put your nose into my business, Dan."

"I didn't try to. All I did was step outside, and Nora called out to me. What was I supposed to do but come tell you?"

"You did more than tell me. You tried to make me take her back."

"She's with child and in a bad way."

"She's brought her own condition on herself."

"Not the baby. She said she was used by some men."

"That's her tale. No cause to believe it. I know that woman better than you, Dan."

"I suppose you do. But this talk about her killing Pyler House . . ."

"It's the truth. She confessed it to me herself long ago and laughed about it."

"And that's what drove you apart? That was the secret thing about her you never would tell me before?"

"Aye. That's right."

"You believe she would really have killed her own father? You know how he doted on her, watched out for her like she was a treasure."

"That was the very thing she killed him over. She said his ways choked her. Made her feel like she couldn't live her own life except the way he wanted. She drank some of his whiskey one night, got the ax out of the corner, and sank it in his head while he was sleeping. She claims she drug his corpse out and threw it down a hole inside a cave."

Daniel thought about it, tried to picture Nora House doing such a thing. When he thought of her as she had appeared last on the street of

Salisbury, he couldn't see it. But when he thought of her as she had been most of the time he had known her, it was a more believable picture. Now that Nora was a shattered woman, she was humble and pitiful. Before, she had been hard and mean, except for that brief time at the beginning of her marriage to Nate, when she and he had both seemed happy, when both had brought out the best in one another.

"I wonder where she went," Daniel said. From the time she had fled from the tavern front, no one had seen a sign of Nora House Meriwether.

"I don't care where she's gone. To blazes with her, as far as it concerns me," Nate said.

Daniel said nothing, wondering if Nate could really mean such a harsh thing. There was a time when Nate had loved the woman, when he himself had talked about getting rid of Pyler House to stop the man's intrusions into his love affair with Nora. Nate had talked big, vicious talk then, but now Daniel realized that talk was all it had been. He knew that from the way Nate had responded when he'd learned that Nora had actually put the deed to his own words. In his heart Nate was a man who strongly believed in right and wrong. If he was capable of occasional cruelty and heartlessness, surely part of the blame for that had to lie in the losses he'd suffered and the cruelties that life had inflicted on him and his late brothers. It was no justification, but it was a partial explanation.

Daniel was in no humor to chide Nate for what he had just said. "Wherever Nora went, I hope for the sake of her child, if no one else, that she finds help. If she had come to my door, Nate, I'd have given that help, even if it made you angry."

"I know. And that would be only right. But she ain't bedeviled you as she has me."

"Whatever's to be said, Nate, I want to set matters straight with you. I was wrong to strike you, and I repent of that . . . though that's not to say that I believe you were right to send Nora away in the state she was in."

Nate held his silence, thinking. Daniel was surprised when Nate's eyes suddenly reddened and became wet. His jaw quivered. "I know," he said softly. "It's weighed on my mind ever since. If I hadn't have been so drunk, maybe I would have not been so . . ." He trailed off.

"What's behind is behind," Daniel said. "We'll hope that help came to Nora from some other place. But whatever happened, or does happen, I want to remain your friend and neighbor for a long time to come, with nothing between us."

"There's nothing between us," Nate said. "You're still my friend, and I expect to remain your neighbor until folks grow so tired of putting up with me that they run me off."

"I doubt that will happen," Daniel said, grinning just to break the somber atmosphere.

"A man never knows," Nate replied, and he wasn't grinning.

WHEN NATE LEFT the Yadkin less than two weeks later, it was not because any other person had driven him away. He left the area of his own volition, heartsick, sad, and laboring under the weight of a terrible sense of guilt.

Nora's body had been found by James and Jesse Boone and a neighbor boy as they were out setting rabbit snares. A six-inch snow had fallen a day before but had melted rapidly the next morning when the sun came out hot in a clear sky and the temperature rose. Jesse was the first to spot the corpse, lying face up near the road, an expression of pain on the cold and unmoving face. Jesse had been so startled, he fell back and rolled into a creek.

Racing back to the Boone cabin a mile away, the boys had brought out Rebecca. She examined the body without letting the children see the horror she was feeling. A crusted pool of blood, only partially washed away by the melting snow, told her that Nora had bled from the birth canal, her delivery obviously having begun early and wrongly. The thought of the poor woman dying by the roadside in the darkness, bleeding and suffering alone, was incomprehensibly horrible. It became even worse when Daniel, told of the find when he came back from chasing down a strayed cow, made a further surmise: "She must have been trying to reach our house when it happened."

They buried her the day she was found, she and the baby that had known nothing of life but the dark warmth of the womb. Nate cried harder than anyone, all his anger toward Nora gone in the horror of what had happened to her and her child. It was his fault, he declared. If only he had forgiven her when she asked him to and taken her in, this terrible fate might not have befallen her.

Daniel gave what comfort he could, but Rebecca had no kind words for Nate. As far as she was concerned, he was every bit as guilty as he said he was. And she happened to know that most the folk in the neighborhood felt the same.

Daniel tried to defend Nate as best he could, reminding Rebecca, and others who held views similar to hers, that Nora was herself a murderer, guilty of the terrible sin of patricide. What happened to her was awful, but surely it was the failure of her marriage that had put her in a position to suffer as she had, and for that failure she had to bear much of the blame.

His argument carried no weight. Rebecca herself countered it by pointing out that they had only Nate's word that Nora had killed Pyler House—perhaps Nate himself had done it, and it was Nora who had turned away from Nate, not the other way around. Or maybe she did kill Pyler, but in circumstances that were justifiable. Whatever had happened, it didn't blunt the tragedy of her own death and that of her baby, nor did it nullify Nate's failure to take care of his own wife.

Nate told no one but Daniel that he was leaving. His land, a small parcel that abutted part of the Bryan property, was Daniel's to use as he saw fit. What livestock he owned, his furniture, anything left about the place, was Daniel's if he wanted it, or anybody's if he didn't. Nate no longer cared.

"Where will you go?" Daniel asked.

"I don't know. Away from here."

Daniel didn't dare speak the fear that was in his mind: that Nate would go off alone and end his days in the same way his brother Clive had. Nate looked into his face and seemed to read the thought.

"I know what you're thinking," he said. "Have no fear. I won't harm myself. I've not got the gumption and manhood even for that. The thought did come to my mind, I'll admit, but I can't do it. I bear a guilt worthy of dying for, but all I can do is try to live with it, far away from here."

Daniel watched Nate ride away, his old hound trailing after him and a single packhorse carrying the few goods he took with him. When he was gone, Daniel felt as empty as the cabin Nate had left without even bothering to close the door behind him. It was cloudy and cool, threatening to rain, and a more dismal day Daniel Boone had never seen or felt.

January, 1765

THE GLOOM in which Daniel moved through his life for the next few weeks was like a night that wouldn't quite yield to dawn. He was continually overwhelmed by an ominous feeling. He could imagine trouble and sorrow around the next bend of every road.

His father grew sick around the year's end, and Daniel began worrying over him and dreaming about him. Usually it was simply a dream of the old man approaching him, either with a smile or a deep frown. As December passed, the dream-image frowned more than smiled, and the real Squire Boone grew more and more sick.

By the end of the year it was evident Squire was going to die. Daniel couldn't make his mind accommodate that fact. His father had always seemed immortal to him, and with the passing years Daniel somehow failed to notice how the man had aged and declined like any other. On his sickbed he was a hollow, withered shell of what he had been. On the first day of January, Daniel's mother sent word to all her brood in the community to gather at her home. Squire Boone was evidently in his last hours.

Daniel sat up all night at his father's bedside, waiting after each labored breath to see if another would be drawn. They came further and further apart, strained and smothering even to listen to, until finally, shortly after dawn on January 2, Squire Boone breathed no more.

Daniel helped dig the grave and put his father to rest. They had a stone carved and stood it above his resting place. It read:

Squire Boone departed this life they
sixty ninth year of his age in thay
year of our Lord 1765 Geneiary tha 2.

Standing by the fresh grave, Daniel thought back over his father's life: the miles he'd covered, the different places he'd lived. Squire Boone told Daniel the story many times, so that the details of it were fixed clearly in his mind. The thirdborn in his large family, Squire had first lived in the English village of Bradninch. But at the age of sixteen, he left his native country to come to the American colonies with his older brother and sister, George and Sarah, sent by their father (also named George), an Anglican who had left the Church of England in 1702 to become a Quaker. The elder George Boone had heard of a new colony being created by another Quaker, a man named Penn, and wished to know whether it would be a land worth living in. To find the answer to that question, he sent his three oldest children on the dangerous voyage from the Old World to the New.

Squire was never to see his native land again. He and his older siblings were pleased by the Pennsylvania country, but only George returned to England to give the positive report to their patriarch. In the year 1717 all the Boone clan made the eight-week voyage, sailing out of Bristol, the total cost of their passage being thirty-five pounds, which the elder Boone had earned through his work as a weaver and from the sale of their goods and property in preparation for the voyage.

The family first lived at Abington, then the North Wales community, and then Oley on the Schuykill River. George continued his weaving and also put his strong back to the blacksmithing trade. In 1720 Squire took a wife, Sarah Morgan, and began a family of his own, and a life that would gradually inch him further and further from the Quaker faith.

Hat in hand, Daniel stood by the grave, pondering the life his father had lived. Squire had been an enterprising, hard-working man all his days, but he'd never acquired much wealth. And it seemed that no one had been content to let him live his life his own way, at least during his Quaker days in Pennsylvania.

Life on the frontier had been different from that in England, where pacifism could be preached and practiced without the constant Indian threat Pennsylvania Quakers had to live with. Squire never had been a man to run from a challenge, and he stood up to threats rather than back down for the sake of peace. That independent spirit was passed down to his children, and their stubborn refusal to abide by Quaker rules of marriage and behavior finally drove old Squire out of the fold of the Friends.

Daniel couldn't regret it. He had only vague memories of being a Quaker, but he did recall that the confession didn't sit all that comfortably with him. The requirements of Quaker living seemed out of place in a land in which a refusal to fight could mean death, and in which a man had to think and act for himself if he was to survive.

Squire eventually had left Pennsylvania, moving through Virginia, finally into North Carolina. Except for the time the Boones had vacated into Virginia during the Cherokee uprising, they had been Carolinians ever since.

Squire was a weaver all his life. For a time he had operated a tavern in his home, and during another stretch served as justice of the peace in the Rowan County court. Never fully satisfied, always restless, always looking for something new. Daniel recognized much of that in himself.

He left Squire's grave with reluctance, facing a world now in which he had no father to guide him. How many questions he might have asked, if only he had got around to it! How much more he might have learned.

Squire's death only added to the unsettled feeling Daniel was suffering through. More and more, the Yadkin was becoming a place he longed to leave. The game was growing thin and scarce; people were crowding in closer all the time; the courts were continually after him because of his debts; his friend Nate was gone, his very memory evoking the bitter taste of tragedy. And now his father was dead. It was time to move on. Every circumstance demanded it.

Daniel presented the idea to Rebecca. He told her of the high meadow where he and Nate had hunted. It would be a fine place for a home, a land where a man wouldn't be crowded, where the game could keep his family fed and put money in his pouch besides. They could move there and set up residence. True, they would be squatting on land that wasn't theirs, but the Boones had been squatters before; even now, their own house sitting on Bryan land. Would she consider moving to the high meadow?

Rebecca's answer was swift and definite. She had no desire to leave the Yadkin. There were enough people there to make her feel safe, and her family was close around her. That mattered dearly to her, especially considering that she was pregnant again. If they moved to the western mountains, they would face the same dangers of isolation that she had always dreaded, and treaty or not, there would be Indian dangers in such a remote place. No, she didn't want to go to any high meadow, no matter how fine and beautiful it was or how much better the hunting would be. She was happy with life as it was right there.

Daniel was deeply regretful; his hopes had been high. But he held his peace. He wanted Rebecca to be happy; and if she wouldn't accept a move to the high meadow, then perhaps there would be some other place she would accept.

It was increasingly evident to Daniel that she would have to accept some move, at some time. However much Rebecca might love their current circumstances, it was growing almost impossible to make a living there, and so crowded that sometimes he felt he could scarcely breathe. For the time being he would hold his peace, but somewhere down the road the Boone family would have to move on.

He wasn't sure where they would go, but he did know one thing: it would be toward the West.

CHAPTER 19

Late December, 1768

REBECCA BOONE was not prone to be philosophical. Only occasionally did she think much about the broad principles of life and the ways of the world. She was much too busy for a lot of idle reflection. And what few times she did philosophize, she didn't realize she was doing it. To her own mind she was simply "thinking things through," a process usually prompted by some mundane event, such as churning butter—the task she now was doing. The more she thought about it, the more it seemed to her that the process of butter churning provided a good illustration of the process of inevitable change that goes on all through life.

When she first sat down to churn, the cream inside had been liquid and soft. The dasher moved easily through it. Easy work, but cream was a long way from being butter. Plenty of arm-tiring, dreary, dull up-and-downing lay ahead. Only when the butterfat began to congeal and the task was at its most difficult did the final good—rich, creamy butter—come into being. Good things came only with hard effort. And they came only through change, like rich butter coming from thin cream.

Rebecca grinned at the thought; it sounded like something that should be in the Bible, though of course in much grander language than she could hope to dream up. Maybe it was in the Bible; you couldn't prove it either way by her, unable as she was to read. She thought of her illiteracy and felt the pang of regret that personal shortcoming always aroused. It would surely be a fine thing to be able to actually pick up a Bible, or one of Daniel's cherished books of history, or his tattered copy of *Gulliver's Travels*, and actually read the words in them for herself. As it was, she was dependent upon others to read to her, and there was certainly little time for that. What a dream it would be to lose herself in a story and live some other life than the one she now faced day to day! She loved her life, loved her family, and most of the time even her domestic duties, but everyone needed an escape. Daniel had his reading and his blessed times of "contemplation" in the forests. Rebecca had no escapes at all.

The butter began to thicken. Shifting positions, she leaned forward a little to put more muscle to the plunger.

Some of these days, I'll have to make Daniel sit down and teach me to read, she thought. *It will be hard, I reckon, but all good things in life come hard, just as I was pondering on. They come hard, and only at the cost of change.*

Rebecca knew a lot more about change than she had four years ago. Over that time she and her family had undergone several changes. Rebecca had given birth to two more daughters: Levina in March of 1766, and Rebecca, her namesake, in May of sixty-eight. And the Boones had moved away from Sugartree Creek, Daniel having at last gotten his way on that always delicate issue between them. Gotten his way several times, in fact. Late in sixty-six the Boones had moved to the region of the Brushy Mountains. They had lived there only one winter, though Daniel hadn't been around much. He had gone off on a winter hunt—a financial necessity—but it had left her alone for several months. She hadn't enjoyed wintering in that crude, small cabin near the Yadkin, and in the spring Daniel had returned and moved them farther up the river to a cabin about a half mile up Beaver Creek. The threat of flooding at that site had led them to move a third time, up to a cabin at the mouth of the creek and on the northern side of the Yadkin. This cabin was tighter and warmer than the previous ones, and the fact that Daniel was keeping his winter hunting closer to home this year made the place all the happier. Daniel hadn't given up his long trips—indeed, he couldn't, for long hunts provided much of their livelihood—but ever since the birth of Jemima he had been more mindful of Rebecca's needs and spent more time at home. The fact that they had moved farther west, closer to the unsettled wilderness, made it easier for him to stay closer at hand.

Daniel was much more satisfied in the new locations than he had been in the last year or two on the Sugartree, and Rebecca hadn't minded them nearly as much as she would have, if some of her and Daniel's kin had not moved into the same regions about the same time. Daniel's younger brother, George, who would be celebrating his thirtieth birthday on the second day of the coming month—which also happened to be the fourth anniversary of old Squire Boone's death—moved with his wife's kin, the Linvilles, up near Daniel and Rebecca's new home. Neddy Boone and his new wife, Martha—Rebecca's own sister—had also joined the migration, as had Daniel's brother Squire and his family, and his sister Hannah and her husband, John Stewart. Daniel was particularly pleased to have John Stewart in the vicinity, because the two had taken to hunting together quite often and in Daniel's estimation made a fine team. As often as not, James Boone went along with them; the boy seemed to have almost the same devotion to the wilderness as his father.

Having old kin and neighbors still living nearby minimized the sense of change the Boone family moves brought Rebecca. Matters were different, but not so different as to be unendurable. Certainly things could have been much worse—would have been if Daniel'd got his way about moving to the Florida country. He and John Stewart had made a lengthy jaunt to Florida back in sixty-five, going along with some old Culpepper County neighbors who had stopped by on their way south from Virginia. They'd talked enticingly of free land available, courtesy of Florida's British governor, to Protestants who would move there. As impulsive as always, Daniel had not only made the journey but had actually put down a payment on a lot—in town, of all unlikely places—in an ancient Spanish settlement called Pensacola. He actually would have moved the family there if Rebecca hadn't put her foot down when he got back home. Sometimes she couldn't figure out her man. Whenever she thought she had all his ways ferreted out, he did something she never would have anticipated—just as he had in Florida. He hadn't particularly liked the Florida countryside, which was full of strange creatures and crawled with blood-sucking insects, yet he had come home ready to move there. That was Daniel, always eager for a new adventure. On that score he hadn't changed a bit with the years.

Certain other of his characteristics hadn't changed, either, including his chronic indebtedness. There had been more law suits against Daniel over in the Rowan County court, humiliating and troubling to Rebecca. She was at first grateful that Daniel had found legal help in the person of a man named Richard Henderson, some sort of judge or barrister or some other legal authority—Rebecca had only a vague understanding of such things—who was a friend of Cedric Winston of Virginia. Henderson had once been part of the Virginia gentry himself. But he hadn't been able to fully extricate Daniel from his financial troubles, and sometimes Rebecca wondered if he really had helped much at all. From time to time Henderson would file his own suits against Daniel for debts owed. More often, however, he intervened on Daniel's behalf to obtain new loans to pay off his old ones . . . but, of course, that left the new debts to worry about.

Odd and inconsistent as the relationship between Henderson and Daniel was, Daniel liked him, and Henderson likewise held Daniel in high regard, for reasons Rebecca didn't fully grasp. It all had something to do with the men's friendship with Cedric Winston, but there was more to it than that. Daniel had dropped a few tantalizing comments about Henderson's "big plans, having to do with land," but when she pressed him for explanation, he grew oddly silent.

She quit her churning; the feel of the thickened butterfat told her the job was finished. Not any too soon, either; her arm felt as if it might fall off, and though she had quit churning, her muscles were still tightening and loosening, tightening and loosening. She brushed back a string of hair from her forehead and tucked it under her cap, the laced flaps of which hung down over her ears. She lifted out the clotted dasher, scraped the butter into a bowl, and washed it in cold water. After pressing the butter in one of her molds, she would have a few pretty, round cakes of it to put on the table. As fine as this particular butter looked, she expected a deal of difficulty in keeping the boys from gobbling it down too quickly.

Daniel came in the door, slipping off his hat and hanging it on a peg beside the door. "The boys have snared some rabbits and are running them down—I seen them crossing the south hill," he said.

"Oh, I hope they don't come busting in a-yelling and carrying on, and wake up the baby!"

"Best get outside to meet them, then, or else they surely will. Why, Becca, that's fine butter there. Prettiest this year, I believe."

"Yes, I think it is. And I'd best stop the boys indeed, else they'll come in and sling rabbit blood all over it, just you wait and see." She wiped off her hands with the tail of her apron and headed for the door.

When she stepped outside, she saw the boys with rabbits in hand, but they were no longer dashing down to the house. They were turned, facing the road, watching a man coming toward the cabin. He rode one horse and led three others, all three heavily laden with some of the oddest-shaped bundles Rebecca had seen.

"What is it, Becca?" Daniel asked behind her. He fingered off a chunk of butter and put it into his mouth while her attention was diverted.

"Peddler, I believe," she replied.

"That right? We see few enough of those out here." He came to her and looked over her shoulder, his hands resting on her upper arms. Suddenly his grip tightened and he drew in a fast breath. "Becca, I know that man. I swear I do. It's been a lot of years, but I swear that's none other than John Findley himself!"

"Who?"

"John Findley—an Irishman who wagonered with me for Braddock! You've heard me talk of him—he's the one who's been to Kentuck!"

He pushed her aside, none too gently in his excitement, and squeezed past her and out the door. She had to grasp the door frame to keep from falling. "John!" he shouted, loping out toward the road. "John Findley! Is that you?"

He's the one who's been to Kentuck. Those words roused a certain dread deep inside her. She watched as the peddler leaped down from his horse, a look of great surprise on his face, and ran toward Daniel with his hand outstretched. The two men shook hands and slapped shoulders, big, broad grins on their faces. The boys with their rabbits still in hand were running down to join them.

Rebecca took it all in, then turned her back and went into the cabin to mold butter. Generally, she was pleased when traveling peddlers came by, but she wished this one had taken some other road. It was just a feeling, something to do with the eager way Daniel had said those words: been to Kentuck.

"IT'S BEEN A HARD LIFE I've lived since last we knew one another, Daniel," Findley said. He was seated by the fireside, his weathered features both lit and shadowed by the moving flames. He was leaning forward, elbows on his knees, eyes turned toward the blaze, a cup of tea steaming in his hands. "Though, I must say, it's not been as hard as that led by our poor old Nate."

Daniel had just recounted Nate's various sufferings to Findley. As usual when he repeated the lie about the mode of Clive's death, he felt wicked and vulnerable, as if his lie would be instantly detected by all who heard. Age hadn't improved his lying any more than it had his luck at the games of dice and cards he sometimes took part in behind Rebecca's back. What had become of Nate was one of the first matters Findley had questioned him about. Findley well remembered having helped pull Nate's tooth that long-ago day along Braddock's Road.

"Did you go trade in Kentucky again, after Braddock's defeat?" Daniel asked.

"I've made many a good try," Findley replied. "My fortunes have turned black on me a time or two, but I still believe in Kentucky. It's a land that will make a rich man of me or kill me, one or the other."

"But have you traded with the Indians there lately?" This came from Daniel's brother Squire, now a handsome fellow twenty-four years of age. Squire happened to come by about an hour after Findley's arrival, planning to talk a horse trade with Daniel. When he heard who Findley was, he forgot horse trading and attached himself to the Irish peddler with the same eagerness as Daniel. Squire had Kentucky dreams, too, and had been hunting with Daniel a few seasons back when they had abruptly decided to find a land route into the fabled Kentucky meadow country by way of the Big Sandy River. The winter had closed in and held them back from their goal, a bitter disappointment to both.

"I've traded, not nearly as successfully as I could have," he replied.

"Only last year I went down the Ohio and traded furs, but a man can carry only so much in a canoe. If I had come in by land, with a long string of horses and enough money backing me to keep me in business for a long while, why, there's no telling what level of wealth I might have brought out of that country!"

"Is Kentuck really so fine a land as the stories say?" Squire asked.

"Every bit as fine, young man. I can't imagine how any man with spirit and sense could help but thrive in that country."

"Daniel and I didn't see anything much wonderful when we were there."

Findley sat up straight. "You've been to Kentucky?"

"Well, Squire believes we were within it," Daniel said. "I think perhaps we were close. The winter trapped us on the Big Sandy. We saw nothing of the Big Meadow that's talked about so much."

"Well, perhaps you were closer to it than you think, even though I can't swear to that. I confess that I'm no true man of the forest," the Irishman said. "Trails and such confuse me. But I do know there is a land route, because the Cherokees have come up from the south and fought the northern tribes. There's a warrior's trail leading into Kentucky, and it's my belief it must pass through the same gap that Dr. Walker explored—what?—nearly twenty years ago, has it been?"

"I've hunted in country that can't be many miles from that gap," Daniel said, a hungry look in his eyes as he gazed into the flames.

"I'm going back to Kentucky," Findley said. "I'll not rest until I've made my fortune there. I've come so close, so often, but always there is ill luck. I was signed on to a trading fleet on the big river, but the blasted boat foundered, and when they lightened it, me and my trade goods were part of what they cast off. Up in the Illinois country, we were. Now I make my living, such as it is, very humbly, roaming from house to house and selling whatever wares I can pack on my horses. But someday—someday there will be Kentucky again for me, and wealth that will let me enjoy my old age in ease."

Daniel eyed Findley. Old age . . . from the look of the man, it was already nearly upon him. How old would Findley be now? He had been in his thirties on Braddock's Road. By now he was approaching a half century of life, an old man by many standards. He didn't look particularly healthy, now that Daniel examined him. For a few moments he was struck by doubt about Findley's veracity. Was he just an old dreamer and tale spinner, or had he really found an Eden beyond the mountains?

Squire and Findley fell to talking intently, the young Boone eagerly absorbing Findley's descriptions of Kentucky. Daniel smiled to himself, recalling how he himself had been so entranced the first time he had heard Findley's Kentucky talk.

Rebecca was farther back in the cabin. Daniel gave her a covert glance.

Her face was stern and unsmiling. He could imagine what she was thinking: that this talkative old Irish peddler was going to lure her husband away for God only knew how long, looking for some fabled land that, if found, he would probably become enamored with and eventually want to emigrate to.

If she was thinking so, she was right. Daniel did want to go to Kentucky, had been wanting to well before John Findley came wandering back into his life. It might be that Findley had been providentially sent to spur him to make an exploration that Daniel had been destined for since birth. Had he not told Rebecca back in their courting days that he had always thought his destiny lay in the West? Even without taking such an exalted view of all this, there could be no question that if he was going to Kentucky at all, it made sense to take along someone who had been there, someone who knew the Indians and enjoyed good relations with them.

Of course it all made good sense, and it fit right in with certain matters he had been discussing with Richard Henderson. Daniel opened his mouth to speak his thoughts, but his eye turned again to Rebecca, and he held silent.

Findley would be with them for the winter, selling his wares by day, stabling and boarding there by night. There would be plenty of time to reveal the scheme taking shape in his mind, and he had no doubt that Findley would leap at the idea.

The real challenge would be selling Rebecca on the notion. Before he opened his mouth to anyone else, there would be a lot of talking to be done with her.

He remained mostly silent the rest of the evening, listening to John Findley talk about Kentucky.

SHE RESISTED his arguments at first, knowing that yielding would mean saying good-bye to him for a year, maybe more. But from the beginning she knew that finally she would give in, and he knew it too. The truth was that the matter was out of their hands. It seemed that Richard Henderson, Daniel's benefactor and creditor, had been developing a plan for some time now, which would have involved Daniel making a lengthy exploration of the Kentucky country. Daniel was in no good position to turn him down even if he wanted to, which he didn't. If the kind of things Henderson talked of actually came about, Daniel told Rebecca, why, the future for them would be bright indeed—so bright that the shadow of a few months apart would seem like, in Daniel's words, "nothing at all."

"Nothing at all?" Rebecca replied. "Do you know what it is to be alone, to have the lives and good of all your children resting on your shoulders alone? Do you know what it is to have the little ones ask where their father is and when he will return, and there's naught at all, nary an answer, that you can give? Do you know what it is to lie in bed and pray that your mate hasn't lost his life and hair to some savage?"

"I must go, Rebecca. I've promised Dick Henderson, and this is the best opportunity I'll find. I owe the man, wife! And more than that, I owe us the chance to dig ourselves out of our debts and find a new home where we can live free of burden."

"Another move? Is that what you have in mind for us?"

"Well, why not? You want to stay in Carolina forever, the way things have gone for us here? You know of all the trouble and restlessness—there's plenty of folk not happy with the way affairs are being handled in this colony."

Rebecca did know, however imprecisely. In the towns and centers of government, there was talk of rebellion against the oppression of aristocratic courts, anger over governmental affairs. Rumors of a coming "regulation" by those angry enough to take up arms. But such things seemed distant there in the northern Yadkin country. To Rebecca they had little reality at all.

"I'm happy here, Dan. My people are around me. We've moved now to please you three times. When will you be satisfied?"

"When I am free of debt, and when I can live without being crowded or taxed to death. That's what Kentucky could be for us someday, but first it will have to be opened and settled. A journey there on Henderson's behalf would be the start of that."

"How? Kentuck is Indian country. I heard from George there was a treaty in South Carolina."

"Hard labor. The Treaty of Hard Labor. The king has said that Kentucky is Cherokee land. But don't you see, Becca, that makes what Dick Henderson is wanting to do all the more important? Now the Cherokees will have to be negotiated with if Kentuck is to be bought."

"Bought? Is that what Dick Henderson aims to do?"

Daniel glanced around as if the subject were too sensitive even for this private a discussion. "Aye," he said. "He wants to buy it from the Indians and set up a colony of his own. And I'm to be one of his agents, exploring, talking to the Indians on his behalf."

"Oh, God!" she exclaimed, distraught. "Now you're not even going to hide yourself from them! You'll be seeking the savages out!"

"When the time is right. The first thing we need to do is to explore and to bring back every piece of fur and pelt I can, and put us square with our creditors."

She was losing her will to fight a battle she already knew was lost; her head slumped and her shoulders grew stooped. "I suppose you'll go, whatever I say."

"It's that I must go, for all sorts of reasons."

"Then go."

"Do you mean it?"

"I mean it."

He smiled and kissed her. "It will be our salvation, Becca. You'll see that soon enough. Our salvation, and the start of our brightest days." He beamed, looking away from her, not noticing the tears beginning to slide down her face. "Kentucky! Old Kentuck itself! You'll come to love the very name of it, Becca. You'll love to say it, just to feel it roll out of your mouth. Kentucky!"

CHAPTER 20

In March, Daniel Boone went once more to court in Salisbury. He despised the humiliation of standing in the dock, hearing himself chastised for the lack of payment of some debt, then being handed down deeper into debt. This time, however, he didn't dread his courtroom ordeal nearly so badly. He had bigger matters to distract him, and besides, the court date gave him the chance to bring along John Findley and John Stewart and have an important, secretive meeting with Richard Henderson.

Henderson was intrigued by Daniel's talk and thrilled to meet John Findley. Heads close together over a table in the back of a local inn, Henderson, Boone, Findley, and Stewart came to an agreement. Henderson would provide financing for the Kentucky exploration in return for as much detailed information on Kentucky as Daniel could bring back. Hands were shaken, and the deal was done.

The month of April was taken up with making final preparations, hiring camp keepers, and gathering the extensive supplies the party would need. Much had to be done around the Boone house, too, and Daniel went at it with a vigor he seldom displayed at agrarian pursuits. He planted a vast garden and big corn crop, and killed all the game he could. Fortune provided him an unusually fat buck and a huge bear, and Daniel made sure that James was with him, getting the best instruction he could. As the oldest son, he would shoulder the responsibility of providing meat for the table. Jesse and Jonathan were older, but it seemed to Daniel that James, as a true blood son, should have the privilege of greatest duty. James accepted the mantle proudly.

On the first day of May 1769 all was ready. After saying good-bye to his tearful family and making sure that his brother Squire fully understood the part of the plan he would carry out some months later, Daniel Boone and his companions set off, packhorses and dogs trailing along after the riders.

"I'll take care of them all whilst you're gone, Pa!" James called after Daniel. Daniel turned and smiled back at his son, who, at just over a decade of age, was doing his best to stand tall and manly. A tear rose in Daniel's eye. "I know you will, son! I know you will!" Then a final glance at Rebecca and a lifting of the hand, and he turned back to the hills and would not allow himself to look again at those he was leaving behind.

Altogether there were six of them going to Kentucky: Daniel, John Stewart, John Findley, James Mooney, William Cooley, and Joseph Holden, the latter three being the camp keepers hired with some of Henderson's money. These three would have the duty of dressing out the skins, hunting game for eating, and cooking all the meals. Daniel, John Stewart, and John Findley would do most of the hunting for hides and the trapping once winter came, and John Findley would also serve as guide, and, if necessary, interpreter and diplomat with any Indians they might encounter. Daniel had some experience with Indians himself, having run across and sometimes hunted with parties of Cherokees during some of his winter hunts off the Yadkin, but the more northern Indians who hunted Kentucky he did not much know. He could only hope that Findley's standing among the Indians with whom he had once traded was sufficiently strong to gain them some goodwill and accommodation. There was every possibility that they would meet no Indians at all. Kentucky was far more a hunting ground than a place of Indian residence.

Following Elk Creek, they climbed the mountains and crested the Blue Ridge. Working north, they followed the contours of the rugged landscape, penetrating one mountain gap after another, until they reached the Holston country. There they came upon the Warriors' Path that ran through the region, and followed it west over hilly terrain, traveling through Moccasin Gap, a deep notch that provided the only good way to pass through the long ridge of Clinch Mountain.

They soon reached the Clinch River, and forded it. Ahead loomed Powell Mountain, and just beyond that, Wallen Ridge. Traversing a gap in Powell Mountain, they bore west, climbing diagonally up Wallen Ridge, then over and down into the beautiful valley of the Powell River.

Here, to their surprise, they met a score of white men, settlers under the command of one Joseph Martin, a Virginian of Albemarle County who was trying to develop a settlement on behalf of Dr. Thomas Walker, who had explored the region so many years before. Encountering the beginnings of settlement so far into the wilderness was vaguely disappointing and anticlimactic to Daniel, but it also gave impetus to their mission. A settlement this close to the gap of the Cumberland Mountains, which loomed just north of them like a great, impenetrable wall, was a sure omen that before long men would penetrate Cumberland Gap itself and begin settling Kentucky lands. Martin's men had already ranged through the gap, and even over the mountains at the area of the White Cliffs, which shone beautifully in the sun.

Boone and company stayed only briefly at Martin's Station, gaining what news they could of what lay ahead, and then pushed on. There was no difficulty in finding the way; all a man had to do was keep the huge Cumberland Mountains to his right and thrash his way as best he could across the timbered landscape.

They encountered an old Indian road that wound up toward the mountains, and then they were at the Cumberland Gap itself. Daniel paused and looked up at the natural gateway he had so long desired to see. Now that he was there, he was awed by the size of the precipice rising on one side of the V-shaped gap, facing lower slopes on the other. How many warriors and native hunters had passed through this mountain depression since time had dawned? How many feet had beaten down the trail that led so clearly up to it, and over? Daniel felt small there beneath the ancient cliffs, and aware of how short a man's life span really was.

Once through Cumberland Gap, they traveled northwest to Flat Lick and found signs of old Indian campgrounds and salt-making works. Leaving the Indian path, they headed west along a trail marked by earlier parties of long hunters under Elisha Wallen, for whom the famous ridge was named. At last they came out of the mountains and into view of the lands they had so long sought: the splendid knobs and levels of the true Kentucky country.

They made a camp at the place the Shawnees called Ahwahnee, or "deep grassy place," and dubbed the creek that ran past it Station Camp Creek. From there Daniel, Stewart, and Findley set out to explore the region, following the cane-lined waterways, the narrow animal trails, and the wider, road-like trails made by buffalo.

Stewart, less a woodsman than his brother-in-law, despite an impressive hunting record, turned his attention to helping the camp keepers put the station camp in order. Daniel and Findley explored alone. Findley sought and found the site of Eskippakithika, the trading village where once he had bartered with the Indians, but the town was empty, its houses burned. The stockade around it still stood, however, and by that he confirmed that he was indeed in the right place.

With a better grasp on the terrain now that he had found a landmark, Findley led Daniel up a trail to the top of a huge overlook knob and spread his arm to the spectacular view that greeted them. Daniel gazed in silence for a long time, taking in hills that faded into blue, streams that sliced a rich landscape upon which a vast herd of buffalo grazed, more abundant in the wild than farmers' domestic cattle were in the valleys and woods of the settled borderland.

"What do you think of it, Dan Boone?" Findley asked.

"I think that we are richer than Boaz of old, John. We have here the cattle on a thousand hills."

December, 1769

IT WAS IMPOSSIBLE, yet Daniel could not deny it: the man striding toward him with a familiar gait was none other than his father. Squire Boone looked exactly as he had about a year before his death. His death. But if he was dead, how could he be there, approaching Daniel Boone on the rich Kentucky land?

"Pap . . ." Daniel smiled and put out his hand. "I'm happy to see you, Pap."

The old man reached him just then and shot him an angry glare. He stretched his hand toward Daniel's, but not to shake it. He pushed his son's hand away and walked on past, leaving Daniel shocked and suddenly frightened.

At that moment Daniel Boone woke and sat upright in the half-faced shelter. The fire burned before him, warming his feet, and the others snored in their bear and buffalo skin blankets all around.

A dream. It had only been a dream.

Daniel lay back down again, not sure whether to be relieved or disappointed. It had seemed so amazingly real. The image of his father's face had been so vivid, it hardly seemed possible he had merely imagined it. Yet he knew that he had imagined it and, in a way, was glad that was all it had been. Seeing his father looking so angry, and feeling him push aside his extended hand, had been terribly disconcerting. Old Squire Boone had hardly ever treated his son that way, in life. The few times he had, it had made Daniel feel just as stunned and fearful as he felt now.

Fearful. The first real fear he experienced since he entered Kentucky.

He rolled over onto his side, worrying. That dream had been an omen, sure as the world, and not a good one.

Trying to shake off the sense of foreboding settling on him like his buffalo hide blanket, Daniel reeled off all the reasons not to be concerned. The hunt had so far gone very well, the land as rich as Findley had promised, or almost so. They had brought in deer hide after deer hide, turning them over to the camp keepers for straking down, packing, and scaffolding. Bales of skins were piling up all around the original station camp, and several other camps they had set up at hidden spots around their hunting region. Every bale represented a debt that could be paid off as soon as they returned to the markets, or a new rifle, or good dresses for Rebecca and the girls.

In all the months they had been there, they had seen no trace of Indians, even though all had kept a careful watch. Daniel had long since decided that they really were going to make it into Kentucky and out again without a single encounter with the older race of hunters who had known this land long before the white men had come. And no one had seriously hurt himself or been ill, except for an early round of fever suffered by John Findley, and that had been easily shaken off.

But that dream . . . the fear it roused wouldn't let him go. He closed his eyes and tried to sleep, and failed.

He told John Stewart about the dream in the morning after breakfast. The pair were setting out together for a day's hunt. Stewart frowned at Daniel's story and shook his head.

"I wish you hadn't a-told me. Now I'll be expecting to see a redskin or some other piece of bad luck come out of every bush and canebrake."

They hunted through the day with fair success. The sky was bright and clear, the wind brisk; and by the time they made for camp after tracking along a buffalo trace that sliced through a wide canebrake near the Kentucky River, both men managed to laugh off Daniel's "omen" dream. Just the foolishness that comes to mind in the night-time, that's all it was.

They crossed a hill, stepped into a clearing, and came to a dead halt. Emerging from all sides around them were Indians. Shawnees. Daniel's legs went weak as he felt not only fear, but deep shame at letting himself be surprised. He had always thought himself too good a woodsman for that. But there he was, facing Shawnees, some of whom looked threatening with dour expressions, others just as threatening with smiles.

One Shawnee stepped forward and gestured toward himself. "Amaghqua," he said. "I am Shawnee, from Chillicothe town. The white men call me Will Emery, or Captain Will. That is the name I like best. Captain Will."

Daniel, relieved that Captain Will spoke English, decided to try an approach that had worked well a time or two when he had encountered Cherokees in the Holston country. "Howdy, Captain Will. I am Boone. This is Stewart. We are glad to meet such a fine group of hunters as you."

"You have not known we were near, Boone," Captain Will said, smiling. "We have surprised you. But you have not surprised us. You leave much sign behind you, like you are buffaloes and not men." Captain Will laughed, the Shawnees laughed, and Daniel Boone laughed too. Stewart, looking very scared, gave a sidewise glance at his brother-in-law, then joined in the laughter.

"You are fine woodsmen," Daniel said. "My friend and I could learn much from you."

"There is something you will teach us, Boone," the Shawnee leader said. "You will take us to your camps and show us how many skins you have taken from lands where you have no right to hunt."

"This is a broad land. We have not taken more than a few skins, not nearly enough to hurt the hunting of our Shawnee brothers," Daniel said, carefully phrasing his talk and making sure he kept a friendly tone and smile. "We have not meant to offend you."

Captain Will's own smile faded—not a good sign. "We have known that white men would come," he said bitterly. "The Iroquois have told the white men that this is their land and have given away lands south of the great river to the north of us. They had no right to do this. This is the hunting ground of the ancestors of the Shawnee. It is not open for white men to hunt."

"We did not understand this," Daniel said. "I thank you for telling us the truth."

"Now you will take us to your camps," Captain Will said. Daniel's face was still bright and placid, but inwardly he was distressed. Who could predict what would happen when the Shawnees reached the camps? No doubt they'd take every skin so laboriously gathered, dressed, and baled. All the work done so far would be erased. Worse, they might do violence to the others, especially if any resistance was raised.

"I will gladly lead you," Daniel said. It was the only option he had.

He glanced at Stewart. The face looking back at him was gaunt, fearful, pleading, and utterly helpless. Daniel gave Stewart a quick smile and simultaneous frown with his eyes. Getting the message, Stewart wiped the terror off his face and forced the closest thing he could render up to a look of friendliness.

Sick to his soul but not showing it, Daniel led the Shawnees toward the closest camp. He knew better than to try to lead them astray; most likely they had already found the location of at least some of the camps and were testing him to see how honest he intended to he. He knew that William Cooley was at the closest camp and feared for what would be done to him if they found him. Daniel began talking loudly, making as much noise as he could the closer he came to the campsite. When Captain Will raised a tomahawk and suggested that Daniel quiet his voice a little, Daniel smiled, nodded, then launched into a loud and utterly convincing coughing fit, apologizing between spasms for all the noise he was making. Captain Will looked at him coldly, suspicious of this continuing noise, but beneath the ice in the Indian's eye Daniel caught a flash of something that gave him hope. Captain Will was amused. He was coming to enjoy the company of Daniel Boone. Even though he surely sensed what Daniel was up to, he was putting up with it.

They reached the camp and found Cooley gone—the furs gone with him. Daniel did his best not to show his relief. Obviously the noise he had made had warned Cooley just in time to let him get away. He would certainly rush to the main camp, give warning, and all the others together should be able to cart away most or all of the fur bales before the Shawnees arrived. Daniel intended to lead them in the most roundabout way possible, and slowly.

He was shocked when they finally reached the main station camp and found that not a single bale was gone. Even the horses were there, even the rifles and ammunition, the men having fled in panic into the forest. Daniel couldn't believe it. He tried not to show his dejection as the Shawnees gathered the peltries, laughing and hooting at their success. More than half a year's worth of work, effort, expense, danger—all that, and it had come to this.

DANIEL HAD BEEN RIGHT about Captain Will. The Shawnee had taken a liking to him. Many Indians Daniel had met through the years seemed to take kindly to him, maybe sensing in him much of their own attitude and spirit. For several days Captain Will kept Daniel and John Stewart as his prisoners but didn't abuse them too badly. The huge cache of peltries that had been seized had put the Shawnee in a good humor.

"What will happen to us in the end?" John Stewart asked Daniel at one moment when the pair had a chance to talk privately.

"Don't know. I'm hoping the old coot will let us go," Daniel replied.

"God, I hope so. I hear they do terrible things to people they kill."

"They ain't going to kill us. I feel certain of it."

Again Daniel was right. The next day Captain Will announced abruptly that the prisoners were to be freed. Not only that, they would be given two pairs of moccasins apiece, a little powder and shot, some doeskin patching, and a small, low-quality trade musket to kill game for themselves along the way home.

"Don't come here to hunt again, brothers," Captain Will said. "Go back home and stay. This hunting ground belongs to the Indians, and all the pelts and animals that come from it are ours, which is why we have felt free to take what you have gathered. If you are foolish enough to come back here, you will not find the mercy you have seen today. The wasps and yellow jackets will sting you very severely."

Hands were shaken all around—Stewart looking downright amazed the entire time—and the Shawnees vanished into the forest, leaving the two white men alone.

"Well, Daniel, are we leaving now?" Stewart asked.

"Don't know about you," Daniel said, "but I don't aim to go nowhere."

Stewart was aghast. "Didn't you hear him, Dan?"

"I did. But I know why I come here, and it wasn't to go home poorer than when I commenced."

"We'll die here if we stay," Stewart said. "I can feel it."

"I don't aim to die, neither."

Stewart studied Daniel solemnly. "I wish I was as fearless as you, Dan. You ain't afraid of nothing."

Daniel was flattered by the compliment, but that night he proved it false. He dreamed he was being attacked by very large, very fierce yellow jackets. They swarmed around him, stinging, refusing to be brushed off. Daniel awoke screaming, and from then on John Stewart knew that the fearless one was in fact afraid, too.

Oddly enough, the realization that they were in similar spirit gave them heart, and together they set upon a brazen plan. They would follow Captain Will and his men, and take back their horses, if nothing else.

It was a daunting notion, but so was that of having to tramp through Kentucky on foot, with nothing to haul the skins and pelts they still intended to collect. They found the Shawnees' trail and followed it, and with stealth actually managed to regain five of the stolen horses. Mounting two of them, leading the others, they rode hard an entire night, covering all the distance they could. As dawn began to break, they finally stopped, weary but proud of their success. Captain Will may have thought he had played a fine joke on Boone and Stewart, but they had managed to turn part of it back on him.

"I ain't nearly so skittery as I was before," Stewart said. "It 'pears we have turned the turn on old Will a right smart way!"

Daniel was kneeling, tightening the snap of one of his moccasins. "Hush!" he said suddenly, lifting a hand and cocking his head. He lowered his ear toward the ground, listening.

"What is it, Dan? You hear something?" At that moment a mounted, armed band appeared over a nearby hill, riding in hard. Now Stewart heard the rumble in the ground that Daniel had detected.

At the head of the riders, familiar faces to the last man, was a grinning, rifle-bearing Captain Will. He lowered his rifle, thumbed it to full cock.

"Howdy, Boone," he said.

"Howdy, Captain Will."

Without another word the Shawnee squeezed the trigger, and the little hillside was filled with sound and smoke and fire, and a cry that rang up hoarsely from John Stewart's throat as he sank to his knees, hand groping to his heart.

CHAPTER 21

JOHN STEWART ROSE slowly, face reddening in embarrassment. "Thought I was shot through," he muttered, and grinned weakly.

Captain Will glanced at his companions, and all roared with laughter. Daniel eyed Stewart sympathetically, glad that it wasn't he who had made such a dramatic blunder. A look at Captain Will's laughing face made it clear that he hadn't been trying to shoot either of them, only to frighten them. Stewart hadn't let him down.

When his laughter had subsided, Captain Will began reloading his rifle, still on horseback. Others of his group dismounted and collected the horses Daniel and Stewart had taken, then led the weary beasts back to be tied to their own mounts.

"Steal horses, Boone?" Captain Will said as he slid the ramrod back into the thimbles of the reloaded rifle. "Boone likes horses—maybe we'll see what kind of horse old Boone would make, huh? And Falling Man, too," he added, pointing at Stewart.

The other Shawnees laughed and nodded as Captain Will slid off his horse. Daniel kept a calm expression, but suddenly he was worried. Evidently Captain Will had some kind of sport in mind for his prisoners. Whatever it was, Daniel was certain it would be at his and Stewart's expense. If the Shawnee was more angry than he was showing, the sport might even have a painful or fatal end.

Captain Will approached Daniel, pulling something from under his deer skin shirt. It was a horse bell, one of those Daniel and Stewart had slipped off the horses when they had stolen them from the Shawnee camp. Captain Will carried it up to Daniel, swept Daniel's hat from his head, and hung it around his neck. Pulling a second horse bell from his shirt, he did the same with Stewart. "Now," he said, "Boone and Falling Man will give Captain Will a ride." Daniel would never forget how humbling it was to walk around on all fours while Captain Will rode his back, whipping him with a switch and forcing him to nicker and snort like a horse, the Shawnees laughing so hard they gripped their sides. Then it was Stewart's turn to be ridden. Daniel rose and stood aside, trying to be inconspicuous while Stewart suffered through his turn, but one of the other Shawnees pushed him to his knees, then rammed his face into the ground.

"Grass," the Shawnee said. "Boone will graze the grass now with his wide horse mouth."

If he was forced to play the object of scorn, he might as well do his best in the role. Daniel made a fine show of ripping up grass with his teeth, chewing it, swallowing it with difficulty. Captain Will hopped off Stewart's back and made him "graze" awhile too, then forced both men to prance about, making equine sounds, the horse bells jangling around their necks. Only after almost an hour of continuing humiliation had the Shawnees extracted all the amusement they could from their prisoners and allowed them to stand, remove the bells, and become men again.

"That's the worst humiliated I've ever been," Stewart whispered.

"We had it easy," Daniel whispered back. "They could have peeled our thatch. Good thing for us Captain Will likes his jokes."

The Shawnees seemed almost jovial now. The display had satisfied them, and they apparently held Daniel and Stewart in high regard because of their courage in retaking the horses and almost getting away with it. Captain Will told the pair that they would have to remain with their captors awhile longer now, since they had proved themselves untrustworthy. "Besides, Captain Will is a good horse trader. He may trade his new 'horses' in Chillicothe."

Daniel wondered if that indicated he and Stewart were to be taken all the way up to the Shawnee towns and kept as prisoners of Captain Will. Prudence kept him from asking, but the northward course the group now took seemed to back up that idea. As the group camped that night, Captain Will came to Boone and knelt beside him.

"You are a clever man, Boone, and I do not trust you. But don't worry—Captain Will likes you and will not see you hurt. But you must remain with me until we cross the river and are in our own country. Then you will be free, and Falling Man too."

Daniel was relieved. Captain Will seemed the type to hold true to his word. At least the prospect of a long Indian captivity didn't lie ahead. Daniel shared the news with Stewart, and the pair slept.

For days they remained with their unwanted companions, acting cooperatively and even passing up a chance or two to bolt for freedom—chances Daniel suspected were deliberately set up by Captain Will as tests of their cooperation. The Shawnees hunted deer and buffalo, making camp along streams and near canebrakes. Most of those sites showed the sign of earlier hunters' camps for many years back. As Daniel observed the ease with which the Shawnee collected game, he noted anew the natural wealth of the Kentucky country, and understood the determination of the Indians not to lose it to the encroachment of an alien race.

DANIEL AND STEWART made their escape when they came within a half day's journey of the Ohio River. The Indian band was camped near a sprawling canebrake. By then they were so accustomed to their white-skinned companions, who after all had made no attempt to bolt, that they had grown complacent about watching them. Daniel and Stewart were tied, though loosely, and the Shawnees were distracted with making camp and planning for the river crossing the next day. Daniel glanced into the canebrake, and a smile stole across his face.

"John, take a look," he whispered.

"If you're eyeing them rifles stacked in the cane, I already seen them," Stewart replied. "Powder horns and shot pouches already strung onto them and everything! Our friends have turned careless on us. If we can slip these ropes —"

Daniel grunted softly, straining. He slipped the cord around his left wrist, and quickly tore the slackened bond from the other and pulled his hands from behind his back. Stewart turned to give Daniel access to his own tied wrists, and soon he was free, too. No one noticed them.

"Ready?"

"Ready."

They rose in silence and moved quickly into the canebrake. Each snatched a rifle, horn, and shot pouch, and then they were off, plunging deeper into the canebrake. Moving carefully among the tall, leafy canes, they lost themselves in the midst of the thick growth, heading toward the far side of the brake, which edged near the forest.

Soon they heard shouts that indicated their absence had been noted. They were still inside the canebrake, and darkness was falling. Daniel touched Stewart's arm, then motioned for him to drop. They would pass the night there; it was unlikely the Indians would search the canebrake in darkness.

For a time it appeared Daniel might be wrong about that. The Indians circled around the canebrake and explored its edges, but as night fell, they soon returned to their camp. Stewart asked Daniel in a whisper if they should leave the cane and go into the forest, but Daniel said no. It was possible not all the Indians had returned to the main camp. Some might still be around the edges of the canebrake, waiting for the fugitives to emerge. The best thing to do was wait for morning.

Stewart wasn't pleased by the idea, but went along. And when morning light came filtering through the tall canes, the wisdom of Daniel's decision was evidenced by the sound of the withdrawing Indians. They were heading north to the river, ready to cross.

"Good-bye, Boone!" The voice of Captain Will was thin and distant and muffled by the cane. "Maybe someday we will meet again!"

Daniel and Stewart waited until they were sure the Shawnees were gone, then left the cane and plunged into the forest. All in all, they had come through their brief captivity rather well, still alive, still with their scalps, and even with rifles and ammunition. But they had lost all their skins and furs and horses. They were separated from their companions, and a long way from the station camp. They had much ground to cover, no prospect of food except what they could kill along the way, and no guarantee that when they did reach the station camp, they would find any of their companions there to meet them.

And they didn't. Days later when Daniel and Stewart, exhausted, bedraggled, and hungry, strode into the old station camp, they found it empty. Disappointed, they stood picturing how it must have been: their companions, scared to the soul, nervously gathering what few items the Indians hadn't taken with them, then fleeing. Which way? Probably southeast, back toward the Cumberland Gap and the wilderness routes to the settlements that lay far beyond it.

Collapsing, the two men rested. Daniel rose in the afternoon and killed a buck he found foraging in a thicket. Slicing away all the meat he could, he carried it back to the camp, built a fire, and roasted a big meal of meat without seasoning and without bread. He and Stewart gorged themselves, then rested through the night. The next morning they headed along the same route they presumed their friends would have taken if in fact they were returning to the settlements.

They pressed hard and traveled fast, and soon began finding sign that indicated others had come that way not too long before. Encouraged, they increased their speed even more. Whoever was ahead of them—and who could it be but their old companions?—they would soon overtake them.

DANIEL TOOK A SECRET devilish delight in watching the encamped men leap to their feet and grapple clumsily for their rifles when he strode into the camp clearing, Stewart right behind him. It hadn't been hard to locate them. Their trail had become all the more obvious the farther he and Stewart had followed it, and along the final stretch they had actually been able to find them by listening to their voices—voices raised in what sounded like a full-fired argument of some sort.

Grinning, Daniel stuck out his hand to the rising John Findley, whose face had gone white as the landmark rocks atop the Cumberland Mountains as soon as Daniel had shown himself.

"John Findley, how are you faring?" Daniel asked. Turning, he nodded to the others—all of whom were there, scalps intact—then his grin turned to a look of astonishment as an unexpected face appeared before him.

"Squire!" Daniel exclaimed. "Squire, is that you?"

"Howdy, brother," Squire Boone said. "Lordy, I'm proud to see you alive. I was fearsome worried about you with all the things these men here have been telling me."

Another new face intruded itself, and a hand was thrust into Daniel's. "Howdy, Dan. We was mighty fretful about you."

"Alex Neely!" Daniel said, greeting Squire's old friend. "Good to see you. I'm surprised through to the marrow. When did you come to Kentucky? I wasn't expecting to see you until the spring. Squire—and Alexander—I wasn't looking for you at all."

"Set down over here and have some victuals, if you're empty," Squire said. "We'll tell our tale, but only after you've told yourn. I'm primed to know what's happened to you."

The others were just as eager, and Daniel hardly had time to wolf down a gourd of stew before he was pressed into the role of storyteller. He told them everything from the original encounter on through to the final escape, even including the humiliating incident involving the horse bells and Captain Will's devilish sense of humor. The recounting brought much laughter, the pure, purging laughter of men greatly relieved from a substantial worry.

John Findley spoke next, telling what happened from the point of view of those who had not been captured by Captain Will. It wasn't a tale made to flatter its subjects, and the hired camp keepers kept their heads low as Findley talked, none of them denying what he said.

"When Will Cooley came a-tearing into the camp declaring that you and John had been took by the Shawnees, it roused a terror in us all," Findley said. "I include myself in that, but the fact is I wasn't so fearful as our hired men here, which would be expected, considering I had dealt with the Indians before in my trader days. I spoke up and says, 'The thing to do is to gather our hides and furs, leaving just enough to fool the Shawnees into thinking they've got it all, and hide the rest with the horses until the danger is past.' "

"That was what we had hoped would be done," Daniel interjected.

"I'm afraid fear had the better of us," Findley said, graciously including himself in the blame, but giving a subtle flick of the eyes toward the sheepish hired men, showing Daniel where the real fault lay. "We left the camp as it was and fled for our lives. When we returned after the Indians had gone, they had taken it all. But that, I'm sure, you already know."

"Aye," Stewart said glumly. "Upwards of a half year's work, gone to the devil because of the fright of a few . . ." He cut off his words, which had already brought William Cooley's face snapping up to gaze into his own, anger replacing the fear in his eyes. Stewart held his gaze but said no more, and after a moment Cooley looked down again.

"It was suggested we should seek to retrieve you from the Shawnees, but the notion didn't seem to please all of us," Findley went on. "There was then nothing to be done but to begin the journey back to the settlements and leave you two to the grace of providence and your own cleverness to free yourself—something you've done very admirably."

"It was while we were heading home that we encountered Squire and Alexander, here, riding in with horses and supplies."

"I'll tell it from here," Squire said. "Dan, we was getting worried about you back home. You'd been gone for months, and no word had come back of your welfare. It came to mind that maybe it would be best for me to come in to resupply you a mite sooner than we'd planned it. Alex here was curious as to how you were getting on and curious to see the Kentucky lands besides, so he come along. We were blessed with decent weather and no real trials, and Dick Henderson helped outfit us good with horses and traps and such, so we made fair time and figured on meeting you up in the meadow country. We was mighty fuddled in mind when we met John and these other three coming back, telling tales of your being captured by the Shawnees and all the hides being gone.

"John was happy to see us and ready to turn back and go find you, which was what me and Alex wanted to do as well. There was some arguments made to the contrary." Like Findley before him, he side-glanced at the camp keepers. Cooley muttered an oath under his breath and rose to stalk away to the farthest edge of camp, where he paced and looked deeply unhappy. Squire Boone watched him, shook his head a little, and went on. "The arguing was still going on when you brought an end to it just now by walking in amongst us. Who would've figured we wouldn't have to go find you at all—you were coming to find us!"

"Well, we've felt the hand of the devil and the touch of the good Lord all in the same journey," Daniel said. "We've lost what we had, but our lives are still ours, we're supplied again, thanks to Squire and Alex, and there ain't no reason not to go on just like we had been."

Squire grinned. "I figured you'd feel that way, Daniel. I was a-counting on it. Alex and me are ready to stay on if you aim to keep hunting."

"Glad to hear it, brother. John, are you of a mind to stay, too?"

Stewart sighed. "I'm fool enough for it if you are. If I've survived the Shawnees once, reckon I can do it again."

"Why, we'll likely not lay eyes on another Shawnee," Daniel said, his spirits rising. "John Findley, you with us too?"

To the surprise of all, Findley sadly shook his head. "No, not this time. My spirit's broke for this season, Dan. I reckon age is getting to me. I figure I'll head back to Carolina and give word to your people that you're alive and well."

Daniel said, "Them three there can do that, John." He waved at the hired men. "I don't even have to ask if they're staying on—I can see from their sneakish looks that they're going back."

"They'll need a guide," Findley said. "Otherwise they'll likely wander to Florida trying to find the Yadkin." His listeners grinned at the disparaging comment, all but Holden and Mooney, who now rose to join Cooley . They meandered about, muttering to one another, a trio of very humiliated, unhappy men. "Besides," Findley continued in a softer voice, "you don't know what tales them three would tell about you and what happened if they were left to tell it alone. I don't think any of us stand high in their favor right now."

Daniel felt a wave of true sadness. "Hate to see you go, John Findley. I sure wish you'd rethink it."

"I've done my thinking. What I'll do now is get back to Carolina and rest these old bones for a bit. After that, who can say? I figure I'll be back in Kentucky. I still ain't made that fortune this here land has promised me."

The groups parted company the next day, Findley and the three somber former camp keepers heading back toward Cumberland Gap; Daniel, Squire, Neely, and Stewart returning to their old station camp. They didn't remain there, but scrounged what notched logs they could, picked up the camp kettle, which the Indians had either overlooked or not wanted, and headed on to more remote camping grounds. They had been careless, Daniel decided, in selecting a campsite so close to the Indian hunting trail. This time they would not make such a blunder.

They set up camp near the deserted old Shawnee hunting encampment called Blue Lick Town. The hard winter settled upon them before they had barely finished, bringing snow and frozen waterways and nights spent on ground that could be kept warm only by burying coals in it and sleeping atop the rising heat. They strung traps along the streams; fished the cold waters; killed deer, bears, and buffalo for meat; and filled their new camp with a mounting harvest of beaver and otter pelts. Bit by bit the pain of their financial loss to Captain Will's Indians began to fade, and Daniel began to grow optimistic. It would take longer than he'd originally anticipated, but he could leave Kentucky a wealthier man than when he had entered it. Unlike John Findley, he wouldn't back down.

But what about Rebecca? There was the question that troubled. He thought of her there, awaiting his return. At the time he left home, she had just come to believe she was pregnant again. He pictured her there alone, handling all the domestic duties, then giving birth to another child without her husband close by. It was a heartbreaking image.

Yet even that couldn't sway him in the end. He was there for reasons beyond a mere desire to hunt and explore. It was his duty to stay until the job was properly done. Rebecca would have to be patient awhile longer. Someday he would make it up to her, somehow.

January's snow gave way to rain as the month neared its end. The four men developed a pattern to their hunting and trapping; Stewart and Daniel working together, Squire and Neely the same. They would venture out from their base camp, sometimes for only a day, other times for several days on end, then come back with whatever pelts their traps had fetched, and sometimes a deer hide or two, though most of those were so poor as to be nearly worthless that time of year.

The rains ended at last, and moving about became easier. Daniel and Stewart headed out as usual at the tail end of one rainstorm, moving through a sodden but beautiful winter-brown land. Daniel had come to love Kentucky dearly in the time he had been there, not only for personal reasons but for practical ones. Findley had not exaggerated long ago around the campfires on Braddock's Road, when he described the region's wealth. The rivers and creeks were filled with mullet, rockfish, perch, eels, garfish. The bigger rivers held catfish, salmon, and buffalo fish, all huge. The cane lands, marshes, and bottomlands were rich with geese and ducks in their season, and various exotic-looking, long-necked herons and other waterfowl. Turkeys roamed the woodlands, and the trees and grasslands were filled with ravens, partridge, quail, and pheasant. At night, huge owls haunted the trees, sometimes emitting cries that sent a chill down the spine of human listeners—cries that sounded like phantoms. Buffalo, rarely seen now in the Holston and Clinch countries, were in such abundance that herds seemed to stretch into infinity across the rolling grasslands. Their meat was delicious, especially the tongues and humps, and the hides made excellent robes that blocked out the most biting cold.

The rivers intrigued Daniel particularly, being a vital consideration for possible sites of future settlements. For his own reasons, and for Richard Henderson's, he made copious mental notes of various waterways he explored. The Great Kenhawa lands were hilly and uninviting, but those about the Licking much better. Decent land was also to be found on the southern branch of that stream, with many good sites for mills. He found promising locations in the Elkhorn country and the Kentucky River basin, though the latter river ran through some of the wildest country Daniel had seen, with great cliffs rising along it to hundreds of feet in height.

He examined the soil as well, judging it by the type of growth it produced in its natural state and based on his own experiences as a farmer in Carolina. The more he looked, the more he became convinced that much of the land would produce excellent crops of corn, rye, wheat, barley, or oats. Settlements could thrive there, if unhampered by the Indians.

Stewart and Daniel were talking about such matters when they reached the banks of the swollen Kentucky River. They stopped there, and Stewart cupped his hand over his eyes and looked across the water. "I believe I'll go across and see what I can find beyond the places we've yet been," he said. "You want to come, too?"

"Not today. I figured to head upstream on this side. You go ahead."

"I'll be back at camp in a day or two at the most, and maybe by tonight," Stewart said. He slapped Daniel on the shoulder, told him to watch himself, and was off, crossing in a bark canoe they had constructed. Daniel watched him until he was out of sight, then turned to his own explorations, feeling oddly unsettled.

John Stewart did not return that night, or the next, or the next. A week passed, and Daniel knew something was wrong. He crossed the Kentucky and found the canoe where Stewart had moored it. The sight of the empty, gently swaying little craft only increased his disquiet. He headed into the forest, looking for sign, feeling very worried.

He found sign, days old, that led him to an empty camp with burned-out coals at the fire site, now cold and crumbling. Nearby he found John Stewart's initials carved into a tree. He looked farther, but what sign he could locate seemed to lead nowhere. He searched, even risked calling out for Stewart at the top of his lungs, but there was no response.

Turning back, he took the canoe over the river and rejoined the others, hoping he would find Stewart with them. He wasn't there. Daniel had little hope left now. Stewart was not the kind to remain away longer than he had promised—a thought that suddenly made him see himself as Rebecca surely must, and therefore a thought he didn't allow himself to linger on for long. When he pushed the image of Rebecca away from his mind's eye, it was replaced by that of his sister Hannah, weeping because now she was widowed and her husband would never return to her from the wilderness.

That night Daniel Boone wept, too. He had come to feel closer to Stewart than he was to many of his brothers. It was impossible to conceive of him as gone. Worst was not knowing what happened to him, and how the end had come.

CHAPTER 22

JOHN STEWART'S DISAPPEARANCE threw a terrible fright into Alexander Neely, the most skittish of the four hunters. Surely Stewart had been killed by Indians, he declared, and if so, the thing to do was for the entire group to head home immediately.

"I'm not inclined to go," Daniel replied. "There's much work yet to be done, and so far not enough peltries to justify a return."

"It's my own pelt I'm worried about," Neely replied forthrightly.

The group conferred, and in the end Neely alone decided to return, to bear to families and neighbors the welcome news that the Boone brothers were well, and the sorrowful news that John Stewart had disappeared, apparently for good. Nervous about his coming lone journey homeward, but also eager to be off, Neeley took his share of the peltries and enough supplies to see him through to Carolina, then departed.

The wilderness seemed a larger, wilder place with their numbers suddenly reduced by half. Yet alone with Squire, Daniel thought back to his own youth, when Squire had been just an eager boy, and how he had hoped that someday the pair of them would be able to explore and hunt together in the wild country across the mountains. And there they were, fulfilling that very plan. Though he grieved deeply for John Stewart and was beginning to feel hollow and lonesome for his family when he lay down to sleep at night, Daniel was happy on another level. Squire was a comfortable partner, and the two of them were made for the wilderness.

Squire wasn't so satisfied. Though not edgy in the wilderness like Neely, he nevertheless had a good appreciation for a warm cabin, a hot fire, and good family close by. He would put up with the deprivations and dangers of the wilderness, but he did not relish it as Daniel did.

If Daniel Boone was courageous, he was not reckless or foolish. He and Squire took many precautions, doing all their cooking at night by hidden fires, frequently changing the sites of their camps, and covering their trails. From time to time they found sign of Indians near them, and would lie low for a day or two until they were sure danger had passed.

Spring came, and shot and powder ran low. Squire packed up the bales of furs and pelts they had taken, loaded them onto the horses, and headed home for more supplies. When he was gone, Daniel stood alone, looking around, wondering if there was another man of his race anywhere within hundreds of miles, save for the solitary homeward-bound figure of his own brother Squire. The loneliness was awesome, heavy as iron—yet for Daniel, strangely thrilling. There was a special joy to be found in solitude, in "contemplation," as he like to put it.

For three months he hunted alone, building up another store of peltries, but only a meager one, for he couldn't spare enough ammunition for large-scale hunting. He concentrated more on simple exploration, making mental notes for Richard Henderson and also for himself. He lived frequently in caves in the cliff country along the rivers and was more careful than ever about keeping his presence hidden from the Indians. Yet sometimes the solitude was too much for even him to bear, and he would talk aloud to himself, or read aloud from his copy of *Gulliver's Travels*, or sing some of the old songs that Nate had so often boomed out in their past excursions together.

He was singing "The Wagoner's Lad" at full volume, stretched flat on his back on a deer hide in a clearing, the day that Virginia hunter Caspar Manskar came upon him. Though embarrassed to be caught incautious, Daniel was delighted by the presence of another white man and passed an enjoyable time with the long hunter, then reentered his solitude refreshed. He kept up with the passing days, notching them off on a stick, while awaiting the appointed return of Squire.

He encountered only one hostile band of Indian hunters. Shawnees, they were, and they chased him nearly a mile before he evaded them by flinging his pouch over the edge of a bluff and into a treetop, then hiding himself beneath an overhang on a ledge just below the cliff's edge. The Indians passed right above him, spying the pouch dangling in the treetop, and concluded that the fool must have jumped. They went on, and Daniel crawled out, grinning at how he had tricked them. It took him the rest of the day, however, to retrieve his pouch from the treetop.

Afterward he wondered with amusement if the Indians might now be talking of him in some awe. A white man who could survive a leap from a cliff top to a treetop! Quite a feat, most likely impossible, or nearly so. It would make a fine tale, however, both for the Indians who thought it was true, and Daniel Boone himself, who knew it wasn't.

HE APPROACHED the figure slowly, rifle at ready. From all appearances the Indian was old, asleep maybe, or even dead. One couldn't be sure, however. The old man might have been put there as a ruse, to draw Daniel close so that others hidden somewhere nearby could rush out to capture or kill the white intruder. Or maybe the old man wasn't as old as his look and posture suggested, and would rise to do the killing himself.

Daniel came within ten paces and the Indian didn't rise. Nor was there sign of any other Indians about. Kneeling, Daniel examined the ground and found footprints, but they were at least two days old. When he stood, the old Indian was looking toward him, eyes small and marble-like, seemingly blind. Daniel lowered his rifle and closed the lock. The sound it made caused the old Indian to start and make a strange noise in his throat. He began a moaning, odd chant. Daniel stood silently, growing sad as he considered the tragic end to which this man's life had come.

The Indian had been brought here to die. His people had left him, old and sick, to find the end of his days alone. Daniel wondered how many years the old man had lived, how much he'd seen, how many miles he'd covered, how many children he'd raised. "Old man, I will bring you meat," he said. Again the Indian started, but did not cease his strange song.

Daniel turned and went back the way he'd come. Half a mile back he had killed a deer and cooked the best of its meat for himself, but the rest he'd left behind. Finding the remains still unmolested by scavengers, he cut away more meat and returned to the old Indian. The chant had ceased, but when he heard Daniel approach, he began it again.

"I'll cook food for you," Daniel said. He built a fire and roasted a good portion, cooking it well, making it easy to chew with old jaws and worn-down teeth. He let the meat cool, and put it in the hands of the old man.

"Eat," he said, though he knew the old fellow wouldn't understand. "Eat, so you will be strong for your journey. I believe you will go soon."

The old man stopped singing and ate some of the meat, tearing it off in strings and lifting it to his mouth with shaky fingers. When he was finished, he fell asleep, head lolling to one side, blind eyes closing. What remained of the meat fell from his lap onto the ground beside him.

Daniel picked up the fallen meat and brushed off the dirt with his hand. He laid it on the Indian's lap and put one of the old man's hands atop it. Then, silently, he slipped into the woods.

That night he dreamed of the incident, but this time it was not an old Indian he found in the woods, but his own father. Squire Boone had looked up at his son, a stern expression on his face, and said, "My boy, there are those of your own who will take their own journey out of this dark land, too, and the heart will surely be torn from you." Then his father had put his fingers on his own chest and they had sunk into the flesh of it—a horrible sight that stunned Daniel.

Immediately he awakened, disturbed. By dawn he went back to the place he had left the old Indian, and found him dead. He had eaten a little more of the meat before passing away. Daniel thought of burying him, but he had no good means to do so, and there was something about the place that sent a shiver right through him. He left the old man sitting as he was and hurried away.

SQUIRE RETURNED in July, bearing welcome news. "Rebecca is well—and she's bore you a new son. He bears your first name, Dan, and Morgan for a middle one. A fine, strapping lad."

"Daniel Morgan Boone," the father repeated, testing out the feel of the name. "It's a fine name. Fine." He stood thinking about his growing family, and at that moment felt lonelier than he had even without Squire.

But now was not the time for a return. Squire had brought new supplies. There was enough powder and lead to make a serious hunt. Bales of deerskins began to pile up in hidden places as the summer rolled past. It was a good summer, very productive. The heat wasn't unbearable and humidity was low. Daniel thrived, enjoying his situation. As for Squire, he put up with it, but enjoyed it much less. Daniel was made for this life in a way few men were, and Squire didn't pretend to fully understand it.

In the fall, Squire left again for home, carrying the summer's harvest. Daniel might have gone too, but there was more exploring to do, and good hunting when the winter came. In December, Squire was back with traps, horses, more supplies, and news that all the Boones were well, though Rebecca sorely missed her husband.

"She'll have me back come spring," he said. "I've been gone long enough."

Squire smiled and nodded. He couldn't have agreed more.

They hunted through the winter, living often in caves along the Kentucky River and sometimes chipping their initials in the walls of them. Daniel, forced to kill a wolf that had entered their camp, found the pups and attempted to tame them, thinking of taking them home as a surprise for his children, but the wolves wouldn't domesticate and wandered off as soon as they were old enough.

Winter came and went, and a damp, rich springtime came over Kentucky. Daniel and Squire packed up the several hundred dollars' worth of skins and pelts the season had given them and headed down through the Kentucky country toward the gap of the Cumberlands. After an absence of two years Daniel Boone was going home at last.

They left the rolling meadow country and entered the dark, brooding mountains. Along the winding trace through the wilderness they passed, until they reached the Yellow Creek valley. Ahead loomed the tall Cumberlands, rocky and massive. By afternoon they crossed through Cumberland Gap into the valley of the Powell, where they made camp.

Now that Kentucky was behind him, Daniel was more eager than ever for home. He couldn't get Rebecca out of his mind, and he was filled with anticipation at seeing his new son. And the other children—how much would two years have changed them? Children grew so fast he might hardly recognize them now. For that matter, they might not recognize him. He was as bearded as an old goat, and his hair was shaggy and uncut, hanging between his shoulders and tied with a rawhide whang.

He ate a hearty second helping of the squirrel stew that Squire had cooked and then lay back, staring at the darkening sky. Nearby the horses nuzzled at the fresh April grass. As the arc of the sky turned black, stars appeared. A shooting star flashed across, south to north. *Heading into Kentucky*, Daniel thought. *Just like I'll do again one day, with all my kin. And once there, I'll stay for good. No leaving, no running out. John Findley was right. There's no finer country. One day it will be my home.*

"Hist, Daniel." Squire's quietly spoken word of warning broke into Daniel's thoughts. He sat up. A moment later six faces appeared at the edge of the circle of light cast by the fire. Daniel did not let any reaction alter his features. Standing slowly, he smiled, then spread his arms in a symbol of welcome.

"Come in, brothers. You have smelled our food? There is plenty for you all, and whiskey too."

Silently, they entered. Squire fetched all the bowls and cups they had and filled them with the stew. He was smiling, just like Daniel, but his eyes had an unusual intensity and sharpness in which Daniel read his younger brother's fear.

Without a word the visitors ate. Cherokees, Daniel determined. He looked from face to face and thought he recognized one of them. Yes . . . an older fellow he had seen sometime before on the long hunts with Nate. With an inner start he realized he was one of the Indians who had chased him the time he had hidden beneath the waterfall. He wondered if the Indian would recognize him, too. If he did, he wasn't showing it.

The other Indians were strangers. The youngest of them, a lean man in his mid-twenties, was the finest-looking specimen. He ate slowly, eyes always in motion, shifting from Daniel to Squire and back again. From time to time he would look at the stack of fur bales piled near the horses and covered with a bearskin. The Indians ate until the kettle was empty, then sat back, looking at the two white men.

"Fetch out the flask, Squire," Daniel said. Squire went to his pack and took out a flask of whiskey, nearly full. He had brought it from Carolina on his last resupply trek into Kentucky, and he and Daniel had drunk sparingly from it. Unstoppering it, he handed it to the nearest Indian, who took a big swallow, swiped his hand over his mouth, and handed the flask on to the next one.

"Hunters?" one of the oldest Indians said, waving at the fur bales.

"Yes," Daniel said.

"You have been beyond the big gap?'" the Indian said in a mix of English and Cherokee.

Daniel knew enough of the Cherokee tongue to communicate. But he didn't want to say too much. These Indians might not be kindly disposed to the idea of white hunters exploiting Kentucky.

"Yes. Some through the gap. Not far."

"Many hides."

"Yes."

The Indian turned and spoke to his companions in their own language. Daniel missed the relevant portion, but the Cherokees all laughed heartily. Only the youngest one didn't laugh; he asked to have the statement repeated. When it was, he turned his head oddly as he listened, then laughed. Daniel realized that the young man was deaf in one ear.

"Good rifles, good hunting," the Cherokee spokesman said. He had a very amicable tone.

"Yes." Daniel replied, beginning to grow more at ease. "Good rifles."

The man lifted his own weapon, a short trade musket, "Bad shooter. Shoot, make big noise, miss deer, deer run away. Bad shooter."

"Muskets are not as good as rifles," Daniel said, grinning and nodding. He glanced at Squire, who still had his smile plastered across his face, his eyes wilder and keener than ever.

"We trade," the Cherokee said abruptly.

"What?"

"Trade. We give muskets, you give rifles. All go away happy men."

Daniel licked his lips. To trade his fine rifle for a cheap trade musket was absurd. He would make some other offer.

"No trade. You take the whiskey, and lead. Gifts for our friends."

"Trade muskets for rifles."

"No trade," Daniel repeated, still smiling.

The Cherokee stood, very swiftly. He no longer acted at all pleasant. "No trade, then we will take."

Squire said, "Daniel . . ."

"Easy, Squire."

"Should we try to . . ."

"No. Too many of them." Then to the Cherokee, "Yes. We will trade. Your muskets for our rifles."

"Daniel, what are you doing?" Squire asked urgently.

Daniel could not reply without the others hearing. By now all the Indians had risen. The one with the deaf ear strode over to the furs and pulled back the bearskin. The spokesman came over and examined them. Other Cherokees began looking over the horses.

"No, no trade," the spokesman said. "Too late for trade. We will take what we want."

Daniel looked sadly at his brother. There was no need now to explain why he had made the last-moment agreement to trade. He had realized that if the Indians took the rifles by force, they would take everything else too. He should have accepted the trade offer to begin with. Now it was too late to backstep. The Cherokees were taking what they had actually had their eyes on all along: the cache of furs and the horses. The Cherokees were warmed by the liquor they had consumed and had a pleasant time stripping the two white hunters of all they possessed. Horses, furs, guns, pack saddles, even food—they took it all.

The one who had spoken for them grinned at Daniel as he sat mounted on the horse that had been Daniel's, holding the rifle that had been his as well. "This is Indian land, given to us by the Great Man Above. You white men, your land is yonder." He pointed the rifle barrel toward the east. "Go back to it and don't come again here."

Unexpectedly, the Indian raised the rifle and fired, the ball sailing just past Squire's head and thunking into a tree trunk. The Indians rode away, laughing and hooting. Daniel and Squire stared after them a long time.

"All our proceeds gone to savages," Daniel said. "I'm impoverished, brother. Two years of my life gone, all that work, and I'm impoverished."

"But you're alive," Squire replied. "You can be grateful for that." He paused. "Besides that, Dan, it's a lot worse for me than for you."

"Why?"

"Because you ain't made water down your leg like I did when he shot off that rifle."

Daniel turned to look at his brother's somber face by the light of the dying fire. Squire shrugged and grinned slowly, and Daniel chuckled. The chuckle grew to riotous laughter, both men deadening the pain of the blow they had just suffered with the buffer of hilarity. They guffawed until they sank to their knees and flopped onto their backs—two absurd, lonely figures there in the Powell Valley night, laughing into the cold, starry heavens above them until it hurt too much to laugh anymore.

REBECCA BOONE BOUNCED little Daniel Morgan on her knee in time to the scratch fiddle music coming from the far side of the big bonfire. All her children were about, running here and there, James successfully flirting with a neighbor girl and Israel trying to do the same, but without any luck. Jemima, bright and pretty at age ten, was beginning to show the first signs of developing into a fine specimen of young womanhood herself. It would not be long, Rebecca thought, before the Yadkin Valley boys began flirting with her.

Daniel Morgan began to cry and squirm, and Rebecca discreetly opened her dress and put the baby to her breast. The fiddler had just launched into "The White Cockade," a favorite tune of hers, and she began to hum along. Dancers reeled all around, men laughed and joked out in the darkness beyond the firelight, and sparks from the blaze rose heavenward with the fiddle music.

"Ma'am, I'd right enjoy sharing a dance with you."

Startled by the deep voice, Rebecca looked up. A tall man stood before her in terribly ragged clothing, smelling none too good, with a long, unwashed beard and hair that had needed a cutting months back.

She recoiled. "Sir, I'm a married woman, and I don't know you. I'll not dance with you."

The tall man smiled. "There's no cause to refuse me, considering all the other times you've took lively steps with me."

Her eyes widened. She rose slowly, the baby still at her breast. Laughing, the tall man reached out and took the child. "So this is my boy, is it?"

"Oh, Daniel! Daniel, you've come back!" She burst into tears, wailing so loud that the fiddle music stopped. She pressed into her husband's arm, crushing her face against his chest. He squeezed her and patted her, kissing her atop her bonnet, still balancing the baby on his other arm.

All around the bonfire voices rose. Neighbors and friends crushed in, but their press couldn't keep out the Boone children who broke through and surrounded their father, arms stretched out to him.

"How was Kentucky, Daniel?" someone asked from the perimeter of the crowd.

"Fine. Fine country."

"Did you bring back many furs?"

"Cherokees took them, all but what Squire brought in on a couple of runs," he answered.

More questions peppered him, but he answered no more. Lifting Rebecca's tear-streaked face, he kissed her lips as his neighbors cheered.

"I'm hungry as a bear," he said. "So's Squire—there he is, coming in off the road there."

Attention turned to Squire at that point, and Daniel slipped away, his family with him, Rebecca still squeezed up wonderfully tight and close.

It was good to be home again.

CHAPTER 23

FROM THE TIME of Daniel's return from Kentucky, life was not the same for the Boone family. Two years of trial and separation had changed them all. The children had matured, which pleased Daniel, but also made him think of what he had missed by being away from them during that period of growth. Rebecca was different, too. Tougher, more stoic, more accepting of the fact that her husband could no more change his roaming ways than a cat could make itself into a dog. Somewhere in her time alone, the will to argue and plead with her husband had left her.

And Daniel himself had changed. Though glad to be back with his own, he had known from the first moment he set foot in Carolina that this could not be home for him as it had been before. Long months in Kentucky had infected him with a love for that land and a determination that it would become his home. Furthermore, during his Kentucky sojourn a court edict had come down, seizing his property as payment for debts. The family continued to live on the land, but no longer was it really their own. They were like squatters, a status that made Daniel all the more restless. Surely there was something better for them than this.

He met with Richard Henderson and told him in detail of his Kentucky experiences. Henderson's eyes gleamed at Boone's descriptions, and he talked all the more seriously about the possibility of negotiating an actual purchase of Kentucky lands from the Indians. Did Daniel think such a scheme, which until then had seemed a far-fetched dream, might actually work? Yes, Daniel declared. There were Indians who would oppose such a thing to the end, but there were still others who could be persuaded. Kentucky could be settled; he was sure of it, and ready to lead such an effort as soon as it could come about.

Henderson urged patience. At the moment he was over-occupied professionally; there was nothing he could do. Someday, though. Someday. He hadn't helped finance Daniel's expedition for nothing. He was serious about establishing a colony in Kentucky. Not yet. In a few years.

A few years. Unwelcome words to Daniel Boone. Patience already straining, Daniel wrote a long letter to Cedric Winston in Virginia, trying to stir his interest in entering such a venture. As subtly as he could, he reminded Winston of his pledge to be of help to him if ever he needed it. Such a time was now.

Winston's reply arrived sooner than Daniel had anticipated, but disappointed him severely. Winston was intrigued by Daniel's suggestion but lacked the financial ability at the time to carry off such a massive enterprise. Further, he was growing old and had no desire to become a land speculator on such a scale this late in life. And there was the delicate matter of his friendship with Dick Henderson. This plan was really Henderson's; for Winston to preempt him would be uncouth, to say the least. He was sorry, but he couldn't accommodate Daniel's request. If ever he needed anything else, however.

Winston's letter closed with an unrelated postscript. There had been a murder over near the Chesapeake Bay some days before Daniel's letter had come. Two men had been caught in the act of breaking into the home of a wealthy landowner. A struggle broke out, shots were fired, and the landowner was killed. But before he died, he managed to fatally shoot one of his two assailants through the head. That assailant was Willie Kincheloe, one of the two Kincheloes that Daniel surely remembered. The other assailant, presumably Lucas Kincheloe, escaped unharmed. The pair had been imprisoned because of their beating of the slave Joe, but had been freed long since. Winston thought they had headed back into North Carolina after the close of the Cherokee war, but either they returned to Virginia sometime later, or they'd never really left at all. Winston thought Daniel would like to know about it.

Daniel was mildly interested, but so overcome with disappointment at Winston's declination that he paid little heed. Tearing up the letter, he cast it to the ground, took up his rifle, and went off for two days of hunting.

That disappointed him, too. He found that the Yadkin country had become even more populated since he had left for Kentucky. Valleys where once he had hunted in isolation now held farmsteads and cattle pens and cornfields. It was downright disgusting.

Daniel came home, made one more visit to Richard Henderson, then announced to his family that the Boones were moving. They would head across the mountains into the big valley southeast of Clinch Mountain and northwest of the Holston range. There they would build a cabin and live where a man didn't have to worry about hitting a neighbor every time he spit out his back window.

Daniel's words were vehement. No one argued with him. Secretly, Rebecca wasn't eager to go, but she comforted herself with the fact that at least Daniel wasn't moving them to Florida, or off into Kentucky, or some other place terribly wild or distant.

They packed up their goods, said good-bye to friends and kinfolk, and by the end of 1771 were living on the far side of the mountains in a new settlement called Watauga. This was land Daniel had hunted while it was still empty wilderness. Now it, like the Yadkin country, was filling with people and cabins and cattle. But at least it wasn't nearly as crowded, and provided a far better base from which Daniel could conduct the special work that had led him there.

DANIEL'S LAST VISIT to Henderson had been impulsive but purposeful. He told Henderson that he was weary of life in Carolina and had no hope at all of making a good living there. If he couldn't yet go to live in Kentucky, he would at least move into the upper Tennessee region. From there he could begin to make contacts in earnest with the Cherokees, toward the proposed Kentucky purchase. Would Henderson back him and officially designate him his agent?

Henderson didn't disappoint him. Daniel came away from the meeting with a renewed sense of purpose. As far as he had it planned, his days east of the mountains were over. Daniel Boone would be a westerner from there on out, working toward one firm goal: the procurement and settlement of the rich Kentucky country.

From his little cabin in Watauga, Daniel spent much of 1772 and early 1773 in a mix of hunting, exploring, diplomacy, and farming, though he left the latter mostly to his sons. He traveled to the Cherokee towns and spent long days there, meeting the headmen and talking to them of the great plans of a man named Henderson, who was willing to pay them well for rights to the Big Meadow country far to the north. He became a friend of the Cherokees, hunting with them, impressing them with his woodcraft. The white hunter with the friendly manner and the wide mouth became a popular figure, and many north-ranging Cherokee hunters began leaving the trail of game long enough to seek out Daniel in his own cabin in Watauga. An image that implanted itself firmly in Daniel's mind was the sight of his beloved Jemima staring with eyes that seemed as big as her young, pretty face at the imposing figure of the prominent Cherokee known as Hanging Maw as he sat at the Boone table, talking quietly with her father. There were plenty of other Cherokee visitors to awe and impress her, too, one of them an exceptionally ugly man named Big Jim, who managed to look more menacing the more he smiled and who seemed more interested in food than in true friendship. Once, during one of Hanging Maw's stops, a young and good-looking Cherokee man named Crow visited. Daniel was both startled and amused to recognize Crow as one of the Powell Valley band who had robbed him and Squire of their furs, horses, and equipment after their return from Kentucky. Crow didn't act as if he recognized Daniel, however, and Daniel thought that perhaps he was wrong about the Indian's identity until he saw from Crow's actions that he was deaf in one ear. That confirmed that he was indeed one of the band of robbers. Daniel slightly resented having now to play host in his own home to someone who had done him such a wrong. Under the circumstances, though, he could do nothing else, and if all his diplomacy worked, the Cherokees would soon be ceding over a wealth far greater than that he and Squire had lost to them before.

During this period Daniel explored extensively, hunting bear all the way to the big French Lick on the Cumberland River, and visiting Kentucky with a party of hunters. He was disturbed by the infiltration of surveyors and land agents into the Kentucky country. When would Henderson make his move? With the population growing and settlement already pushed to the brink of the mountains, it would not take long for the swell to crest and Henderson's chance at Kentucky to be lost.

Others were also worried about the rising tide of land speculation, among them the royal governors, whose task it was to stifle illegal moves across the settlement boundary line. And more significantly still, the Indians were worried. They saw the mounting white population looming like a specter in the east, bound to break over the peaks and infiltrate their country. They found the flags of surveyors marking lands that before had been their hunting grounds.

Daniel's restlessness grew until he felt he might burst. He could no longer wait for Henderson. If Kentucky was to be gained, the time was now. He heard rumors that Virginia's Captain William Russell wanted to gather a party to move into Kentucky, but needed a guide. Someone who knew the country and the Indians. Someone who had explored Kentucky before and was ready to return for permanent settlement, and soon.

Someone precisely like Daniel Boone.

September, 1773

ISRAEL BOONE LEANED on his rifle and looked across the busy, crowded panorama of people, horses, carts, and livestock that stretched before him. At age fourteen he was strong and tall, muscled by long hours of work in the fields that provided the means for the Boone family's livelihood beyond the harvest his father brought in from the forests. He didn't generally mind farming much—certainly he didn't despise it as his father did—but farming had no rewards to offer that even came close to comparing with this. In all his days Israel had never felt such an excitement as was now filling him, as the family prepared to set out for Kentucky.

Kentucky! He could scarcely believe he was actually going there—to live, no less! His father's Kentucky stories had enthralled him for two years now; often he'd begged to hear them told, over and over again, until his mother could bear no more of it and demanded that storytelling cease. Kentucky had become a distant and fantastic land in Israel's mind. Soon it would become a real and present place, and he could hardly wait. A baby's cry caused Israel to turn his eyes toward his mother, who was seated on a blanket spread beneath a sycamore tree. Little Jesse Bryan Boone, born back in May to bring the number of Boone children to eight, not including Jesse and Jonathan, was fussing while Rebecca changed the "hippens," or diapers, that he had soddened. Israel grinned, but his grin faded as he saw his mother was crying right along with the baby.

A chill rippled over him, filling him with dread. What could be wrong? Why tears on such a happy day as this?

He remembered then that older folk don't always see the world through the same eyes as the young. His mother had been, at best, ambivalent about this move to Kentucky from the first time it was mentioned. But she hadn't cried—not until now. Was something else wrong?

Israel went to his mother as she finished with the hippens and put the baby to her breast to suckle. He knelt, rifle resting on its butt plate beside his right foot. "Ma, what's wrong?"

Rebecca swiped at a tear and tried to smile, but it was a weak effort. "Israel, do you not see the sadness that's happening here today?"

"Sadness . . . I don't see nothing sad, Ma. We're going to Kentucky together—even your own people are with us!"

"Not all of us will be together. Jesse and Jonathan will be going away from us here. They'll not live with us anymore. Had you not known that?"

He had known it, but until this moment the reality of it hadn't struck him. Jesse and Jonathan, now grown, had been like brothers to him, but they had opted not to join this migration to Kentucky with the Boones, Russells, Bryans, and a few others. He realized abruptly that he might never see his two cousins again, and was jolted.

"And look there, Israel. See your father and his mother? It's not only in my eyes there are tears."

Israel looked. Daniel Boone stood with his arms around his old mother, Sarah, hands stroking her thin, stooping shoulders. She was crying in quiet, shaking sobs, and streams of tears were running down Daniel's face from tight-shut eyes.

Israel had never seen his father cry in his life, and the sight of it now was no less than horrifying. "But why?" he asked his mother. "Why should they be sad?"

"Because this is likely the last day this side of the grave that mother and son will see each other's faces," Rebecca replied. "Your grandmother is old, Israel. In a few years, a few months, she will be dead, and most likely without having ever seen your father again after today."

Dead . . . Israel had never even thought of the possibility of his grandmother dying. Not even the death of Squire the patriarch had made him associate mortality with beloved old Sarah Boone. The sense of horror inside him grew. Now he understood why the old woman had insisted on making the first part of this journey with them. She hadn't wanted to part from her son and grandchildren.

"Ma, I . . ." Israel felt the urge to speak, yet could think of nothing to say. Turning, he stalked away, tears brimming in his own eyes.

In the course of a few moments his view of this Kentucky quest was all but reversed. He felt childish, foolish, for not realizing the sad aspects of the great adventure his father and Captain Russell had cooked up together. Until now, Israel had been swept away by the sheer excitement of it all, especially as the plan had grown. First his uncle Squire announced that he and his family would join the migration. Ben Cutbeard, married to one of Israel's cousins, signed on, and then several of the Bryan family, his mother's kin. There were other men going along, too, mostly old friends and hunting companions of his father's, such as the short-statured but very tough Michael Stoner, a German crack shot from Virginia.

All the talk and preparation had been fun and invigorating, and the fact that certain beloved people—Jesse and Jonathan, Grandmother Sarah, various others—would never see them again simply hadn't seemed real. Now, suddenly, it did, and Israel was crying.

He was past his tears when they called for the train of people, carts, packhorses, and livestock to begin moving forward again. But when Daniel called aside some of the men to fire a salute to his departing mother and those with her, a huge gush of emotion swelled inside Israel and he sobbed out loud, ashamed but unable to stop. He was grateful when they set off. It was easier to hide his crying when everyone was distracted by travel.

The babies of the party rode in big hickory baskets strung over the backs of horses, one basket on each side. There were no real wagons, the way into Kentucky not being wide enough to accommodate them, but packhorses, handcarts, and narrow horse-drawn barrows were abundant. Poultry was carried in big wicker cages on the backs of horses. Cattle, hogs, and extra horses were driven in a herd, under the control of James Boone and several others. The noise was enormous, and plenty of dust was raised, but for that Israel was grateful, because the ruckus and grit took his mind off sorrowful partings and reinvigorated his excitement.

Though at first they moved in a sort of long, imprecise clump, they soon spread out over a long distance because of the narrowness of the trail. Daniel and most of his family were in the lead party; James Boone, his companions, and the livestock were coming in behind them; and a third party of travelers followed. All in all, there were about fifty people in the party, including several slaves, a few of whom were with James to help tend the cattle and hogs.

For days they traveled, crossing the Clinch, going over the mountains, finally reaching the valley of the Powell. There a great excitement overwhelmed the group. Not far ahead was the Cumberland Gap—and just beyond, the forested, mountainous country that eventually gave way to the meadow country Daniel regarded as the true Kentucky.

On the night of October 9 Israel lay awake, unable to make himself calm down. He wasn't sure just why. Perhaps it was the closeness of Kentucky, the strain of the travel they had done so far, or the unusual day that had just passed. He and some of the other boys caught a young man of their party stealing from a pack belonging to another family. They told Daniel and some of the other men about the incident, and the thief was severely rebuked, though not put out of the party. The whole thing caused far more stir than it was worth. As Israel lay open-eyed, he decided that was what had him unsettled.

Finally, he did sleep and awakened hours later. Instinctively he felt it was nearing dawn. Someone had risen a little earlier and put more wood on the fire to knock off the nighttime chill. Grateful, Israel scooted his blankets a little closer to the blaze and settled down to sleep again.

He heard movement across the camp. Quietly, he craned his neck and took a look. Jakey Bledso, the fellow caught thieving, had risen and was creeping away from camp. At first Israel thought about standing and raising the alarm, figuring this fellow was up to no good. He stopped himself when he realized there might be nothing more to this than a man heading to the woods to relieve himself. Settling, Israel waited to see if he would return.

Five minutes or so later, the man had still not returned. Israel considered rising and going to tell his father, but the thought got mixed up with an image of himself walking up the side of a tree and milking a cow there. Then the treetop became the old stable back at the cabin on the Watauga, and it led straight into the bed loft where he and his brothers had slept. *I'm dreaming*, he thought, and that was the last sensible thought he had before sleep finally overcame him.

He woke up again when the dawn came but had forgotten about seeing Bledso leave. Almost an hour went by, filled with breakfasting and getting ready for the continuation of the march, when someone noted the empty blanket and asked what had become of thieving Jakey

Bledso. Then Israel remembered, and turned to search for his father to give him the information.

At that moment there was noise elsewhere, and someone called out Bledso's name. Israel saw a wild-looking figure—Bledso, racing in with pale face and wide eyes, hair blown crazily by the wind of running. In the center of camp he fell to his knees, leaning forward, gasping. "They're . . . they're . . . all of 'em . . ." He was too winded to get out his words.

Daniel approached and knelt beside him. "Catch your wind, Jakey, then tell us."

Bledso took in three or four good gasps and calmed himself just enough to speak.

"They're dead, Mr. Boone . . . Indians . . . killed them."

Israel's eyes widened, and he felt a great ache rise in his stomach.

"Indians killed who, Jake?"

"All of them . . . killed them all, I think." He gasped a couple of more times. "I came through . . . where the herds is . . . still was dark . . . saw bodies, cut up bad they was . . ."

Daniel rose, face like granite. "Squire," he said, "go back, take a look."

"I'll go too, Pap," Israel heard himself say.

Daniel wheeled on him. "No! Stay right here, boy—you understand?"

Taken aback by the ferocity of his father's reply, Israel nodded and backed away. He felt very much the child right then. Looking back the way Bledso came, he could think only one thing: James. Over and over again the name of his brother passed through his mind. James . . . James!

He wondered why his father had sent Uncle Squire back to investigate rather than going himself. James was his own son, and he might be hurt, or even dead! Resentment toward Daniel Boone rose, until he stepped back and watched what his father was doing. His face an ashen gray, Daniel moved among the people, giving direction to them in preparation for an Indian attack. Israel realized then that even at a time of personal fear and possible great loss, his father thought first of the people who were in his charge. Israel felt ashamed then of his own ill feelings.

No Indians came, but it wasn't long before Squire came riding back, his expression and pallor telling the story before he spoke. Israel burst into tears, as did the other Boone children. Daniel Boone told them to hush, but his voice broke as he did, and tears came to his own eyes.

Rebecca walked up to Squire and put her hands on his shoulders. "My boy?" she asked.

"Yes," Squire whispered. "God, I'm sorry. He's gone, Rebecca. He's gone."

Daniel heard it too and closed his eyes. The sound of cries and wails rose through the camp. William Russell appeared, coming in behind Squire.

He, too, had a son back with the cattle and had gone in himself to see what happened. He rode up to Daniel and dismounted, tried to say something, then broke into loud sobs.

"I'm going to go to him," Daniel said to Rebecca. "I'm going to bury my son."

"Wait," Rebecca said. "Wait, husband."

She went to the packhorses and dug out a pair of linen sheets, which she gave to Daniel. "Don't bury my boy in the bare dirt," she said. "Wrap him before you lay him under."

"I will," Daniel said. "I'll wrap him good, so's he don't . . ." His voice faded out. Israel stood staring at him, thinking, *God, he's old.* And right then he looked it. Looked as old and tired and sad as the mountains themselves.

THE MIGRATION ENDED after the dead—six of them—were buried. The travelers had not reached Cumberland Gap. No one had the will to go on, though Daniel feebly pleaded with them to continue. He'd sold his lands, left his possessions behind. There was nothing for him except Kentucky.

He did not argue hard, his spirit having left him. Even as he pleaded to go on, Daniel hardly heard his own words. All he could think of was James as a little child, huddled beneath his cloak on winter hunts back on the Yadkin. James's dead body, marked with the signs of Indian torture, seemed unreal to him. A damaged sculpture of wax, pale and cold. The body he wrapped in Rebecca's sheets and buried seemed to have no connection to the firstborn son he had loved so dearly.

The description of what had happened came from a slave named Adam, who'd managed to hide in driftwood nearby and watch the terrible scene. The Indians had come upon the encamped herdsmen with the first light of dawn and shot them with no warning. Both James Boone and the Russell boy died hard deaths, first falling wounded, then dying slowly under the carving knives of their attackers. James cried out for his mother before he died.

And he called a name, too: Big Jim.

Daniel felt ill when he heard that. Big Jim . . . a Cherokee who had been his guest, eaten at his table. James had died at the hands of a man he knew. Daniel imagined the ugly, grinning Indian leaning over his helpless son, and felt the greatest hate he had ever experienced toward another human being.

A friend of Russell's offered the Boones a cabin back near the Castle's Woods settlement where Russell lived. With nowhere else to go, Daniel accepted. They spent a hard, sad winter there, Rebecca frequently weeping for her slain boy, and Daniel overwhelmed with a sense of guilt. If not for his endless drive to go to Kentucky, James would still be alive. He couldn't help but feel responsible.

Even so, Kentucky still attracted him. With all it had cost him, he still longed to go there. He didn't dare speak of it to Rebecca, but when he looked at her, he saw that she already knew.

He hunted and trapped along the Clinch River, seeking healing in the solitude while he hunted meat for his family and pelts to put a few coins in his pouch. The meat was sufficient, but typically for Daniel Boone, the coins were far too few to cover his living expenses. He began to slide into debt at Castle's Woods just as he had along the Yadkin.

In the early spring Daniel set out alone along the same route his failed expedition to Kentucky had followed. The closer he came to the place where James had died, the deeper grew the sorrow that had been with him since October of the year before. The day was cloudy and dark; a storm was coming in. With his heart like lead in his chest, he found the place where he had buried his son.

God in heaven, he thought, *the wolves have dug in the grave*. Rebecca would never stand for that. He knelt and began gouging at the disturbed dirt with a spike he had in his saddlebag. Overhead the sky grew darker and thunder rumbled. At length the slow digging exposed the body of James, wrapped up in a sheet with the corpse of Henry Russell, Captain Russell's son. With a sense of dread he pulled back the sheets. James's features had decayed beyond recognition, but his light hair distinguished him from the body of Henry Russell. He was relieved that the wolves had not dug deeply enough to reach the bodies.

For several minutes Daniel stared at the body of his firstborn. Tears flowed abundantly. As lightning flashed to the earth in the distance, he covered James's corpse with saddle blankets he had brought along and reburied it more deeply. He laid Henry Russell away in a separate grave, then covered both graves with stone and wood to keep foraging animals from bothering them again.

Weary, he sat on the ground, staring blankly as rain fell softly upon him. He had never felt as empty and sad as at that moment. Always he had thought of himself as in control of his own life and destiny, but now things were different. He felt now like a leaf in a stream, being carried along every turn and twist, with no means of determining where he would go or what would happen to him.

He recalled the nightmare he had suffered in Kentucky after finding the old, dying Indian. Vividly he remembered the words the image of his father had spoken to him in that dream: *My boy, there are those of your own who will take their own journey out of this dark land too, and the heart will surely be torn from you.*

Had it been a prophetic dream, warning him in advance that James would die? It felt so—yet it couldn't be. James had died before he reached the "dark land" of Kentucky. Just a dream, that's all it had been. Just a dream.

Sitting there, he traced in his memory the days behind him, watching his life pass as if viewed through a veil of gloom. Even his happiest moments now seemed tainted with a pervading darkness. Looming in the background of every image was tragedy, loss, death.

He thought of Nate Meriwether. How long now since he had seen him, even given him much thought? Was Nate even living, or had his sense of guilt over the sad fate of his Nora finally destroyed him? Would he ever lay eyes on his old friend again? The thoughts sank Daniel even deeper into depression. It seemed to him that the sorrows and tragedy that overwhelmed Nate and his relations were but particularly vivid examples of the ultimate sorrow that awaited every life, including Daniel Boone's.

During the bright days of his youth Daniel had sometimes felt that the world was a thin veneer scarcely managing to hide a reality too bright, marvelous, and beautiful to comprehend. Now that happy notion seemed a sham, the very opposite of the truth. At this moment reality seemed a mocking thing, with sorrow rather than joy at its heart.

Eventually he moved some distance away and made a camp, but rest would not come. The storm struck, hammering the forest with rain and making the trees moan in the wind. When it faded away, Daniel fancied he heard movement and voices—Indians, hunters? It didn't matter. He had no desire for human company. Rising, he slipped the hobbles from his horse, took up his rifle, and rode away into the depths of the black forest.

Part 3

Conquest

"Reconstruction of Boonesboro" undated photo from Miriam & Ira D. Wallach Collection,

CHAPTER 24

March, 1775

DANIEL BOONE HEFTED his belt ax and hacked a mark in the side of a big straight-trunked poplar, then paused to catch his breath. From behind came the sound of chopping, of brush breaking, of occasional trees falling into the woods, splintering branches and saplings into pieces as they descended. Removing his flop hat to wipe sweat from his brow, Daniel drew in a deep breath and thought that now he had a clearer idea of how hard the advance woodsmen had worked making a way for the armies of Braddock, and then Forbes, back in his younger wagon-driving days.

Fact was, he thought, *they had it harder than us. At least the way we follow here has the semblance of a trail already, and sometimes much better than what we had when we hit the buffalo roads*. And he knew this route, having followed it more than once now into these wilds of Kentucky.

A yell and loud cracking noise made him turn. Another great tree crashed to the earth about two hundred yards behind him, rousing a weary, low-volume cheer from the party of ax men who had felled it. That had been perhaps the largest tree felled yet. For the most part they had managed to go around the really big timber and hack their road through the brush or saplings.

Road . . . the name hardly fit most of the narrow trace Daniel and his ax men were leaving behind them. Only when passing through natural, open glens or along the larger game trails and buffalo paths did this wilderness way really qualify as a road. Much of the way would be impassable for a freight wagon, and even a narrow cart would have a hard time of it at spots. Daniel had to smile ironically as he imagined how Richard Henderson would gripe and swear when he and his party actually traveled this trace. No doubt he would have some choice commentary for Daniel when they finally reunited at the end.

Daniel advanced, rifle in one hand, belt ax in the other. The day seemed unusually warm and humid for so early in the season, weather to make working up a sweat aggravatingly easy. They had been in damp cane country for the last few days until entering this belt of forest. It had given them respite from the canebrakes, but no break from hard work.

Blazing off a mark on another tree, Daniel took secret, guilty comfort in the fact that his part of the job was somewhat less strenuous than the work being done behind him. As leader and "pilot" of Henderson's ax men, his main duty was to blaze the route, keep his eyes open for Indian sign, and bring in daily meat to feed the hungry ax men. The bulk of the actual clearing of the way was left to the thirty-some-odd ax wielders behind him.

Actually, the intensity of the work for the ax men varied greatly from place to place along the way. Sometimes there was little required of them but to score an occasional blaze mark on a tree alongside a good game trail; at those times they covered miles at great speed. Other times they had to cut away groves of trees, slice a passage through canebrakes, hack through vast mats of vine that grew as thick as a man's waist, or pile logs across streams too deep to ford. At those times they moved very slowly. The swampy areas made for the hardest going; there was little that could be done to make passage of those mucky, stagnant stretches anything better than a hard trial for man or beast.

They had begun their task about the tenth of March, starting out from a stockade called the Blockhouse, near the Long Island of the Holston River. The advancing line of the road moved from its origin at the Long Island, through the Clinch range at Moccasin Gap, past the lowlands of Little Moccasin Creek, and on to Troublesome Creek. It crossed the Clinch River, ran along a creek beyond to the Natural Tunnel, across a rise and into the valley of the Clinch's north fork. The natural curves and contours of the land set the course through Powell Mountain at Kane's Gap, over Wallen Ridge, and into Powell Valley. There the route passed Martin's Station, which had been destroyed by the Cherokees since Daniel had seen it last and was now being rebuilt, and on to the landmark White Rocks and Cumberland Gap. Daniel was glad to get past that region, where James had died a year and a half back. He could almost feel the presence of his lost boy there, and the effect was devastatingly sad.

Beyond Cumberland Gap the road crossed through the Yellow Creek valley two miles beyond, then ran on to the Cumberland River about thirteen miles farther. There it joined the famous and ancient Warriors' Path, which it would follow for fifty miles or so, all the way to the mouth of the Scioto River. At the Scioto it would diverge from the north-running Indian route and bear more westwardly along a buffalo trail to the Hazel Patch region and the Rockcastle River. A further game road that followed a creek and passed through a gap would take the trail makers to Otter Creek, which flowed into the Kentucky River. And there, at the creek mouth, this road in the wilderness would finally reach its end.

Daniel blazed another tree. The cutters were well behind him now, working hard to keep pace. Slipping the short ax back into his belt, he dug a bit of jerked buffalo from his pouch and chewed on it, mentally retracing their route and seeking to get his bearings on their exact location. The best he could judge, they were near the end of the mountainous country. Before long the hard-driven men would have the pleasure of seeing the first of the rolling, open meadow country, where the going should be much easier and the end would almost be in sight.

The end. Daniel anticipated it joyfully. He had waited for this moment a long time. The effort to move to Kentucky, so tragically aborted back in seventy-three, seemed to be off to a much better start in seventy-five. This time Daniel wasn't acting alone, as he and William Russell had the first time. He had the backing of a land company, the support and employment of Richard Henderson, and the advantage of a written agreement freshly signed by the Cherokees themselves, giving Richard Henderson ownership rights to the best Kentucky lands, and right-of-way to allow him to enter them. This wilderness was no longer Indian country, the treaty declared. It was the property of Richard Henderson's Transylvania Company and open for settlement.

That the Cherokees had a slender claim at best to any right to sell Kentucky, that the northern tribes would certainly not consider any Cherokee-made bargains binding upon them, and that even the government of Virginia, in whose legal domain the Kentucky region lay, strongly opposed Richard Henderson's plans, were facts Daniel tried not to think about too much. He was in Kentucky to stay, and that was what mattered. His dream was becoming reality. And there was too much hard work to be done to waste time fretting over the eternal disagreements among Indians and the legal nit-picking of powdered-wig bluebloods back east.

Daniel was pleased with the tireless effort his men had put forth through inhospitable terrain. After fording the Cumberland River and reaching the Rockcastle, they'd come upon country filled with brush still dead from the winter. For twenty miles or so they struggled through that barren countryside before hitting tangled cane lands for another thirty. It was hard labor forging through the thick stalks, and Daniel had made every effort to minimize the difficulties by moving from game trail to clearing to open glen to buffalo trace, a course that sometimes zigzagged crazily in the short run, but which utilized every natural advantage the terrain offered.

Before long the ax men caught up, and Daniel declared it was time for rest and food, news welcomed by all except, perhaps, his daughter Susannah, who had married Will Hays, one of the ax men, only a few days before the road making had begun. Susy Boone had come along with her father and new husband as the cook for the company, a big job for a small-framed, slender young woman. So far she had managed very well, cooking most of the meat her father killed into fatty stews that satisfied the raging hunger of the workers.

That night the men seemed more weary than normal, eating in silence, not even bothering to joke and cajole one another as usual. Only when Daniel announced that the hardest part of the work was nearly behind did they show much spirit. Smiles broke out, and banter. It didn't last long; exhaustion quickly took over. Daniel went to sleep with a now familiar chorus of rough snores rising all around him. As usual the group slept in a sequence of small camps spread back along the trail they were making. It was safer that way in case Indian attack came; any attackers would have to spread themselves thin to get to all of them.

The next day brought them into reeds and cane again as they encountered what Daniel was increasingly sure would be the final stretch of rough country. Sure enough, before the day was through they reached a pass that gave them a view of a very different kind of country beyond: vast clover meadows, rolling hills, beautiful plains. They would move much more quickly from there on out.

On the night of March 24 Daniel lay down again for sleep. Nearby was his brother Squire, noticeably more muscular because of the long days of ax swinging. They were close to their destination now. It was a good feeling. Squire and Daniel talked for a few minutes about the progress of the day, then closed their eyes for rest.

They slept very soundly. Daniel hardly stirred until near dawn, when something made him bolt upright and suck in his breath, terrified. Indians. He knew it instantly, even before his eye caught the rapid movement of the attackers in the dim light of the nearly burned-out fire. A loud, ragged fusillade of gunfire erupted; he heard someone scream.

Daniel grabbed his rifle, from which dangled his powder horn, shot pouch, and moccasins. He plunged into the nearest foliage, glancing around in time to see Squire doing the same in an opposite direction.

Daniel could see little of what happened, but he could tell from sound alone that the entire camp was in panic. There were shouts, shots, thuds, crashes, terrible screams. Advancing to the edge of the thicket, Daniel picked out a target and fired, but without success. A moment later someone approached him from behind, and he wheeled, seeing only the dark outline of a figure. He was raising his rifle when he heard Squire say in an urgent whisper, "I left my powder and bullets in camp . . . can you spare me some?"

"Course I can—help yourself." Squire had already fired off the load in his rifle. Quickly he reloaded out of Daniel's supplies, and Daniel did the same. The gunfire continued, and dark, quick figures, tomahawks in hand, flashed like living shadows between them and the light of the red-coal fire.

SO NOW IT HAPPENED. Daniel had hoped that his venture could go through without interference, but once again it was obvious the original exploiters of Kentucky's rich lands were not going to stand by and allow their prized hunting ground to be infiltrated by settlers without resistance.

For Daniel, the machinations that had led up to this settlement effort had started in earnest about the end of 1774. The terrible pain that had lingered with Daniel since the death of James had faded to more bearable proportions by that point, and there was plenty of intervening activity to take his mind off the tragedy. Indian warfare, for one thing—a conflict that became known as Lord Dunmore's War, after Virginia's Governor Dunmore, who had ordered the campaign. Daniel was called into service as commander of forts along the Clinch River, and had entered Kentucky early in the conflict to warn surveyors in danger of being caught unawares in the coming trouble.

Dunmore's War brought violence to the Clinch country, but Daniel came through it unscathed—and with his name known more widely, and his reputation as a leader greatly enhanced. He also came out of the war with the commissioned rank of captain.

An October 10 battle at Point Pleasant, on the Ohio River, brought the war to an end when the Shawnees, successful at Point Pleasant, but facing the prospect of long, overwhelming warfare thereafter, opted for peace. Daniel, not a participant in the Point Pleasant battle, was released from service in November, and a new prospect arose to gain his attention.

Richard Henderson's term as Superior Court justice in North Carolina ended in 1773. With the close of the Dunmore hostilities, he was ready to implement his old scheme as soon as possible and called on Daniel to help.

The timing was good all around. The end of Daniel's military term freed him to set out again for the Cherokee country, and the submission of the Shawnees made the opening of Kentucky seem all at once much more feasible. So Daniel met again with Cherokee headmen and diplomats, such as the brilliant, diminutive Attakullakulla, and blunt-featured, stocky Oconostota. "Carolina Dick" Henderson, he had told them, was now ready to do what had been talked about before. Already he was laying in store many good supplies for his Cherokee brothers, to be given to them in payment for their agreement to give him legal ownership of the lands of Kentucky and the Cumberland River. Daniel did his best work, playing on his natural understanding of the Indian mind and the respect that his own woodsman's prowess had earned from them.

His blandishments paid off. A delegation of Cherokees, led by Attakullakulla, had agreed to meet Henderson and Boone in the western mountains of North Carolina and examine a sampling of the goods that would be paid for the land. The samples impressed them. When 1775 dawned, plans for a formal treaty negotiation were in place, Henderson was already advertising for settlers interested in Kentucky lands that were "about to be purchased," and Daniel Boone was setting up a body of ax men who would cut a passable road to the planned point of settlement at the mouth of Otter creek on the Kentucky River.

In March the Cherokees came to the flats of Sycamore Shoals, near the cabin the Boones had occupied while living in Watauga, and began the formal negotiation of the largest real estate transaction anyone there had ever participated in. Henderson plied the Cherokees with liquor and presents and kept the six wagon loads of trade goods constantly in view, but feelings about his proposal were mixed among the Cherokees. While Attakullakulla and others clearly leaned toward the agreement, some, particularly Attakullakulla's own son, Tsiyu-gansini, or Dragging Canoe, vehemently opposed it.

Dragging Canoe had managed to rouse a burst of chilling doubt even in Daniel Boone himself, when the brave rose at one point in the negotiations and told Daniel that any purchasers of Kentucky would find it a good land, but dark and bloody, a land over which a dark cloud would hang. The words stirred back to Daniel's mind the old dream of his father warning him that kin of his own would die on Kentucky soil, and for a few minutes all the pain of James's slaying and the dreadful prospect of other such losses all but overwhelmed Daniel's desire to go on with the plan.

But Dragging Canoe had turned away and left the treaty ground, and Daniel had gone on. Well before the deal was completed, he was at the Blockhouse of the Long Island, assembling his crew of ax men. They had no time to lose. As soon as the treaty was signed—there appeared no reasonable doubt by then that it would be signed—Henderson would assemble a settlement party and begin the trek along Boone's road. By March 10 the ax men had all been assembled, and the actual hewing, blazing, and clearing out of the road began.

And all had gone well—up until this early morning, when the camp rang with gunshots and cries, and the predawn dark grew fearsome and fraught with mortal danger.

THE SOUNDS OF BATTLE gave way to a silence broken only by the moans of the wounded. Daniel strode through the camp, his face as gray as the ashes of the smoldering fire. On the ground before him lay the dead, burned body of a black man named Saul, the slave of Captain William Twitty of North Carolina, one of the ax men. He had been struck by a bullet in the initial attack and died even as his body pitched over into the campfire, where it lay sizzling and smoldering until the fighting was done.

Sad-faced, Daniel stepped across the body and went to the place where Captain Twitty himself lay in great suffering, both knees shattered by rifle balls. Twitty had been asleep in his tent when the Indians came. Two burst in upon him as he lay wounded, but a bulldog that Twitty kept with him wherever he went leaped to his master's defense. The brave dog drove away the Indians, but only at the cost of a tomahawk blow. Now the dead creature lay near the man whose life it had saved. If ever Daniel thought an animal seemed noble, it was this bulldog.

Young Felix Walker moaned and writhed nearby, drawing Daniel's attention. He went over to the young man and knelt. "Try not to move too much, good fellow. You'll fare well if you rest and let yourself heal."

The truth was, Daniel didn't know if Walker would survive. He had been wounded in the hip and saved himself only by crawling away into the brush in the confusion of battle. If his wounds festered, there was no guarantee he would live. Daniel concocted an herbal ointment for the wounds in an attempt to save him.

Daniel conferred privately with Squire. They had lost camp supplies and horses to the Indians, and several men had been robbed of their personal baggage. Another attack seemed likely. The best response at the moment would be the erection of a stockade both to protect the wounded and to provide a defensible place if a second attack occurred.

Daniel ordered the stockade built on a nearby hilltop. It became a makeshift hospital for Walker, and a place of eternal rest for Twitty, who died a few days later, and was buried within the seven-foot-high walls.

Hunters were sent out to find food and discovered that other white men were also in the region and had also been attacked. These were led by Captain James Harrod, who had earlier put in a small settlement on the Salt River and was now returning to that place. Two of Harrod's party had been killed by the raiding Shawnees.

Days passed, and Walker continued to hover between life and death. With the help of his new son-in-law, a decent wordsmith, Daniel composed a letter to Richard Henderson, who was advancing behind on the trail, and sent it back by a courier. Daniel told Henderson of the "misfortune" that had struck them and that he had directed all the party to converge at the mouth of Otter Creek for the sake of safety.

A portion of the letter stated:

My advise to you, sir, is to come or send as soon as possible. Your company is desired greatly, for the people are very uneasy, but are willing to stay and venture their lives with you. Now is the time to flusterate the Indians intentions and keep the country, whilst we are in it. If we give way to them now, it will ever be the case.

DANIEL LAY ON HIS BACK, looking at the underside of the temporary tent roof stretched across his little cabin shelter. Fire flickered in the fireplace, some of it escaping out the unfinished stick chimney, some of it streaming back into the cabin to cloud the air. Daniel didn't mind; he was used to the smoke, and a snap of unseasonably cold weather made the fire a necessity.

Many days had passed since he'd sent the letter to Henderson, and affairs at the would-be settlement—already called Boone's Fort by the men building it—remained uncertain. The Indian attack struck fear in several, causing them to flee back toward the Tennessee country. Daniel could picture Richard Henderson's frantic reaction to the sight of frightened people streaming out of the very land he was entering, telling disturbing stories and urging everyone to get out before it was too late.

Rolling over, Daniel sighed wearily. He had never been through such an exhausting time in his life. It was hard on mind and body to deal with the daily strains of settlement making. Problems everywhere, it seemed.

Some matters had turned out well, he reminded himself. Felix Walker survived, and now was moved by tandem litter to the convergence site at Otter Creek. No major Indian attack came, despite continued harassment and even the death of one more man. Those who had fled were overreacting. The stockade was going up, however slowly. And the men had already seen some evidence of the lush richness of Kentucky in the number of buffalo grazing around the big lick at the creek mouth when they arrived there, and the fat turkeys that seemed to strut everywhere.

Henderson's colony in the wilderness was becoming a reality, bit by bit. If only they could hold out until their roots were firmly planted in Kentucky, there would be ample reward. The acreage Henderson had pledged for Daniel in payment for his work would make him a man of some means at last.

Holding out would be the hard part. Though most of the men held him in great respect, evidenced most clearly by the fact they'd named the settlement after him, Daniel knew he was no unassailable authority figure to them. Typical of frontiersmen, the Boone's Fort men considered themselves kings over their own lives. They might do what Daniel told them, might not. As often as not, it was the latter. Sometimes Daniel could find only a handful willing to work on the stockade; everyone else had other affairs to mind, and simply refused.

A few disliked Daniel outright. Colonel Richard Callaway, one of the road makers with a slightly aristocratic background, seemed to resent Daniel's leadership from the outset, and was now moving in the background like a serpent in shadows. As a man who had held higher militia rank than Daniel ever had, he clearly despised being under Daniel's authority on the way up from the Tennessee country. Now, Daniel figured, he was stirring others to discontent.

Daily, Daniel grew more eager for Henderson to arrive; perhaps his recognized authority would overcome all the vying and sniping that had begun to occur. With all the obstacles still facing them, they couldn't afford to be divided.

Particularly aggravating was the stubborn refusal of some to stand guard at night. Every man seemed either too weary from his labors, or too preoccupied with scouting out good land sites, or too convinced that he was bearing more of the brunt than his partners, to cooperate for the safety of them all. Daniel was forced to the conclusion that the human race would do quite well if it wasn't so burdened with human nature.

But such difficulties would pass, he figured. When everyone was on site, when an assembly could be called and rules set down, squabbles would decline. And then, eventually, he would be free to go fetch his family. Rebecca Boone would at last become a resident of the country her husband had longed for through so many years. A country whose attempted settlement had already cost her her firstborn child.

Daniel knew that Rebecca was not eager to be a Kentuckian. She had not stood in the way of his work with Henderson or tried to dissuade him out of his Kentucky dream . . . but still he knew. He was eager to get her there and show her that Kentucky could be a fine place, the best place, to live. She had to reach that conclusion, simply had to. Daniel wanted life there to be happy and family relations cordial.

He pinned every hope he had on Kentucky. If Kentucky failed him, there might never be another chance for him to find the life he wanted for himself and his own. He would work hard to make this settlement grow and thrive, and to make Rebecca come to love it as much as she loved him.

CHAPTER 25

DANIEL DUCKED OUT of the doorway of Richard Henderson's cabin and strode a little faster than normal across the clearing in front of it. At that moment Squire Boone happened to be peering down the length of a long, thin sapling pole he intended to use as a hoe handle, to see if it was straight enough. Daniel strode into his sights, as it were, and Squire lifted the pole to his shoulder like a rifle and shouted "Bang!" so loud that Daniel was startled.

"Squire, what the devil? You turning child again and playing rifle-gun with sticks?"

Squire lowered the pole and laughed. "What's the matter, brother? You look sour as turned milk."

Daniel veered over to Squire's side and thumbed secretively toward Henderson's cabin. "Him again. Can't get a lick of help out of the man sometimes. Sits in there and thinks big thoughts and leaves the troublesome matters for me to work out. You ought to hear some of the things he says about his people here! 'Rascals,' he calls them." He paused. "Of course, I can't blame him much, the way folks fuss and feud around here."

Squire gave a sympathetic nod. Indeed, there had been little harmonizing of the dissonant atmosphere around Fort Boone since Henderson had arrived in mid-April.

All the pomp and showmanship of the great real estate transaction at Sycamore Shoals had given way to a gritty reality once the festivity was past. The journey to Kentucky had been hard going for the former Carolina jurist and his settlement party. First the party was forced to abandon its wagons at Martin's Station because of the poor quality of the road from that point on. In the meantime other independent settlers with no sense of subservience to the Transylvania Company came swarming past, going on through the Cumberland Gap while Henderson was stalled at Martin's. Then snow had come and delayed Henderson further.

When at last the abandoned wagons were safely sheltered at Martin's, the baggage and supplies were shifted onto pack horses, and Henderson's settlers were on their way again, they had faced the dismay of encountering deserters from the Boone party, and many of the independent immigrants who had come by while they were stranded at Martin's, now coming back again, faces white with fear and tongues wagging about Indians.

Fearing that Daniel himself would give up and bring back his party—effectively ending the entire venture—Henderson sent his wagon master, William Cocke, forward with word that the settlement party was on its way. As payment for his risky messengering, Cocke was promised ten thousand acres of good Transylvania Company land. Henderson was so dismayed with fear that his dream was about to crumble that he had actually wept aloud while urging Cocke to make the journey.

Cocke was a capable woodsman, and made it through to Boone's Fort on April 17; Henderson and the others arrived on the twentieth, coincidentally Henderson's fortieth birthday. Henderson's tears had dried up by then. He had reached his destination. When Daniel led his men in firing a salute to the arriving party, Henderson beamed with joy. His coming was an important event, and he knew it.

In May word reached the isolated settlers about another important event that had occurred far away, the day just before Henderson had ridden in. In New England, colonial militiamen had fought with British soldiers at Lexington and Concord, launching a revolution that ultimately would have a far greater impact on the Transylvania settlers than Henderson's arrival ever could.

Initially, Daniel was relieved to have Henderson on hand. As overall head of the enterprise, maybe he could gain better control of the group than Daniel had. Henderson got off to a promising start by quickly making several major decisions, such as shifting the location of the stockade by a few hundred yards, opening a store stocked with the goods he had brought, and throwing out orders right and left. There was a decent response: trees felled, lots cleared, the new stockade beginning to take shape within a week of Henderson's arrival. Then the novelty of it all began to wear off, and it was back to business as usual. The later arrivals grumbled to the earlier ones that all the choice land had been snatched up, some fussed over the fact that Henderson had moved the fort location, and others fought for a public lottery for property—then complained when the lots they drew didn't suit them.

All these things Squire Boone knew as well as his brother. But they didn't affect him as much, because most of the weight of discontent fell onto Daniel's shoulders. Especially now. Lately Henderson had grown discouraged and took to drinking more than he should, closing himself up in his cabin to brood. When Daniel came to him with some question or another, as he had today, he often came out again with no good answer. Daniel found it irksome. Henderson had declared his appreciation for Daniel's holding out in the midst of danger while awaiting the settlement party's arrival, but lately he hadn't actually shown much admiration by exerting firm leadership. But did people complain about it to Henderson? Very little. They poured out their woes and complaints to Daniel.

"Cheer yourself, Dan," Squire said. "This is a new country. We've stirred the stream, and it will take time for the silt to settle."

"I sometimes wonder if it's settling at all," Daniel replied. "Seems that every day there's something new to kick it all back up again."

"And so it will go until—well, until it stops, whenever the good Lord decides that will be," Squire said.

It did go on, but so did progress, however slowly. Other settlements were taking shape around the region—somewhat disturbing to Henderson, because they had an uncertain relationship at best with his Transylvania Company, and some of them, such as Harrodsburg, were led by men who had actually occupied the Kentucky country before Henderson had got there. Besides Henderson's settlement, there were three other major settlements in the area: Boiling Springs, Logan's Station, and Harrodsburg.

In May a general convention was called beneath the spreading boughs of a great elm, and delegates were chosen to represent the various settlements. Laws were enacted addressing matters ranging from the day-to-day system of government to conservation measures aimed at preserving game and range land, and bills to improve horse breeding and to ensure that the Sabbath was not broken. The conservation laws were pressed hardest by Daniel and Squire, both of whom were delegates from Boonesborough. Already hunters noted a sharp decrease in the game that originally had frolicked without fear around the river and salt licks.

The convention ended with the symbolic ritual of "seism," in which a chunk of turf was handed to Henderson by John Farrar, who had served as attorney for the Cherokees at Sycamore Shoals. The act symbolized the official taking of land ownership by Henderson and his company.

With the lawmaking convention behind, Daniel felt much better about the status of the new settlement. Now the place felt like a real settlement. It had form and law and an aura of permanence. It was now being called Boonesborough—Henderson had preferred a less militaristic name than Boone's Fort—and its stockade stood nearly complete, except for a few places where palisades were not yet in place and gates not yet finished. It took up about an acre, and had blockhouses at each corner, one of which Henderson was making his home and official headquarters. About thirty cabins stood around and within its walls. The Kentucky River ran about fifty feet away from one wall.

The time had come for Daniel to fetch Rebecca and the family. And he needed to hurry. He had left her pregnant back at the old homeplace, and if he got there in time, he could see the birth of his newest child.

In early June he set out. With him were several of the settlement's younger men, who would travel as far as Martin's Station to pick up salt supplies and other such goods, stored there when Henderson had abandoned his wagons. Daniel would go on farther, to his kin. Richard Callaway would go on, too, parting from Daniel to go fetch his own people in Virginia. With Callaway would be another man, several years younger than him or Daniel. His name was James Carrick. Like Callaway, he had left a family back in Virginia. And, like Daniel Boone, he had left his wife pregnant, but her pregnancy had started much earlier. By the time Jim Carrick returned to his bride, she would have a new babe in her arms, whether a son or a daughter he did not yet know.

FROM THE MOMENT he saw Rebecca's face, Daniel knew that all was not well. Her features were pale and puffy, splotched with red, and her ankles, wrists, and fingers were terribly swollen. Even the swell of her midsection looked outsized and misshapen. So startling was her appearance that Daniel had scarcely been able to hide his shock behind the smile he forced out.

Rebecca's smile was not forced. She wept with happiness to see Daniel, her happiness and relief so sincere that it brought tears to his own eyes. As he held her, he realized how much he had missed her and how the passing years only made her more dear. Too much time had gone by since they were wed back on the Yadkin. Daniel was now twoscore years old, and Rebecca was only a few years behind him. How much had he given her so far, besides debts, endless uncertainty, and worries? Children . . . that was the only treasure he had been able to provide, and even then it was to her that the pain of childbirth and most of the trials of homekeeping had fallen.

"When the baby is born, we'll be together," Daniel told her. "Kentucky is becoming a settled place. Boonesborough, they call our settlement. Boonesborough! You'll be living in a place that bears our name."

"I'm glad," she said, smiling again. It only made her look more weak and wan.

The baby was born in late July, a difficult birth for mother and child. Daniel realized that with her age advancing, bearing children was growing dangerous for Rebecca. They named their newest son William and prayed fervently that he would survive those first difficult weeks, but such was not to be. He was a sickly child, weak and without energy, and within a few days of his birth Daniel and Rebecca had the heartbreak of laying him to rest in a small grave. Rebecca became lost in grief and fell ill for weeks. Daniel struggled to keep his emotions from breaking free at inopportune times, and distracted himself by setting up a new party of soon-to-be Kentucky settlers.

News of Indian dangers in Kentucky kept leaking out, and Daniel found few families willing to sign on. Those who did were mostly single, young, reckless men who were eager for the challenge, their eyes on land, wealth, and influence for themselves that only a new country could provide. Seventeen such eager bucks signed on, along with three families. About fifty people in all were in the group that finally set out under Daniel's guidance in August.

Rebecca was silent and still looked pale and sickly. Daniel wondered if he was doing right, moving her at such a weak and weary time. He decided that he was, mostly because since little William's death she had brooded far too much and lingered far too often beside his grave. He had to get her away from there.

A short way into Kentucky, Daniel overtook Jim Carrick, traveling alone with the family he had reclaimed. Daniel chided him severely for taking such a rash chance by traveling without more company; he ought to have waited for Callaway's party or joined some other larger band of travelers for safety's sake.

Carrick hung his head. "You're right, Mr. Boone, like you generally are. I've always had a faultish manner of taking risks that's too risky to be risked, you know."

Daniel fought back the smile that was trying to reach his lips. He was ever amused by Carrick's odd use of language. The man was always twisting words around in ways Daniel would have never thought of, making even the most somber pronouncements sound funny.

"It has come out well for you this time, at least," Daniel replied. "You can travel with us the rest of the distance. I see your babe there—boy or girl? I can't tell in the swaddle."

"A boy," Carrick replied. "Name of William. A good name, William, and that's why we named him that."

Daniel felt a shudder of sorrow. "Aye," he said. "It is a good name—the same name we gave to our little one."

"I'd like to see your boy. Where he be?"

"He's dead," Daniel replied tersely. "He lived only a few days."

"Oh . . . I'm fearsome sorry."

"Obliged for your sympathy."

"I know the losing of babes right well. My Phebe, she's had a passel of them die afore or just after their borning, and that's why, matter of fact, that after ten years of being husband and wife we've sprouted but two sprouts betwixt the pair of us."

"I'm sorry. I didn't know."

"No way you could have knowed, with you not knowing and all. When you don't know, then you don't know."

Daniel might have smiled again at Carrick's off-kilter talking, but there were no smiles left in him. The death of his child was too fresh a wound to be exposed to anyone for long without causing new pain. He turned away and called the travelers forward, farther up the Wilderness Road.

DANIEL LIKED JIM CARRICK despite his admitted recklessness and for better reasons than his amusing speech patterns. Carrick was a product of the Virginia frontier, a farmer and hunter of great skill. Traveling with Henderson, he earned the respect of his fellows for his uncanny ability to find and kill game, and his willingness to work cheerfully at clearing away from the road the occasional fallen log or bit of brush that Daniel's ax men had missed. Once at Boonesborough, Carrick was one of the few who didn't complain or bicker with his fellows. He put in more hours of labor on the Boonesborough stockade than any other man, and spoke not a word to anyone except to give encouragement or to prompt a laugh at just the time one was most needed. Sometimes he prompted laughs without meaning to.

Carrick was a happy-spirited man, not so much boisterous or jovial, but just calm and content with his situation. Daniel wished there were a few dozen more like him around Boonesborough. With such folk he could build a fine settlement indeed.

Carrick's wife, Phebe, whom Daniel had never met before overtaking the family on the road, was a fine match for her husband. Unusually pretty, she looked delicate, yet handled the stresses of travel without any obvious difficulty. Her care for her new baby was exemplary and touching, though Daniel worried that it would rouse jealousy in Rebecca. In fact, it actually seemed to be good for Rebecca to be around a new baby, even one with the same name as her own lost child. She helped Phebe Carrick care for the child, and also took their older son, eight-year-old Silas, under her wing to such an extent that he was soon calling her "Aunt Rebecca." Rebecca was pleased by that, though she pretended to Daniel that she wasn't.

"Makes me feel old, that boy calling me 'Aunt.' "

"Take cheer, wife," Daniel gibed. "At least he didn't call you 'Granny.' "

Daniel and Carrick, as the best hunters in the party, handled most of the work of bringing in fresh meat for the travelers. Daniel thought Carrick one of the easiest-mannered and capable hunting partners he had ever had, until one day when they were hunting in the vicinity of the Rockcastle River. That day Carrick seemed nervous and distracted, and once actually set off his rifle by accident, a rare negligence for any skilled hunter.

"God's heaven, Jim, what's the matter with you?" Daniel demanded.

Carrick swallowed and said, "It's this place. There's something I found near here when I was cutting away some brush for Henderson. It put a fright into me like nothing I've never see'd. It's an omen for me, I fear. Knowed it as soon as I see'd it. It's a bad omen for me. A pure portential omen of badness to come my way. I didn't show another soul what I had found out of the sheer fearishness of it."

"I don't put too much stock in omens; a man makes his own way," Daniel said, conveniently ignoring his own tendency to judge the future based on dreams. "What was it you found?"

"Let me show you," Carrick said.

The rest of the party was camped some distance back, off the road. Carrick led Daniel toward a clump of trees near the river. "Look in there," he said. "God knows I don't want to see it no more, God knows."

Puzzled, Daniel walked into the little copse. A big sycamore loomed before him. Daniel looked all about and saw nothing. He was about to call back to Carrick to find out just what it was he was supposed to be seeing, when a thought came to mind and he walked around the other side of the sycamore.

It was hollow and split. Jammed into the tight inner space was the skeleton of a man long dead. There was no flesh on the brown bones now, though a few traces of what had been clothing still hung on the skeletal frame. The skull was turned outward, mouth open; this man had died staring out of the tree into which he had squeezed himself. Why would he have done such a thing? Indians . . . he must have been hiding from Indians.

Feeling the chill of awe that only the dead can arouse in the living, Daniel examined the skeleton more closely. One of the forearms was splintered in a way that suggested a rifle ball had struck it. So this poor fellow had been wounded when he hid. Maybe he had bled to death from the arm wound, died of shock or exposure, or perhaps there had been another bullet in him somewhere that hadn't left evidence of itself in a broken bone. Daniel stared at the remains several long moments, wondering who it could be. Then he looked down toward the skeletal feet, still shod in the ghost-remains of decaying moccasins.

There was something between the feet. Daniel carefully reached into the hollow and pulled the object free. A powder horn. Dusting it off, turning it in his hands, he squinted at two initials marked on its side.

J.S.

He mouthed the letters to himself, pondering and then he stepped back, gaping at the skull that sightlessly gazed at him. He was as shocked as if the skeleton had suddenly spoken.

"Oh, John, John Stewart—God above, John, is this what became of you? Poor John. Poor John." Tears washed down his face, and he reached into the tree to touch the skull of the man he had last seen paddling his canoe across the Kentucky River, the brother-in-law and friend who had left and never returned.

PAST THE HAZEL PATCH, about half the travelers said farewell and took a northwesterly branch of the road that crossed through Crab Orchard, Logan's Station, and on to Harrodsburg. Daniel led the rest of them more due north to Boonesborough, arriving the eighth day of September.

He found Richard Henderson in distress. Back east, various legal and legislative threats to the Transylvania Company were developing, and the partners there were eager for a meeting. There were discussions pending, political figures who needed influencing. Henderson had been itching to leave but didn't feel free to do so without Daniel Boone there to take over leadership in his absence. Now that Daniel was back, Henderson hurried to leave, and Daniel found the mantle of responsibility for this still embryonic settlement thrown across his shoulders once more.

Even so, he was happy to be back again, and proud to have his family with him. Ceremoniously he led his wife and daughters to the banks of the Kentucky River and declared, "Here you stand, Becca and daughters, as the first white women ever to set foot on the banks of the Kentucky River." Though the claim wasn't strictly true, Susy Boone having actually attained that honor months before, it was a moment he had long awaited, and its pleasure did not disappoint him.

He found that Squire had gone to fetch his own wife, Jane, and their family, along with various old neighbors of the Boones and Bryans in the Yadkin region. He and his group returned in due course, as did Richard Callaway, bringing his family and about fifty new settlers with him.

For once in his life Daniel Boone was pleased to see the population rising. These were delicate times, given all the revolutionary talk going on back east. Indian dangers would mount in proportion to the political troubles of white society, and every man entering Kentucky would be needed to help deter the likelihood of violence.

The month after Daniel's return to Boonesborough, the Shawnee Indians signed a treaty at Pittsburgh, where Fort Duquesne once had stood, relinquishing their claims to the Kentucky country. Daniel was glad to hear the news, but didn't take it too seriously. Words on paper had never amounted to much in dealings between whites and Indians. Tribal headmen usually had no more success at coercing cooperation from their younger warriors than Richard Henderson had at coercing the same from his own settlers. Indian society, like that of the white frontiersmen, gave high regard to individual independence. Many young Shawnees, filled with the vigor of their age, had vowed that the whites would not occupy Kentucky, whatever treaties the old men had signed. A few Shawnee chiefs themselves encouraged such sentiments, the noted Blackfish among them.

Despite the uncertainties of life in Kentucky, new settlers came to Boonesborough, Harrodsburg, and the other stations. The more people arrived, the less authority the Transylvania Company seemed to have. Many people defied it outright and took land as squatters. Claims were made in every kind of way, from vague jotted-down descriptions of geographical landmarks to initials carved into trees. Others relied on Virginia homesteading law and cleared a little land, erected a half-faced shelter or crude cabin, and threw some corn into the ground just so they could head home to the east and file a "calmer" claim on their parcel, then sell it to some Kentucky-struck soul hungry for land.

Among those who actually came to stay, overlapping claims were abundant, not unexpectedly, and this sometimes led to threats and fisticuffs. Daniel began to suffer serious worries about his own land holdings. Eventually all the conflicting claims would have to be dealt with. That meant the courts would become involved, Virginia courts most probably, and the Transylvania Company's entire legal construction would be scrutinized by hostile eyes. Claim to the two thousand acres he had been promised might vanish like mist.

Winter came, and with it grim occurrences. In December one Arthur Campbell and a couple of young men were attacked by Indians across the river from Boonesborough; shots were fired at them, and though Campbell came through unhurt, one of the boys was killed. The other vanished.

Then right on the heels of that tragedy came another that jolted Daniel Boone himself. Jim Carrick, who had fast become one of Daniel's best friends, went out to look for a missing pet dog, of all things, because his older son was worried about it. Just another case of Carrick's rashness, but this time with a high cost. Jim Carrick did not come back.

Night fell and Phebe Carrick came to the Boone house in the meadow near the fort, telling of what her man had done and worrying that he hadn't returned. Daniel and his oldest sons ventured out a short distance, calling for Carrick, but he did not answer, and they dared not go farther into the woods at night with the current Indian threat. They returned to the house and invited Phebe and her sons to spend the night with the Boone family, if that would help. No, the woman replied. She wanted to be at home when her Jim came back. If he found the cabin empty, he would worry.

The next morning Daniel went to the Carrick cabin and discovered that Jim Carrick still had not returned. Phebe was distraught now, unable to hide her fear. Her face was pale as milk.

"Don't fret," Daniel said as confidently as he could. "He might have got lost, or run into trouble and be hiding until it's safe to return. I'll take Squire and my boys and go find him for you."

He assembled a small group of searchers and searched all day, but nothing of Carrick could be found, not even sign. His disappearance was oddly reminiscent to Daniel of the vanishing of John Stewart, whose skeleton Jim Carrick called an omen of trouble on its way to him.

The irony was so great, it made the back of Daniel's neck ache. Had Jim Carrick's discovery of the remains of poor John Stewart actually portended that he would disappear in a similar way? Could such a thing really be? Daniel could only hope it wasn't, that Carrick would come striding back into Boonesborough very soon, apologizing in his typically garbled way for being fool enough to chase a straying dog for two days.

Daniel and his companions returned to the settlement near dusk. Jim Carrick was still not home. Just as the last light faded, however, something moved out in the dark and came in toward the Carrick cabin. It was the dog Carrick had gone looking for, but Jim Carrick was not with it.

Rebecca and Jemima spent the night with Phebe Carrick and her sons. The young woman grieved like the widow she surely was. No one doubted now that Jim Carrick had died at the hands of Indians. He had gone looking for a lost dog and found the end of his days instead.

There was feeble hope, of course, as long as no corpse was found. Throughout the month of January 1776 Daniel continued to look for some sign of Jim Carrick when he went hunting, but never with success. At the beginning of February the people of Boonesborough gathered around the Carrick cabin and listened as Squire Boone, who had become something of a preacher, read from his Bible and said words of remembrance for James Carrick, deceased, and talked of how he would rise from wherever he now lay on the day of resurrection.

Phebe listened to Squire's words without expression and did not bow her head when the final prayer was voiced. Daniel knew why. Rebecca had told him that Phebe had decided not to believe her man was dead, not until someone could show her his remains. He was out there, somewhere, and someday he would come back.

Daniel was saddened. Her hope was vain, and everyone but she knew it. Many a man fell at the hands of Indians, never to he found. It was only by chance—or the hand of destiny—that Carrick himself had stumbled upon the body of John Stewart. Jim Carrick was dead, and the best thing Phebe could do would be to accept it.

And maybe, Daniel thought, to join the sudden outflow of settlers heading back to more civilized regions. The death of Arthur Campbell's young friend and the disappearance of Carrick had frightened the settlers deeply. With a grim sense of foreboding Daniel watched the number of Boonesborough settlers decline.

Meanwhile Henderson himself was away, embroiled in court and legislative quandaries back east as he sought to avert his land company from veering to shipwreck on legal rocks. A revolution was brewing, Indian troubles were bound to increase with the spring, the population was dwindling, and the very status of the land company that stood at the center of Boonesborough was in question.

There was no doubt in Daniel Boone's mind of one fact: seventeen and seventy-six was going to be an unusual and trying year.

CHAPTER 26

July, 1776

JEMIMA BOONE LOVED Sunday afternoons above all other times, except when the weather was rainy or cold. Sundays were the single day of the week when a person could be calm and lazy and no one raised a scolding voice because of it. In Boonesborough it was against the law to violate the Sabbath day. Jemima was no lover of rules for their own sake, but she did like that one. Enforced idleness! It was truly a wonderful stretch of time, Sunday afternoon.

And this Sunday afternoon was nearly perfect. The weather was good, the river deliciously cool, the trees thick and lush with the green weight of deepest summer. Only two things marred Jemima's otherwise unspoiled state of affairs. One was the pain in her right foot, which she had cut on some sharp cane earlier in the week. The other was her guilty awareness that she was violating one of her father's firm rules by sitting with two female companions on the far bank of the Kentucky River, the rushing water between her and the southern riverside, where Boonesborough stood about a quarter mile up the river. Daniel Boone had strictly forbidden her to wander on the north bank in times of Indian danger.

Not that Daniel Boone was likely to discover her offense. She was sure that at the moment he was laid out across his bed, resting in the cool cabin shade on this Sunday afternoon, no doubt snoring like a pit saw rasping out planks. Daniel Boone loved his Sunday afternoons, too, and often napped them away. A little earlier he had walked with Jemima and her companions down to the river, where the single canoe that served Boonesborough as a miniature Kentucky River ferry was tethered. He helped them climb into it as he repeated his usual admonishment: "Stay away from the far bank." Jemima had promised that they would, and Daniel had wandered back home for his nap.

She hadn't intended to violate her promise, but the current was strong that day and pulled the canoe closer to the north bank than they had planned. When Jemima fretted about it, the others teased her about being afraid of the "Yellow Boys," or Indians. Besides, they pointed out, the north bank was abloom with the most beautiful flowers. Surely it couldn't hurt to pick a few, and to rest on the riverbank. Hadn't Jemima come here wanting to soak her hurting foot anyway? And so Jemima had relented, against her better judgment but without much choice. At thirteen she was the youngest of the three, and the Callaways could be pushy sometimes.

Now she moved her sore foot in the water, letting the gently massaging current wash away the pain. Her sense of guilt was fading as well, along with her fear of "Yellow Boys." She was glad they had gone to the north bank. Nothing was going to happen, and her father would never know she had disobeyed him.

Beside her, Frances "Fanny" Callaway, daughter of the oft-contentious Colonel Richard Callaway, pummeled her older sister, sixteen-year-old Elizabeth "Betsy" Callaway, with questions about her upcoming marriage to Sam Henderson, nephew of Richard Henderson. What kind of dress would she wear? Would she hold flowers like those they had just picked? How would Sam dress, and where would they spend their wedding night? And did she dread the wedding night? What if she got a baby in her? Would it hurt when the baby was born? Would she want a boy or girl?

"God bless you, Fanny, you don't give me a chance to answer—not that I think I ought to answer all them kind of questions anyhow," Betsy said. "I don't know what I'll wear. Something new. And I think I will hold flowers."

"I don't know I'll ever get married," Jemima said, thinking about Flanders Callaway, cousin of Fanny and Betsy, who already had his eye on her despite her youth. So far her father had been very clear in his opposition to anyone courting his favorite girl. Let her have a childhood before she's pushed to being a woman, he would frequently say.

"You'd best marry Flanders before somebody else gets him. Nobody but him would want to marry you no ways," Fanny teased. "You ain't pretty enough, and you got such long hair your husband would get all tangled up in it and strangle."

"I'm prettier than you," Jemima countered. Fanny hadn't offended her. Jemima knew her own attractiveness.

"That's not what my daddy says. He says I'm the prettiest girl in Kentuck."

"He's your father. You think he's going to tell you you're ugly?"

"You saying I'm ugly?" Fanny glowered hotly at Jemima.

"No." Jemima suddenly sounded distracted. She turned her head, brows lowering, ears perking. What was that whisper of sound she had just heard?

"You little girls are so purely silly," Betsy said with a very grown-up attitude.

"Let's get back in the canoe," Jemima said softly.

"Why? You mad and wanting to run home?"

"I heard something back in the trees."

"I didn't," Fanny said.

Betsy touched her sister's arm and shook her head. She looked very serious. "I think I heard it too," she said. "Jemima's right—we need to get away from here."

They climbed into the canoe and set off, Betsy and Fanny handling the oars. Though a talented canoeist, Betsy found the current overwhelming, and try as she and Fanny would, they could not push away very quickly from the north bank. Meanwhile they were drifting farther away from Boonesborough rather than back toward it. "Are there Yellow Boys?" Fanny asked. She was scared now, hunkered down in the canoe looking tiny and childlike. She seemed far too small to be trying to paddle in such current.

There was no time for an answer. They were pushed back toward the north shore again, near some overhanging trees. Just then a lean figure leaped out of the brush into the water, going completely under and then coming up just in front of the canoe. A coppery hand flashed out and grabbed the tug just inside the prow of the canoe.

"Simon!" Fanny yelled in a tone of relief. "It's only Simon!"

The name was that of a friendly Indian who frequently lived right in Boonesborough, and for a couple of moments Rebecca thought that Fanny was right. The wet Indian face looking back at hers was familiar, but she quickly realized it wasn't Simon's face. With fear mounting she couldn't recall where she had seen this Indian or who he was, but she did know that she and the Callaway girls had just drifted right into great danger.

Jemima sent up a loud scream, and the other girls did as well. Fanny lifted her paddle and pounded the Indian across the head, but he ignored the battering and pulled the canoe into the shoreline brush. A second Indian appeared among the leaves. Leaning over, he dragged Betsy out of the canoe and into the water, then pulled her up the bank. Twisting her in his arms so that she faced the other girls, he put his forearm over her throat and lifted a knife to her forehead, implying the action of scalping.

Fanny and Jemima fell quiet at once. They could not dare risk Betsy's life by further noise. But already they had made quite a ruckus enough, Jemima hoped, to have reached someone back at Boonesborough. Noise carried well over water, and they were scarcely more than a quarter of a mile away.

Within moments Jemima found herself being prodded through the woods by six Indian captors. She cast glances continually at two of them: the one who had grabbed the canoe tug and another one with him. Both faces she had seen, and slowly it came back to her. The one who had stopped the canoe was the Cherokee named Crow, who had come with Hanging Maw to the Boone cabin in Watauga . . .

And the other was Hanging Maw himself. She wondered if he remembered her. He was looking at her oddly, as if perhaps he did. He reached out and touched her long hair, which was tied up behind her head, and she fought the impulse to shudder. It was a surprise to encounter Cherokees this far into Kentucky. She wondered if the others were Cherokees, or if Hanging Maw and Crow had taken up with a Shawnee war party. Such tribal intermixing did occur sometimes, especially when tribes found themselves facing a common problem or enemy. Before long the sound of their language would convince her that the others indeed were Shawnees.

Jemima's injured foot shot pain up her leg, and she stumbled. Hanging Maw reached down and yanked her up again, then leaned over and looked into her face. "Boone's girl," he said, then grinned. He gave her a shake to make the others notice her. "Boone's girl."

They all smiled at the news; obviously she was a special prize. Summoning her courage, she spoke up: "Yes, Boone's girl," she said. "The girl Boone loves and protects."

Now, she thought, *ponder on that awhile. You know my father is a great woodsman, and now you know he won't stand idle while his daughter is taken away. Nor will he show any mercy to you if I come to harm. Ponder on that while you grin.*

Of course, she dared say none of this aloud. Hanging Maw grasped her shoulder and urged more speed out of her. Deliberately she fell, making him stop. He pulled her up and she fell again. "My foot is hurt," she said.

He looked behind, then yanked her back to her feet. "Walk fast," he commanded. "Don't fall." Then he pointed at the Callaway girls. Betsy was stoic; Fanny was wailing. "Your sisters?"

"Yes," Jemima replied unhesitatingly. Fanny looked aghast at the lie, but Betsy realized what Jemima was doing and gave her sister a subtle kick. "The daughters of Boone, who has been your friend and would not like his girls hurt," Jemima added.

They went on, the Indians eager to put as much distance as they could between themselves and Boonesborough, as quickly as possible.

MODESTY WAS the last thing on Daniel Boone's mind as he raced stumbling out of his cabin, pulling on his Sunday trousers with one hand as he went. He had laid them aside while taking his nap and then grabbed them up when the stir of noise in Boonesborough awakened him. He was barefoot and hatless, his rifle, powder, and ammunition in his one free hand.

The girls' cries had reached one of Richard Callaway's sons first of all, and he in turn alerted a couple of the settlement's young bachelors, who had been roaming in a meadow together, wearing their Sunday clothing and talking sadly of their dearth of female company. The three raised the general alarm, sending Boonesborough into a frenzy of activity.

There was no time for the men to make good preparation for pursuit. Every passing moment put the Indians and their captives farther away. Daniel was running barefoot, in Sunday pants and shirt; Sam Henderson had his face half-shaved, half-bearded, dripping with soap, and Richard Callaway was wildly trying to load his rifle while running at the same time. He was murmuring and muttering, nearly in tears, talking of his fear that the savages would "use" his girls. At first Callaway made for the river, but then diverted back to get his horse. A sizable group of others, some of them Callaway kin, did the same, mounting as fast as possible and riding for the river ford.

Daniel and several others ran to and along the river until they saw the drifting canoe on the far side. One of the several boys who had joined the wild race shucked his clothing and dived in, swimming to the far side and fetching back the canoe. Daniel was the first to climb in, followed by Sam Henderson and three others. They paddled over the swift river and got out, with Boone shouting back to those still on the south bank that a good number of them should remain behind and guard the fort against attack.

Daniel's face was set and expressionless, his eyes showing only resolve. Inside, though, he was in turmoil. Why had the girls gone to the far bank? And where would they be taken? It was crucial to find their trail quickly. He glanced at the sky, seeing the afternoon sun westering, and swore. Darkness would be upon them far too soon.

He divided his little group at the top of a hill and headed with his division in the upstream direction. At length Callaway and his mounted men galloped up. Conferring, the men decided to send Callaway's band toward the Licking River, where they might be able to cut off the Indians as they headed north toward their distant towns.

A scouring of the area revealed no sign the Indians had come that way, so Daniel and his companions hurried off in the opposite direction. They detected sign there, as well as fresher marks indicating that the small group he had divided off from earlier had already followed the Indian trail. Hurrying along as fast as bare feet and Sunday trousers would allow, Daniel pushed ahead until he met up with the other group at twilight. They had covered about five hard miles, but the Indians were apparently moving very fast.

As darkness came on, the light of a fire flickering off in the trees attracted them, and they discovered a squatter's farmstead occupied by William Bush, an old friend of Daniel's. It was too dark to go farther. A boy who had come along was sent back to Boonesborough for proper clothing and supplies for the men. He was back by morning, at which time the men set out again.

Daniel grew more disturbed as the day went by. The Indians were leaving some sign, but moving very fast. Occasionally the trackers found plants bent or uprooted, scraps of cloth dropped. The girls clearly were leaving sign as best they could, but it was meager, and no doubt the Indians were keeping a close watch on them.

A gnawing fear began to rise in Daniel. It was possible that his Jemima, most beloved of his daughters even though physically fathered by another, might have left his life forever. Indian captivity was like a great dark pool that could swallow human beings so deeply they were never heard from again.

He quickened his pace, trying to make up distance and praying they would not lose the trail.

THE SUNDAY DRESSES the girls had been wearing when captured were ragged tatters now, the skirts cut short, the cutoff remnants wrapped around their calves like leggings, and their shoes replaced by moccasins. Jemima's long hair was drenched in sweat and filled with burrs, leaf pieces, and cobwebs picked up during the mad race through the forest. It appeared to her that no harm was intended to them, and for that she breathed a prayer of thanks. Fanny Callaway was obviously fearful that they would be raped, mostly because one of the Indians, a Shawnee, seemed obsessed with looking at her. But he had not touched her other than to prod her on, and Jemima did not think he had physical assault in mind. It wasn't common for Indians to molest captive women sexually.

Jemima was glad to know that, because otherwise she too might have been fearful. Hanging Maw was paying her much attention, often chortling about how he had played quite a joke on old Boone by taking his girls. None of the Indians had found reason to doubt Jemima's claim that the Callaway daughters were her sisters, even though Jemima didn't think she and the Callaways bore much resemblance. Maybe it was with Indians-to-whites as it was with whites-to-Indians: they all tended to look pretty much the same.

The day passed without sign of anyone pursuing. Jemima didn't let herself believe for a moment that her father hadn't come after her. But what if he couldn't find their trail? These Indians knew how to move without leaving many marks, and their speed and perseverance were extraordinary. And the man named Crow, serving as rear scout, had reported no sight of any pursuers. Jemima noted that he, like Hanging Maw, spoke English fairly well, and suspected he was making a point of frequently reporting in English their apparent lack of followers. Probably he wanted to be sure the girls knew that no one was about to save them. Jemima thought that a cruel bit of mental torture.

The few times they paused to rest, Hanging Maw would remove Jemima's bonnet, take the combs out of her hair, and watch the dark cascade fall down her back. He ran his fingers through it, muttering admiring comments and telling her what an attractive young squaw she was. After picking a louse or two out of her tresses—frontier folk lived almost continually with lice—he would put her hair back into a knot and fix it in place with the combs. He was gentle with her, very affectionate, and Jemima remembered her father's comment one time back in Watauga about the generally decent nature of Hanging Maw.

The farther they traveled, the more weary and heartsick Jemima became. Tied sitting up against trees at night, the girls found it hard to sleep, and the only food for most of the journey was jerked buffalo tongue, which all but gagged them when they tried to chew it down. It was growing hard to think, hard to cling to hope or even pride. When Hanging Maw asked Jemima to kindly finger through his scalp for nits and lice during one rest stop, she did it without complaint, too weary to care.

Her sore foot throbbed, making every step torture. But it provided a convenient reason to stumble frequently to the ground, causing a few moments of delay. Moments added up to minutes, precious time that could aid those who surely pursued. Often she would scream when she fell in case rescuers were within earshot. The screams brought snarls and threats from Hanging Maw, but never did he follow through. In his own rugged way he seemed to be a kind-hearted man, actually affectionate toward his captives. Certainly he was tolerant and did not appear to want them hurt. Without his tempering presence some of the Shawnees in the group would have taken tomahawks to the girls long before, Jemima felt sure. If she was fated to be a captive, she was glad it was Hanging Maw who had taken her, not some gruffer soul.

Even so, captivity was captivity, a thing to destroy hope and joy. Jemima tried to keep up her spirits but soon reached the point where she couldn't do it without fixing her eyes on Betsy Callaway. The oldest captive was making a very brave showing for herself, giving encouraging smiles to the younger ones and whispering to them at night that soon they would be freed.

Eventually even Betsy was struggling to maintain hope. More than any of the others she had managed to leave behind sign, even a few shreds of her handkerchief. Whenever she was caught, they would threaten her, but as soon as they were on the move again, she would be finding some other way to leave tracks, broken sticks, or torn leaves as evidence of their route.

A stray pony found roaming the woods provided the best opportunity for a delaying tactic the girls were to receive. Though all of them knew how to ride, they pretended ignorance of horsemanship, and secretly pinched and spurred the pony to make it buck. The Indians laughed heartily to begin with, then tried to give lessons, but the girls seemed incredibly dull-minded, unable to learn. By the time the Indians gave up their lessons and set the pony free again, Jemima felt encouraged. They had just eaten up lots of time with their deception. Maybe, just maybe, that time was what their rescuers needed to close the gap.

If there were any rescuers. What if they hadn't found the trail, or found it and then lost it . . . ?

She shut off the thought. It would only bring despair. But she couldn't help noticing that the Indians were much more relaxed than before. They laughed freely, advanced a little more slowly, and didn't watch quite so closely to see if the girls were leaving sign. And they were talking of finding some better food, eating a good meal.

Jemima knew just what it all meant. The Indians no longer believed there was much chance they would be overtaken. They had pulled a good joke on old Boone and had gotten away with it.

ENERGY THAT HAD BEEN slowly draining from Daniel Boone for the last several miles returned in a rush as he knelt beside the buffalo carcass along the trail. It had been killed recently and the hump cut away. The blood was still fresh, the exposed flesh only now beginning to draw flies.

"I'll wager they ain't even ate the meat yet," he said. "Next water, they'll cook it. They've been running on poor victuals from the start, and they're ready for some good ones."

Daniel stood, looking north. Sam Henderson leaned wearily on his long rifle, watching him. "I can tell you're mulling on something," he said.

"I am," Daniel replied. "It 'pears to me they're heading for the Licking crossing, sure as the world. But taking a careful way, trying to hide their sign. They're getting more careless, though; this buffler proves that."

"So they don't figure they're being followed?" Sam said.

"Well . . . they're still hiding their tracks, but I believe they're easing up on it. Getting more easy about it."

"So maybe we should leave the trail and . . ." Sam didn't complete his sentence, but Daniel could see he had already picked up his own line of thinking.

"Leave the trail, head straight through to the crossing. Cut 'em off."

"That's a risk," another of the party said.

"It is. But it may be the only way to make up the time and distance they've got on us."

Standing around the dead buffalo, the men talked, debating, questioning, wondering. They knew their decision might make the crucial difference either way in the outcome of all this, but they were too weary to get worked up. It was a peculiarly quiet exchange of ideas. In the end they left the decision to Daniel.

"We'll leave the trail," he said. "If we can cut them off, we can bring home our girls."

"And if we can't?"

"Then we can't. But we will. We will. Now, let's move on, quiet as we can, spread out from one another, and trot fast as lightning."

JEMIMA WAS MORE WEARY than she had ever been in her life, but for some reason she couldn't rest. Crow walked up to her and stared down at her with a look of amusement on his handsome face.

Jemima looked up at him. "How'd you lose your hearing in that ear?" she asked, surprising herself with her forthrightness.

Crow looked surprised, too. Perhaps he hadn't realized that his handicap was so obvious. "How you know?"

"I could tell back when you sat at my father's table in Watauga," she replied. "Once I even slipped up behind you and snapped my fingers at your right ear, and you didn't hear it."

He held silent a moment, then said, "I was born with one ear stopped. It has never opened."

"Where did you learn to talk English?"

"From my mother's brother. An old man, wise man. He knew the talk from the traders and the soldiers. He was fast to learn and taught what he knew to me."

"Where is he now?"

"He is dead. Dead long ago."

"Oh."

Crow smiled subtly. "You have no tears for dead Indians."

"I didn't know him." Jemima was growing weary now that she was seated. She didn't want to talk anymore. There was a fire burning, and buffalo meat roasting. The aroma made her empty stomach ache.

Crow went on, his words as bitter as his tone was matter-of-fact. "No white man grieves for Indians. He is made to think only of himself. He kills Indians like dogs, like my mother's brother was killed."

Jemima closed her eyes, intending only to rest them a moment while smelling the cooking buffalo, and to shut out Crow, whom she now regretted having questioned. In half a minute she was asleep, mouth lolling open. Crow turned away from her and went to the other side of the fire, where he knelt and looked into the canebrake rising just past the camp.

Noise made Jemima jerk awake. One of the Shawnees was dancing about on one foot, grasping the toes of his other through his moccasin. The other Indians were laughing. Fanny had come and sat down beside Jemima while she slept. She put her hand to her mouth. "Oh, he'll kill Betsy for that, sure!" she whispered sharply.

"What did she do?"

"He was rubbing on her hair, and she brushed some hot coals out of the fire onto his foot."

Good, Jemima thought. *Hope it hurt him. Hope his toes fester clean off from it.*

In truth the man wasn't hurt much at all and was dancing about as much in fun as in pain. But Betsy seemed to have lost hold of her ability to restrain her emotions and broke into tears. Jemima and Fanny rose together to comfort her. No longer were they bound in camp; they were thirty miles or more away from Boonesborough, and apparently the Indians were sure they could not, or would not, escape, knowing that to do so would only get them run down and maybe tomahawked.

Silent minutes followed. One of the Shawnees went to the fire and knelt beside it, adjusting the spit upon which the buffalo meat dripped and sizzled. Crow lay on the ground, staring up at the sky. The other Indians were moving about nearby, gathering wood, smoking pipes, allowing the cramps in overstrained leg muscles to relax. Jemima took in the whole scene, and it came to her in a horrifying burst of realization that she might be seeing only men such as these from now on. She would soon be living like an Indian, a captive, maybe a forced servant or squaw for some Shawnee buck. The prospect had seemed unreal until that moment. Now it seemed sickening.

What little hope she had left suddenly vanished. She became empty and sad. Eyes filling with tears, she looked away, up into the brush in a narrow hollow nearby . . . and saw her father.

Her every muscle tensed. Daniel was snaking slowly down through the brush, making not a bit of noise, moving as slow as a stalking panther. Jemima blinked, convinced her mind and eyes were deceiving her. She bit her lip and tried not to cry out in joy. When he gave a hand signal for silence, she knew that indeed her father really was there, really was real, really hadn't failed her after all. How could she have doubted him?

Elsewhere in the woods a rifle suddenly boomed, making Jemima give a little cry. A gush of blood gouted forth from the chest of the Indian adjusting the cooking spit, and he collapsed right into the blaze. The other Indians came to their feet, the girls too.

"Daddy's here!" Jemima yelled as loud as she could. "Daddy has come!"

For several moments all was confusion. Daniel Boone's voice rang out, urging the girls to run. A tomahawk sailed past Betsy's head, narrowly missing her. She ran hard, the other girls after her. Another order sang out: "Fall down!" Again it was Daniel Boone's voice. They did fall, but in their excitement rose again immediately.

Men were rushing into the camp from all sides, and the Indians were doing their best to get out of it. Barefoot, lacking all their clothing and weapons, they were plunging toward the cane. Jemima saw Crow grasp his side; blood ran between his fingers and down his hip and thigh, which were bare; he wore only a breechcloth and short matchcoat. He had removed his moccasins and leggings when they had made camp. He vanished into the looming stalks, Hanging Maw right behind him.

When the tumult was over, Jemima was conscious only of her father's arms enclosing her. She held tight to him, hugging him, weeping, hearing him weep too. One of the other men went to the fire and kicked the dead Indian out of it, commenting that the scent of burning Indian did nothing to enhance the aroma of roasting buffalo meat. Then he went over to the canebrake and examined the lines of fresh blood leading into it, evidence of the severity of the wounds some of the Indians had received.

Jemima paid little heed. She cared only to enjoy the safety and the love of her father at this moment.

They were all tired and hungry. No one felt much inclined to chase the Indians. Now that the girls were back, punishment didn't seem to matter. Before heading toward Boonesborough they devoured the roasted buffalo meat, and Jemima Boone thought it the finest meal she had ever eaten, and the company the best a young woman could ever find anywhere on the whole wonderful earth.

CHAPTER 27

JOY AT THE RESCUE of the captives overwhelmed all other concerns at Boonesborough for a time, but soon Daniel and the other leaders began to consider the implications of what had happened. The presence of an influential Cherokee such as Hanging Maw in Kentucky with Shawnees bore worrisome implication. Might he have come seeking to stir further war sentiment among the Shawnees? Despite the Henderson treaty, there remained plenty of sentiment among Cherokees against white encroachment, and even some who had signed it noted the treaty meant little, because the Cherokees had no real claim on land beyond the Cumberland Mountains. Others, such as Dragging Canoe, had refused to sign with Henderson at all. There were plenty of Cherokees who would be happy to see the Shawnees rise to punish the intruders. If Hanging Maw was urging war, the months ahead might be bloodier even than they were already expected to be.

A happy distraction from the coming troubles was the marriage of Sam Henderson and Betsy Callaway on the sixth day of August. Dressed in Irish linen, she stood beside her man before Baptist lay preacher Squire Boone, who joined them in Kentucky's first white settlers' marriage. Richard Callaway had his doubts about the legality of it all, but went along with it after Sam Henderson signed a bond to have a less questionable ceremony performed at the first chance.

The wedding was a happy time made all the more so by the fact that the bride had narrowly escaped Indian captivity and had been rescued by none other than her own fiancé. It was the stuff of romance and legend, a story every family who witnessed it could pass on to their descendants.

Even during the rescue, however, more reason for worry had come upon the settlements. Nathaniel Hart's cabin had been burned while the men were away. An orchard of five hundred apple trees had been destroyed. Obviously Indian presence in the area was substantial even if unseen, and the settlements were being watched by hostile eyes.

A copy of America's Declaration of Independence reached Boonesborough in August and immediately created another huge stir. Over in Harrodsburg, support for the Declaration was instant and virtually unanimous; the Harrodsburg folk had already formed a revolutionary "committee of safety" some two months before. For some who hailed the Declaration, it was a matter of simple patriotism. For others it was a mix of patriotism and the hope that the rebelling colony of Virginia would note their support and confirm the right of the Harrodsburg settlers to their land holdings. Many Harrodsburg settlers had occupied their parcels before Richard Henderson had signed his treaty, and stood opposed to the Transylvania Company.

At Boonesborough, feelings about the mounting revolution were mixed. Rebecca Boone's kin, the Bryans, included many loyalists, and Daniel himself wasn't quite sure where to stand on the issue. He held a captain's commission from Lord Dunmore's Virginia government and had no intention of giving it up, yet he understood the desires of many to be free of the British dominance that men such as Dunmore exemplified. Hardly had news of the start of the colonial rebellion reached Kentucky before Daniel began to detect tongues wagging about him and eyes casting his way in secret. Everyone wanted to know how he would come down on the revolutionary issue.

The truth was that for Daniel Boone there was not much time to worry about narrow philosophical or governmental arguments. Life in the Kentucky backwoods was a struggle for survival and gave a man more than enough to worry about day to day. Daniel could accept life under any number of types of government, as long as that life could be lived as safely and peacefully as possible. He devoted his patriotism mostly to the local community, not to governments across the mountains. He would be happy to stay neutral in the coming conflict if he could.

What would ultimately determine the feasibility of neutrality would be the actions of the Indians. With Americans and Britons at war with each other and Americans of different political leanings squabbling among themselves, the Indians would certainly act according to their own best interests. And what they considered their own best interests would be to push back the settlers who were taking over their country. They would observe the apparent majority of revolutionists among the settlers. They might seek support from the British in driving those revolutionists out, and the British would probably give it.

If so, Daniel Boone would be forced to fight for his own interests and his own home, just as the Indians would continue to fight for theirs. The probability that he would he able to sit out the squabble between the mother country and her rebellious offspring seemed quite low. It was discouraging. He was a peaceable man and did not enjoy war, especially when it was forced upon him and carried out on terms and scales he could not control.

REBECCA BOONE gently ran a homemade comb of horn through Jemima's long hair, beginning at her scalp and going all the way down to the end of it, near the pretty girl's knees. Jemima's luxuriant tresses were Rebecca's pride and had caught the attention of many a young man, Flanders Callaway in particular. Jemima should certainly have no trouble finding herself a husband. And it wouldn't be all that long now before she would be of marriageable age. Flanders was pressing his case with the family, and if Daniel had resisted initially, he couldn't say much now. Flanders had helped in the rescue and proved his devotion to Jemima unanswerably. Rebecca had little doubt the pair would marry soon. Probably within the year. She was happy her daughter had a good prospect, but a mother couldn't help but be wistful and sad when she thought of giving up her girl. It would be even harder for Daniel, who loved Jemima so deeply.

Jemima had turned fourteen almost three months before. Now it was the last day of the year 1776. Long gone were the autumn breezes, clear skies, brilliant oranges, mellow russets that Rebecca loved. Winter was firmly settled in, and with it, fear. She dreaded the coming year deeply. With her back to her mother, Jemima could not see that Rebecca's tears. Jemima herself, who had become quite the proud, fearless young woman after surviving her brief captivity, was jabbering with excitement, but Rebecca didn't listen to a word.

Jemima's excitement stemmed from the presence of many new people in the Boonesborough stockade this day. They had come from McClelland's Station, a fort north of the river that suffered an Indian attack on Sunday, December 29. Though the McClelland defenders had driven the Indians off and killed the Shawnee chief named Pluggy, who had led the attack, they had not felt it safe to remain isolated at their own station and had come to live temporarily at Boonesborough, as other settlers from smaller stations were expected to do soon. And some folks from Harrodsburg had been attacked on Christmas day as they had set out to fetch ammunition that had been hidden from the Indians here and there around Limestone on the Ohio River.

Even before that there had been other Indian troubles. Lone hunters had left and not come home, vanishing just as poor Phebe Carrick's Jim had vanished. Others had faced attacks and survived, coming in with terrible reports about the number of Shawnees lurking in the region. And those of a superstitious bent were clicking their tongues and talking about how ill it was that they were about to enter a year with three repetitions of the same number. The Year of the Three Sevens, it would be. A bloody year, terrible to endure.

And so Rebecca stood combing and silently crying. Despite her natural savvy and the experience of her ordeal, Jemima just didn't understand how terrible it all would be. She was still childish enough to believe that her father would always find a way to fix anything that was wrong. He would keep them all safe, somehow. Rebecca could not blame Jemima for thinking that way, considering that Daniel had, in fact, saved her from her captors.

But Rebecca knew better. Daniel Boone was just a man. A capable one, a survivor. But still just a man. He had brought them all out there into the wilds and swore he would protect them. They would be safe, he had declared. But had he not also declared, back in seventy-three, that they would make it safely into Kentucky? And had not James Boone paid the price at the hands of Big Jim, the Indian that Rebecca hated more than any other man walking the earth, the man for whom she desired a hard, bloody death?

She turned her head and wiped her tears as the cabin door opened. Phebe Carrick walked in, carrying her youngest. Rebecca smiled and hoped Phebe would not see the redness of her eyes. Phebe was such a sad person that Rebecca always tried to be bright and cheerful in her presence. Now she forced a big grin as she said her hello to Phebe.

"You've been crying, too, I see," Phebe replied.

Jemima turned her head and looked up at her mother. Rebecca shook her head, still smiling. "No, I've not been crying. Something's blown into my eyes, that's all it is."

Phebe did not answer. Her own eyes were red and looked even sadder and hollower than usual. "My oldest has been asking me if we're to die and be scalped now that the Three Sevens year is upon us."

"Someone has been filling that boy's head with nonsense," Rebecca said. "You ought to tell Silas not to listen to such as that."

"He asked me if his father had been scalped when he died. I told him I didn't know." Fresh tears filled Phebe's eyes, and she sank down onto a three-legged stool near the fireplace, stroking the soft hair of her little one.

"It's the coming of these McClelland's Station folk that has him worried, and you too," Rebecca said. "It puts a fright into everyone."

"Were you really crying, Ma?" Jemima asked.

"Hush, girl. Don't twist about if you want me to comb you. No, I've not been crying. I see nothing to cry about." Odd thing, how I turn right away to lies about such things, she was thinking even as she spoke.

"I wish I had never come to Kentucky," Phebe said. "My children would be safer elsewhere."

"Then go," Rebecca urged. It wasn't the first time she had tried to talk Phebe into leaving Kentucky. "Others are leaving, and many more will soon enough, when the hard times come."

"Hard times? But you just said there was nothing to cry about, Ma!" Jemima said, twisting around again. Rebecca put a hand firmly on her head and turned her away once more.

"I can't leave," Phebe said. "What if Jim was just took captive? He may be alive, and if he is, I want to be here when he returns. He might be hurt. He might need me."

"It's been a long time already, and he ain't come back, Phebe," Rebecca said. "If he did come back, Daniel would come fetch you to him, or take him to you." She paused. "And you know that he ain't coming back, anyhow, don't you? He's been killed."

Phebe stood, growing almost haughty. "You don't really know that."

"No . . . yet I do know. And so do you, in your heart."

"I don't. And I'll not leave Kentucky until I do know, one way or the other." She strode to the door and walked out, slamming it behind her.

"She's mad at you for talking so hard to her, Ma," Jemima said.

"I know. She came in looking for comfort, and I preached at her again." Rebecca paused, combing out a tangle. "But the truth is she has no call staying in Kentucky, a single woman with young ones. She's had a few offers of marriage, yet she won't take them. If she's set on staying here and refusing to marry, I don't see that she's got call to come whining about her condition. Stubborn, that woman is. Purely stubborn."

"You sound like you don't much like Phebe, Ma."

"I like her. I love her dear, and feel for her deep. But she ain't doing the best thing for herself or her young ones. She needs to leave Kentucky, put all the bad behind her, and find herself a good life in a safe place."

"With the war and all, is there a safe place?" Jemima asked.

"Many places safer than Kentucky," Rebecca replied. Then she realized that kind of honesty didn't jibe with the false comforts she so routinely voiced to her offspring. "But don't you worry," she added. "We'll be safe."

"I know," Jemima said brightly. "We'll be safe as can be, as long as Daddy is with us. And Flanders. Flanders is a good man, don't you think? He wants me to marry him, you know."

"Yes. I know." Rebecca returned to combing, saying nothing more.

REVOLUTION'S TIDE in the east became problematic for the western settlements in many ways in 1777. With troubles on their own doorsteps, the easterners had little time for concerns about distant backwoodsmen. Though Virginia had created Kentucky County at the end of 1776 and authorized the shipment of ammunition, there remained a dangerous lack of manpower and firepower on the frontier. A strong leader named George Rogers Clark had been put in charge of the Kentucky militia, but a feeble militia it was, just a score or so more than a hundred riflemen, with powder and lead in chronically short supply. And this while the Shawnees were gathering a band of two hundred warriors under the powerful war chief Mkahdaywahmayquah—Blackfish—to strike the settlements.

A sniping incident at Boonesborough in early March killed a slave and wounded another man. A raid near Harrodsburg occurring about the same time caused the death of the stepson of one Hugh McGary, a friend of Daniel's. McGary himself was wounded the next morning when he and several others left the Harrodsburg stockade to chase Indians who had set fire to cabins outside the fort, but they managed to kill a Shawnee dressed in some of the clothing of McGary's dead stepson. Furious, the wounded McGary chopped apart the fresh corpse and fed the Indian to his dogs. From that time on folks whispered that the trauma of it all had affected McGary's mind. He wasn't quite right in his thinking and actions thereafter, nor was his wife, who had taken permanently to bed the moment she learned her son had been killed.

It was a ghastly season around the settlements, Harrodsburg taking the hardest blows. Hunters vanished, field-workers died, and families endured the horror of watching loved ones killed and scalped within sight of the fort walls. Ammunition was precious, and meat hard to obtain because the Indians drove it away. The clearings around fort stockades, created to make it impossible for Indians to creep up to the very walls, now became hazards for the white hunters and farmers who had to come and go across them.

Daniel Boone was a man with much to worry about, but he comforted himself with the fact that he hadn't had it so hard as James Harrod and his people. The first four months of 1777 had almost passed without any substantial attack upon Boonesborough. He was grateful but knew such good fortune could not last.

On the morning of April 24th, the cattle at Boonesborough acted strangely, refusing to leave their pens to go to pasture. A dog of Squire Boone's, known to have a nose for Indians, was sniffing about and growling. Two men of Boonesborough left the fort to scout for Indians and bring back firewood, while a relative newcomer to Boonesborough, Simon Butler, stood at the gate, rifle ready. The wood-toting pair were returning when a round of shots blasted out of a clump of sycamores in a nearby hollow. Daniel Goodman, one of the two, fell, with wood scattering about him. The other man panicked, dropped his wood, and scrambled for the gate.

Goodman was still alive, but badly hurt. Unable to rise, he crawled toward the stockade, but a handful of Shawnees came tearing out of the woods, quickly overtaking and tomahawking him to death.

Simon Butler charged forward, shooting and killing one Indian. The other Indians raced off when Daniel Boone and ten armed men charged out of the gate. Daniel was heartsick over what had happened to Goodman—the brave fellow had gone for firewood at Daniel's behest—and furious that a small band of Indians had been so brazen. A tiny band of raiders had just diminished Boonesborough's meager fighting force by one, and in the current climate of hostility, every man was needed.

Only after they were seventy yards out from the fort did Daniel realize his blunder. A tiny band of raiders? It wasn't the case. Within two seconds a line of at least fifty warriors burst out of the woods and raced into the area between the Boonesboroughites and their stockade.

"Back!" Daniel yelled. "To the stockade and sell yourselves dear!"

The fort gate still gaped open, but to reach it, the men would have to pass through a swarm of Indians outnumbering them five to one. Raising their rifles, the stranded men fired, then charged, shifting their weapons so that they held them by the warmed muzzles. Swinging and butting with them, they darted into the mass of warriors, yelling at full volume, while a few shots peppered out of the fort.

Daniel was racing at full speed when a rifle ball hit him in the ankle. He fell so hard, it drove the wind from his lungs. Pain rippled up his leg, then began to numb away to a nerveless throb. Daniel tried to rise, but a great weight descended upon him. He felt fingers twine themselves through his hair and jerk upward on his scalp. Wincing, he prepared himself for the inevitable slice at the hairline, the rip of scalp from bone. Just as the scalping knife touched his skin, he felt the Indian atop him fall aside. Daniel saw that the swarthy face beside him was covered with blood; someone had struck the Shawnee in the side of the head, very hard.

"Daniel, just hold on and I'll—" It was Simon Butler's voice, but his words were cut off as a second Shawnee came near. Swinging his rifle around, the young man batted the Indian in the skull, crushing his forehead. Daniel began to lose consciousness.

The next thing he was aware of was that he was bobbing along above the ground, arms dangling. He could make no sense of it at first, but then realized he was across someone's shoulder. For the life of him he hoped it wasn't a Shawnee shoulder. Of course, a Shawnee would probably have simply tomahawked him rather than carry him off. With that comforting thought he allowed himself to black out again.

When he came to, he was in the fort, Rebecca at his side, several of his children standing around with worried looks on their faces even now giving way to relief as he opened his eyes. Above and behind them loomed the tall form of Simon Butler, grinning humbly.

He heard the tale of all that had happened. After his wounding it had indeed been Simon who had rescued him, knocking two Indians away with his gun butt and carrying Daniel bodily into the fort. They'd had a narrow escape, with Indian bullets striking all around.

Fortunately, none but Goodman had died. The woundings were significant, however. Not only was Daniel out of action, with a badly shattered ankle, but six others were hurt as well, including the marksman Michael Stoner. Daniel could tell that his own ankle would keep him down for a long time. It was blasted inconvenient, especially with Shawnees about in such numbers; but, by heaven, he was alive, and glad of it.

He looked over at Simon Butler, whose humble face always managed to be homely and handsome at the same time. To this young man he certainly owed his life. "Simon, you're a fine fellow," he said. "You've behaved like a man today." Simon grinned, and a slow flush of red spread up his face. "Your daughter Jemima helped me," he said. "She run out onto the fighting field and helped me get you in the last few steps." He touched the brim of his beaver hat and turned away, heading back out into the stockade yard.

Daniel shifted and winced, then looked at Jemima. She grinned at him almost shyly. "You really did that, Jemima?"

"Yes."

"That was a fool thing, girl."

"You rescued me. I wanted to help rescue you."

He paused for a few moments, then smiled. "Come here, daughter. Give your daddy a hug."

DANIEL'S ANKLE KEPT HIM abed for weeks, his foot hanging in a sling. He despised being laid up; it actually made him feel guilty, being unable to respond to the continuing Indian forays.

Boonesborough itself escaped a truly massive siege. Blackfish had been sufficiently disappointed by the outcome of his surprise attack that he merely skulked around the forest for a time, harassing the settlers and stealing from their cabins, then moved on to Harrodsburg again, attacking there twice in May. Squire Boone, who had been away from the region for a time, had since returned and was near Harrodsburg when he fell victim to a surprise attack in the forest. He survived, but with a wound that took a long time to heal.

May brought more attacks on the stations, including a siege of several days' length at Logan's Station. Harrodsburg saw fatalities, and Boonesborough was pinned down for two days.

As serious as the attacks themselves was the decreasing amount of food and supplies. When trapped in their stations, the settlers depended on cattle, and the Indians naturally sought to kill as much livestock as possible. Boonesborough lost many cattle in the final May raid.

Boonesborough suffered another attack in July, but Blackfish's raiders managed to kill only one man and wound two others. At length they withdrew, destroying crops, and headed back to the Ohio River and their towns beyond.

By now Daniel was up again, walking on a crutch. Scouts roaming the forest found evidence of the withdrawal of the Shawnees. A time of relief was at hand, made all the more secure with the arrival of reinforcements from Virginia in August.

Even without raids and with reinforcements, however, the situation of the settlements was precarious. A spring and summer of violence had made farming all but impossible, and the crops burned by Blackfish in July were a particularly harsh loss. It was too late in the season to replace the crops, and winter would be upon them in a few months. These had been hard seasons with little to brighten them except for the celebration of a double wedding held the previous spring and officiated by Colonel Callaway. Callaway's Fanny had stood up beside John Holder, one of the men who had helped in her rescue, and the other bride was none other than Daniel's own Jemima. Flanders Callaway had claimed his beloved at last. It had been a bittersweet occasion for Daniel Boone, to say the least.

During the fall the men hunted, gathered greens and nuts, foraged for roots, turnips, and potatoes. With great difficulty the people managed to keep themselves fed, but all dreaded the coming of winter, when fresh meat was difficult to obtain. Meat could be preserved, of course, but that required salt, and salt, like most everything else in the settlements of Kentucky, was in short supply at the moment. By the year's end the shortage was severe. When Daniel began talking to Rebecca about gathering a large group of men to go off to the Blue Licks for salt making, she did not voice worries about the danger such a venture would involve. She had eaten all the bland, saltless greens and meat she could stand. If Daniel wished to go make salt, that was very fine by her. Kentucky was difficult enough to abide; at least they could enjoy some decent food.

CHAPTER 28

LADEN WITH four hundred pounds of buffalo meat, Daniel Boone's horse moved very slowly through the bitterly cold February day. Overcast and gray, the sky was like a low ceiling above him, and a fresh snow had piled higher than ankle-deep. His breath and the horse's came in great white puffs, and the buffalo meat itself, tied to the horse with tugs of rawhide, steamed in the cold. Hard going it was, moving in rugged country on such a wintry day.

Back at the salt-making camp at the Blue Licks, there would be a fire to warm his numbed fingers and to roast the meat. And it would make tasty fare. Like any frontiersman, Daniel loved his food heavily salted, particularly his meat. Having gone without salt through the prior fall and first part of the winter, it was delightful to be able to enjoy salted meat again. The pleasure almost made up for the hard labor involved in salt making and the lengthy time it required such a large band of men to be away from home.

This period in the dead cold of winter was certainly the most prudent time to be making salt, however. For one thing, the need was immediate. For another, Indian attacks were less likely at this time of year. Indians usually kept to their towns in the coldest weather, reserving their war forays for the warmer months. Already a few bags of precious salt had been sent back to Boonesborough to add flavor to the diet and to allow preservation of game. And of course the salt makers themselves reserved a good share with which to season the meat that Daniel, Tom Brooks, and Flanders Callaway brought in from their daily excursions. The approximately thirty Boonesborough salt makers certainly earned their rations. All the wood-chopping, fire-tending, and boiling work they did in these harsh conditions was nothing to be taken lightly.

Daniel stopped suddenly, listening to the forest around him. He turned his head, peering through the endless field of barren trees. Perhaps he was wrong, but he thought he had heard a noise that didn't quite fit.

Unable to see anything, he went on another few steps, then turned abruptly and looked behind him. To his surprise and dismay he saw a handful of Indians creeping through the woods on his trail. He couldn't see them clearly because of intervening foliage, but he could tell they were Indians advancing quietly, with stealth. He saw no change in their stance or movement to indicate they had noticed that he had grown wise to their presence.

Daniel swore beneath his breath as he assessed his options. With the horse laden down with meat, he couldn't ride away, but he was loath to give up such a quantity of food. Nothing to be done for it, though. He tried to untie the tugs and let the meat fall, but the tugs were frozen. Furthermore, he couldn't unsheath his knife to cut them: it had frozen in place in its hide sheath.

To the devil with it, then; he would run. He left the horse standing where it was and set out on a lope. A glance over his shoulder showed that the Indians—Shawnees, almost certainly—had seen him make his break and were coming after him with no attempt to hide themselves.

They reached the horse; one stopped to secure it and remove the buffalo meat. The other three Indians came on after Daniel, who loped through the woods like an antelope. A rifle cracked and a bullet plowed the snowy ground behind his heel. Another shot, and a ball sang past his ear thunking into a maple ahead. He glanced back and saw the Indians reloading on the run.

Daniel ran for a long time, as hard as he could go, but it seemed no use. Every time he looked back, he saw they were closer to him than before. Fleet fellows, these were, and young. And he doubted that four Indians had come into Kentucky alone. They were probably part of a larger group—a terrible thought.

Another shot rang out, and though it also missed him, Daniel decided that to continue would be fatal. If he made a stand, he could kill only one of them at best before dying himself. And if he kept on running, they would certainly catch him within minutes.

He had little time to take anything more than a matter-of-fact attitude about his momentous decision. Daniel ducked behind a tree, then set his rifle out in full view. They would know from that sign that he was giving up. Icy air slicing painfully into his straining lungs, he leaned against the tree, gasping, and waited for them to reach him.

They approached him with big grins, glancing at each other with the expressions of men who had just stumbled upon a great treasure. Daniel looked from face to face, shook his head, coughed, and said, "Howdy."

"Howdy," one of the Indians replied.

"Too dang cold . . . for an old man like . . . me to be running young bucks like yourselves," Daniel panted out.

They said no more. Rifles leveled on him, they prodded him out of his place and back toward the waiting horse. Daniel was so weary, he could hardly keep on his feet, and only now did the somber reality of his situation settle upon him. He was a prisoner of the Shawnees, and there was every possibility they already knew about the salt makers at the Blue Licks. They might even have already captured them, or be on their way to do so. Nearly thirty of Boonesborough's best men . . . What would become of the people left behind if all these were killed or taken captive?

A rifle poked his spine, urging him on. Still panting, he stumbled down the low slope toward his waiting horse and the Indian who held it.

DANIEL HAD A DISHEARTENING notion of what all this was about as he moved through the snowy woods with his four captors. Word had recently come that back in November the great Shawnee chief Cornstalk, who had often led efforts for peace between red and white, had been murdered by a mob of angry whites around Point Pleasant. Cornstalk was a beloved man to his people, and it could be that the Shawnees had come into Kentucky on a vengeance quest. If so, matters could turn very sour for Daniel very soon. He might pay the price for the murder of Cornstalk with his own torturous death.

His eyes widened when he was led into the Shawnee camp. He could scarcely believe the size of the Indian band—a hundred men at least. No, even more than that! And their faces were painted for war making. Surely this indeed was an expedition mounted in vengeance. He looked at the Indians and saw that all were young warriors. Eager and bloodthirsty, no doubt, the kind of young men who would have cried loudest for revenge upon the death of Cornstalk.

Daniel's arrival brought a great hail of exuberant yells. The warriors crowded around him, eyeing him, and talked among themselves. He wondered if he was recognized. Daniel Boone was a well-known name among the Shawnees. Though despised in the way any persistent white encroacher was despised, he was also respected as a woodsman and a courageous fighter. He hoped that respect would save him here. Looking about at the swarm of faces, he tried to pick out someone familiar.

But they all were strange. His heart sank, and he wondered what death would come to him, and how quickly. Then the crowd shifted, and hope leaped within him as a face he did know appeared before him.

"Captain Will!" he said. "Howdy!"

The jovial face of the former captor of Daniel Boone and "Falling Man" John Stewart gazed in confusion, brow furrowed. "Who are you?"

"Do you not remember Boone, who pranced in horse bells for you years ago and ran from you into the canebrake?"

Captain Will brightened, and a big grin split his face. "Boone! My old friend Boone!" He came forward, putting out his hand to shake Daniel's.

This first open identification of the prisoner brought a new round of loud vocal response all around. Boone himself, captured! The man whose very name marked the fort on the Kentucky River was now in Shawnee hands! It was a great day for the Shawnees indeed.

"You have not heeded me about wasps and yellow jackets, Boone," Captain Will said. "Now you are stung, eh?"

"It was many a year ago you gave me that warning, Captain Will, and all is different now. Today I'm commander of a fort. My people wish only to live there in peace and be brothers to the Indians."

There was no more time for talk. A few moments of hand shaking—the Shawnees seemed eager to touch the flesh of the man they considered a worthy and honorable enemy—and then Daniel was hustled off and brought before a stocky, rather short man of obvious importance. Beside him stood a tall black man with a haughty face. Daniel would later learn that this fellow had been captured by the Shawnees in Virginia and raised among them. Now he was a translator for the tribe and went by the name Pompey.

A glance past the stocky Indian provided Daniel with a surprise. Two white men were there, dressed in heavy, hooded capotes, knitted voyageur's caps of coarse buffalo wool, and buffalo mittens. They looked like French Canadians, and Daniel figured they must be there under hire—but under hire of whom? The British, most likely. This too, was a distressing sign and a confirmation of the general fear that the British were supporting Indian incursions against the frontier settlements. He feared anew for his men at the licks, feared for the unknowing, nearly defenseless people of Boonesborough. His expression, however, did not alter.

He was not surprised to hear that the stocky Indian before him was Blackfish. Daniel stood as tall as he could, looking down at the face of the man who had been the bane of Kentucky settlers all the previous year.

Blackfish spoke tersely, and though Daniel understood most of his words, he waited for Pompey to translate the Algonquian.

"Hello, Boone. I have heard much of you."

"Hello. I have heard much of Blackfish as well."

"There are men at the licks with kettles and fires. Who are they?"

"They are my men."

"I am glad to know they are your men, for that means they have come from Boonesborough, and there are fewer rifles there to oppose us."

Daniel could hardly stifle the shudder those words roused. "You have come to destroy my fort?"

"Yes. We must avenge the death of Cornstalk. The young warriors are bitter for his murder."

"I am sorry that Cornstalk is dead. He was a great chief who wished our peoples to live in peace together, as I wish."

"There can be no peace now. Cornstalk's blood cries for revenge."

"My town on the Kentucky River is filled with women and children. To harm them would not be a worthy revenge for Cornstalk."

"That is why we will go to the licks and kill your men before we take prisoners at your town." Pompey gave a faint, smug smile as he translated those words to Daniel.

Daniel's mind worked frantically. Somehow he had to dissuade Blackfish from his plan. Virtually making up his scheme even as he spoke, he said, "There is a better way that will please you, Blackfish."

"Tell me."

"Take me back to my men at the licks, and I will surrender them to you if you will give me your pledge not to harm them or make them run the gauntlet. If I tell them to give up, they will not resist you. They are strong men who would make good prisoners, but if you go to battle them, they will kill many of your warriors before they die. If you pledge their safety and let them surrender, you can take them back to your towns."

"But what of those in Boonesborough?"

"Already the women and children there are hungry. If you attack them, you will be able to take them prisoner, but they would eat your food all the way back to your towns. There are few men left at Boonesborough, and they are weak and hungry and ready to give their allegiance to the British. In the spring I will lead your warriors back to Boonesborough, and all there will gladly surrender to you."

Pompey translated slowly and precisely. Blackfish listened to every word and stood in silent thoughtfulness for a full minute before he spoke again.

"I will do as you say, Boone. If your men surrender, they will not run the gauntlet or be tortured. But if they resist us, all will die."

"They will not resist," Daniel said confidently. But he wasn't confident. He had no idea at all of how his men would react to the arrival of the Shawnee band. He wished he could have come up with a better scheme.

But it was as his father once told him: "It's hard to render a perfect tune when you have to make it up while you're already whistling."

THIS, THOUGHT DANIEL, *is the hardest thing I've ever done and I don 't know for certain I can do it.*

He was seated in a circle of Shawnee warriors, not far from Blackfish himself. Off to the side his glum-faced men sat on the cold ground, surrounded by Indian guards. Several of his men stared at him with something disturbingly close to hatred, as if he were a Judas who had betrayed them in the worst possible way.

The terrible fact of it was, he might turn out to have been just that. Despite Blackfish's promise of protection for the prisoners, what was going on was no less than a debate about whether the salt makers would be spared, or their blood would be spilled here at the lick, and their fort on the Kentucky River attacked forthwith.

The give-and-take was hard to follow, even with Pompey translating into his ear. Daniel realized he was fortunate to be part of this council at all; it was only at the invitation of Blackfish that he sat in the circle. And it was that invitation, given before his men, that accounted for the obvious conclusion of some that they had been betrayed by their own leader.

There had been mutterings from the very moment he had ordered them to lay down their arms before the big Shawnee warrior band that appeared at the lick with Daniel at their lead. Daniel could understand how disturbing a sight it must have been, him in company with a body of their enemies. His words must have disturbed them much more: "Don't fire—throw down your rifles and surrender, else all will be massacred! If you surrender, you'll be spared, and no harm will come!"

Some had been reluctant to give up their weapons, but in the end all had done so. He had heard murmurs of the word "Tory," and grumblings that perhaps his well-known respect for "savages" might have run a lot deeper than anyone had realized. Hard words to hear, those, though an understandable sentiment under the circumstances. But what else could he have done? How could the twenty-seven men at the salt lick have held out against a foe that so outnumbered them? And he had, at least, negotiated an agreement of safety and a pledge to leave all their kin at Boonesborough unmolested for the time being.

Now Daniel felt betrayed himself, not by Blackfish directly but by the very nature of Indian government. He should have taken it into account in his earlier thinking, he realized, but he had been doing the best he could, making it all up as he went along.

Blackfish was chief, but his authority came by the agreement of those he led. Indians were notoriously independent; a man could pretty much opt in or out of decisions made by others, and the will of the whole was decided by consensus. In other words, Blackfish's promises to Daniel meant nothing if the warriors themselves chose to override them.

The argument went back and forth for hours, wearying the ear and straining at the mind and emotions. Daniel did his best to keep up and felt hope alternately wax and wane. He had no idea of how the final decision would go. He felt a bitter fury at the two French Canadians, who confirmed their ties to the British by the fervor with which they sought to turn the will of the warriors toward a slaughter of the prisoners and a quick attack upon defenseless Boonesborough.

At last Blackfish turned to Daniel and, through Pompey, told him it was his time to speak. Daniel would have the chance to give his own argument about why the men should be spared. He was pleased to hear this and eager to speak—eager, but with one qualification. So far the speeches had been in Algonquian, incomprehensible to all the white men who heard them. But Daniel would be speaking English, and through his words the men would come to know for the first time that what was being debated there was their mortal fate.

"Brothers!" Daniel declared. "What I have promised I can much better fulfill in the spring than now. Then the weather will be warm, and the women and children can travel from Boonesborough to the Indian towns, and all live with you as one people." He paused, giving Pompey time to translate, then went on. "You have all the young men here. If you kill them, as some have suggested, it will displease the Great Spirit, and you could not then expect future success in hunting or war. If you spare them, they will make you fine warriors, and excellent hunters to kill game for your squaws and children."

He paused again, and as Pompey talked, heard angry murmurs among the white men. It would be difficult now to convince some of them that he had really obtained a promise of their safety before surrendering them. If he had such a promise, why was he having to plead for their lives now? He could only hope they would understand Indian ways well enough to realize it wasn't his fault.

Clearing his throat, he spoke again, his words accompanied by steamy gusts of his breath: "These young men have done you no harm. They surrendered on my assurance that such a step was the only safe one." He spoke his next sentence just a little louder, to make sure all his own men heard it. "I consented to their surrender on the express condition that they should be made prisoners of war and treated well. Spare them, and the Great Spirit will smile upon you."

He sat down then to await the decision. He had done all he could do to keep his men alive and Boonesborough free from attack. Now the outcome lay in the hands of the Indians and the Great Spirit whose name Daniel had twice evoked.

It was difficult to keep the tears from his eyes when the final decision was announced. By the narrowest of margins—two votes—the Indians had decided to keep Blackfish's promise. The men would not die, not run the gauntlet, and Boonesborough would not be attacked.

Daniel drew in a deep breath and exhaled very slowly. Trials lay in the future for all of them . . . but at least there was going to *be* a future. For a while he hadn't been sure about that at all.

HE'D SAVED HIS MEN from the gauntlet, but he made one significant omission from the agreement: himself. He stood now at the beginning of a long double row of grinning, eager warriors. He would have to run between them, struck by their clubs all along the way. If he came out on the other end, well and good. If he fell, odds were worse than even that he would not get up before being beaten to death. Standing there awaiting the start, Daniel made a wry mental note: *Next time I work out a bargain to keep folk out of the gauntlet, I'll surely remember to include Daniel Boone.*

He did his best to seem good-humored about the ordeal. He realized his failure to exempt himself might have been what swayed the vote in favor of life for the prisoners. Perhaps those who felt that sparing the prisoners violated the late Cornstalk's right to blood vengeance for his murder ended up going along because they knew they could at least have the pleasure of beating the famous Boone to death in the gauntlet. So much the better for the other prisoners. So much the worse for Daniel Boone.

A blow struck his buttocks and almost knocked him flat. Catching himself, Daniel surged out in a dead run, trying out a survival strategy as he went. He dodged left, coming so close to that line of warriors that they couldn't find space to draw back for a solid blow, and staying out of reach of the right-hand line. When the left-hand line began to pull back to get a better swing at him, he dodged to the right and crowded that row as well. Then back the other way, and back yet again . . .

It worked fairly well. Daniel made it halfway down the long line before anyone hit him too hard a lick. Then a club flashed above his eyes and stars burst in his vision, washed away by a red flow of blood pouring down over his nose. Someone managed to smack him on the crown of the head with a war club, and it laid open the skin. Grimacing in pain and fighting dizziness, he fixed his eyes on the end of the line and surged on.

Time played tricks on him. He seemed to be moving very fast and very slow at the same time. Blow after blow rained down, some hard, some deliberately soft, reflecting the attitudes of the individual punishers. He was vaguely conscious of passing Captain Will in the left row. Captain Will gave him only a friendly slap and shouted encouragement. Struggling to keep his feet, Daniel saw the end come nearer, nearer . . .

Then a big, smiling man stood before him. One of the Indians had broken out of the line and stood directly in the center, club uplifted, ready to come down and end the life of Daniel Boone. Into Daniel's mind flashed the memory of another big Indian years before, a Pennsylvania bridge across a deep and watery gorge, a knife drawn, a threat of death—and as he had during that solitary encounter during Forbes's trek toward Fort Duquesne, he lowered his head and butted directly into the man's midsection. With a grunt the Indian fell back, and Daniel lunged right across him, his ankle nearly grabbed by the man he had just humiliated.

And suddenly he was through. There were no more Indians on either side of him. Wiping blood from his eyes, he came to a stop while the Indians closed around him, slapping his shoulders and cheering at his success. He heard similar accolades rise from the clump of white prisoners who had stood watching. *Glad to know some of them haven't lost faith in me*, he thought. He couldn't keep himself from grinning. It felt good to be alive, and good to have earned the respect of his captors. Owning that respect might keep him and his men safer and get them better treatment when they reached the Shawnee towns.

They departed the next morning, the prisoners treated like beasts of burden. Some went along without complaint, but others argued. James Callaway, nephew of the colonel, belligerently pointed at his own head and defied a warrior to sink an ax into it if he didn't like the fact that Jim Callaway didn't carry a kettle for any yellow savage. To Daniel's surprise the warrior didn't accept the invitation, and Jim Callaway was spared both death and overburdening. One William Brooks might have been tomahawked had not Daniel talked him into agreeing to accept his burden. As a gesture of support Daniel took some of Brooks's baggage on his own shoulders despite the fact they were already overburdened.

It was a difficult journey, and cold. With hardly a break the men were driven north for ten days. There was nothing to eat but dog meat, decent fare from the Indian point of view but repulsive to most of the white men. Hunger and weakness threatened to drop many of them where they marched, but Daniel offered continual encouragement, told them to cinch up their belts and keep plodding no matter what. He had endured worse hunger than this many a time and got through.

They were finally given some venison brought in along the way, but first were made to eat a repulsive jelly made from the deer guts. The mess was hard to keep down, but what seemed to be cruelty by their captors wound up having been motivated by kindness. The men had been so long without meat, the Indians explained, that eating venison without ingesting some of the jelly first would have killed them. Daniel didn't believe that notion was necessarily true, but kept his mouth shut. What counted was that the Shawnees believed it and were trying to keep their prisoners alive and reasonably healthy. A good sign.

They reached the Ohio River and ferried across, twenty at a time, on a buffalo hide boat. At last they reached the town of Chillicothe. Nearing the town, the prisoners were made to remove their clothes and sing loudly as they drew near, shivering, white, humiliated. They passed between rows and clusters of Shawnee cabins, not sure what would befall them now that they had reached their destination. The unpredictability of Shawnee sentiments had already been proved to them by the near change of tune concerning their fate at the salt lick.

Daniel himself wasn't sure what would happen now. He was happy to see that the town's population was diminished at the moment, with many of the summer residents wintering elsewhere. If any gauntlets were formed, they would be short ones. He was even more grateful that no squaws had appeared with black paint for the prisoners' faces, which would indicate they were doomed to the stake.

If fortune smiled, many of the captives would be adopted into the tribe to replace fallen warriors. Those men would be treated well, as if they were naturally born Shawnees. Others would remain prisoners and slaves, living lives of uncertainty and misery.

As for his own fate, Daniel had every plan to survive as well as possible. He had already made many friends among his captors, joking with them, professing his conversion to their cause and that of the British, and acting as if he could think of no better situation than to be among their people. He already had developed an inkling that no lesser a man than Blackfish himself was thinking of adopting him.

Should that happen, Daniel would be as well situated as he could hope to be to carry off the plan already forming in his mind. He had no intention of leading any Shawnee force to Boonesborough in the spring or urging any more surrenders. He planned to make his escape as soon as the time was right and get back to the settlements to give warning. But the time wasn't right yet. He needed to learn more about the strength of the Shawnees and the level of support they were receiving from the British. And most of all he needed to know when they planned to attack.

He hoped Blackfish would adopt him. As Blackfish's "son" he would be trusted and able to learn what he needed to know.

There was a problem, however. From Pompey he'd already learned that Blackfish had a son before, but he was dead now. How had he been killed? Daniel asked. Pompey looked at him with a deeply ironic expression as he answered, "The son of Blackfish was killed when white men fired into his camp in Kentucky in the past summer. He and some others had kidnaped three girls from your fort on the Kentucky River."

CHAPTER 29

THEY MARCHED DANIEL BOONE and ten other prisoners to Detroit in mid-March to show them off as prizes to the British. By now Daniel knew he was indeed to be adopted by Blackfish, and, with his typically pliable approach to life, accepted his status readily. There might even be something to enjoy in living as an Indian for a while. Hadn't people always told him that he was as much Indian as white in his attitude toward life?

He was paraded before Lieutenant Governor Henry Hamilton, a hated British official becoming known to the settlers as "Hair Buyer" because he paid British bounty on rebel scalps brought in by the Indians. He paid for prisoners, too, Daniel observed as several of his fellow captives were "sold" to the British by Blackfish.

The general antipathy toward Hamilton notwithstanding, Daniel found him a distinguished and pleasant gentleman, very British in manner and look. His rather florid, smooth-skinned face showed nothing that appeared diabolical. Daniel discovered he actually liked Hamilton, and in the ten days he and the Shawnee delegation spent there, Hamilton grew to like Daniel in turn. Most of the time was spent with the Indians giving intelligence to Hamilton or his underlings, and at one point Daniel was extensively interviewed by Hamilton himself. During this time Daniel continued to play his role of Tory convert and made a point of showing Hamilton his commission as militia captain under Dunmore, a document that the Indians had allowed him to keep. It was a handy item to have around, allowing him to show instant evidence of British allegiance anytime it was prudent. Hamilton was so taken by Daniel that he actually tried to buy his freedom from Blackfish, intending to free him and send him home.

The return to Chillicothe was slow and winding, with Blackfish making stops along the way to visit other Shawnee villages and even several other tribes. At each stop Blackfish talked openly about his plan to attack Boonesborough in the spring. Daniel listened with a look of pleasant concurrence on his face, but the words confirmed in him the need to escape and give warning. When they reached their home base again, Daniel was slightly amused—and slightly disturbed—to discover that one of the prisoners slated for tribal adoption had vanished. Andrew Johnson, a short, unimpressive-looking man who had managed to fool his captors into believing him a simpleton, was a fine woodsman but pretended total ignorance of woodcraft and feigned a lack of any sense of direction. When he fired his rifle for the Indians, he always squeezed his eyes closed and missed his mark widely, and when asked which direction he would flee to get to Kentucky, inevitably pointed the wrong way. Called Pequolly by the Shawnees, he had quickly become a kind of human mascot, a simple jester whom the Shawnees found endearing.

They were actually worried now that Pequolly was gone. Daniel knew that he had certainly escaped, but the Indians naturally felt otherwise, not believing him mentally capable of such a thing even though at the same time he had vanished, so too had a coat, knife, rifle, and ammunition. The evidence couldn't convince them; they were sure that poor Pequolly must be lost and roaming, probably dead by now. They searched for him but, strangely, could find no tracks. It was as if he had vanished like a phantom. Shawnee grief over the loss of the supposed simpleton was sincere and widespread.

Daniel thought it funny that Johnson fooled them so easily, but one thing worried him. In his pretense of British support and eagerness to live as a Shawnee, Daniel had managed to fool some of his own companions as well as the Indians, and he never got the opportunity to explain his ruse to all of them in private. Johnson was one of these. Daniel suspected that Johnson thought him a true Tory and traitor, and when he got back to Boonesborough, this would be the story he spread.

Nothing gained by worrying about that now, he decided. Whenever he made his own return to Boonesborough, he would just have to be all the more persuasive. At least Johnson would be able to reassure Rebecca and the children that their husband and father was still alive. No doubt the capture of the salt makers had been detected long ago, and the people left behind must now be sorely worried.

DANIEL STOOD NAKED in the cold river, fighting off his white man's sense of modesty as Shawnee women scrubbed him from head to toe until his skin was nearly raw. Already his hair was shaved off except for a scalp lock at the top. It was all part of the official ceremony making him a Shawnee and son of Blackfish.

As he stood enduring his washing, which was designed to symbolically scrub away his whiteness and leave him Indian, Daniel's eyes fastened upon an Indian man standing on the bank, watching. It was none other than Crow, the Cherokee who had helped Hanging Maw capture Jemima and the Callaway girls. Daniel was surprised to see him there; Hanging Maw had long ago headed back to his own home in the Cherokee country. Daniel nodded solemnly at the Cherokee, who nodded back. There was no look of friendliness on his face, but neither was there hatred, as Daniel might have expected, considering that Crow had been wounded during the girls' rescue.

As Daniel was escorted out of the river, he saw a young Shawnee woman come to Crow's side and slip her arm around him. Now he understood. Crow had probably been brought to Chillicothe to heal from his wound, and while there had met and fallen in love with one of the local young women. Now, Daniel expected, the pair were husband and wife. From time to time members of one tribe would marry members of another. Daniel himself knew that the Cherokee named Savanooka, known more commonly as the Raven of Chota, was by birth a Shawnee, but he had married a Cherokee woman and lived as a Cherokee thereafter.

After the river ceremony Daniel was dressed and taken to the council house, the largest structure in the impressively built and well-organized Shawnee town. There he smoked the pipe with Blackfish and others, went through the ceremonial actions they directed him to perform, and ate until he was fuller than he had been in months.

When it was all through, he was no longer Daniel Boone, but Sheltowee, meaning "Big Turtle." He was now the son of Blackfish. He would be expected to live as an Indian, to think as one, to fight as one. Blackfish already told him there was a squaw who wished to claim him.

When the ceremony was done, Daniel stood in the midst of Chillicothe, looking around and thinking to himself that his situation there was not really bad in itself. He had respect, company, even some degree of status. The life of the Indians fit him well in most ways, and there he would probably be better fed and kept than at Boonesborough. A part of him could actually consider the unconsiderable, could actually make the transition from white man to . . .

No. *No.* As much as the freer part of his spirit might be tempted by the Shawnee life, he remained Daniel Boone, a boy raised as a Quaker in Pennsylvania and now a settler of the fine country of Kentucky. No amount of river scrubbing could change the color of his skin or the basic allegiances of his heart. If there was any question of turning away from them, it was answered at once when he thought of Rebecca and his other loved ones. He could not forsake them, and all his big bluffing talk of leading them there in the spring to become Indians themselves was so absurd, he could hardly imagine how even Blackfish had taken it seriously.

He was thinking about these things when he turned and saw Crow striding toward him. The Indian man looked him squarely in the eye as he came up, then stopped about three yards away.

"Howdy, Crow," Daniel said. "It has been many a year since you and Hanging Maw sat at my table in Watauga."

"Yes," Crow said, turning his head very slightly so that his hearing ear was toward Daniel. "But not so long since we saw each other last, when you came firing your rifles into our camp."

"You had stolen my daughter from me, and the daughters of another man of my fort. We had no choice but to take them back."

Crow nodded. "I hold no anger over it, Boone. When there is reason, men must fight and sometimes must kill as well."

"You called me Boone. My name now is Sheltowee. I have been adopted by Blackfish."

"So now you are Shawnee?"

"Yes."

Crow said nothing, but his face revealed skepticism. *A perceptive fellow, this Crow*, Daniel thought.

"I don't understand why Blackfish has adopted you. His son was one of us who stole your daughter. It was he who fell dead into the fire when you fired your rifle. Does Blackfish not know this?"

"He knows, though I will tell you what I told him: several of us fired our rifles. I don't know that it was my bullet that killed his son."

"But it could have been, and even if you had known it was Blackfish's son, you would not have held back from killing him."

"No. But again it is as I told Blackfish himself when we talked of all this. The capture of the girls had put us at war, and in war men must do what they would not do other times. These things can only be forgotten."

Crow considered the words and nodded. "Yes. You speak correctly, Sheltowee. But I know your race. The white man kills even those who are living in peace. He murders the old and sick and seeks to murder even the young boys. I know this from what I have seen with my own eyes."

Daniel had no idea what Crow was talking about and said only, "I am no longer a white man. I am a Shawnee."

Crow studied him in silence, turned away, and walked off. Daniel observed him until he was gone, feeling oddly disturbed, as if Crow had managed to look through the veil he had cast about his own thoughts and read them easily.

Such a thing was impossible, he knew, but even so, he decided that from there on out he would keep a close eye on the Cherokee.

Easter Sunday, April 19, 1778

DANIEL TRABUE'S EMPTY STOMACH sent forth an embarrassingly loud grumble as he rode toward the stockade of Boonesborough. He and the men with him hadn't eaten a bite since Thursday, and that day all they had eaten was a few morsels of bacon. And Trabue hadn't got his full share even of that, because he had shared part of his with a strange, bearded, unspeaking man his party had encountered among empty cabins in Powell Valley, vacated by settlers fleeing Indians.

There was a general commotion within Boonesborough at the arrival of the Trabue party. Loud shouts of greeting and whoops of delight arose as people spilled out toward the riders. But what ragged people they were! Daniel Trabue was taken aback by the sight. Dressed in tatters, thin and obviously hungry, there was nothing bright about them except the broad smiles the arrival of this little band of strangers had generated.

Trabue dismounted and shook hands all around. His smile masked the disturbance the sight of these impoverished people roused in him. And where were the others? They had been led to believe there were more people resident at Boonesborough than this seemingly handful. Apart from the military men, there didn't look to be any more than eight or ten families' worth of humanity about the place.

Trabue's older brother, leader of this band, introduced himself to the men of the fort. "I'm James Trabue, come from Charlotte County, Virginia, with the rank of lieutenant under Colonel George Rogers Clark. I was enlisted foremost to help him enlist volunteer troops. This is my younger brother, Daniel, one of my enlistees. The others with me, with the exception of the boy Negro and the tattered fellow mounted at the rear yonder, are also enlisted. The tattered fellow is a poor injured soul we found hiding amongst empty cabins in Powell Valley. On any road, we've come to join ourselves with Colonel Clark's force. A good number of my earlier enlistees were thought to have already reached this fort." James Trabue looked around. "I see no sign of them. Where are Thomas and William Brooks?"

"Well, it's clear you haven't heard of our latest sorrow," came the answer from Flanders Callaway. "Tom and Will were among them who was taken prisoner by the Shawnees at the Blue Licks while they was out making salt. Nigh thirty men took by a hundred or more cussed savages, judging from the tracks, and leaving us here with hardly a defense."

Daniel Trabue was stunned. This was the first information that had come to their party concerning the capture. He drew closer to hear the story, what there was known of it. Tales of Indian encounters held a special morbid fascination for him at the moment. After the Trabue party had left Powell Valley and gone through Cumberland Gap, they had run across a small group of Indians, chased them away, and taken as booty five bows and arrows, three shot bags and powder horns, several new hunting shirts, leggings and breechcloths decorated with silver brooches, a brass kettle, and several other fine items. It had been his first meeting with Indians, and he had not known how brave a showing he would make for himself. In fact he had done quite well, leading the charge that had driven the Indians away and outclassing one braggart who had declared his bravery and then hid among the horses. But it had been a frightening experience that had made Kentucky's infamous Indians a reality instead of campfire phantoms. The thought of a hundred or more Indians capturing the bulk of Boonesborough's defensive force raised his hackles and made the land around him seem suddenly fraught with danger.

The Trabue party was told that the disappearance of the salt makers had been discovered by Flanders Callaway and a companion who had been away from the salt lick hunting when the capture occurred. The empty camp and various sign on the earth told clearly what had happened. Simon Butler had traced the sign all the way to the Ohio River. There was no doubt that all were prisoners, but there had been no sign that any had been wounded, killed in a fight, or put to death. It seemed obvious they must have simply surrendered. What had become of them since, no one knew. The fear was they had been put to death in the Shawnee country across the Ohio River.

"Turned over by the damned Tory Boone, the way I see it," one man grumbled.

Flanders Callaway turned and faced the speaker. "I know the kind of opinion that has developed among some of you about Captain Boone, and I know that my own father considers the man nigh a rascal. But the truth is that Captain Boone would never do anything that wasn't necessary to save lives. He's no Tory, that I can tell you."

"That's right," someone else said sarcastically. "Keep up the good word for *Daddy Boone*." The indirect reference to Flanders Callaway's son-in-law relationship to Daniel Boone seemed to anger the young man. He turned. "Who said that?"

No answer.

"Next time anyone has a thing to say to me in such a manner, by hell, let him say it to my face like a man!"

"Calm yourself, Flanders," a weary-sounding feminine voice said. "There's nothing gained by such anger."

The clump of people parted to let a slightly slumped, middle-aged woman come through. It was obvious she was a woman given some deference there, though even now there were faint grumblings from some, out of which the word "Tory" came through. James Trabue swept off his hat as she came to Flanders Callaway's side and put her arm around him.

"Hello, ma'am," James Trabue said. "My name is Lieutenant Trabue."

"I am Rebecca Boone, wife of the late Daniel Boone," the woman answered. "Welcome to Boonesborough."

"Don't say he's dead—you don't know it!" Flanders scolded.

"He's dead. I can think of him as no other way until I'm shown otherwise," she said. She looked past James Trabue and the others, fixing her gaze on the tattered man at the rear. "What's the matter with that man?"

"I believe he was injured by Indians and rendered mute," James Trabue answered. "He was found wandering among empty Powell Valley cabins like that demon-possessed man in the Bible who roamed among the tombs. He is a stranger. When he was first seen, he nearly scared our darky boy to death—the boy grabbed a pistol and took a shot at him, thinking he was an Indian." There was a titter of laughter; the black boy dropped his head, ashamed. "See the man's right ear, there, with the lobe missing? Shot clean off, it was, by the pistol ball."

Rebecca left Flanders's side and walked slowly up to the silent man, who still sat his horse. He looked back at her, his eyes brighter now than before, as if some nearly extinguished spark of life and reason was beginning to flare again.

"This man is no stranger to me," Rebecca said. "I've known him for years." She reached up her right hand, and to the surprise of all, the silent man reached out and took it. "Hello, Nate Meriwether," Rebecca said.

Nate's whiskered lips parted, revealing rows of yellowed teeth, minus one that had been pulled out by Daniel Boone many years before beside Braddock's Road. His words were so slurred that most hearers could not make them out, but Rebecca understood.

"Hello, Rebecca Boone," he said. "I'm mighty happy to see you again."

JEMIMA BOONE CALLAWAY sat beside her mother, their hands entwined. Both were watching Nate Meriwether sleeping on a rope bed in the corner. He snored softly and slept very deeply. "He comes and goes and comes again," Rebecca said. "There's a mark on his head, mostly healed now, where he was struck. From the look of it I believe he was hit with the bowl of a tomahawk pipe. There's a round circle of bone pushed in just a little."

"But is he. . . well, what he was? Is his sense gone?"

"As I said, he comes and he goes. I'm thinking he'll be the Nate Meriwether he once was when that bone rights itself."

"Has he told you what happened?"

"Naught but a bit of jabber about having a family and then losing them. Indians, I gathered."

"Like his brother in Pennsylvania, the one you told me about . . ."

"Yes. There was another brother, named Clive, killed by highwaymen. He had turned to drinking, but put it aside with the help of your father."

The mention of Daniel caused Rebecca to choke off. Jemima looked at her sternly. "Daddy is alive, Ma. You have no call to believe he's dead."

"Yes, I do, girl. For if I don't believe that, then there's doubt and question and hope that's almost sure to be ruined. To me he is dead. The Shawnees took him to their town and killed him, and now I'm widowed. There's naught left for me but to sit in this terrible place and feel my own hunger and hear the babble of them who say your father was a traitor."

Jemima pulled her hand away from her mother's and stood. "I'll not listen to you talk so sorrowful, Ma. It's never been your way, and there's no call for it now."

"You think there ain't? Not even after all the time I've told Phebe Carrick to quit clinging to a fool's hope that her man is still living? Now it's my man gone, and I'll not act the fool as she has. I'll never see my Dan again."

Jemima stamped her foot. "Then why don't you leave? Go back to Carolina, or wherever you want, and quit spreading sorrow to those of us who don't think it foolish to hope as long as we can!"

Rebecca lifted weary eyes; at that moment she looked very old. "Perhaps I will go. Yes. I think I will. And you and Flanders, you can go too."

"I'll not leave here," Jemima declared. "I'll stay here until the day my father comes walking back through the gate, and I throw my arms around his neck. And then I suppose it will be up to me to tell him that his own wife declared him dead and left him."

Rebecca shook her head and smiled condescendingly. "Poor Jemima," she said. "Poor, hopeful Jemima."

It was all Jemima could take. "To the devil with you! Straight to the bloody devil!" she yelled as loudly as she could, a deliberate effort to startle her mother. But Rebecca just kept smiling and shaking her head as if Jemima were a sad, misled child. The only one startled was Nate Meriwether, who rolled over, mumbled, and drifted back to sleep again as Jemima stormed out the door, mad as a teased hornet.

IN LESS THAN A MONTH Rebecca proved she was serious about refusing to hope for the best. Andrew Johnson had shown up in Harrodsburg, reporting that Daniel was still alive the last time he saw him. The last Johnson had known of Daniel, Blackfish was taking him and some other prisoners north to the British outpost at Detroit. By the time he fled, they had not returned.

"He's dead, then," Rebecca said flatly. "The British have killed him."

Jemima was both confused and infuriated. She couldn't understand why her mother seemed so intent on clinging to the belief that Daniel was dead—indeed, why she seemed to want to believe it. Rebecca's answer was that she had spent too many years of her life fighting to maintain hope her husband was alive, wherever he was. She was tired of that struggle. Even so heavy a burden as bereavement was not as crushing as that of uncertainty.

Later on Jemima would realize there were other factors that encouraged Rebecca's departure from Boonesborough. Andrew Johnson was openly declaring that Daniel Boone had acted as a Tory, forcing the surrender of his own men when many had been willing to stand and fight. He had joked and acted friendly with their Indian captors and gone off to Detroit in a seemingly content and cooperative manner. It surely seemed the man had betrayed his own folk, and Johnson had nothing good to say about him. People picked up on the talk and did a lot of whispering that it was the Tory-sympathizing Bryans who had corrupted old Boone. Now he was of no more account than they were. Why, old traitorous Boone had actually promised Blackfish that he would lead the Shawnee army against Boonesborough in the spring! Hurt by such gossip against her kin, Rebecca left with her children and William Hays, who had married Susannah. They went back toward North Carolina, the region where Rebecca had lived her happiest days in what seemed like a former life.

Jemima was left alone at Boonesborough with her husband to await the return of Daniel Boone. She confidently declared her belief that he was alive and defied all who dared question his patriotism in her presence. It was quite a delicate position to hold, considering that her ever-grouchy father-in-law was among Daniel Boone's most strident critics. Colonel Callaway was a generally miserable person to be around those days, but then so was most everyone else. Food was all but nonexistent, clothing consisted of rags draped in whatever way possible around thin human forms, and no one dared hunt or farm any more than necessary because of the Indian danger. There was no salt, no bread, few vegetables and fruits, and no liquor. The people subsisted entirely on what meat the hunters could bring in. The Trabue party had remained at Boonesborough only about a week before heading on to Logan's Station, which was reportedly in much better condition as far as food and supplies were concerned, but in the time they were on hand, they brought in several deer and turkeys. These were fast consumed, however, and poverty returned.

With Rebecca gone, Jemima took Nate Meriwether into her own house. Slowly he was recovering, his speech improving, his periods of vacant staring and silence lessening in duration and frequency. Twice he went through terrifying convulsions, but these were short and seemed to do no harm. The most difficult thing about dealing with Nate was his rising emotionalism. As his injured head healed and his "sense," in Jemima's term, slowly returned, he began bursting into tears at unexpected moments, repeating names that she supposed were those of his family members, and occasionally shouting in fury. Jemima was distressed by this, and Flanders soon declared he had endured about enough of having a stranger laying about his cabin and getting his wife all tormented. But Jemima was unwilling to turn Nate out. He was hurt, and obviously coming to grips with a great loss that he probably hadn't been able to comprehend until now. It was their duty to tend him until he was well. He was an old friend of her father's, after all.

"And there lies the true reason for all this Christian charity, I believe," Flanders would say. "It's for your father's sake you tend this poor fellow."

A solution to the difficulty walked through the cabin door in mid-May in the person of Phebe Carrick. Rebecca had pleaded with Phebe to come to Carolina and leave Kentucky behind, but Phebe had refused, stubborn as ever. She was the opposite of Rebecca, who opted to give up hope until shown a reason to hold to it. Phebe still held out the feeble hope that somehow her missing Jim was still alive. Maybe he was a captive of the Shawnees, like the salt makers. Maybe some of them had actually found him in the Shawnee towns and would someday bring him home.

Phebe had initially paid little attention to the stories about a hurt man named Nate Meriwether who now was being tended in the Flanders Callaway cabin. She had not laid eyes on the fellow; she rarely emerged from her own cabin anymore, terrified by fears of Indians and worried for the welfare of her children. For the first time she was beginning to consider the possibility that she should leave the place. Her Jim really wasn't coming back. She started regretting that she had not listened to Rebecca Boone's urgings to go with her to Carolina.

Phebe was ready to admit her change of heart and find a way to leave, when something happened to change her mind. She heard details about Nate Meriwether that made him suddenly interesting to her.

She was told how his family had apparently either been killed or captured by Indians in Powell Valley, as best anyone could surmise from the scraps of things he had said. He obviously had been struck down himself, but had not died. He had become a solitary, mute relic of a man, roaming among ruined cabins, grieving for his lost loved ones.

The story had a quality of romantic tragedy that struck a chord with almost everyone, but especially with Phebe Carrick. So much of her own story seemed embodied in the experience of this Nate Meriwether. Many times she had perceived herself as a lonely wanderer, left alone and hopeless.

Jemima was cooking a meager supper of bear meat and wild greens when Phebe appeared at her door. Nate was asleep again—he slept a lot as his head injury healed. Phebe nodded in greeting, went over to Nate's bedside, and peered down at him for a time. Jemima watched her, puzzled.

Phebe turned. "I've come to help you care for this poor man," she said. "If you'll let me."

Jemima felt a great burst of relief. Phebe had come at just the time she was beginning to feel overwhelmed. She was weary of stockade life, missed her mother, worried for her father, and feared her own husband could walk out of the fort at any time and never return, just as Daniel and the salt makers had, just as Jim Carrick had. She knew tensions were no less for her mate. Flanders Callaway's home had been invaded by a wounded stranger whom his wife was so busy caring for that she hardly had time for him. So Phebe's abrupt offer seemed a gift from heaven.

"Yes, Phebe, I'll let you help me," she said. "I surely will." She put down her stirring stick and slumped into a chair, feeling more like an old woman than a fifteen-year-old bride. "I need help more than ever I have before."

"Then you have it," Phebe replied.

CHAPTER 30

DANIEL BOONE LOOKED around to make sure he was not observed, then knelt and reached into the hollow of a leaning sycamore. From it he withdrew a small hide pouch, well greased to repel moisture. Opening it, he dropped another couple rifle balls inside. Four of them now, and in the horn also secreted in the sycamore, enough powder for five or six shots. Hiding the pouch again, he stood and quickly moved away from the spot, concerned lest anyone should discover it.

Powder and ball . . . but no rifle with which to fire them. Even such a fine woodsman as Daniel Boone would not wish to enter the wilderness without a rifle. Boonesborough was a long way; a man making the journey there on the run would need a rifle for protection and sustenance. So far Daniel didn't have one, at least not permanently. He had gained enough of Blackfish's confidence now that he was allowed to hunt with a rifle on his own from time to time, but he always had to return it. A couple of times he had considered sneaking off from such hunts but had not done it. Several of his fellow Boonesboroughites were still prisoners or adoptees there, such as William Hancock, who had been adopted by none other than old Captain Will himself. Daniel would much rather make the break with all or as many of his fellow captives as he could.

So he held fast, waiting for a group-escape opportunity and letting several other chances go by. In some ways the waiting wasn't all that hard. He had managed to charm or talk his way out of most of the work Blackfish initially had put his new "son" to, such as hoeing and wood hewing. And he had even finally pleaded free of a squaw who had been more or less forced upon him. No desirable partner, this squaw! Old and ugly, she used him as a slave and got great pleasure out of whipping and tormenting him. He would have rather kept company with a meat ax than that squaw, and had breathed several prayers of thanks that she had not wanted him for anything more than labor and aggravation. The thought of physical intimacy with her was more than Daniel could bear thinking about. He had asked Blackfish to get him free of the woman, and somehow he had, though he hadn't seemed to understand why Daniel wasn't pleased with her. After that Daniel lived in Blackfish's house and was much more content there.

Daniel had come to like Blackfish and his family very much. Married to a quiet, kindly woman, the Shawnee chief had two appealing young girl-children Daniel delighted in giving small gifts, usually little wooden ornaments or sculptures he whittled out. In the evenings, they would tease and play chase with Sheltowee while Blackfish watched, nodding and smiling in lazy approval. All in all, being the adopted son of Blackfish was no bad bargain.

There were occasional chances for sport, mostly shooting matches that pitted Daniel against Shawnee men. He was a hard competitor and shot well, impressing his opponents. Only when he detected that his opponents were beginning to grow irked at being outshot did he hold back some and let himself lose. It was easier to remain popular that way, easier to earn more trust and favor.

One competitor he actually did have trouble outshooting was Crow. The Cherokee had a steady hand and eye and rarely missed his mark.

"How do you shoot so fine?" Daniel had once asked Crow after losing a match to him.

"I look at the mark and see it as the heart of a white man," Crow answered coldly.

Daniel had left the hollow sycamore far behind now, and slowed his pace as he entered town. He was satisfied, confident he had not been seen. It had been no easy feat, stealing those rifle balls. They had come from the pouch of Blackfish, taken when no one was looking. One of the other two had been left over from a hunt, as had all the powder he had saved up, and the last bullet he had palmed during a shooting competition. He hoped to obtain several more before escaping.

His eye turned toward one of the windowless Shawnee cabins. Leaning against it, staring hard at him, was Crow. Daniel nodded a greeting and Crow nodded back. As often happened, Daniel felt unsettled. He had never been able to shake off the feeling that Crow knew his every thought and plan. Something in those dark, unflinching eyes was disconcerting. Thinking back, Daniel remembered having felt similarly in the days that Crow had visited his Watauga cabin with Hanging Maw. Even then Crow had been able to stare at him so probingly, it troubled.

Daniel walked on past, whistling softly to himself and trying to ignore Crow. It was growing late and he was hungry, wondering what kind of food Blackfish's wife had boiled up in her kettle today. He hoped it was good solid food, not the pasty, thin stews he sometimes had to settle for. Turning a corner, he glanced behind him and saw Crow still staring at him. He had watched him stride all the way down the dirt avenue.

Daniel thought about Crow that night as he lay down to sleep. He began to tally up the other times he had seen Crow staring at him and was surprised at how many there were. No question about it: Crow had some definite, special interest in Daniel Boone. Whether it was anger over his ignoble wounding during the rescue of Jemima and the Callaway girls, or something running deeper than that, Daniel could not guess.

When he slept, he dreamed he was in his boyhood haunts in the Pennsylvania backwoods, hunting with the old gnarled throwing stick he had used in those days. In the dream he was trying to creep up within throwing distance of a rabbit, but the rabbit scampered away when a great black crow suddenly cawed at Daniel from the sky and swooped down among the treetops, trying to reach him. He knew in the dream that if it did break through the branches, it would peck out his eyes, and so he ran. But everywhere he went, the crow was always just above him and always getting closer.

DANIEL HAD COME TO understand much of the Algonquian tongue during his captivity, and now he and Blackfish could converse with relative ease, even without Pompey around. This afternoon, however, it strained all Daniel's meager skill in the new tongue to understand Blackfish's fast-spoken words. The chief was wrought up, a state Daniel wasn't accustomed to seeing him in.

He had good reason to be disturbed. Early in the day Blackfish had gone hunting with several other men of Chillicothe, and unexpectedly they had come under fire from another band of men. No one in Blackfish's party had gotten a good look at whoever was shooting at them, but they had to be Indians from some other Shawnee village. White men didn't roam in this country; it was filled with Shawnees and too dangerous.

"We knew there was a mistake," Blackfish said, pacing back and forth before Daniel and his family. "We shouted at them, 'We are Shawnee!' but they did not stop shooting. They killed two men—two!—and drove off many of our horses, and still I do not know what Indians they were!"

Daniel sat silently, confused, but with a dawning suspicion in his mind.

"Why did they attack us?" Blackfish went on. "Who would have reason to make war on us now? Did they attack us only to take our horses?" From outside the open door came the sound of wailing—women mourning for the two slain warriors. Blackfish continued to pace, muttering beneath his breath.

Suddenly Daniel sat up straighter, cocking his head.

"What is it, my son?" Blackfish asked.

"Someone is coming on horses," Daniel replied.

Moments later all could hear the sound of galloping hooves. Blackfish went to the door just as four riders came to a stop in front of his house and leaped gracefully down. The lead rider was Crow. He walked up to Blackfish, who had just stepped outside. Daniel went to the doorway and stood behind Blackfish, listening. Crow cast a quick but significant glance at him before addressing the chief.

"We have seen the men who attacked you today," Crow said. "They are not Indians, but white men."

"White men!" Blackfish repeated in astonishment. "Never before has any white man dared to attack the Shawnees at their own towns!"

"This was not merely any white man," Crow went on. "With my own eyes I saw him: Pequolly, riding at the lead of a group of whites, the stolen horses being herded across the river before them!"

"Pequolly!" Blackfish mulled it, then chuckled. He shook his head. "No, no. Pequolly is a little fool. He could not lead men against us; he is not capable. Sheltowee himself told me Pequolly is no woodsman, just a fool."

"Sheltowee was wrong or perhaps Sheltowee tells lies," Crow replied, turning his gaze directly on Daniel now. "It was Pequolly. I am not the only one who saw and recognized him. He was no fool, but a liar and a rogue who pretended before us, then fled at his first opportunity. Now he is leading raids against the Shawnees, laughing at us for having believed him. He and those with him were dressed as Shawnees, but they were white men, every one of them, Pequolly at their head. He knows our country now and uses what he knows against us."

"I wish you could have captured Pequolly and brought him here to Chillicothe," Blackfish said. "He should be killed for what he has done."

"We could not reach them and did not have the numbers to stop them, Blackfish," Crow said. "I would have enjoyed fighting and killing them, but it could not be. We came directly to you because we knew you would want to know what we had seen."

Blackfish fell into brooding silence. He turned and looked at Daniel rather sadly, then sat down. "I will think about this," he said. "Leave me alone now." He waved the others away, but pointed for Daniel to go back inside the house. Daniel did not think that was a good sign.

Blackfish sat thinking until darkness fell and then came to Daniel, who had been doing some very intense thinking of his own. Obviously, Andrew Johnson had made it back to the settlements and now was leading incursions in retaliation for the capture at the salt lick. White men raiding near the very Shawnee villages . . . it was unprecedented, and Daniel was not sure what effect it would have on those remaining captive. Andrew Johnson was an impulsive, action-oriented man; there was no telling what he might do.

Daniel wished Johnson wasn't quite so daring. His action had not only revealed his own pretense but also that of all his fellow captives who had gone along with it before the Shawnees. How would it affect their status? Daniel was wondering that very thing when Blackfish came to him and sat down facing him.

"You have told your father lies, my son?" Blackfish said.

"What lies, Father?"

"About Pequolly. You said, like all the others, that he was a fool when in fact he was not. Why did you not tell me the truth?" Daniel gave the best answer he could.

"When I and the others saw that Pequolly was pretending to be touched by the spirits, we did not dare tell otherwise for fear that he might be hurt for pretending. We could not know he would escape and do what he did today. If I had known he would come later to war on our people, I would have told you the truth, Father."

Blackfish thought on Daniel's answer for a long moment, his eyes tuned upward toward the soot-encircled smoke hole in the center of his cabin roof. Daniel kept his gaze firm and unblinking, hoping Blackfish would think him truthful. He had carefully chosen his words, deliberately calling the Shawnees "our people," as if he now thought of himself as one of them. He knew that Blackfish was very fond of him and probably predisposed to accept his words. The perception proved correct.

"I understand, my son," Blackfish said. "All is well between us, then."

"I'm glad, Blackfish. I am proud to be your son and would not want you to be unhappy with me."

Abruptly Blackfish asked Daniel a question he had not expected. "Do you miss your white squaw and children?"

Daniel paused, then said, "Yes."

"Will you run away to see them again?"

"No, Father. This is my home now, and I know that when the time is right, we will go to Boonesborough and they will surrender and come to be with us here, as Shawnees. I will see them again then."

That seemed to be what Blackfish had wanted to hear. He nodded and grunted affirmatively. "Yes. Soon they will be with you. I will treat them as my own children and grandchildren, and your sons will be good Shawnee fighting men."

"When will we go fetch them, Father?"

"Soon. Very soon. Now that the whites are beginning to attack us here, we will not be able to wait for long."

Daniel nodded. His heart hammered so loudly, it throbbed in his ears. It seemed that the conversation was over, but abruptly Blackfish spoke again. "There is one other thing I still do not understand," he said. "You have told me that the white men are weary of being poor and now wish to live under the British king and as neighbors to the Shawnees. Why, then, did Pequolly attack us?"

Daniel was a fast thinker, but this time he was caught with no ready answer. It seemed Blackfish was not quite as simpleminded as Daniel had sometimes thought him to be. His question had cut right to the bone of the issue.

"I don't know, Father," was all Daniel could say. "Perhaps Pequolly is a fool after all." Blackfish did not respond. He got up and left the cabin. Daniel was unsure whether he himself was now free to do the same, but since he had been inside the place all afternoon, he decided to take his chances. Leaving the cabin, he walked out onto the thoroughfare and let the cool night air calm him.

He had been sweating, even though the evening wasn't hot or humid and he had done nothing for hours except sit in Blackfish's cabin. It was a nervous, cold sweat, drawn out of him by an unfamiliar feeling much like panic. The situation was changing, growing much more precarious.

No longer could he look for a chance to help the others escape with him. The likelihood of that was too small. He thought it probable that Andrew Johnson would continue to lead attacks in the region, and that would push the Shawnees to quicker action against Boonesborough. The warning had to be given. He would have to escape alone, the quicker the better. He needed to get his hands on a rifle, and soon.

THERE WAS NO DOUBT in Daniel's mind over the next couple of days that Blackfish was keeping a closer watch on him. The doubt that had arisen in the old chief apparently hadn't been fully assuaged by Daniel's explanations. And it seemed to Daniel that everyone was looking just a little askance at him now.

Blast Andrew Johnson—why couldn't he have left matters alone? He had introduced an element of mistrust into a situation Daniel had been handling till then and increased the likelihood of a major assault on Boonesborough. No sensible Shawnee could have confidence that the whites were eager to surrender as long as Pequolly was still chastising the towns, striking and stinging like an angry little bee. And this he did, several times, each time going away with Indian horses and sometimes leaving behind wounded or dead warriors.

Daniel did his best to go on with life as if nothing had changed, but clearly he no longer enjoyed the general trust he had before. All the assurances he might give that he didn't intend to escape would bear little weight now. He decided that what was needed was a demonstration, not mere words.

He was part of one of Blackfish's hunting parties one night when a plan came to him. All the Indians were sleeping soundly around him, their rifles leaned against a tree near the camp. Silently Daniel rose and went to the tree. Part of him ached to steal one or two of the rifles and make his break right then, but given the current level of their mistrust, he knew they would quickly give chase and catch him the next morning.

What was needed now was some act to show them they didn't need to worry about him. A bullet screw lying at the base of the tree where the rifles were leaning would provide a means for such a demonstration. Working slowly and very carefully, he withdrew the bullets from each rifle and tucked them under his shirt. He leaned the guns back exactly as they had been before, then crept to his bed. The next morning, the men breakfasted and rose to begin a new day's hunt. Stretching, Daniel yawned, then said to Blackfish, "Well, I'll be heading to Boonesborough now."

Blackfish was astounded, then suddenly angered. "No you won't—you go and I'll shoot you."

"Go ahead, then," Daniel said, and, turning, he loped away. The Indians dived for the rifles, raised them, and fired. Daniel turned, snatching at the air as if catching bullets. At the same time, he dug beneath his shirt with his other hand for the bullets he'd extracted the night before. He came trotting back to the others, and put the balls into Blackfish's hand, laughing. "Don't worry, old Boone ain't going nowhere," he said.

The Indians gaped, astonished that Sheltowee had apparently caught flying rifle balls out of the air. Only when Daniel explained his trick did they understand they had been duped, and laughed admiringly at the jest of Sheltowee. Daniel noted that Blackfish made a quick count of the rifle balls before giving them out to be reloaded into the guns. One ball for every rifle. Daniel had not sneaked himself any ammunition.

The hunt went very well. Daniel enjoyed it greatly. He could tell from the attitude and actions of his companions that he had regained the trust he had lost. They would not watch him so closely now, and if fortune was with him, soon he would be able to make his flight.

Daniel Boone was a skillful gunsmith, not quite as talented at it as his brother Squire, but certainly more skilled than anyone else in Chillicothe. From time to time he routinely repaired guns for Blackfish and other Indians. He knew it was an ominous sign, however, when he was suddenly presented with a large pile of damaged weapons needing quick repair. It could mean only that Blackfish was ready to call for the Boonesborough attack at last.

Daniel repaired the guns and received an opportunity he had long been waiting for. Among the weapons was a stockless rifle, complete with lock.

Old and of little account, the barrel and lock had been thrown in as afterthoughts; Daniel was to carve out a stock for them if circumstances allowed. He made sure they didn't, tucking the thing away with his packet of possessions. It wasn't much of a weapon, but better than nothing.

Around the first of June, Blackfish gathered his family, including Daniel, along with a delegation of warriors, and began a mission that combined diplomacy and practicality. The diplomacy involved visits to the various other Shawnee towns and also towns of the Mingos, where he officially announced that the Boonesborough attack was at hand. The practicality involved the making of salt in the Scioto River region; this is why Blackfish had brought along his family.

Daniel's gear was packed on a horse, with the stockless rifle carefully hidden. Also on the horse were the kettles for salt making—seized from the Boonesborough salt makers, Daniel wryly noticed.

Throughout the mission Daniel felt restless and tense. The time was at hand, and if he didn't make his break for freedom, he might never get another chance. He began to imagine what it would be like if in fact he didn't get away. He would be marched to Boonesborough along with the Indian force, made to call out to his own people to give themselves up—no. It was intolerable even to think about. He had to escape.

Yet, for days he was unable to do so. There was never a time when at least one of the warriors wasn't close at hand. Most often it was Crow, who continued to act as if he could read Daniel's intentions in his eyes. Daniel found it intensely frustrating. Blackfish went off on his official visits, and for two weeks the women made salt. Time dragged on, and the chance to get away continually evaded Daniel.

They were on their way back toward Chillicothe, their work and visits complete, when fortune changed its hand. Daniel was leading his packhorse, laden with the salt kettles and his own gear, including the rifle, and the Shawnee men were riding ahead. All were hungry, but there was no meat to be had, until Blackfish suddenly pointed out a distant flock of turkeys. Impulsively all the warriors hefted rifles and rode off to hunt turkey, and Daniel found himself left alone with the women. Even Crow had abandoned the scene.

The women were talking among themselves and watching the men ride far away when Daniel slipped a knife from his belt and cut the straps holding the kettles on his horse. The sound of the falling kettles made the women turn; they looked at him in confusion.

He pulled out the hidden rifle and then cut away the tugs holding all but his own packs. By now the women were looking concerned; Blackfish's wife stepped forward toward Daniel.

"Sheltowee . . ."

"No, Old Mama, no. I miss my squaw and children. I must go see them."

The old woman's eyes teared, and she reached out toward him. He felt a sincere wrenching of his emotions. Not until that moment had he realized what deep affection he had developed for his Shawnee family. Nor had he understood how much affection Blackfish's wife had for him. Patting to make sure he had his powder and bullets safely tucked under his shirt, he swung onto the horse's back and rode off. The last sound he heard was the wailing of Blackfish's squaw as she watched her "son" ride away from her, back to a life he had been snatched from, back to people he had known and loved long before he had known her.

HE RODE THE HORSE into the ground and leaped off it, heading off on a hard run with his weapon in hand. Eventually he slowed his pace to a lope, then to the long, steady, mile-eating stride that every good frontiersman mastered. He took every precaution to minimize his sign, running along logs and occasionally jumping from rock to rock. It was good to be on the run at last, but also unnerving, and he fancied many times he heard the Shawnees just behind him. He hardly let himself look back. He just kept loping along.

Hours fell away and no one overtook him. He moved on through the night, not stopping, heading for the Ohio River. He reached it the evening of the seventeenth, put his rifle and ammunition on a log, and held to it as he floated into the river and finally across. He came up on the other side and plunged into the forest, where he found a hidden place and lay down to rest, eat a few bites of jerky, and nurse his blistering feet. He slept a little but soon forced himself awake and carved out a crude stock for his rifle barrel, tying it in place.

He rose and kept moving. The country was becoming more familiar, and he thought it a fine thing to be in Kentucky again, even though he was too exhausted to appreciate it fully. He doubted the Shawnees had chased him that far, but he couldn't assume he was safe yet.

He killed a buffalo with the rifle and thought it the finest bit of hunting he'd ever done. His brother Squire was always inventing gadgets and odd tools; wait until he saw this rifle! He thought it quite a fine weapon.

He butchered the buffalo and ate some of the meat, roasting it just enough so that it was no longer raw before wolfing it down. Cutting away the tongue, he smoked it over the fire and tucked it away. If he didn't eat it himself, he could give the delicacy to his children.

A day later he reached the ford of the Kentucky River and crossed. Boonesborough was so close now, he could literally smell it. His impulse was simply to race in and greet his family and friends, but he couldn't do that with his hair cut away in Shawnee style and his clothing that of an Indian. Nor could he assume that he would he universally welcomed at the fort, considering the stories that Andrew Johnson might have spread. He could easily imagine what hateful old Colonel Callaway must think of him now! Traitor, Tory, friend of savages . . .

He refused to let himself dwell on that. His family was less than a mile away now, and he would let nothing spoil his reunion with them.

His heart rose to his throat when he first cast eyes on the settlement. There was the stockade, the cabins nearby, smoke rising from various chimneys, cattle milling about in the clearings and into the forest. He stopped and gazed at it all for long moments, drinking in the welcome sight. And though he wasn't a formally religious man, keeping his simplified Christian beliefs mostly private, he dropped to his knees and thanked his Maker that he had made it home.

Then he stood, brushing away a tear, and called out as loudly as he could: "Hello the fort! It's Boone!"

Nothing happened. He repeated the call. People began to show themselves at the stockade gate. A couple came around from behind one of the exterior cabins, and at the edge of the woods a boy appeared with stick in hand, driving in a pair of brindle milk cows. The boy stopped and put out his hand over his brow, looking up at what appeared to be an Indian who now waved vigorously back at the fort.

"That you, Boone?" someone shouted.

"Aye, it's me! I've broke free of the Shawnees and come a hundred and sixty miles in four days!"

"Well, bless your soul, come on in here, then!" the voice called back. He loped toward the stockade, his face beaming. Looking back at him were lean and dirty faces, some smiling, others cold. His own smile trickled away. He sensed he had run smack into a wall of hostility harder and more solid than he had anticipated. He stopped, looking around.

"Howdy."

"Howdy, Captain Boone."

"Hello, sir."

"Boone."

The greetings were quiet and cool. Daniel brushed sweat from his brow and leaned on the makeshift rifle, feeling it give against its leather ties under his weight. "I'm mighty weary . . . Where's Rebecca?"

"She's gone, Captain. Lit out to Carolina under the belief you was dead."

"Dead . . . but didn't Andrew Johnson get word here that I was alive?"

"He got word out about you. Yes, indeed he did."

"Then why did she leave?"

"Maybe she was ashamed of what that word was saying."

Daniel felt an emotion that would have been anger had he not been so weary, and had not grief already begun to rise, rapidly shutting out space for any other feeling. He had so looked forward to wrapping his arms around the shoulders of his wife and to squeezing his children to himself. But they were gone.

"Welcome back, Dan," a younger voice said. "*I'm* glad to see you."

"So am I," said another person, this one a man. "I trust you. I ain't believed a word said ill against you."

There were a few other voices of support after that, however feeble, and the crowd moved in toward him, the friendly and the hostile together. Most of them put out hands for a shake. Whatever the truth about Daniel Boone's loyalties, he had just made a remarkable journey to get home. Any man who had covered forty miles a day, carrying a rifle that looked like a boy's stick play-gun, had earned a handshake. Perhaps not trust just yet, but at least a handshake.

They peppered him with questions, but Daniel brushed them off. There would be plenty to say later. For the moment he wanted to visit his cabin.

"But it's empty, Dan."

"I know. But I want to rest my bones there a spell, just to let them know they've truly made it home."

The empty cabin looked terribly hollow there on its weedy lot. Daniel went inside and looked around at the undecorated walls, the stripped interior, the places where once furniture had been. People had already come and helped themselves to what Rebecca had left behind, figuring no one else would ever be claiming it.

Something brushed Daniel's ankle. He looked down and saw a thin, patchy calico cat that had been one of Rebecca's pets. Apparently it hadn't followed its owner to Carolina. Kneeling, Dan picked up the cat and scratched it around its ears, listening to it purr while he continued to look sadly around the empty cabin.

"Daddy? Daddy? Are you in there?"

He put down the cat and rose, turning.

"Jemima? Is that my dear little Duck I hear calling?" he said. He hadn't called her that childhood pet name in a long time.

She burst through the door and threw her arms around him, kissing his grimy face, which was hirsute with four days' worth of beard. While among the Shawnees he had kept himself shaved, but on the run there had been neither time nor need for it.

"Daddy, I knew you would come. Ma said you were dead, but I

knew you weren't. I told her you'd be back!"

"I am back, dear girl. I am back. Did your ma really think me dead?"

"She was afraid to think anything hopeful for fear of disappointment. But I never lost hope, Daddy. I knew you would come back. I wish Ma was here to see I was right."

"So do I. Lord, it's good to see you, Jemima. I've missed my family mighty bad."

She pulled back, looking at him with dampened eyes. "You look like an Indian!"

"I've been one, or as good as. But not no more. I'm Daniel Boone again, and it's as Boone I'll live from now on. I'm home, and home I intend to stay."

CHAPTER 31

DANIEL SAT ON a log-section stool, leaning forward, his elbows on his knees and pleased astonishment on his face. His return to Boonesborough brought him several surprises, from the absence of his family to the remarkably negligent way the fort's residents had let the stockade decay, but no greater surprise had he encountered than Nate Meriwether. Daniel had not known for many years whether Nate was even still living.

Nate stood by the doorway of a stockade cabin given over to him a few days before, when he had grown strong enough to live on his own. He was smoking a pipe and looking for the most part his old self, though his graying hair had made a significant retreat, and nature had added some baggy flesh beneath his eyes. The biggest change in the man was his voice. His speech was impeded now because of the blow to the head he had received, slurred and a little hard to understand until one grew accustomed to hearing it. But even in the few days Daniel had been home, he had detected a significant improvement in Nate's speech and an even more noticeable heightening of his spirits and physical strength. Jemima, perceptive well beyond her years, had commented on the same, and given a likely reason: "It's because of Phebe. He thinks the world of that woman, and it's no marvel, the way she's cared for him."

Though weary, Daniel had come to Nate's cabin tonight because they hadn't yet had time for a good talk, and he was curious to know what had happened to his old friend since he'd left the Yadkin country after the death of Nora House. But so far they hadn't really talked, just exchanged pleasantries and eyed one another, getting used to the remarkable fact that fate had brought them together again after so many years.

Nate drew on his pipe and sucked the strong smoke into his lungs, blowing it out through his nostrils as he eyed Daniel. "I believe some of your hair is beginning to sprout again," Nate said. "I'm glad to see it. I don't like that Indian look."

"I don't mind it so much myself, though I do have to be careful not to surprise nobody. I could be took for an Indian in the shadows and have a bullet through my headbone before I had the chance to say my name."

"It's the truth." Nate puffed again, growing thoughtful. His face became pinched and tight. "I hate Indians, Dan. Hate them more than I ever did before. Everything good I've ever had in life I've lost to savages."

"I've found good and bad both among white and Indian all the same," Daniel replied. "You can't dump out the whole apple barrel because there's worms in some of the apples."

"I'll leave it to you to defend them yellow bastards," Nate said sharply. "Is it true what folk around here are saying about you, Dan? Have you gone over to the Indians and the bloody Brits?"

"The 'bloody Brits'? Odd words from a native-born Englishman, who always seemed proud of his homeland in the early days."

"Them days are past," Nate said in his slurred voice. "The minute the British began paying the Indians for scalps and trying to turn them against God-fearing settlers, I made my choice of sides. I'm against the Crown clear through to the entrails, Daniel. Any nation that would stir the savages to war against folk of their own kind ain't worth my allegiance." He paused, then pointedly added, "Nor that of any good man."

Daniel was on the verge of telling Nate he met "Hair Buyer" Hamilton himself in Detroit, but the fervor that had risen in Nate made him hold silent. Clearly this was a heartfelt subject for the opinionated Nate Meriwether, whose emotions were still a little unstable, despite his physical improvement.

A change of subject was in order. Daniel asked the question he really came for. "What happened to you in Powell Valley, Nate?" Daniel asked. "They tell me the Indians killed your family and left you hurt and roaming."

Nate cast down his eyes and removed the pipe from his teeth. "Aye. Just like it was with Clive and his brood. They came upon us, struck, and left me alone in this world." He snapped his fingers. "Like that, it was. One moment I had a good wife and children, the next, nothing."

"I'm mighty sorry, Nate." The words sounded almost embarrassingly inadequate. Daniel searched for something comforting to say. "At least the Indians spared your life."

"Spared me? Ha!" Nate turned and knocked out the ashes from his pipe against the frame of the door. "If I was spared, it was out of no goodness of the savages. They had already pounded me in the head with a pipe tomahawk and broke a circle of bone loose, and would have give a death blow if they hadn't been run off. As it was, the hurt they had already done me and the sorrow of losing my family took away my ability to speak for the longest spell. It wasn't until I reached this fort and saw your Rebecca that I was able to find my voice again. And you can hear I ain't yet talking quite right."

"Who drove the Indians off? Neighbors?"

"Neighbors—neighbors in body, but not spirit. Them same neighbors run off and left me there to die, figuring I was grave bound anyways and not wanting to burden theirselves with a man in my condition. They just up and left me there, helpless and alone, and there I stayed until a party of men enlisted under Colonel Clark found me. They took me in with them, and it was a joy to hear them saying we was going to Boonesborough. I knew I'd be seeing my old friend Dan Boone. You've did well for yourself, Daniel. You're a famous man now. I've heard much talk of you these last two or three years."

"I ain't done a thing worth speaking of, the way I see it. And let's not talk about me. It's you I want to hear about."

"You've heard it all."

"But what about after you left the Yadkin? Where did you go?"

"South Carolina. Hunted and farmed there but never much liked it. Then I was up in Pennsylvania for a little spell and nigh got married, but that didn't fall out like I hoped, and we called it all off. I moved to the Sapling Grove settlement and met me another girl, Mary Creed by name, and we did marry. Had a couple of children. It was a fine life for me, best I had known. We settled next in the Powell Valley, and it was there the Indians come and . . . you've heard the rest." He paused, regaining the composure that had begun to slip away. "That's my tale, all there is worth the hearing. I'm halfway or more through my life, and just as worthless and alone in the world as I was back when you and me were hunting together in Carolina."

"I don't believe you're alone any longer. Seems to me that Phebe Carrick has a right keen interest in you."

Nate grinned and looked uncomfortable. "I don't know. I've heard about her own tragedy, her husband disappearing and all, and I figure maybe she's just kind-hearted toward somebody else who has suffered loss."

"Maybe. But my Jemima thinks different, and she's clever at reading people. She's certain Phebe had become smit with you."

"Is she, now? Well!" Nate scratched under his chin and self-consciously tried not to smile.

Daniel was glad to see Nate's pleasure. If he and Phebe could find happiness in each other's company, all the better for them. They were both bereaved, both in need of someone besides themselves to think about and care for.

"Nate," Daniel said in a more serious tone, "I want you to do something for me."

"What's that?"

"Take Phebe Carrick and her boys and get them away from here. Take them back to Carolina, where they'll be safe. You seem healed up enough to make the journey. It won't be long before the Shawnees come and attack this fort, and there's no need for Phebe to be here."

"You think I'd leave now? I won't do it."

"There's no cause for you to stay."

"Indeed there is, and you've done said it. There's Indians coming, and I won't miss the chance to kill my share."

"What if they should overrun us? What would become of Phebe? If you care for her, get her off to a safe place."

"Do you care for your Jemima?"

"Of course I do."

"Then why ain't you getting her off somewhere else safer?"

"Because . . . well, she likely wouldn't go, and . . ." Daniel had no good answer. Nate had hemmed him in. "Nate, you've done took to outfoxing me."

Daniel rose and prepared to leave. Clapping a hand on Nate's shoulder, he said, "I'm glad to see you again, Nate. Glad you're healing so good, and I hope you and Phebe up and marry each other."

"You're pushing that cart way too fast, Dan," Nate replied. "Not that it's a bad notion. Here now—you ain't leaving, are you? You ain't told me about all that's happened with you."

"I'll tell you another time. I'm ready for some sleep."

"But you never answered my question. Have you really gone over to the Brits? There's folks here saying you promised the Shawnee king hisself that you'd turn over the fort when they attacked."

Nate was just as a unflinchingly to the point as he ever had been. "Do you believe I'd turn over this fort, Nate?"

"I don't want to believe it. But they tell me you turned over the salt makers."

"I had no choice. It was that or death for a lot of innocent people. If I hadn't gone along with them and pretended to have turned to their side, they'd have killed every man at that salt lick and burned this fort to the ground right after. What would have become of the folk here I don't like to think about and at that time my own family would have been among them. There's plenty of folk alive right now who would be dead if I hadn't done what I did and that includes big-mouth Andrew Johnson, who's spread such poison about me. And Colonel Callaway, too. He'd be moldering as a corpse if I'd not talked Blackfish into delaying his attack. But our situation is different here now. We know they're coming. We're strengthening this stockade and I believe we can hold out. I don't intend to surrender this fort unless it's demanded by the people of this station, and I don't think they're going to demand that. And hang it all, even if they did, it wouldn't be me who'd surrender the place. I'm not the ranking officer. What it comes down to, Nate, is that I'm true to my people, and all I've ever done is what I had to, to keep them alive and safe. Do you believe me? Or do you think I'm a traitor, too?"

Nate solemnly said, "I believe you, Dan. I just wanted to hear it from your own mouth."

"And so you have," Daniel replied. He grinned, feeling a touch of embarrassment as he realized how impassioned he must have sounded. "Good evening. Sleep good."

"You too, Dan."

AS DAYS PASSED, Daniel could still sense widespread distrust of him at Boonesborough. Despite that, the people were cooperating with him in preparing for the coming attack, and he believed he detected that more people trusted him now than had when he had first returned.

He continued forthright in his warnings, telling the Boonesborough residents that the Shawnee army coming against them would be larger than any they had seen so far. Maybe as many as four hundred warriors. Constantly he urged preparedness.

Despite the confidence Daniel had voiced to Nate, the fort was still not ready to hold off attackers. Some sections of the palisade had decayed, and work was needed to strengthen, and in two cases, to complete, the four corner blockhouses. The gates were weak, and the single well provided only an insufficient puddle of water. Daniel stirred the people to work, strengthening the walls, cutting logs to add to the blockhouses, and digging the well. They cut away brush that had grown up in the clearing around the fort, and the women worked at making bandages and molding bullets. Men went by pairs to the fields to work the corn, hoping desperately that the attack would be delayed long enough to lay in a good supply of food inside the stockade.

Days went by and no attack came. Daniel was puzzled, glad that his prediction hadn't come true, but irked that his detractors used that as supposed further evidence that he was playing some sort of deception game. He labored to ignore their whispers and encouraged all to use the unexpected extra time to their advantage. If the attack hadn't come sooner, it didn't mean it wouldn't come later.

His biggest ally and hardest worker turned out to be Nate. True to his word, he stuck by Daniel and defended him vigorously to those who criticized him.

Meanwhile, Nate and Phebe had become a true couple. They were together almost all the time. When Nate wasn't working, he was either keeping company with Phebe or playing with her children, who dearly loved him. Phebe seemed to love him, too, and despite the tensions of the time and place, was as full of smiles and cheer as she had been of gloom before Nate had come.

Work went on. Every day scouts patrolled the woods, looking for indications that the Indians were on their way. Every evening they rode in again, shaking their heads, and relief would mix with puzzlement and hope. Maybe there would be no attack at all. Maybe Daniel Boone had misunderstood Blackfish's plans, or maybe those plans had been dropped.

Changed maybe, Daniel conceded, but surely not dropped. Blackfish had been too definite, too dedicated to the idea of taking Boonesborough. It was far too early to assume the threat had vanished.

Boonesborough was benefitting from the arrival of new men. Squire Boone had moved to Harrodsburg, but now he returned, bringing his family and some other men as reinforcements. Logan's Station also generously provided a few extra defenders, even though they had no excess of help themselves, and the slaves and older boys of Boonesborough were outfitted for fighting. William Hays, who had taken Susannah and Rebecca and the other Boone children back to North Carolina, returned to Boonesborough and the happy surprise of seeing his father-in-law again. Other good men present included Sam Henderson, John Holder, and Daniel Wilcoxen, a nephew of Daniel Boone's. All in all there were about sixty fighting men to hold the fort against Blackfish, if Blackfish would ever come.

They found William Hancock, former adopted son of Captain Will the Shawnee, lying naked on the far side of the Kentucky River. Nate Meriwether, out scouting, was the first to hear his cries, and when he found the man, was certain that Hancock was dying. Scraped, bloodied, bruised terribly, clad only in a crust of dirt that covered every inch of him, he was hardly distinguishable from the earth upon which he crawled, being too weak to walk.

Nate covered him and ferried him over the river to the fort. Hancock was given food and water and nursed back toward health. As soon as he was able, he told his story.

Nine days before, he had made his own escape from captivity. Captain Will had come in drunk one night while Hancock lay pretending to sleep, and Hancock took advantage of it to get away. Like Daniel, he had distressing news that needed to get to Boonesborough.

The Indians were indeed coming, though the escape of Daniel Boone had caused them to delay their plans. Now the story around Chillicothe was that the attack was to come sometime in August, and the British were going to provide the Indians several small swivel artillery pieces capable of knocking down the stockade. Then the people of Boonesborough would be given the chance to surrender, as Boone had promised they would, and go live under British rule in the north. Otherwise, the women and children would be taken prisoner and the men massacred.

Hancock's chilling words struck fear into the settlements and put deeper division between the pro-Boone and anti-Boone camps. Some credited Daniel with having delayed the attack by his escape; others declared he had probably worsened matters and drawn the British deeper into the planning. But at the moment the disagreement mattered little. What mattered was that the attack was really going to come.

Hancock's story of escape was harrowing and included one detail that caused the more religious-minded among the populace to say that a divine hand had saved Hancock's life. He had fled without clothing and no sustenance but three pints of parched corn that proved insufficient. He had made it all the way to the Ohio River and tried to get across by clinging to a piece of floating wood, but the springtime current was swift and carried him about twenty miles downstream before he was able to make it all the way across. This was country he did not know, and he wandered for days without hope as his corn supply gave out. He had lost all hope at last and fell down to sleep, and perhaps to die.

Then came his miracle. Opening his eyes, he saw his own name carved into a tree. He knew where he was then, for he had carved the name himself months before on a hunting trip. He was within a half day's journey of Boonesborough! Regaining strength with that realization, he rose and staggered the last few miles until he collapsed on the north bank of the Kentucky River, where his shouts for help had finally revealed him to Nate Meriwether.

Work on the stockade redoubled and corn harvesters went out in great numbers, loading up carts of corn to be stored inside the stockade. The cattle were watched closely and grazed heavily so they would be at their fattest when they were herded into the stockade just before the attack, whenever that might be. More bullets were molded, more bandages prepared. And in the rare moments when he wasn't involved in defensive preparations, Squire Boone spent his time splitting and hollowing out a stout log he had dragged into the fort. Whenever Daniel asked him what he was up to, Squire merely winked and said he was making a surprise for old Blackfish and his boys.

Two days after Hancock came in, Nate rode back in from a scouting expedition with an apparently dead Indian hanging over the rump of his horse. As he entered the stockade, he created quite a sensation, people gathering around to gape, some to act panicked and declare that the attack was upon them.

Daniel came loping up just as Nate rudely dumped the limp Indian man onto the ground. The fellow rolled over onto his back and groaned, eyes shut. He was only semiconscious, bruised and swollen around the face and shoulders from an apparently fierce beating, and his lower leg was bleeding from a bullet hole just below the knee.

A babble arose—"God, he's still alive!"—"His leg bone is busted by the bullet!"—"Somebody take a knife to the yaller savage and end his sorry days!" The latter came from a woman who had lost a son to Indians in Virginia years before.

"No," Daniel said. "Nobody hurt this man. I know him."

"One of your damned Shawnee friends, Boone?"

"I doubt he'd consider me a friend, and he ain't Shawnee, not by blood. He's Cherokee-born, and his name is Crow."

"I'll be!" Nate said. "I never had a notion I'd found me a yellow boy that you knew, Dan."

"How'd you find him?"

"He was sleeping out in the woods. By hisself. I was able to creep right up on him before he heard me. It was like he was deaf."

"He is," Daniel said. "In one ear."

"I was about to kill him, but then I figured he might know something about the attack. He might be a scout for Blackfish."

Daniel said, "Haul him over yonder into that cabin."

"That's my cabin, Dan!"

"Well, haul him yonder to mine, then, dang it! And why'd you shoot him, Nate?"

"He sprung up and come at me with a knife."

"Looks like you beat him half to death, too."

"Had to. He was still coming at me even after I shot through his leg bone. Hopping and waving that knife and squalling, just like this."

Nate jumped up on one foot and leaped about, waving an imaginary knife while saying "Eeech! Eeeeh! Eeech!" which drew laughter from all but Daniel.

"Somebody help me haul him."

Daniel's helpers were not at all gentle carrying Crow, who groaned and fell into deep unconsciousness after his shattered leg flopped out loose, putting great pressure on the point of the fracture. They laid him out on the floor, and Daniel took advantage of Crow's unconsciousness to examine the wound. The ball had cracked the bone and then angled out to the right, almost emerging through the skin. It sat just below the skin's surface, a hard, distorted lump of lead. Daniel flipped out his knife, cut through the skin, and let the ball fall out. He picked up the ball and handed it to a man nearby. "Keep that and we'll melt it down again. And somebody bring me a couple pieces of straight wood."

When Crow's leg was splinted and bandaged—"A waste of good bandages," someone declared—Daniel had him moved aside. He gouged out a hip hole in the dirt floor and spread a saddle blanket over it. With Squire's help he moved Crow onto the blanket so the bulge of his buttocks fit into the hip hole and his shoulders, back, and legs were firmly supported by the ground. "He'll be as comfortable as can be expected that way," Daniel said.

"Why do you think he was out yonder alone, Dan?" Squire asked.

"I suspect he came to find me and kill me, if he could," Daniel said.

"Why?"

"I ain't sure. All I know is that he had some resentment of me while I was still with Blackfish. It may be because he was one of them who captured Jemima and the Callaway girls. He was shot in the side as he fled that camp."

Squire whistled in surprise. "He was one of them? It didn't seem none of the others out there recognized him."

"No. If they had, they might have killed him right there. They may kill him yet, unless I can persuade them it's worthwhile to keep him as a hostage to use to bargain with Blackfish."

"I'd already thought the same thing," Squire said. "Think he might really be useful?"

"I don't know. I doubt that Blackfish would halt a siege for him."

"Well, if you want to protect this Indian's life, I don't believe I'd say that where anybody else will hear it."

"Believe me, Squire, I don't aim to."

DANIEL WAS AT CROW'S SIDE when he regained consciousness. The Cherokee gazed straight up, looking bewildered, then twisted his head and tensed when he saw Daniel.

"Sheltowee." His voice was weak and hoarse.

"That's right, Crow. You're in my fort now. Why did you come?"

Crow frowned. "I followed the white son of Captain Will. But I lost his track when he crossed the great river."

"You lingered hereabouts a long time after not catching your man."

"Yes. I stayed to see the fort, its strength, the number of its men."

"Is Blackfish close behind you?"

"No. But he will come. He will come."

"I don't doubt he will. In the meantime I'll be hard-pressed to keep some of those here from killing you, especially if they recognize you from the capture of our girls. There's a man here named Colonel Callaway, and two of them girls was his. He's a man with a fierce temper, and he won't be swayed by me. He despises me. Thinks I'm a traitor and Indian lover."

Crow said nothing. He squeezed his eyes tightly closed, obviously in pain, though he was trying to hide it.

"I splinted your leg. It will be a long time before you'll walk on it."

"Do not try to help me. I don't wish your protection. If they kill me, they kill me. It's the way of white men to kill Indians when they are hurt and unable to fight."

"I've heard you say such as that before. What do you mean by it?"

Crow said nothing.

"Why have you had such an interest in me, Crow? Why did you watch me so close in Chillicothe?"

Still only silence.

Daniel sighed and said, "I'll go fetch food for you. Don't try to get away from here, Crow. You'll never make it on that leg, and there's men here who would be glad of an excuse to shoot you. I'll be back with some of them soon, and I'll want to know all you can tell us about Blackfish and his warriors. When they will come, how many there are, such as that."

He rose and went to the door.

"Sheltowee."

"What?"

"The man who captured me today—who is he?"

"I don't believe I need tell you that."

Crow turned his head and stared straight up, lying still as a corpse. Daniel left, closing the door behind him.

"Squire," he called, "come fix this door to bar shut from the outside, if you would. We'll be using it to hold our prisoner."

CHAPTER 32

Of all those who interrogated Crow, Colonel Callaway was the harshest and most threatening, but even he couldn't shake the Cherokee's stoic calm, nor gouge from him any information beyond what Daniel's and Hancock's reports had already revealed. Daniel was finally convinced that Crow truly knew little. Callaway and some of the others declared themselves ready to kill Crow as a piece of useless baggage who would only consume precious food during a siege, but Daniel presented his argument that Crow would be valuable as a hostage, and carried the day. He fancied that Crow gave him a faintly grateful look afterward.

Daniel sent a message to Virginia military figures, asking for reinforcements if they could be sent, and telling what was anticipated from Blackfish. "We shall lay up provisions for a siege," part of the communiqué said. "We are all in fine spirits and have good crops growing, and intend to fight hard to secure them." The Indians, it noted, were expected to attack within two weeks. If Virginia was to give aid, it would have to do so quickly.

But again the attack didn't happen. The time came and went with no sign of Blackfish. Daniel puzzled over the matter, growing impatient, then on impulse developed a plan that startled almost everyone.

"I'm weary of waiting for them," he said. "I propose we show them something of our strength and see if we can't make a great speck of horses and peltries and such at the same time."

He proposed striking a Shawnee settlement on Paint Creek across the Ohio. Small and vulnerable, this town could be attacked with complete surprise, lots of booty taken, and they could all be safely back at Boonesborough well before Blackfish's attack came.

Colonel Callaway and several others could see no sense in the plan, and even those tempted by it had to admit it was foolhardy. In the end temptation proved stronger than caution. How many horses had the people of Boonesborough lost to the Shawnees during their time in Kentucky? How often had Shawnees wantonly killed livestock, destroyed crops, harassed and even murdered men tending the fields? William Hancock had come back from his captivity telling an infuriating story of how his Indian "father," Captain Will, had ridden a horse Hancock knew had been stolen from Boonesborough. When Hancock mentioned this to him, Captain

Will had calmly declared that every horse, even every man, in Kentucky was rightly his as a Shawnee. Such an arrogant and possessive attitude on the part of an Indian didn't sit at all well with the men of Boonesborough. Daniel's reckless proposal was accepted.

Callaway was furious. He and those others who most deeply distrusted Daniel nursed their deepening anger and declared that surely even more of old Boone's Tory treachery was hidden somewhere in the plan.

Daniel and his companions ignored Callaway. After Daniel arranged for Nate to remain behind and make sure Crow was not harmed in his absence, the Paint Creek raiders set out on the last day of August. Some of them came riding back the next day, having developed doubts about the wisdom of leaving the fort with only half its usual number of fighting men. The others rode to the Ohio and swam their horses over, spirits exhilarated. The Indians would never expect them to do something as bold as this. Let old Blackfish, captor of salt makers, planner of sieges, get an unexpected taste of the white man's stealth! If this excursion bordered on the mad, it also promised to be satisfying, and if they were lucky, rewarding to boot.

All but two came hastening back on the evening of the sixth day of September, telling tales of creeping through the forests of the Shawnee country, of encountering Indians, of Simon Butler shooting two of them off one horse with a single bullet that passed through one and into the other, of a fierce little battle in the woods that netted them a victory and several good horses as booty, and of the startling fact that they had found the town on Paint Creek empty of warriors.

At the time all they could suppose it meant was that the Shawnee men were away on the warpath, heading for Boonesborough. Leaving Simon Butler and Alexander Montgomery behind as scouts, they raced back home and beyond the Ohio River found confirmation of their suspicion. Blackfish and his warriors had already crossed the river and were making their way toward Boonesborough along the Warrior's Path. Daniel and his raiders were cut off from their own stockade by an Indian army of about four hundred in number, supplemented by a band of French-Canadian militia probably sent by Governor Hamilton. The Indian force was well armed, but at least no one had seen any of the dreaded swivel guns.

Daniel and his raiders took to the woods and found their own way back to the fort across untrailed country. They made it just in time. Blackfish and his army would arrive the next day, and the long-awaited, occasionally doubted siege would be under way.

That night final preparations were made. The routine was familiar, but the feeling entirely different. This time it was real. Every person in the fort, down to the children, had some task to do, whether it be gathering water, making bullets, or chinking up cracks between the stockade logs to avoid giving the Indians any handy targets.

Four hundred well-armed Indians, with official British military support, facing off against about sixty stockaded riflemen, a dozen women, and a score of children. Not the best of odds numerically, but the stockade itself did much to even the balance. Historically, Indians had seldom fared well in assaults against stockades. Daniel reminded the people of their advantages as he urged along the final preparations, but nothing could stanch the fear burning in the back of every throat, including that of Daniel Boone himself.

The Boonesborough residents worked through the entire night and greeted the clear dawn with dread. The morning passed in unusual silence, people going about their chores with one eye always on the forest.

Moses and Isaiah Boone, sons of Squire, were outside the fort watering horses and were the first to detect the approach of riders. At first they took them to be the Virginia militiamen who had been requested. Happy and eager to greet them, they leaped on the bare backs of two of the horses and rode to meet the approaching band.

"Boys!" The voice was that of their uncle Daniel, who had seen the approaching group from the rifle platform of the stockade. "Come back—that's Shawnees!"

The boys wheeled their horses and rode pell-mell back toward the fort, wheeled again and rode back to get the other horses, and in a cloud of dust and rumble of pounding hooves, finally rode through the stockade gate, which was promptly closed behind them. Catching their breath and shaking as they realized how close they had come to riding into the very arms of the foe, they joined Squire Boone on the rifle platform watching silently as the Indians began to appear.

In a long line the Indians emerged from the forest, then the uniformed militiamen. Behind them was a train of packhorses bearing food and supplies. Daniel studied the cluster of leaders and picked out the familiar forms of Pompey, the black interpreter, and Blackfish. There too was Chief Moluntha, and with the militia, Lieutenant Antoine Dagneaux de Quindre, and Black Hoof, who had been present when Braddock was defeated. Other faces he either couldn't recognize immediately or couldn't attach to a name; they included the trader Peter Drouillard, and the Chippewa chief named Blackbird. Standing on the rifle platform and looking over the palisades, the men of Boonesborough talked quietly among themselves, commenting in grim tones about the army assembling against them no more than three hundred yards away. Already a group of Indians was putting up an arbor in the peach orchard. A lone figure bearing a truce flag on a stick came out from among the Indians and walked about half the distance to the fort, where he mounted a fence, waved the flag, and called out, "Boone!"

Nate, standing beside Daniel, asked, "Who's the hollering darky?"

"His name's Pompey," Daniel said. "He's interpreter for Blackfish." He cupped a hand to his mouth and yelled, "Howdy, Pompey! How's your health?"

"Good, Boone! How is yours?"

"Very well! Good to see you again, Pompey! Is there something I can do for you?"

Another voice, coming from among the Indian army farther back, carried thinly across the distance. "Sheltowee! Sheltowee!"

"I'll be danged!" Daniel muttered to Nate. "Blackfish hisself is calling for me."

"You hear the voice of your father, Boone?" Pompey yelled. "He has come to see you. He is ready for you to keep your promise to surrender your fort. He wants to meet with you!"

"Where?"

"At the arbor in the peach trees."

"I'll meet with him, but not there. You tell him I'll meet him at yonder stump." He leaned over the stockade and pointed.

Pompey nodded. "I will tell him." He turned and walked back toward the Indian lines.

Nate gaped at Daniel. "You ain't really going out there, are you?"

"Surely am."

"God, Dan! They'll kill you, or at the least take you hostage!"

"They might. If they kill me, there'll be nothing for the rest of you to do but fight. If they take me prisoner, we've always got Crow to bargain with. Don't know if it will do any good, but you can always try. The fact is, I trust Blackfish for now. He'll want to talk before he'll want to shoot."

"I don't believe that. Don't go out there, Dan."

"No choice. Look—there comes Blackfish already. And Moluntha—several of them coming. Wish good fortune for me, Nate." He dismounted the rifle platform and went to the gate. They opened it enough to let him out, then closed it behind him. For two minutes there was nothing but dead silence as a handful of chiefs and a lone white warrior approached each other in the clearing.

"He'll surrender us," one of Boone's doubters declared. "Within an hour, every one of us will be marching as prisoners before them yellow savages!"

"Hell, no, we won't!" Nate said loudly. "Within an hour we'll be piling that clearing full of dead redskins. Daniel Boone will never give us up! Within an hour—you mark my words."

IT TURNED OUT that both men were wrong. Within an hour nothing happened at all except that Daniel sat with the chiefs talking back and forth. Though Daniel had become fairly adept at the Shawnee language while a captive of Blackfish, Pompey served as official interpreter to make sure all accurately understood each other. The first meeting consisted mostly of greeting and solemn talk. From the fort Nate watched as Daniel was presented a letter, which he read, folded, and tucked under his shirt. Then Blackfish brought out a broad wampum belt and began going over it with Daniel, like a schoolmaster helping a pupil with his reading slate. Daniel talked some more, sometimes nodding, sometimes shaking his head, and finally all the negotiators rose from the blanket on which they had been sitting, shook hands, and went their separate ways. Blackfish and his delegation trudged back to the arbor in the peach orchard, and Daniel came back to the fort, where he was given entrance. He bore seven buffalo tongues in a pouch, a goodwill gift from Blackfish.

"Leave the gate open," he said. "Right now we need to show some good faith and trust—I'm hopeful of talking our way out of a fight."

Daniel told what had happened and showed the letter, written by Governor Hamilton himself. It urged the surrender of the fort and pledged safety for all residents, who would be given pardons, protection, and guidance to Detroit, then safe haven as supporters of the king. The belt Blackfish showed, Daniel explained, said basically the same thing in symbols, featuring a white line symbolizing a peaceful trek back to Detroit.

"There was a black line, too. Death to us all if we resist," he added.

"What will we do?" a man asked.

"I leave that to the men of this fort," Daniel replied. "I'll stand beside whatever decision comes."

A great argument ensued. It quickly became apparent that for all the dark gossip about Daniel Boone conniving to surrender, there were plenty of men there who would have been ready to go right along with it if he had. About half the men present argued in favor of surrender, but the other half, led by Callaway, Squire Boone, and various others of iron nerve, declared no surrender was acceptable. Callaway even threatened to kill any man who dared seriously propose it.

"I'll fight to the death, myself," Squire Boone said. "But I'm not loath to a reasonable treaty, if one can be struck on better terms than that letter offers."

That sentiment wound up being the only one the men could agree on. Daniel refolded and put away the letter. Standing, he said, "I'll tell Blackfish that we have talked and will not surrender to him. But I'll also ask for more talk and the chance to negotiate terms. I believe he'll grant it, at least for a time. The old boy doesn't seem intent on destroying us, and all the time we can buy gives our Virginia reinforcements more time to reach us."

"Does Blackfish know we have an Indian hostage?" Flanders Callaway asked.

"Yes. But I saw no evidence from him that his thinking was changed by knowing it. When I told him, he just lifted his eyebrows and said, 'So that's what happened to Crow! His squaw has been grieving for him since he disappeared.' "

Grumbling followed that announcement, and mutterings that Crow might as well be killed and thrown over the stockade, for all the good he was. No one took that seriously, at least not yet, knowing that a murder would end all chance at successful negotiation.

Daniel turned to Major William Bailey Smith. "William, if you'd put on that Virginia militia uniform of yours and come with me, we'll go talk some more with Blackfish. And be sure to wear that plumed hat. It gives you the look of a mighty big military man, and Blackfish, he responds to such as that."

NATE MERIWETHER was growing disgusted. It was now Wednesday afternoon and everything still seemed to be stalled. The Indians had appeared Monday morning, and since then there had been nothing but talk and bluster and continual nerve-gnawing waiting. Daniel had met with Blackfish, the other Indian leaders, and Governor Hamilton's representative de Quindre at great length, and earlier in the day the women of the fort had actually set out a great banquet for the leaders of both sides, right outside the fort walls. It had been wonderful fare: buffalo tongue, vegetables, venison, bread, cheese, milk, all laid out on tables with fine dishes and tableware for the sake of giving the impression that Boonesborough was so well lardered it could afford to host such great feasts. Nate understood the ploy, but still found it deeply troubling to see Indians treated as guests. All he could see when he looked into the eyes of Blackfish and his fellows was the reflection of the faces of his family members, slain by Indian hands. He was ready to fight, ready to kill, but so far not a shot had been fired.

The Indians still didn't have a clear idea of the number of fighting men inside the fort. The Shawnees had been falsely informed well before their arrival that the Kentucky forts were better manned than they actually were, and Boonesborough's leaders had done all they could to keep the illusion alive throughout the long, tiring negotiations of the previous two days. The women of the fort had dressed in men's clothing, their hair hidden under flop hats, and paraded back and forth past the open door to give the impression there were more fighting men there than really existed. Other times the children had been put to work on the rifle platforms, holding up hats on sticks on either side of them, while lifting their own heads high enough to show the hats they wore, so that from the outside one child gave the impression of three men. And Daniel, Major Smith, Colonel Callaway, and the various others actually involved in the talks had consistently lied about their strength.

The situation was particularly hard for Nate to endure. Blackfish was in the midst of some showy oratory in his native tongue, his voice ringing out like that of a preacher as he seemingly spoke to the world at large. Nearby him sat the most recent Boonesborough team of negotiators, who to all appearances had struck some kind of agreement with the Indians at last, prompting Blackfish's burst of speech making. The Boonesborough delegation consisted of Daniel Boone, William Buchanan, Colonel Callaway, Squire Boone, William Hancock, Flanders Callaway, Steven Hancock, and Major Smith. They all looked ill at ease, while pretending to listen appreciatively to Pompey's translation of Blackfish's speech.

"I'd like to put a bullet right through that bigmouthed chief right here and now," Nate said to William Stafford, a keen-eyed marksman who stood beside him. They were among twenty-five marksmen Daniel Boone had ordered to man the bastions, ready to fire.

"I've done got my eye on the one I'll shoot," Stafford replied. "See that chief-looking redskin sitting there apart from the rest, with that moon-shaped medal on his chest? If the signal comes, that'll be the one I kill."

"That's a long shot."

"I'll make it. First wave of a hat, and that yellow boy is dead."

The "wave of a hat" Stafford had referred to was the pre-designated signal worked out by the negotiators to indicate the fort's riflemen should fire into the clump of Indians.

At the first sign anything was going askew, the hats would be waved and the battle would begin. Though the purported reason for the meeting outside the fort was for the delegates from both sides to sign a peace accord, a general feeling prevailed that something duplicitous was under way. If peace came, fine; if not, the fort's riflemen should be ready to fire.

"What if we strike one of you?" Nate had asked.

"It's a chance we're ready to take," Major Smith had replied. "The number of Indians will exceed that of us, so just fire into the clump and we'll live with the odds that it's Indians who will most probably be struck."

Nate chewed a little strip of wood he had peeled back off the sharpened palisade and watched Blackfish waving his arms toward the treetops. The chief's voice rose, then suddenly fell, and he headed back toward the clump of negotiators.

"Done talking, finally," Nate said with relief.

"By gum, I believe they've really come to terms!" Stafford said. "The Indians are all putting out hands for shaking. . . . Wait a minute, though—something don't look right here . . ." Nate had already lifted his rifle. "That ain't like no hand shaking I've ever seen!" he declared.

Stafford raised his rifle, too, and sighted at his selected target. Meanwhile, down at the treaty site, Blackfish had taken a firm grip on Daniel Boone's arm, and another Indian was approaching to grasp his other one. The other Boonesborough delegates were being similarly surrounded and grasped, and it appeared that Colonel Callaway was on the verge of being dragged away. It was Callaway who pulled free first and whipped off his hat, waving it wildly.

From the walls and roofless blockhouses of Boonesborough, rifles fired in almost perfect unison. Stafford grinned through gun smoke. The Indian he had targeted had fallen dead, shot through the chest. Stafford hurried to reload.

Nate swore; his shot had missed entirely. He had seen dirt kick up near Pompey's feet just after he fired. He, too, scrambled to reload. Below in the fort the livestock were bawling, nickering, bleating, virtually stampeding about, terrified by the sudden explosion of gunfire. The confusion was no less out at the treaty site, with the white men now broken free of their would-be captors and racing back toward the stockade, Blackfish was on his back—wounded? Knocked down by Daniel as he made his escape? It was impossible to tell right away and it seemed to have the Indians buffaloed at the moment.

Across the fort a hundred different things happened at once. Tice Prock, a Dutch potter who had never expressed any eagerness for fighting, was discovered by Colonel Callaway's wife hiding beneath a bed. She chased him out, calling him a coward, and he made no attempt to deny the charge. He leaped into the unfinished well and cowered there, trembling yet seemingly unashamed.

Meanwhile, Ambrose Coffee had just undergone an experience he would thereafter remember as a miracle. He had been lying atop a wall of the unroofed blockhouse, watching the negotiations, when the fight suddenly broke out. He was a fine target for hidden Indian marksmen, and came tumbling down suddenly into the blockhouse, his clothing shredded by bullets. Springing up, he looked about for the expected gushes of blood and found none. Not a single ball had struck him, every one of them merely cutting his clothes and breezing right past his skin.

Outside, Daniel Boone took a blow from a tomahawk as he ran for the fort. He winced as a two-inch cut opened in the back of his head and another wound in his shoulder. He kept running, blood flowing down his back.

Squire Boone, meanwhile, was jolted to the ground by the impact of a bullet that hit him in the shoulder. He rose and ran toward a smaller door that opened through the stockade into one of the cabins, the main gate already being shut. The small door received him, then was shut tight and barred.

The battle for Boonesborough began, ironically, in the wake of a just-signed peace treaty. No one had time to mull the wonder of it or even ask themselves if they were surprised. There was too much fighting to do.

THE NEGOTIATORS MADE IT back into the stockade except for one man, and only Squire Boone had suffered serious damage. His shoulder wound was bad enough to force him to his bed, where he lay with a broadax at his side, ready to swing it at the first Indian who broke through. Not that an actual invasion of the stockade was likely. The riflemen were doing a good job of holding back the first onslaught, and all the strengthening of the stockade that Daniel had ordered was proving worthwhile.

The man who had not made it back inside was still alive, hidden behind a stump that protected him from Indian gunfire. It was frustrating for all of Boonesborough to see him there and know there was nothing to do but try to keep the Indians from reaching a position from which they could hit him. As the afternoon dragged on, the man stayed where he was, waiting for nightfall.

Colonel Callaway was alerted by his wife to the cowardice of the potter, and he went to the well and made Prock's ears ring with his denunciations of his cowardice. "If you won't fight, you chicken-hearted Dutchman, then at least you can work! As long as you're hiding down there, dig!" He tossed down a shovel, and Prock went to work to deepen his own hiding place, no doubt hoping he would never strike water and be driven from his refuge.

The fighting eventually lulled, and Daniel Boone, who had so far ignored his own tomahawk wounds, explored the fort and assessed the situation. Despite the fact that he was out-ranked by Callaway and Smith, he was the man ultimately in charge, and everyone knew it. Even those who mistrusted him could not deny that he had done no treachery since the arrival of the Shawnees. He had already declared his intention to fight through to the end, and there was no cause to doubt him.

Daniel paused at Squire's cabin long enough to gouge the bullet out of Squire's shoulder and to inquire if he had finished his "surprise" for Blackfish. Squire grinned through his pain. "A couple more wagon-wheel bands around it, and it will be ready," he said. Daniel had already examined Squire's invention and ascertained what it was: a log cannon, made to fire rifle balls and scrap, held together by tightly encircling metal bands.

"I'm hoping they'll be gone before you have the chance to fire it," Daniel said. "You rest in here. We've got enough riflemen to hold them for now. Come out only when you feel strong enough to do it."

He left and encountered Jemima, who had an embarrassed expression on her face as she clutched a bloody rag against her backside. "Daughter, what happened?"

"I was struck in the rump by a bullet," she said. "Don't worry; it didn't lodge. When I pulled at my skirt, the ball fell out. It barely broke the skin, but it's bleeding fierce and making me feel mighty bashful." She grinned, but then looked shocked. "Daddy! There's blood on your neck!"

"It's nothing."

"Let me see."

"No time, girl. Get on into Squire's cabin here until your bleeding stops."

She reluctantly obeyed, looking worried. A moment later Daniel chuckled when he heard Squire's pain-racked laugh erupting from his cabin as he realized the nature of his niece's minor, but humiliating, wound.

Daniel went on to the cabin where Crow was imprisoned. Knocking on the door, he called in, "Are you well in there?"

"Come in and let me kill you, Boone," Crow replied.

"Sound hardy enough to me," Daniel said, and went on.

The fighting continued in spurts, but for the rest of the afternoon there was no onslaught to match the initial one. All in all, Daniel was pleased with how they had fared. The Indians now knew they could not take the stockade by sheer force. He hoped they would soon grow discouraged and withdraw, as so often happened in sieges such as this. He went next to a cabin in the center of the stockade yard. There the children had been hidden, guarded by the women.

He found the lot of them in physical safety but mental distress, the young ones crying comfortlessly, some of the women hardly any better off. They feared they would be stormed by the Indians, they told him, and Daniel alleviated their fears by laughing as he described how poorly the Indians had done so far. "They've rushed the gate time and again, but your daddies and uncles have showed them this fort ain't going to fall. You ought to see them falling back under that rifle fire! Don't you fret—it takes more than Blackfish and a gaggle of Indians to bring down Boonesborough! And just you wait—my brother Squire has him a surprise for Blackfish that'll tickle you plumb silly." Winking, he left the cabin, which now held a much more comforted collection of people, and a lot of children now very curious about what "Mr. Squire" had up his sleeve.

The gunfire died away at dark, and the man who had been stranded outside made a successful dash for the stockade and was admitted through the gate. All the fort's men were accounted for then, except for William Patton, who had been out on an extended hunt at the time of the attack and had not returned.

Thursday morning brought another wave of assault and a wearying day of almost continual rifle fire. The results for the Shawnees were dismal; it was more and more evident that they could not prevail against the stockade walls. That night, therefore, they sought to get rid of them in the only way possible without heavy artillery: flame.

Even Indian-hating Nate Meriwether had to admire the courage of the warriors who raced toward the stockade bearing flaring torches, with which they set afire piles of flax that had been left to dry near the stockade wall. They dragged the burning flax along the base of a fence that connected to the stockade. The fence caught fire then ate its way toward the wall—the first truly serious threat the fort faced.

Hard-cursing John Holder, famous for his profane and blasphemous language, grabbed a couple buckets of water and left the fort, running toward the blazing fence with Indian bullets smacking all around him. Cursing at full volume, he dashed out the fire and kicked down the part of the fence connecting the stockade. He made it safely back inside, still swearing, only to be upbraided by Mistress Callaway for cursing when he ought to be praying. His only response was more cursing and a declaration that he had no time for praying.

Friday brought a decline in gunfire on both sides during the day, but an unexpected turn of events when sentries at the fort noted unusual movement and unexplainable digging sounds that seemed to come from the bank of the Kentucky River, at low flow there in the late summer. The bank was about ten feet high at that point, and whatever activity was going on was being done out of sight of the fort, the bank itself hiding the diggers. Soon a brown, dirty stain showed up in the river itself, dirt being dug from the bank and thrown out.

"I'll be hanged!" Daniel said to the men around him. "De Quindre has 'em digging a tunnel!" The implications were serious. If the Indians managed to undermine the fort, or to tunnel close enough to it to plant explosives that would blast away the wall, the fort could be taken.

"What can be done to stop them?" Nate asked.

"I suggest a countermine," Callaway said.

"Exactly so," Daniel replied. "We'll dig beneath the cabins so that if they do reach us, they'll be forced into a narrow space one at a time, and we can make it plenty hot for them."

The work got under way at once. One cabin floor was completely hollowed out, and a tunnel begun that would run beneath the entire row of other cabins. Once complete, the tunnel would allow riflemen stationed in the hollowed-out cabin to fire down the row at any Indian who dared gopher his way out into the countermined tunnel.

That night the Shawnees surprised the fort defenders with a new daring attempt to burn the stockade. Yelling Indians bearing gunpowder-imbued torches of shell-bark hickory defied the riflemen by racing up to the fort itself and casting the torches onto the roofs. Other warriors fired flaming arrows from a distance. Though most of the torches failed to catch anything ablaze, a few did set flame to roof shingles that had to be knocked out from beneath with poles or put out with water. The inventive Squire Boone, now recovered enough to be back in action, quickly improvised squirt guns made with old rifle barrels and fired with plungers made from wrapped ramrods. Water could be drawn up into the barrels, then squirted out again onto the flaming shingles.

Squire also brought out his black-gum log cannon. Hefted into one of the blockhouses, it was propped and fixed in place, then loaded with rifle balls. "Back away," Squire warned those closest around. "She may go up like a powder keg." The first blast was wonderfully loud and lit the sky like a lightning flash. Indians who were gathered just out of rifle range yelped and scattered as rifle balls ripped into their ranks. Squire laughed uproariously and scurried to reload while the people of Boonesborough sent up a great cheer.

The second shot ruptured the cannon and ended its military career forthwith, but the episode had cheered the folk of Boonesborough at a time of great danger. Soon, however, the Indians renewed their assault, and the night was filled with the light of dozens of rifle flashes and a continuing rain of torches and arrows, and with the screams of charging Indians and crying fort children.

Boonesborough lost its first man that night. A slave named London bravely tunneled under the wall to put out a fire that threatened to catch the stockade ablaze, and was shot by an Indian. The death cast a sobering pall over the frightened people.

The next day saw the start of a new and more psychological aspect of the siege. The Indians began taunting the fort with insults and obscenities, which were in turn fired back by the fort riflemen. This kind of exchange was common in such warfare, but not designed for sensitive listeners. One Shawnee took the abuse further by exposing his backside to the fort, but this game ended when a marksman overloaded his rifle and managed to put a bullet into one of the man's buttocks.

"That one was for me," Jemima Boone Callaway joked to her husband, touching the still-tender spot.

Of all those who taunted the fort, the most infuriating was Pompey. Born in slavery and treated much better by the Indian race than the white, he took great delight in angering the riflemen. He would pop his head up and hurl an insult, then duck again before anyone could take aim and shoot him. Eventually Nate leveled his rifle and kept it aimed at the spot Pompey had last risen from, hoping he would come up at the same place again. He did, and Nate fired at the first flash of movement.

Pompey flung out no insults that time, and as time went by, Nate began to believe he had hit him. "Where's Pompey?" the men on the rifle platform began yelling.

"Pompey's sleeping!" the cry came back. "Howdy, damned white men, fire your big cannon!" Since the explosion of Squire's log gun, the Shawnees had delighted in bringing up the matter.

"Where's Pompey?" they called back again and again, until finally the Shawnees admitted the truth. "Pompey is dead." Nate was a hero from that moment on. He had quieted the taunting interpreter forever, and a welcome relief it was for those who had been forced to listen to him for hours on end. "Where's Pompey?" they continued to call, even after they knew the truth. "Tell Pompey we want to hear him talk to us some more!" Then they would laugh and heave stones across the wall, trying to hit the Indians who still worked around the mouth of the tunnel they were making, a tunnel that came closer to the stockade every day, so close now that the sound of digging could be heard through the ground itself.

On the night of Thursday, the seventeenth of September, Daniel Boone set Crow free. The Cherokee had not left his cabin prison since he had been captured. His food had been meager and of poorest quality, and as the siege heightened, sentiment in favor of killing Crow increased. Daniel was sorry to see that Nate was at the center of it.

He slipped away to Crow's cabin as the Shawnees launched the most fierce assault they had yet made against the fort. Screaming, firing rifles and arrows, throwing torches—the Indians seemed ready to climb the very walls and lay Boonesborough to waste. And the riflemen were more hard-pressed to stop them now, because long days of shooting had depleted supplies of ammunition and powder. Their every shot had to be carefully placed; yet the Indians seemed to have an endless supply of powder.

Crow sat up when Daniel entered with torch in hand. The yellow light played along the swarthy face of a man expecting to be killed at any moment, but hiding any fear he might have felt behind a stoic veneer. Daniel tossed him a shovel. "Dig. You can cut your way out under the wall, and if you can drag yourself away on that bad leg, you can live."

Crow could not disguise his surprise. "Why would you save me, Sheltowee? There are others here who have shouted through my door that I am to die."

"I have no desire to see a man murdered within any stockade that bears my name."

"Not even an Indian?"

"Not even an Indian."

Crow looked skeptical. "You are trying to make me escape so you can have a reason to kill me."

Daniel waved the torch to illuminate the far wall and floor. Already a depression was scooped out. "If I was wanting you dead, I could kill you here and claim you attacked me. No one would doubt it. But I've got no time to talk more with you. There's your shovel. Dig your way free, and maybe you'll make it away from here alive. If not, I doubt I'll be able to stop others from killing you. Good-bye, Crow."

He closed the door and barred it, then ran across the stockade yard to take his place on the rifle platform.

CHAPTER 33

THE NIGHT'S FIGHTING was nothing less than hellish. The Shawnees were putting their full effort into the assault, and Daniel was soon convinced that this was the pivotal moment in the siege. If the Shawnees were repulsed that night, he wouldn't be surprised if the entire thing came to its long-overdue end.

Daniel was busy through the night: moving among the riflemen, giving encouragement to the women who fought the fires set by flaming arrows and thrown torches, doing his best to quiet the fears of the screaming children, and firing his rifle at furtive targets in the clearing until his shoulder ached from the pound of the recoil. Several times he feared that the Shawnees were going to succeed in setting the fort afire, but then the skies opened and a soft steady rain began to fall—not a downpour, but enough to dampen shingles and palisades as well as any hope the Indians had of catching the fort afire. When the rain intensified to a full storm, the Indians gave up trying to burn the fort.

Yet even then they fought with tremendous intensity and therefore greater recklessness, and the cost to them was the loss of many lives, more than all who had died in the siege up until then. By the morning the clearing around the fort was stained with rain-diluted blood, and the bodies of those fallen Indians who had not been dragged away by their comrades lay still and ugly in the mud.

All was oddly quiet as the morning light heightened. The men in the bastions looked hard for Indians but saw none save the dead. An hour passed, and the gate was cautiously opened. Daniel and a dozen others ventured out.

The tunnel that had been dug two thirds of the way from the river to the fort had fallen in, collapsed by the dirt-softening rain. The arbor in the peach orchard was half blown down and empty. There was no sign of the enemy force, and tracks in abundance indicated they had left.

It was over.

Squire Boone drew in a deep breath and leaned wearily on his rifle. "Men," he said, "I believe we owe our Creator a prayer of gratitude right about now." Closing his eyes, he prayed aloud right there, and even profane John Holder bowed his head and murmured an "Amen" when the prayer was done.

When Daniel returned to the stockade, he went to the cabin where Crow had been held. It was empty. A shallow hole just big enough to accommodate a man had been scooped out under the outside wall. Crow had taken the shovel with him. At first Daniel felt a warm, grateful feeling that Crow had been so thoughtful that he hadn't left the shovel behind as evidence that someone had helped him to escape, but then he realized the crippled Cherokee had probably merely taken it along to use as a crutch. That made more sense. Crow seemed far too hostile a man to have done anything out of kindness for any member of the race he obviously despised.

Crow's disappearance—which to Daniel's pleasure aroused no suspicions—made little difference to most of the people, who were happy to be rid of him, but it appeared to disappoint Nate very much.

"What did you have in mind, Nate? Killing him for sport?"

Nate grunted in reply and strode off to find Phebe and her children.

BOONESBOROUGH WAS SAFE for now, but there were no guarantees for the other nearby stations. As women and children collected spent rifle balls in and around the stockade—an astounding 125 pounds of reusable lead—a big party of Boonesborough's successful defenders marched to Logan's Fort, where they received an unexpectedly hostile welcome hollered from the stockade rifle platform: "Damn you, come on!"

The reason for the hostility soon became apparent. William Patton, the Boonesborough-based hunter who had been away from the fort when the siege began, had come back during the height of the siege and watched the worst of it from a hiding place in the woods. Hearing the screams of the women and children and the war cries of the attacking Shawnees, and seeing the night brightly lit with rifle fire, he had concluded that Boonesborough was being overrun and had fled to Logan's Fort to give the grim news. When the Boonesborough party approached Logan's, the people there thought they were Shawnees until they were close enough to be recognized.

Rejoicing was abundant throughout the settlements as news of Blackfish's withdrawal spread, but it was tempered by the lingering presence of small bands of Indians haunting the forests. This was to be expected after a major siege, especially one that had left the attackers unsatisfied with the results. For a long time hunters and farmers had to he cautious, wary of every unexpected movement in the brush or odd-sounding birdcall.

Daniel Boone was gratified that his unswerving leadership during the siege seemed to have alleviated the suspicions many felt about him. Even so, certain ones, particularly Colonel Callaway and Benjamin Logan, remained extremely hostile. Daniel realized just how hostile when official charges were brought against him by the two men. He was brought up for court-martial and tried at Logan's Fort before a jury of militia officers.

Young Daniel Trabue, a witness to the trial, recorded the charges on paper and later in a journal. His would be the only direct written record of the episode that would survive the years. Boone was charged with four counts: that he had voluntarily surrendered the salt makers to hostile Indians, that while a prisoner of the British he had agreed to surrender his people for removal to Detroit under British jurisdiction, that he had weakened Boonesborough by taking many of its men away on his reckless venture to the Shawnee town on Paint Creek, and that he had endangered the officers of his fort by bringing them into the presence of the enemy on the pretense of making peace.

The latter charge was specifically Callaway's; he had not forgotten the terror of being grabbed by Shawnee hands and almost dragged away just before the shooting began.

Daniel defended himself against the charges by admitting their technical truth but explaining his motives. He had voiced his defense informally many times since his return from captivity, and now he presented it with great force, angered particularly at Callaway. Any apparent cooperation he had given the enemy had been nothing but "stratagem" and "policy," designed to "fool" the British and Indians and save lives. What he had done bought valuable time for the forts to strengthen themselves and almost certainly accounted for Boonesborough's successful defense. Surely, if his intention had really been to betray his own people, he could have done so any number of times, rather than fighting like the devil and risking his own neck against the very enemy he was accused of supporting.

Callaway and Logan were chagrined when the verdict came down overwhelmingly in Daniel's favor. He was acquitted on all charges and his rank elevated to major to boot. This was more than mere vindication, and for Callaway and Logan it was blatant discreditation.

Callaway declared that he would never have another word to say to Daniel Boone for the rest of his life, and he kept his promise. Daniel didn't mind. He had nothing more to say to Callaway, either.

Daniel was a weary man by then, and lonely. With the distractions of Indian attacks and courts martial behind him, he wrote Rebecca a long letter, telling her that he was indeed alive, and of all that had happened to him since last he saw her. Soon he would see her again, he wrote, and the family would be together, as they should be. He could hardly bear to wait.

He set out for North Carolina the day after Nate Meriwether married Phebe Carrick. He would be back before long, he told his friends. Maybe not back to live at Boonesborough, where the sting of earlier doubts and accusations would eternally be present, but back to the region, and with his family.

He had invested too much sweat and blood in Kentucky to abandon it now, and even though Richard Henderson's wilderness empire was being beaten to pieces in the eastern courts, Daniel still had hopes of gaining title to a big piece of Kentucky. He said his good-byes and rode south, taking his daughters Jemima and Susy and their husbands with him.

September, 1779

THE COLLECTION OF PEOPLE, livestock, and packhorses stretched back so far that it looked like an army to Rebecca Boone. The sky was clear, the road ahead open, and the Boone family course too firmly set to change now, even though she would not be unhappy at all to do just that.

Rebecca could hardly believe she was Kentucky bound again, not after all that had happened there, and all the time that had passed. When she had left Kentucky, Daniel still an Indian captive and in her opinion dead, she had never intended to set foot there again. She had come back to her own people and settled in the home of her brother, expecting to remain among the Bryans the rest of her days.

Then had come the rumors that her Daniel was still alive and back at Boonesborough, rumors confirmed by the arrival of a long letter brought by returning hunters. Soon Daniel himself, with Jemima and Susy, had shown up, looking older, battered, and very thin. She had welcomed him as if he had returned from the dead, a comparison that almost perfectly matched the facts as she experienced them.

But as so often happened between her and Daniel, differing visions of their ideal future quickly arose between them. Daniel was ready to return to Kentucky as soon as he could gather a new party of emigrants, but Rebecca loathed the idea. Kentucky had brought them nothing but danger, poverty, and trials. She was happier in Carolina, among people she loved.

The arguments between them had gone from quiet discussions to severe disagreements, and the fact that the Bryans entered the fray didn't calm any waters. Many Bryans were open Tories, a matter sensitive to Daniel, considering what he had gone through. They wanted Rebecca to remain among them for her own happiness and protection. Months dragged by as Daniel sought to persuade his wife to return with him to Kentucky while her blood kin did their best to persuade her to stay. Kentucky was far too dangerous a place, they declared. Even now returnees from the region were telling of new Indian violence, and of Colonel

John Bowman's big raid against Chillicothe. The Shawnee town had been burned to the ground, and among the Indians who died had been none other than old Blackfish himself—hard news for Daniel, who even through the Boonesborough fight had felt affection for his Shawnee "father."

Ironically, it was politics and land affairs that finally swayed the question in Daniel's favor. The local community began making matters hot for Tories like the Bryans, and the distant refuge of Kentucky began to look more and more inviting to Rebecca. Furthermore, Daniel learned that the Virginia Land Commission would be sending representatives into Kentucky to hold land hearings at the various forts in the region. With the Transylvania Company in ruins, settlers who wished to confirm their claims would have to appear before the commissioners at the appropriate stations to gain title.

Daniel could not let his land holdings slip through his fingers while arguing with Rebecca and the Bryans. He would have to be at Boonesborough by fall at the latest if he was to claim his lands.

So Rebecca relented, and soon she was sitting astride a big horse with its nose turned toward Kentucky. She could scarcely believe she was really going back there. At least she was far from alone. Daniel had recruited quite a band of travelers off the Yadkin: the families of all his brothers and sisters not yet in Kentucky, a family named Lincoln, and even quite a few Bryans, who had dramatically changed their anti-Kentucky rhetoric when local sentiment toward Tories took a harsh turn. All in all, there were a hundred or so people heading to Kentucky, a band large enough that even the most skittish travelers felt reasonably safe. No larger single party of travelers had ever embarked upon the trace since Daniel and his ax men had blazed it out in seventy-five.

Everything was on packhorses, the way still too rough and narrow for wagons. The largest single load was two heavy swivel guns given by a man planning to launch his own settlement, but these proved too cumbersome and heavy, actually killing the big horse upon which they were packed. Other methods of conveyance also proved ineffective, and the guns finally were hidden alongside the trail. Daniel mentally marked the place, hoping to come back and retrieve them someday.

By late October the big party reached Boonesborough, a place greeted with mixed feelings on the part of Daniel and Rebecca alike. After all he had endured at the settlement, and for the settlement, Daniel could not forget the embarrassment that Callaway and Logan had caused him. He had no desire to live there now and did not intend to do so any longer than required to make solid his land holdings. There was plenty of other good land around, and he would make a station of his own.

Rendering Boonesborough even less appealing were the squalor and disrepair of the place. There was little sign anyone had lifted a finger to repair damage done during the siege. Even though Daniel understood that the fort's inhabitants were busy simply keeping their own homes safe and provisioned, it bothered him to see the stockade in such shambles.

The brightest spot in the gloom was greeting Nate, Phebe, and their family again. They had acquired some acreage along the Kentucky River and built a stout little cabin with a tall stockade fence around its front. Nate and Phebe both looked healthy and happy. Daniel was glad for them and believed that surely they had been brought together by some providence that pitied them in their earlier misfortunes.

Daniel saw his land claim approved by the commissioners in December and departed from Boonesborough on a bitterly cold Christmas day. He took several of his kin and friends across the frozen river to a new site northwest of Boonesborough. He couldn't care less what name was attached to the place and suggested none, but others called it Boone's Station.

He might not have moved so quickly to the new site had he realized how fearsome the winter's weather would be. No one could recall such a cold season. Days were so cold it was hard to find a drink, because every bit of water was frozen, and nights were colder still. Making it worse was the lack of decent shelter at the new place. The families lived in half-faced camps, warmed in meager, temporary shelters only by big bonfires that had to be kept burning continuously. Game was not hard to kill when it was found, the weather having so weakened the animals that they could scarcely flee, but the beasts were starved and gave little meat. Daniel was grateful for the corn he had brought in from North Carolina, but it didn't last the full season. The winter was harsh and terrible and drove Rebecca's spirits very low.

By spring the situation was somewhat better. A few cabins had been erected and stockaded, and warming weather improved the game situation. Daniel built a large double cabin on nearby Marble Creek and moved his family there, along with six of Rebecca's young cousins, whose mother had died. With five of Daniel and Rebecca's own children still in the home, the double cabin was quite a crowded place.

When the winter had fully broken, Daniel settled in to farming, hunting, raising livestock, and gathering land through petition and preemption. He was forty-five years old and beginning to feel his age. The time had come for him to grasp what prosperity he could, or it would be too late.

DISASTER STRUCK when it seemed financial affairs were at their most promising. Daniel was a widely trusted man, and several of his friends put into his care some fifty thousand dollars in cash to purchase land warrants in the Virginia capital of Williamsburg. He took Nate with him on the trip, the cash stuffed into his saddlebags. When they reached James City, Virginia, they stopped at an inn for the night. Taking a meal downstairs, the two men sat with the saddlebags at their feet between them and attempted to make conversation with the only other customer, a hairy, bearded, toothless man who seemed skittish and unfriendly. Daniel thought he had seen the man before, but for the life of him couldn't recall where. When the man left abruptly, Daniel asked the landlord who the stranger was.

"Oh, that's naught but old Lukie. He lives up the road a couple of miles, back in a hut in the woods, and I feed him when he comes in. He's a sorry sort, prone to thieving and such, and I find it keeps my possessions safe to be kindly to the man. Here, gents, have you another drink."

That night they locked the door of their room tightly and put the saddlebags at the foot of the bed. Daniel fell asleep content that all was well. He felt warm and happy, almost dizzy. As if the drink might have been . . . and then he was asleep.

He dreamed some hours later of his father, walking toward him with a scowl, pushing aside the welcoming hand he extended. The same familiar old nightmare, one that had always portended trouble. He awakened covered in sweat, daylight in his eyes, much later than he usually woke. Nate was still sleeping soundly and did not even move when Daniel called his name and jostled him.

Looking down at the foot of the bed, he saw that the saddlebags were gone. For half a minute he was paralyzed, staring in disbelief. The money—fifty thousand dollars!—gone. He woke Nate only with the greatest effort and realized they had been drugged. The innkeeper was the one person who could have done such a deed. He must have realized there was something valuable in the saddlebags and made sure that his two patrons would sleep soundly enough for him to sneak the bags away.

Nate had drunk more of the tainted liquor than Daniel had and could hardly stand up without staggering to one side or the other. Daniel had to grab his shoulders and talk right into his face to make him understand that they had been robbed.

Making their way downstairs, they found the landlord was nowhere to be seen. Not a sign of him anywhere! Daniel headed outside, still clad only in a long, closed-front hunting shirt that hung loose like a dress around his white, thin knees. Looking furtively around, he began to shudder as the full truth sank in.

"What about that stranger at the table?" Nate asked. His doped condition had brought back some of the slur in his voice that he had overcome since his wounding in Powell Valley. "He might have took it."

Daniel doubted it; this robbery had all the appearance of having been pulled off by the landlord, the only one who could have tampered with their drinks. The scoundrel might have even made the accusation of thievery against the bearded stranger in order to divert in advance any suspicion about himself. But every possibility had to be considered.

"We'll dress and go looking for that stranger," Daniel said. "Landlord said he lived a couple of miles up this road."

They threw on their clothes and took their horses from the inn stable, noting that the landlord's big roan, which had been there the day before, was absent. More proof the man had robbed them and fled. Daniel looked for hoof prints and found them leading in the direction they themselves were intending to go. And a second set of hoof prints, too. Mounting, they followed them. Some two miles out they veered to the right onto a little horse path leading to a log hovel that blended almost invisibly into the woods behind and around it.

No one was there. Daniel had little doubt they had found the residence of the bearded man. Suspicion arising, he studied the ground and saw that two fresh sets of hoof prints also led away from the house, then diverged from each other out on the road. "They were in it together," he said to Nate. "The landlord drugged us, and his thieving friend did the robbing. I'd wager all I own on that." He winced at his words. All he owned . . . what would he own now, having lost fifty thousand dollars of other people's money, a debt he would have to repay?

Daniel and Nate spent days trying to trace down the thieves, but without success. A deep knot of tension settled into Daniel's midsection, hurting and burning him. He dreaded having to face those who had trusted him and lost out because of it. He had to find the money. Had to.

But he didn't. The landlord and his bearded partner "Lukie" had succeeded. Daniel had never known such a deep fury.

And something else about the theft kept nagging at him, too—the familiarity of the bearded man's face. He knew he had seen that man somewhere before. Lukie . . . what kind of name was that? Lukie . . . for Luke, probably, or Lucas . . .

He knew then. It had been many years since he had laid eyes on Lucas Kincheloe, but the face beneath that beard had indeed been his. He wondered if Kincheloe had recognized him, too, if he laughed to think that he was stealing from the man who had humiliated him so many years ago in Fredericksburg and got him tossed into prison.

It was too much to take. Daniel was embarrassed to shed tears in front of Nate, but he couldn't help it. Here at middle age he had been struck one of the hardest blows of his life, and he wasn't sure that this time he would be able to overcome it.

WHEN THE TERRIBLE NEWS got out to those who had lost their money, Daniel was moved to tears several times again, but for a happier reason. Several simply forgave his debt. They knew his character, and that if it had happened to him, it would have happened to anyone in the same circumstances. They were confident he had guarded their money the best he could. Who would have anticipated being drugged at an inn?

Others were not so forgiving and insisted he compensate them for the loss. He agreed to do it, though he knew it would take many years of effort and sacrifice.

In the summer a happier surprise came to the Boone family when Rebecca discovered she was pregnant. At age forty-one she had believed herself past her childbearing days, a saddening thought to a woman who hated to see her youth slip ever further into the past. Daniel coddled her gently, urging the children to carry most of the household workload so that nothing would endanger Rebecca or the unborn one. The memory of infant William's death still hurt after five years. This time both he and Rebecca were determined that all would go well.

In late summer Daniel and Nate volunteered as scouts under General George Rogers Clark when he raised a force of more than a thousand troops, most of them reluctant draftees. On August 7 the army struck the Shawnee town of Piqua, routing the occupants in a fierce battle that brought atrocities all around and left the Shawnee crops burned and the town itself beaten to the ground and destroyed. Daniel found no pleasure in the fight. He was reaching an age where he longed only for a peaceful life away from warfare, away from creditors, away from the constantly unsettled state his life seemed to be in.

After the campaign Daniel returned home and set out on a hunt with his brother Neddy. Now just approaching the age of forty, Neddy continued to be a favorite uncle of Daniel's children, though in Jemima's case the uncle relationship was symbolic, of course, rather than fact. All the older children knew the truth about Jemima's parentage and accepted it with the same forgiving calm that Daniel did. There had never been discomfort between Neddy and Daniel, even from the first days after Jemima's birth.

The brothers hunted for a few days near the Blue Licks and headed home, Daniel feeling more at ease and free of worry than since the loss of the land-warrant money. But as they paused to rest and graze their horses near a walnut grove, Daniel grew uneasy.

"Let's not linger here," he said. "I have the sense of Indians about."

Neddy laughed. "You are far too fretful, brother. Look there at them walnuts! Bushels of them. I'll crack us a few." Lacking any solid reason to feel edgy, Daniel didn't argue, but set off to chase down a bear he spotted heading toward a canebrake some distance away. He was near the canebrake when he heard the crack of a rifle behind him. Wheeling, he saw Neddy lying on the ground, a Shawnee kneeling over him with knife in hand. Another couple of Shawnees were running toward him.

Daniel turned and ran into the canebrake, plunging in deep and then dropping to hide. He heard the Indians reach the edge of the brake, heard them talking, heard the name of "Boone." Had they recognized him when he'd run into the cane? The next sentence told him the truth: "We've killed old Daniel Boone! We've killed Blackfish's Sheltowee!"

He was heartsick. Cowering in his hiding place, he recalled something Rebecca had told him after the birth of Jemima, how she had yielded to Neddy's advances in a time of loneliness, partly because Neddy's looks were so like his own. Now that same similarity had fooled the Shawnees into thinking they had just killed the most famous Boone of all.

Killed . . . Neddy was dead. Daniel couldn't make himself accept it. A moment ago he and Neddy had been walking and talking together, happy and unworried . . . and now Neddy was dead.

My boy, there are those of your own who will take their own journey out of this dark land, too, and the heart will surely be torn from you. Old Squire had said it himself, years ago, in Daniel's dream. For years Daniel had wondered if the dream-prophecy would come true. Now it had. Perhaps it would again.

The Indians sent a dog into the brake to find him, and he was forced to shoot it. He backed up farther into the cane, reloading as he went, then dropped onto his face among the stalks, watching as the Indians came in, following the sound of the shot. They found the dog, cursed and muttered among themselves, then turned and left. Whoever it was in the canebrake hardly mattered. They had killed Blackfish's Sheltowee, and any additional prize was too small to worry over.

Daniel remained in the canebrake a long time, then finally left. He found Neddy's body cut and mutilated. They had taken away his head, no doubt planning to display proudly to their fellows what they thought to be the dead face of their old admired enemy, Daniel Boone.

Daniel paused and wept by Neddy's body only a few moments,

then pressed on to Boone's Station. It was a twenty-mile journey and took him all night. Giving the terrible news to his loved ones, he gathered his son Israel and a party of other men and made the same journey in reverse. Neddy's body had already been partially eaten by wild animals, but there was no time to stop. They pursued the Indian trail all the way to the Ohio River before realizing they could not catch up with Neddy's killers.

Sadly, they turned back, picked up what remained of Neddy Boone, and began the sorrowful journey back to Boone's Station. When Rebecca Boone saw the pitiful remains that had once been Neddy, she sobbed like a woman widowed, and nothing anyone could do seemed to comfort her. Daniel observed her grief sadly, but if it roused any jealousy in him, he hid it very well. He told her years before that he would not hold her at fault for what had transpired between her and his brother, and Daniel Boone was a man of his word.

CHAPTER 34

August, 1782

ISRAEL BOONE RUBBED his stiff neck and winced at the pain. *Blast it all*, he thought, *when will these sore muscles quit their aching?* He had been sick for nearly two weeks now, and though he was much better overall, his neck still had the most annoying crick, and sitting horseback didn't do a single thing good for it.

Shifting in the saddle and balancing his long rifle horizontally before him, he vainly tried to find a comfortable position. He sighed and wished he were anywhere else in the world except there on the bank of the Licking River in the midst of an army of Kentucky frontiersmen numbering something less than two hundred. It wasn't that he was afraid, he thought to himself—while deeper in his mind a voice admitted that yes, he was afraid, unusually so—it was simply that he didn't feel well. His joints ached, his neck was stiff, and he had no energy. The hot late-summer day was making sweat pour off him, trailing down his skin beneath his lightweight hunting shirt and soaking through at the armpits.

Israel heard his father's voice, rising loud in argument with the other officers. Hugh McGary, hot-tempered, irrational, maybe even a little insane, was shouting in Daniel Boone's face, leaning forward, fists clenched and arms straight, bellowing something or other. Israel grinned a tight-lipped, mirthless grin. No one could rouse Daniel Boone's ire like McGary.

Israel himself had managed to rouse his father's ire mere days ago when Daniel had discovered that he had not signed the register of volunteers at Boone's Station when a company was formed for an expedition. He still stung when he remembered his father's words to him at the breakfast table. "Israel, I didn't hear your name called among the volunteers signing in at the station yesterday. I would have thought it would have been one of the first named."

"I've been sick in bed," Israel replied. "Otherwise I would have enrolled."

Daniel hadn't seemed to listen. "I hate to consider that I've raised a timid son."

Mentally replaying that exchange was enough to bring color to Israel's face. How could his father have embarrassed him that way in front of all the family, especially when Israel had a perfectly good reason for not having enlisted? Ever since the court-martial episode four years back and the loss of the land-warrant money in Virginia, it seemed that Daniel was overly touchy about public perceptions of Boone honor. Israel wished that he would ease up on such worrying. The Boone name in general—and Daniel Boone's name in particular—had suffered no great damage in the minds of most. Daniel had even been elected to the Virginia legislature and put in good service in the assembly since the events that had so embarrassed him. Yet he would often discount such evidence of his good public standing and worry over anything to do with the Boones that might cast a negative light. Even the death two years ago of his most backbiting critic, Colonel Richard Callaway, who had been killed and mutilated by Indians on the Kentucky River, had not seemed to bring Daniel any relief from worries over his reputation.

Israel's humiliation before his brothers and sisters had led him to leave the house right after the meal and ride into the station, where he'd put his name on the enlistment sheet. He had hardly felt up to doing even that, much less actually riding out with the company, but he wouldn't stand by while his father thought ill of him. At age twenty-three he was a stout and brave young frontiersman, and he'd be whipped and hanged before he would let any impugn his courage!

Whatever personal grudge he felt toward his father regarding this expedition, he agreed with him fully that it was a justified foray. The first part of the year had been bloody and violent. The slaughter of almost a hundred Christianized Delaware Indians by a band of rangers from the Monongahela tribe had led to retaliation by other Indians of the Ohio country. Throughout the summer there had been raid after raid, and no one had been able to catch the raiders. Reports had it that one of the leaders of the raiders was the white man Simon Girty, who had taken on the Shawnee way of life and continually urged his adopted brothers to violence against the "Long Knives." Another raider frequently seen had been the Cherokee-born Indian named Crow, the very man who had managed to dig his way out of the Boonesborough fort the last night of Blackfish's siege back in 1777, when Israel was still living with his mother and most of his siblings among the Bryans in Carolina.

The Bryans were Kentuckians now, of course, and in fact, an attack by Girty and his raiders against the Elkhorn River fort of Bryan's Station, named after Rebecca's kin, had been the catalyst for the present military outing. The volunteers now hanging fire here on the banks of the Licking had first raced to Bryan's, only to find the Indians already gone. The officers had gathered and argued, much as they were right now, about whether to follow or to wait for more volunteers under Colonel Ben Logan. Hugh McGary had advocated waiting for Logan, but John Todd, leader of the militia under whose auspices Daniel, Israel, and the other

Boone's Station volunteers had enlisted, sneered at McGary's caution, calling it "timidity" and declaring that the Indians should be pursued before their trail grew cold.

McGary had been humiliated. Israel had seen it in his face, even from a distance. He knew the ways of Hugh McGary enough to know that Todd's perceived insult would not be forgotten or forgiven.

Israel had ridden near his father all the next day, suffering greatly from the crick in his neck and the pain in his joints, but saying not a word. He was determined to prove himself as stout and uncomplaining as any man there. He would prove to all, and particularly to Daniel, that Israel Boone was not "timid." He would make sure his father noticed.

The farther they tracked the Indians, though, the less Daniel seemed to notice anything except the trail left behind, which was surprisingly obvious and even marked here and there by blazed trees. Frequently Daniel stopped and examined the sign on the ground, frowned, then looked around at the tree blazes and other clear markers the Indians had left behind. Israel had joined him upon the fourth such stop, knelt on aching knees beside his father, and immediately saw what had him worried.

"They're stepping in each other's tracks!" Israel said. "Trying to hide their numbers."

"That's right, and that can only mean there's a danged passel of them and they don't want us to know it. Now, ask yourself, son: why would an Indian army hide its numbers and at the same time leave such a clear track behind?"

The answer that came to mind chilled Israel as he spoke it. "Ambush."

"That's right. They're trying to draw us after them and to make us think they're but a small band. They'll draw us in somewhere ahead—beyond the Licking, I'll wager—and drop on us like snakes into a canoe."

The army pressed on. Israel knew Daniel would express his worries to the other officers when the time was right. As he sat watching the officers argue on the riverbank, he figured that this must be the time.

He wondered what had McGary so worked up. He was still yelling into Daniel Boone's face, a face growing ominously red. If McGary pushed too hard, too far, there was no telling what Daniel would do. Any amusement Israel felt over the scene faded, and he watched with concern. After a few moments he edged his horse a little closer, where he could hear what was being said.

McGary's voice boomed out. "We have men aplenty to take on any Indian force thrown against us! For us to come this far and then to hold back to wait for Logan—! It contradicts all the big and brave talk you were doing back at Bryan's Station, by godly!"

"There is every sign that they intend to ambush us!" Daniel shot back. "Have you not read their invitations spread all along the way here?"

"I've read clear sign that Indians are across the river, and it's Indians we've come to kill!"

"It's we who will be killed if we proceed without caution," Daniel said.

"Caution? Caution, by godly!" McGary fired back. "Now who speaks of caution? When I spoke of caution back at Bryan's, I was called 'timid.' Now it's old Boone himself taking the shakes! I've never known you to be a coward before, Boone!"

Israel's eyes widened. No man had ever faced his father and called him a coward. No worse charge could be laid to a man on the frontier. Daniel's face grew even redder, and he stepped toward McGary, finger in his face. "No man calls me coward, McGary. I can go as far in an Indian fight as any man here!"

"Then let's do it!" McGary bawled. "And cease this foolish jabbering!"

Colonel Todd, whose gibes at McGary at Bryan's Station were the indirect cause of the current tension, stepped forward. "Gentlemen, calm yourselves!" he said. "The men are observing us." He turned to Daniel. "What if we go on? What tactic would serve us best, in your opinion?"

"I would advise dividing in half, sending one half across here, the other farther upstream, and bring them together like the two sides of a wedge moving to a point. If the Indians intend ambush, they'd be faced with two groups. It might be we could squeeze them between our two sides."

It sounded as good a plan as anyone could devise, but McGary immediately cut off any hope of following it. He went to his horse, leaped into the saddle, and rode down into the river. Turning, he waved his rifle above his head and shouted, "Them that ain't damned cowards follow me! I'll show you where the Indians are!"

He spurred his horse across the water. A muffled yell rose among the waiting troops. Most of those already mounted galloped down to the water and followed McGary across. Unmounted men scurried to their horses and came after them. Israel looked at his father, who threw up his hands in surrender to the inevitable. "Let us go, then!" he said, and went to his own waiting horse.

At the edge of the water Daniel Boone paused and turned, waving his own men forward. "Come on and show your best courage!" he yelled. "We are all slaughtered men now!"

Israel thought those to be the most ominous words he had ever heard. His neck suddenly aching all the worse, he spurred his horse forward and followed his father to the other side, full of dread.

ON THE FAR BANK most of the troops dismounted, and Daniel, Todd, and Colonel Stephen Trigg quickly split the force into three divisions. Israel was glad to be under his father's command. He always felt safer in times of danger when his father was close by.

Quickly, the three bodies surged forward, climbing a wooded hill. At the lead were McGary and twenty-four other advance men. Israel did not envy them. He could sense that the Indians were near, could feel them as if their breath were breezing against his sweating face.

Daniel Boone turned and looked at Israel. "I wish I'd not urged you to enlist in this," he said. "I fear for what will become of us here. But be brave, son, and stay close. I believe the Indians will be upon us soon."

Almost as if triggered by those words, a loud whoop sounded at the hill, followed instantly by a far louder volley of gunshots. Israel heard men scream and saw more than a dozen of the advance scouts fall writhing to the ground.

"Ambush!" someone yelled.

"Forward!" Daniel Boone shouted. His face looked fearsome and atypically pallid. He ran forward, and Israel discovered that he, too, was running. It was as if his motions were no longer under his control, but happening of their own accord.

An Indian rose from behind a fallen tree and leveled his rifle. At almost point-blank range Daniel turned and shot the man through the heart. The Indian grunted and fell to the side, blood spurting. Daniel had already started to reload by the time the man shuddered into death.

Israel saw another Indian bound up out of a ravine, and he raised his own rifle. He fired and the man spasmed and fell back into the ravine, out of sight. Breathing hard and fast, Israel reloaded his rifle and ran on after his father.

The situation was terrible. The Indians had appeared in huge numbers on both sides of the advancing white army. Israel fired again, reloaded, moved forward. To his surprise the Indians seemed to be pulling back. The Boone division was moving ahead with surprising speed. Israel sent out a whoop of delight. His fear was gone now, and his neck didn't hurt him anymore. This was a real fight, hot and deadly, but he was still alive, still making progress right along with his father and fellow troops.

Hugh McGary appeared, racing back toward them. He halted at Daniel's side and grabbed his shoulder. "Retreat, man, by godly!" he yelled. "Don't you know that they are all around us? Trigg and Todd have already given way, and now the damned yellow boys are at the horses!"

Israel turned and saw that McGary was right. Indians were racing down to seize the horses left by the river, and others were coming up behind, firing and yelling. The air was filling with smoke and dust, and now the screams of dying men rose with new volume and intensity.

"Retreat!" Daniel Boone shouted. "Into the woods, then make for the river!"

A riderless horse, its saddle wet with the fresh blood of the man who had died upon it, appeared through the fog of gun smoke. Daniel snatched it. "Israel, climb on and ride out of here!"

"I'll not leave you!" Israel yelled back.

"You must!"

"Not unless you come with me!" Daniel swore and turned, looking for another horse. Israel fired his rifle at a running Indian, then set the butt against the ground to reload. Something hit him hard in the side of the neck, and he fell to the right. Rolling onto his back, he moaned, then felt his mouth flood. His neck burned and he couldn't breathe. *Oh, God help me*, he thought, *I'm shot*! He tried to get up and couldn't. His best effort only made him thrash on the ground. Blood poured from his mouth and down his throat. He tried to breathe and felt the hot liquid fill his lungs.

His father's face appeared above him. "Israel!" He tried to answer but no sound came out. A dark circle began to form around the perimeter of his vision, then closed down, narrowing to frame the distraught face of Daniel Boone. He reached up, groping for his father's shoulder, but he could not find it. The dark circle closed down tighter and Boone's face faded away, becoming an intensely bright point of light, very far away and down a long tunnel. All sound was gone, and his neck did not hurt now. He ceased his struggle and felt himself pulled into the tunnel, moving at an amazing pace toward the light.

There was only time for one last thought about the life and world he was leaving: *I hope I have died bravely, without timidity, so Father will not be ashamed of me*.

NATE MERIWETHER had not been at the Battle of the Blue Licks. He had remained behind as part of the force left to guard the stations. The terrible news of the battle's outcome had shocked him deeply, and he told Phebe that he believed he had been wrong to stay behind.

"No," she remonstrated. "No. I've lost one husband to the Indians, and I am not ashamed of being glad I haven't lost another." Then she told him she wanted to leave. Already others were fleeing Kentucky, heading for safer areas, and she wanted to be among them. Nate shook his head. He could not leave now. To do so would be to desert his friends and neighbors and leave them with one less man to fight for the conquest of the land. "We have to win this land or see it taken from beneath us by the very savages who murdered Israel Boone and all them others at the Blue Licks. The very savages who must have killed the man who was first your husband. The ones who took my whole family from me in Powell Valley."

"But how many must die before it's won?"

"I don't know, Phebe. No one knows. Very many, I figure. But the more of us who run away, the more will die. That's why we must stay."

"I don't care about winning this land. Let the Indians have their country! All I want is to live in peace." She threw up her hands in exasperation. "Why must we always be fighting them? Is there no other way? When we kill them, they kill us, and then we kill them again in turn. If we show the Indians mercy, maybe they would show us mercy as well."

"There is no mercy in the Indian heart," Nate replied. "I have never seen nor heard of an Indian showing mercy to any human being except their own kind. That's why they must be wiped out."

A few days after the corpses were buried in a mass grave near the Licking River, Nate rode to the Boone house. He found Rebecca there alone with her children, Daniel being at the Boone's Station stockade. He was disappointed; he'd come to give his condolences to his oldest friend.

"I'm awful sorry about Israel," he said, looking at a woman who seemed far older than her years and at least ten years older than the last time he had seen her only weeks before. "I know what it is to lose children."

Her eyes grew red and she looked down at the baby in her arms. This was Nathan, the unexpected addition to the Boone family that had come along the prior year. She hugged the child close to her. "Yes, Nate, I know you do." She began to cry, and he went to her and put his arm around her.

"I know you never thought much of me through the years, Rebecca," he said. "But I've admired you from the time we were young back on the Yadkin. Always so pretty and kind and good. Daniel did well for hisself."

Rebecca quaked under his arm, crying. She reached up suddenly and kissed his bearded cheek. "Thank you, Nate. Thank you." She paused, thinking. Her body grew tense. "He made Israel enlist, Nate. Shamed him into it right at our table. Said he'd be ashamed to have a son who was afraid to fight."

"Don't hold him at fault for that, Rebecca. This is a land where the worst that can happen to a man is to be thought a coward. If Israel hadn't have gone, there would have been others who would have called him coward. Daniel knew that and wanted to spare him from it."

"If Israel hadn't have gone, he'd still be alive."

"Maybe. Maybe not. A man never knows when or where he'll die.

Israel could have stayed here and died at the hand of a skulking savage. He could have died from the sickness that took him. As it was, he died a hero."

"A hero . . . a dead hero. Where's the glory in it?"

"You sound much like my Phebe." Nate looked up, squinting into the distance. "I'll be—there comes Dan right now."

Daniel rode in slowly. Nate gave Rebecca a squeeze and dropped his arm from her shoulder. Daniel dismounted and walked up. "Nate, I see you've come trying to steal my woman. I ought to—" He let the feeble attempt at banter trail off. He was still full of pain, with no room yet for jests. It would be a long time before Daniel Boone was in the humor to joke and laugh again. "What brings you, Nate? Can you stay for supper?"

"I'd be tickled to. Thank you. What brings me is just that—well, I want you to know from my own lips how sorrowful I am over your loss."

Daniel nodded. "Thank you." He rubbed his chin, fighting emotion. "But it ain't just me. There's sixty or so other families grieving in loss, thanks mostly to Mad Hugh McGary, bastard that he is! He should have died, not Israel and the other good men. Damn him! Damn him to hell!"

"Daniel, don't swear," Rebecca chided weakly. "I don't want to hear you talk so, with a son fresh dead."

"I'm sorry. I'm sorry—" Still trembling with fury, Daniel scuffed his foot. "But, God, if only they'd have listened to me! I told them there was ambush ahead! Any man with eyes and sense could see it! But they had to go on. Had to show how brave they were. And I followed."

"What's done is done, Daniel," Nate said. "You can't change it. All you can do is avenge it."

"Avenge?" Daniel repeated.

"That's right. Spill the blood of ten yellow devils for every white man who dies. Do it until they're gone."

"I've thought much the same for a long time," Daniel said. "Now I don't know what to think. It hurts even to try." He kissed Rebecca and reached out for Nathan. Rebecca put the boy in her husband's arms and he squeezed him close. "Come on in for supper, Nate. We'll smoke a few pipes and talk about the old days."

They walked into the cabin together.

NATE AND DANIEL participated in the inevitable military sweep against the northern Indian towns in retaliation for the Blue Licks fight. Led by George Rogers Clark, a thousand-member army gathered at the mouth of Licking River and moved against the Indian towns for the first three weeks of November. The Indians seemed to have known they were coming, and the troops met little resistance as they destroyed the already once-burned and rebuilt town of Chillicothe, then did the same to Piqua and four other towns. As usual, they concentrated mostly on crop destruction, the most devastating blow that could be inflicted as winter approached.

Even while Clark's army was advancing, Daniel leading the militiamen from Fayette County, the fledgling United States and Great Britain signed articles of peace. Though the treaty had little to do directly with the old disputes between Indians and whites, the accord did bring an end to British support of Indian incursions. When the news of the treaty finally penetrated into the Kentucky settlements, Daniel Boone would feel the first glimmerings of real hope that the peaceful kind of life he had so long wanted for his family might actually be at hand.

Meanwhile, he began to look at new lands. Even before he heard of the peace treaty he knew that an end of the British-American conflict would come someday, and the Ohio River would grow ever more important as a trade and settlement route. Simon Butler had already begun a settlement on the Ohio, and recently revealed that his true surname was Kenton, a fact he'd been hiding under the erroneous belief that a former romantic rival he had fought with had died of his injuries.

Daniel was eager to develop a new settlement himself. To own good Ohio River land, particularly with a decent landing spot for craft, could make a man wealthy. Though he had come into possession of thousands of acres of Kentucky land already, he was just as continually losing it to pay off his old debts. He would feel more financially secure on the river.

And he could move away from his present habitation, where everything reminded him and Rebecca of Israel.

He had thought that the ache of losing James to the torturing knife of Big Jim was the worst hurt he would know. But with Israel it was even worse. He felt partly responsible for what had happened. It was he who had encouraged Israel to enlist, he who had let Hugh McGary get his goat and force a wrong decision . . . he who had lived while Israel died. He would never be free of the haunting fact that his own actions had led to Israel's death, just as his own over-eager pursuit of his Kentucky dream had helped bring about James's slaying back in seventy-three.

After the scourging of the Ohio towns was through, Daniel explored the Limestone Creek region along the southern Ohio bank. The place seemed to be exactly what Daniel was looking for. Here a man could establish an inn, trading house, and store, and vend lands to those moving into the new country. He could sit back and grow rich! He could forget the trials and losses of the past and live out the last of his years in prosperous peace.

He returned to Marble Creek and told Rebecca that soon they would be moving again. This time there was no argument from her. She was ready to go elsewhere, and Daniel's enticing talk of peace and mounting wealth in their advancing years somehow seemed more believable coming from the lips of a fifty-year old man than had the cloud castles he promised her in more youthful days. Rebecca liked to hear him talk of settling down, of welcoming newcomers, of helping towns and communities grow up. Always before, he had been eager to move on over the next hill. Maybe age and change and even tragedy were having a few positive effects on the man she loved.

And she did love him, though she sensed that he feared he would lose her affection because of what had happened to their first two offspring. She realized she could build a strong case against him and find him at fault for the death of both James and Israel, and she had actually been ready to do so when the sting of Israel's death was fresh. But she would not. Nate Meriwether's words had changed her thinking . . . and who would have thought Nate, of all folks, would be able to do that? His talk about Daniel made her realize her husband had never intended anything but good for his loved ones. The pain of his sons' loss was as deep in him as in her. She could not hold against him offenses he had never intended to commit.

If Daniel was at fault, she forgave him. She did not want to stand at odds with him. She wanted to stand with him, and to lie beside him at night, talking and laughing and dreaming just as they had their first night together twenty-six years before in the tiny loft of the little Carolina cabin in old Squire Boone's yard.

CHAPTER 35

THE HAUNTING OF NATE Meriwether began immediately upon his return from the Ohio campaign. Or haunting is what people came to call the weird series of events that became part of the eerie strain of Kentucky folklore. It was all very strange, explained by some as supernatural, others as a series of coincidences, misidentifications, mistakes. Others saw it as evidence that Nate was as mad as old Hugh McGary himself, whose shroud-wrapped, Indian-slain stepson frequently appeared as a ghost in McGary's cabin to accuse him of cavorting with other women while his wife lay abed, sick and disturbed in the mind because of her bereavement.

Nate's haunting was different. It began with mere feelings that he was being watched while he was chopping wood in his yard or chipping rifle flints out by the spring. Then he began to sense a presence nearby when he was out hunting, though investigation revealed nothing. Nate wondered if he was losing his mind and told only Phebe about what was happening. If he had wanted to keep it a secret, he shouldn't have told her, because she grew terrified and immediately told both Jemima and Rebecca Boone, and they in turn told their husbands. Eventually the word got out everywhere, mostly because Jemima's tongue proved rather loose with the tale.

"Now, that's a right rum thing," Daniel said after Rebecca told him. "Nate's too good a woodsman to be imagining ghosts in trees. If he's hearing something, that can only mean there's something really there."

"But if it's not a ghost, what could it be? If it was a human, and Nate so fine a woodsman as you say, he would be able to find sign."

"Unless whoever is watching him is a better woodsman than he is," Daniel said.

The mystery went on for weeks. Folks joked about it, others worried, Baptist-minded Squire Boone declared that Nate was "hainted by old sins," and children shivered in their beds at the thought that a spirit roamed the woods near the Meriwether place.

Daniel was preoccupied with his approaching move to Limestone and didn't give the "haunting" much serious thought at all—until the day an ashen-faced Nate showed up at his door, looking sick and shaky, and asked for Daniel to serve as a guide to the Tennessee country, where he and Phebe were going to resettle.

Daniel was twice-stunned, surprised that Nate was ready to leave Kentucky after forcefully declaring so many times he would not do so, and surprised as well that he even felt the need of a guide.

"You know the way already. What need do you have of me, Nate?"

"Look at me, Dan!" He held up a hand that quivered like a frightened rabbit. "I fear I'll never make it alone, the way I am. I need a good man with me—my old friend Daniel Boone. And besides—" he looked even more solemn now "—I believe I won't be living long. I ain't sure I'll be allowed to leave Kentucky. Whatever this is that's after me, it's come to kill me. I need your protection."

"Why do you think it's going to kill you?"

"I been finding things. Bird feathers stuck in my door. And dead birds tied above the well. And this morning there was something marked into the ground with a stick. A picture of a man, lying down by a fire with his leg all twisted up funny. I don't know what it meant, but it sent a shiver right to my marrow. There's something out there hating me and wanting me dead. And it's going to have me dead, too, sure as the world, unless I have a guard."

"What's Phebe think about all this?"

"She's ready to leave this place. She's worse scared than I am. Daniel, go with me, please. Guard us and guide us, at least till we're out of Kentuck. I want you to go. You're the best friend I've had, and the fact is I don't expect I'll be alive much longer to keep on being your friend. Make this journey with me and I'll die grateful."

"Shut up all that talk about dying. I don't believe it. Somebody's pulling that leg of yours and you don't even know it. Haints and such don't mark fool pictures on the ground."

"Will you go with me, Dan?"

Daniel sighed. "I'll go with you."

IN BED THAT NIGHT Daniel told Rebecca what Nate had said and asked her what she thought about it.

"About them moving? I hate to see Phebe leave. She's been a good friend and a joy to me, and like a sister to Jemima these last few years."

"That's not what I'm asking about. The marks, the 'haint.' What do you think it is?"

"Not a haint, I can tell you that. I've studied on it, and conclude that a haint wouldn't waste his time on Nate Meriwether. Whatever it is, it's wearing flesh and blood, I'll wager."

"That picture scratched on the ground has me a-pondering. There's got to be some meaning to it."

"I reckon so. Something out of Nate's past, maybe. Something that's supposed to make him think, or scare him. But that's enough talk. Good night, Dan."

"Night, Becca." Daniel rolled over and closed his eyes. Thirty minutes later, having been awake and thinking the entire time, he stiffened and sat up. Rebecca murmured and turned, not awakening.

"Great God of heaven!" he whispered into the dark cabin room. "Could it be that?"

He was not able to fall asleep for another hour and a half, his mind racing with the thought that had stirred him.

By the time morning came, he felt that his midnight realization was rather more likely a weary mind's deception and put the notion behind him, not telling Rebecca about it. He spent the day hunting with sons Daniel Morgan and Jesse, and together they brought in a bear and two deer, quite a day's catch of meat. For the next two days they were busy with skinning, hide dressing, butchering, salting, and so on, and the day after that he spent readying himself for the journey with Nate. He and Phebe, and Nate's two stepsons, Silas Carrick, now about sixteen, and William Carrick, a lively seven with an eye on eight, and the daughter that Nate and Phebe had produced together a year and a half back, Elizabeth Ann Meriwether, would be setting out the next day.

The next morning Daniel kissed Rebecca good-bye and sternly directed his sons to see to the welfare of the family while he was gone, then rode over to the place he was to meet Nate. Nate and his family were already there, waiting, and Nate looked even more scared and worn down than the last time he had seen him.

"It was back last night. The hounds was barking, and I even fired a shot into the woods. I heard a scrambling, and whatever it was took off a-running in the dark. I could hear it."

"Stop this 'it' talk. That's a human being for certain. You can't scare ghosts with bullets. Did you check for sign this morning?"

Nate didn't answer. "He was too scared," young William chimed in. The contribution earned him a reproving sidewise glance from his stepfather.

"Nate, you beat all, you surely do," Daniel said. "Well, folks, I'm ready to head down the way, if you are."

"More than ready," Nate replied.

They set off down the road, everything Nate and Phebe Meriwether owned riding on pack saddles, and Daniel in the lead, his rifle across his saddle.

There was no evidence of followers, ghostly or otherwise, but at nightfall Daniel had to admit that he felt a certain odd sensation on the back of his neck, a vague and nebulous sense that there were more in the vicinity than the six human beings that made up their little band. Nate sat near the fire, gazing furtively around at the dark encircling forest, looking as scared as Daniel had ever seen a man look. It was unnerving just to see him, because he knew Nate well enough to realize he wouldn't be frightened of nothing. If he was this scared, there was something, or more likely someone, very solid and real bringing it about.

That night Daniel lay in his bedroll, pretending to sleep. They were camped at a lonely, isolated place. If someone intended harm to Nate, this seemed a likely spot to inflict it. If that happened, Daniel intended to be awake to respond.

Hours dragged by without event. The dark camp, lighted only by the dim glow of fire coals, brought sad thoughts of dead sons, and Daniel finally fell into a fitful sleep full of sad dreams.

"*Sheltowee*."

He opened his eyes. He had been dreaming of Blackfish . . . had he also dreamed the voice calling the name Blackfish had given him? He sat up and saw Nate rising, picking up his rifle, and knew he had not imagined it.

"Out yonder," Nate whispered, thumbing to the north. "Far out in the woods."

"I heard it, too," Daniel said, also rising.

The others, all but the two youngest ones, awoke. Phebe said, "Nate?"

"Hush, woman. Whatever it is—whoever it is—is out there, and I'll be damned if I'll run scared even another hour. Dan and me will go and find him and settle this. Silas, you fetch up your rifle and guard the camp."

"But that wasn't your name that was called, Nate," Phebe said.

"It was my Shawnee name," Daniel said. "Whether whoever called it is the same one that's been causing Nate trouble, I don't know. I'm betting it is."

Silas had already taken his place beside his mother, rifle already half-raised, eyes scanning all around.

"*Sheltowee*!"

The call came again, borne on the cool night breeze. It was difficult to tell from where it came, but Daniel made his best judgment and plunged into the woods, moving in near silence. Nate followed, seeming to find courage in the company of a man with whom, over the years, he'd spent so much time in the dark and dangerous wilderness.

Phebe moved over and sat between her two sleeping children, watching the forest and praying.

THEY MOVED through the forest with rifles at the ready. It was pitch-dark. Whoever was manipulating this obviously had selected his time carefully. He wanted to move them into the woods at the darkest hour. As Daniel thought about that, he began to think that maybe they had made a mistake to play along with an obviously prearranged scheme. This might prove as foolish as the mad rush into ambush at the Blue Licks had been. "Nate, let's go back," he whispered, "Nothing but ill will come of this."

"Daniel look!" He had already seen it. Off about a quarter mile ahead, a fire burned. A large campfire, flaring in the darkness like a lone star in a black sky.

"He wants us to go there," Daniel said. "He's luring us, just like Girty and his warriors lured us into the Blue Licks."

"Who is he, Dan?" Daniel remembered the bizarre notion that had come to him in the night, only to be rejected in the morning. Now it seemed much more believable again.

"I think I might know, or at least have a good guess," Daniel said.

"Who?"

"I believe it might be the Cherokee named Crow. The one you shot and took prisoner just before the siege."

"Crow . . . so this is revenge for me capturing him?"

"No. Revenge for something that happened much longer ago than that. Do you recall when—"

"*Sheltowee*!"

The cry was louder now. It startled both men. Daniel was grateful for the darkness; he would not be proud for Nate to see the fear he knew was marking his features. But one thing he now was sure of: it was Crow. He had recognized the voice this time.

He had to hand it to the Cherokee. The man was a master of mental warfare. He had tormented Nate for weeks and was managing to rouse stark terror even now. Daniel had never felt so exposed, so manipulated.

"Let's turn back, Nate. That's Crow indeed, and he'll mean you harm."

"Then I'll face him. I'll not run from a damn Indian. I've been through enough of his hell already."

Daniel paused, took a deep breath. "Go on, then. I'm right beside you. But don't step into the firelight hear?"

"I hear."

They went on, both so tense that neither realized Daniel hadn't finished explaining why he believed Crow was waging this strange and private war against Nate Meriwether.

They edged forward, moving slowly toward the flickering fire. Nate was making little whimpering sounds in the back of his throat, faint, barely audible ones, but Daniel didn't tell him to desist because he knew Nate couldn't if he tried. The poor man was frightened beyond measure, but also curious, and determined to bring this to an end one way or another.

They went as far as they could go without entering the circle of firelight. There they stood, staring in confusion and fear at a figure that lay on the ground near the fire.

It appeared to be a human being, but a closer examination showed it was nothing but clothing stuffed with leaves and moss, the head made of a stuffed sack. The figure lay on its back, arms folded across its chest. One of the legs was straight, the other bent crazily.

"That's the same position of the figure drawn in the dirt outside my cabin," Nate whispered.

"Yes," Daniel replied. "A man, lying in a camp with a broken leg. Do you remember now, Nate?"

Nate sucked in his breath suddenly. "Oh, God above! I do remember!" Crow dropped from the tree above them, landing just behind Nate. In the span of a moment he had an arm around Nate's head, covering the eyes and pulling back the head, and a knife pressed against Nate's throat. He shoved Nate forward into the circle of light and wheeled him around to face Daniel. Nate gurgled and moaned and dropped his rifle in utter panic.

"The rifle," Crow said to Daniel. "Drop it."

Daniel lifted the weapon and stuck the sight end of the muzzle right in Crow's face.

"Very well, then," Crow said. "I kill him." The knife cut skin; in the flickering firelight Daniel saw blood trickle down.

"No!" he said, lowering the rifle, then laying it at his feet.

Crow cut no deeper, but neither did he remove the blade from the slit he had sliced into the skin. Blood continued to run out, trickling down the blade to its tip and dripping onto the ground and onto Nate's left moccasin.

"It was when Chillicothe burned that I finally remembered where I had seen this man's face," Crow said to Daniel. "I was there, hiding and watching. I saw him among the soldiers burning the corn, and I remembered. At Boonesborough, when he shot me through the leg and took me captive, I knew then I had seen his face before, but I did not remember where. And you would not tell me who he was, Sheltowee. I lay in that cabin, my leg broken, and tried to remember who he was and why I had hated him the moment I saw him. But I could not remember. When I did remember at Chillicothe, I followed him back to his home to get my vengeance. And tonight I will have it!"

Nate made a terrible squeaking sound, but Crow did not lessen the pressure of the knife.

"Do you remember a time long ago, white man, when you found an old Cherokee lying in camp with his leg broken? You killed that old man and shot the boy with him through the side of his body. I was that boy, and the man was my mother's brother, who had taught me and guided me. He had taken me to hunt with him and broke his leg when he fell in a ravine. He was helpless when you came into our camp and killed him. If not for my deaf ear I would have heard you come . . . but I didn't hear until it was too late. So then you shot me, too, white man, and chased me through a hole in the hill to try to kill me. On the other side I put my knife into you—do you remember me now, white man?"

"Yes," Nate said, his voice strained. "Yes I remember. . . ."

Daniel was surprised Nate didn't try to deny it. Maybe fear had taken his ability to lie, or maybe he realized he would never be able to win any argument with Crow. Daniel realized that a pivotal moment had come. In seconds Nate's throat would be cut and he would be dead, killed right before his eyes, just as Israel had been.

It was an intolerable situation. Daniel stepped forward. "No! No, Crow, do not kill him."

Crow's flashing dark eyes glared at Daniel "Why, Sheltowee? Why should I not kill him, and you as well? There is another one I remember from the time of the murder. There was a man who came to help this one"—he shook Nate roughly—"after I had cut him. That was you, Sheltowee. Your face too has lingered in my mind through many years, unrecognized. Even in the days that I sat with Hanging Maw in your cabin, I knew I had seen you before. I knew it when I helped take pelts from you south of the big gap, and when I helped steal away your daughter and while I was your captive at Boonesborough—all those times I studied your face and tried to remember. Now I do remember."

"So you will kill me, too? No, Crow. You will not have the chance. If you cut my friend's throat, I'll have this rifle back in my hand before he strikes the ground, and your dead body will lie atop his."

"I have no desire to kill you, Sheltowee. It was not you who murdered my mother's brother. It is this man whose throat I must cut and whose scalp I will take."

"Yet it was my name you called when we were in our camp back yonder, me you tried to lure out."

"I called your name because I knew it. This one, I did not know his name, and it does not matter. To me his name is ugliness, it is dung and piss!"

"Don't kill him, Crow." This time Daniel said it like an order.

"I will!"

"No. I gave you your life in Boonesborough. I gave you a shovel and let you escape. Now you give me his life in return."

Crow seemed shaken by those words. Daniel had rightly figured him for a man who sought balance, an evil for an evil, a goodness for a goodness. So Daniel had just presented Crow with a predicament. He could achieve his vengeance only by denying the rightful request of a man who had saved his life. There was motion in the woods behind Daniel. Silas emerged, rifle in hand. He gaped in shock at the sight of his stepfather in the grasp of an Indian, a knife at his throat.

"Nate . . ."

"You should've stayed back at the camp with your mother like you were told, boy!" Daniel said sharply.

"She sent me here. She was worried."

Crow all but yelled, "I *will* kill him! I must!"

A very odd thing happened to Daniel Boone right then. Emotion rose inside him, drawn from old wells and new ones, and tears rolled out of his eyes. Right then the life of the westering frontier, with its endless cycle of war and retaliation, seemed so frustrating, difficult, downright absurd, that he could hardly bear it.

"Put down the knife, Crow. You will gain nothing by killing my friend. And he is my friend, has been for years."

"He is an evil man."

"Sometimes he is. Like you and me and all of us. He ain't good. He has hate in him, and he has been cruel many times. He has wronged you. But he is my friend, and I ask to let him live."

Crow faltered. He looked uncertain but did not let go of Nate.

Daniel waved back toward Silas Carrick, his emotions continuing to mount.

"See this boy, Crow? That man you have at your blade is his stepfather. In his eyes he is as precious and important as your mother's brother was in yours. If you kill his stepfather before his eyes, he'll hate you just as you have hated that man, and he'll kill in turn. He'll try to balance evil with another evil. And then somebody else will try to balance that evil in turn. It's ever been that way with all of us. We kill, you kill, all of us do, again and again, like a great wheel turning over and over. We are all men of war. Men of death. We have been forced to be. But tonight we do not have to be men of death. We can be men of life. The Great Spirit will be pleased with us if we will be men of life. For this one night the wheel of war does not have to turn."

Crow removed the blade from Nate's throat but kept a grip on his head. He was staring at Daniel with an expression that could not be interpreted. Fearing that his words, however heartfelt they were, were failing to persuade Crow, Daniel returned to his first and most straightforward plea.

"I ask for his life, in return for your own at Boonesborough. If for no other reason than that, I plead with you to let him go free."

Crow drew in a deep breath, making his nostrils flare. Suddenly he moved the blade up to Nate's forehead and cut a long line through the skin just below the hairline. Then with a grunt he shoved Nate forward, onto his face. Nate lay gasping. He was crying, too, groping at the scalp he had been sure, only a second before, that he would lose.

"I have spared him for your sake, Sheltowee. That is the only reason. For you, and the life you gave me at Boonesborough. All your other talk is the talk of a soft man, a man who is growing old and becoming a woman. This wheel of war you speak of, it still turns. It will always turn, forever."

At that moment Silas Carrick stepped forward, lifted his rifle, and shot Crow through the forehead. Crow jerked backward off his feet as the bullet exploded through his skull and exited the back. He was dead before he struck dirt.

"Good boy," Nate said in a voice of pain. "Good boy, Silas."

IN THE SILENT MOMENTS that followed, Daniel walked slowly to where Crow lay and knelt beside the body. Crow's eyes were wide-open, glazed and staring. Kneeling, Daniel reached down and closed the Cherokee's eyes with his fingers, then rose and walked away to slump against a tree.

"You can take the scalp, if you want," Nate said to Silas. He had torn a strip from his shirt and had bound it around his cut brow, soaking up the blood. Silas said nothing, only turned and vomited, then ran back toward the place where waited his mother and siblings, who were no doubt in terror now that they had heard a shot fired. Shrugging, Nate stood and headed toward the body himself. Daniel picked up his rifle, lifted it, cocked it.

"Nate," he said, "if you touch his body, I'll kill you. I swear I will."

Nate was aghast. "You'd kill me for scalping a dead Indian that was ready to cut my throat open? A damn Indian?"

"Yes."

Nate shook his head. "He was right about you, Dan. You are getting old. You are getting soft of soul. Weak and womanish."

Daniel lowered the rifle. "In my life I've twice held the corpses of dead sons in my arms. I've seen women and children killed, or treated in ways that are worse even than killing. I've heard wounded men beg to die in fields of battle. I reckon maybe I am getting old and soft, Nate. Such as that can make a man soft. God help us, it ought to. Because if it don't soften him, it will harden him."

Nate gently touched the bloody rag around his head and then dabbed at the small cut in his neck. "I nearly died tonight. I'm obliged to you for all you done." Nate put out his hand toward Daniel, noted the blood on it, and then drew it back, replacing it with the other one. "You've been a good friend to me, Daniel. A mighty good friend for many years. But you've never done a finer thing for me than you done tonight."

Daniel did not take Nate's hand. He couldn't. There was nothing there tonight for any man to be proud of, or to make any friendship strong.

"Go on back to your wife, Nate. Tell her your 'haint' is gone, and she don't need to be afraid anymore. I'll be up later. Maybe in the morning."

"What are you going to do here?"

"There's a cave yonder. I've slept in it hunting a time or two. I'm going to put Crow in it and block the mouth."

"Burying a yellow boy! Hah! They're right about you, Daniel. You are an Indian lover, sure as the world. I can hardly believe you actually helped that devil get hisself free from Boonesborough."

"I did help him. I have no regrets about it."

"You should. If you'd have let me kill him then, none of this would have—"

"Shut up, Nate. Shut up and leave me be. Get back to your wife."

Nate lifted his brows, obv iously offended. Turning, he strode away a few paces, then stopped. "That Indian was right about one thing, you know. That war wheel you was talking about, it will always turn, just like he said."

Daniel looked at Nate sadly. He felt very tired. "Yes. It will, and it's too bloody bad."

He found the cave and laid Crow to rest in it as he had planned, then spent the remainder of the night sitting outside its mouth, lost in thought. When morning came, he went up to Nate's camp.

He found that Nate and Phebe had talked through the night about the possibility of staying in Kentucky after all, now that Nate's "haint" was gone. In the end they decided to go on anyway. They were ready for a new home, and Phebe still found that Kentucky had a pall cast over it. For her, like many, it had been a "dark and bloody ground," as one dissident Cherokee had predicted at Richard Henderson's Kentucky purchase, back in seventy-five.

Daniel went on with them as far as Cumberland Gap, and said his farewells. The parting was solemn, something like the funeral of a friendship that had been killed even as Nate's life had been saved. When Nate and his family rode out of sight, Daniel doubted he would ever lay eyes on the man again. It was sad, but in the bigger sense, perhaps good they were parting ways. Trials had done their work on them both, but made them different men. Daniel's soul was softening, Nate's growing hard. Time would probably only continue both processes, making them more and more different with the years.

So it was good they were parting. And when he remembered Nate from now on, he would try to think of only their earlier days, when both were young men in Carolina, laughing and hunting and climbing the ridges together.

Daniel headed home slowly, hunting along the way. He encountered no trouble or danger, and the time alone in "contemplation" was calming and worthwhile.

He rode home and told Rebecca all that had happened, then packed up the Boone possessions and moved the family off to Limestone on the Ohio River, never once pausing to look back.

About the Author

Cameron Judd is an award-winning newspaper reporter and editor, now working in public relations in higher education. He is the author of over thirty published books, including *The Overmountain Men*, *The Border Men*, *The Canebrake Men*, and *Crockett of Tennessee*. He lives near Greeneville,Tennessee, and is currently at work on his next novel.

http://cameronjudd.tripod.com/

Rachel's Story

A Southern Girl in Pre-Civil War Boston

by Marian Coe

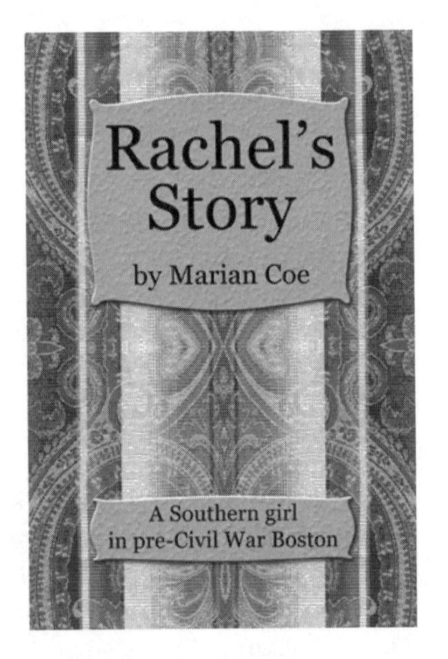

ISBN: 1932158642
pp: 260, trade paperback, $16.95
(Fall, 2005)

Rachel cares for her dying mother in the South Carolina plantation cabin where they lived with her half-breed Cherokee father and younger brother. Now she faces as great a challenge in seeking out the life her mother left behind in Boston. Rachel's search for understanding of the world, both inside and outside herself, and for acceptance of the gifts her Cherokee grandmother prophesied for her, propels her into the political and intellectual vortex of the age. Her guides include Elizabeth Peabody, Thoreau, Phineas Parker Quimby, and Ralph Waldo Emerson. Coe has drawn from the Transcendentalists' own writings and modern sources to create compelling and accessible portraits of the intellects of this pivotal age in American thought.

Marian Coe, a former staffer with the St. Petersburg Times, in Florida, is an Alabama native and a transplanted North Carolinian. She lives on Sugar Mountain with her artist husband, Paul Zipperlin.

Coe is the award-winning author of five books, including ***Legacy***; a psychological mystery set in the Florida Gulf of 1945; ***Eve's Mountain***, a novel about the contemporary Blue Ridge; ***Marvelous Secrets***, an eclectic short story collection; ***Key to a Cottage***, a woman's journey of self-discovery, ***Once Upon A Different Time***, a romantic adventure based on the writings of Charles Dudley Warner, with illustrations by Paul Zipperlin; and the forthcoming ***Rachel's Story: A southern girl in pre-Civil War Boston***.

ONCE UPON A DIFFERENT TIME

by Marian Coe

illustrations
by Paul Zipperlin

ISBN: 1932158537
Paperback, pp. 144, $12.95
Sepia illustrations

Join a spirited group on a romantic adventure along the hills and dales of the Appalachian mountains in 1884, as they travel on horseback from Abingdon, Virginia to the fashionable resort of Asheville, North Carolina.

Novelist Marian Coe and artist Paul Zipperlin have woven an imaginative odyssey based on the true account by Charles Dudley Warner of just such a trip published in the ***Atlantic Monthly*** of the time.

This novel belongs in Bed-and-Breakfasts and well-loved homes along the route traveled by Coe's delightful characters. . . . [T]his one is bound to find a place among its readers' heartstrings. – ***Carolina Mountain Living***

Deftly, Coe interweaves . . . a plot that involves two invented characters - Lily, a headstrong girl, and her chaperone, Aunt Tess (with) an actual journey by Charles Dudley Warner, a writer for Atlantic Monthly. . . . In essence, "Once Upon a Time" reminds us of "The Land of Sky," Christian Reid's 1885 travel romance. – **Rob Neufeld, Asheville Citizen-Times**

Where the Water-Dogs Laughed,

or The Story of the Great Bear

by Charles F. Price

ISBN: 1932158502
Hardcover, pp 304, $24.95

Hamby McFee is a "high-yella" a man of mixed race, whose life experience has rendered him unwilling to fit in with either race. The latest in the award-winning Hiwassee saga continues the stories of characters introduced in the earlier books. Hamby McFee's life and fate is intertwined with that of the Curtis family, the Prices the wealthy Weatherbys and a mysterious giant black bear. Price has provided us with the sage and ageless viewpoint of Yan-e'gwa – the bear – while crafting an ultimately human story.

Charles Price's first book ***Hiwassee: A Novel of the Civil War*** has become a standard in Civil War fiction. His second book, ***Freedom's Altar***, won the 1999 Sir Walter Raleigh Award for the best work of fiction by a North Carolinian. ***The Cock's Spur*** earned Independent Publishers' 2001 Book Award as one of the Ten Outstanding Books of the Year. It also won the Clark Cox Historical Fiction Award. ***Where the Water-Dogs Laughed*** was recognized by the Independent Publishers' Association in the historical fiction category for 2004 and received the Clark Cox Award for Historical Fiction from the North Carolina Society of Historians at the annual meeting in October, 2004.

The North Carolina High Country frames stories of active career women finding love with men as rugged and authentic as their mountains.

Appalachian Paradise

by Maggie Bishop

ISBN: 0971304564,
Trade paperback, $9.95

Emeralds in the Snow

by Maggie Bishop

ISBN: 1932158561
Trade paperback, $12.00

Praise for Maggie Bishop

"**Maggie Bishop** brings a vast knowledge of the Appalachian region ... displays the unique ability to draw the reader into each setting with vivid description, to the point that the reader feels part of the scene ... well-paced, the characters deftly drawn, the chemistry ... searing, and the romantic story teasing enough to leave the reader anxiously waiting for "the moment".
– Christy Tillery French, ***Midwest Book Review***

"Delightful romance with strong main characters the reader will grow to like and admire ... Their hike through the mountains is the perfect time for love to bloom amidst the calm and beauty of the Appalachians, vividly described in colorful detail."
– Astrid Kinn, ***Romance Reviews Today***

"I can think of few better ways to spend a snowy day. A wonderful Mountain Beach Book." – ***Carolina Mountain Living***